*In the second thrilling book of her magnificent McClellan
trilogy, award-winning author Jo Goodman spins an
exciting tale of passion, daring, and revenge that sweeps
from the war-torn Colonies to the elegant drawing rooms
of England . . .*

THE DARING PATRIOT
Bold and beautiful Rae McClellan eagerly seizes a chance
to be a courier for the Colonies, never anticipating her midnight
excursion to a local tavern would lead to murder—and brand
her a wanted woman. Saved from an angry mob of
Redcoats by a powerful stranger, she is swept up into a
tempestuous adventure that will become a battle for her
country, her family . . . and her heart.

THE NOBLE SPY
Jericho Smith curses the moment he became enraptured by
the confounding Rae McClellan—and the feverish desire
she arouses in him. Jericho was one of the Continental
army's most able spies . . . until Rae makes him want
things he never dared desire before, like the love of this
spirited woman and a lost legacy that awaits back in
England. Yet even as Jericho and Rae surrender to an
undeniable passion, a dangerous foe reaches out across
the Atlantic, luring them both into a perilous gambit for
their lives—and their love . . .

D0962914

Books by Jo Goodman

THE CAPTAIN'S LADY
CRYSTAL PASSION
SEASWEPT ABANDON
VELVET NIGHT
VIOLET FIRE
SCARLET LIES
TEMPTING TORMENT
MIDNIGHT PRINCESS
PASSION'S SWEET REVENGE
SWEET FIRE
WILD SWEET ECSTASY
ROGUE'S MISTRESS
FOREVER IN MY HEART
ALWAYS IN MY DREAMS
ONLY IN MY ARMS
MY STEADFAST HEART
MY RECKLESS HEART
WITH ALL MY HEART
MORE THAN YOU KNOW

Published by Zebra Books

JO GOODMAN

SEASWEPT ABANDON

ZEBRA BOOKS
KENSINGTON PUBLISHING CORP.

http://www.zebrabooks.com

For my parents. They never stop encouraging.

ZEBRA BOOKS are published by

Kensington Publishing Corp.
850 Third Avenue
New York, NY 10022

Zebra and the Z logo Reg. U.S. Pat. & TM Off.

First Printing: September 1986
Second Printing: September 2000
10 9 8 7 6 5 4 3 2

Printed in the United States of America

Dear Reader,

When I began writing about the McClellans in *Crystal Passion* I didn't anticipate there would be a secondary character who would require a story of his own. What caught me especially off guard was that not only wasn't the character a McClellan, but that he didn't even have a first name. The more I thought about Smith, the more I realized that Rahab McClellan was meant for him. I'm not giving anything away by telling you this at the outset. If you're familiar with my books, then you already know my heroes and heroines tend to work things out between them and then work together. That's why some readers might find Jericho Smith's behavior toward Rae troubling at different junctures in their relationship. Interestingly enough, I never received one letter of concern or protest when *Seaswept Abandon* was initially published. I imagine this had something to do with what was, if not entirely accepted, at least could be tolerated. I have to wonder what the reaction will be this time around—and I look forward to hearing from you if you have a thought about it one way or the other.

The McClellan trilogy will conclude with the reprinting of Noah McClellan's story in *Tempting Torment* in 2001. Noah was such a nice guy in the first draft I was asked to toughen him up. Men. And they think we're so difficult to understand.

Best wishes,
Jo

McClellan Family

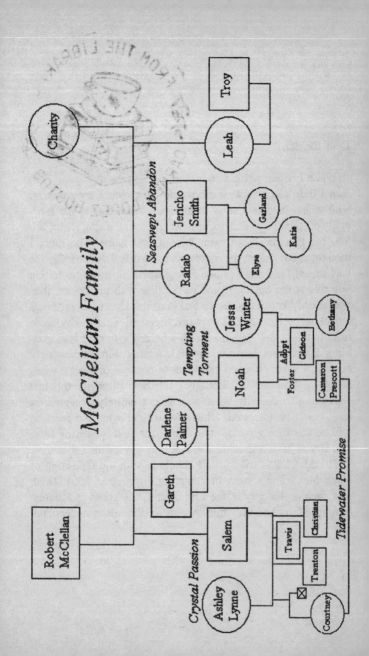

Chapter 1

"Auntie Rae! Auntie Rae! Look at my dress!" Courtney McClellan spun on her small feet, lifting the hem of her frilly pink dress nearly to her knees. "Isn't Mama clever? You can't see where Tommy Miller tore the lace."

Rahab McClellan smiled fondly at the whirling dervish that was her four-year-old niece. Courtney was a near perfect miniature of her mother, and Rae's eyes lifted to her sister-in-law, once again startled by the resemblance between the two. Ashley and Courtney shared thick ebony hair and fair porcelain complexions. They were delicate in stature but long of limb. Mother and daughter had a sweep of jet lashes that outlined clear and laughing eyes. The eyes, so similar in their direct gaze, were different in hue. Ashley's were the color of emeralds, startling green in her fair face, while Courtney's eyes were very much the silver gray of her father's.

Rae did not have to look in a mirror to know her own face had suffered today from the unexpected warmth of the sun. She had refused to wear a bonnet and now there were a number of suspicious-looking brown flecks on the arch of her cheek-bones and across the fine bridge of her nose. Freckles, she thought disgustedly, raising her dark green eyes heavenward. She gently mocked her fate at having been born the only McClellan with this particular curse. Her three brothers were dark, her sister fair. She was neither. The plait of hair at her nape was coiled tightly, the style subduing the flash of red in her heavy tresses, and she pretended it kept her emotions in check. There were times when Rae felt herself a changeling among her less temperamental siblings. Somewhat self-consciously, she drew a slim finger across the path of freckles on her cheek.

Ashley caught Rahab's wistfulness and smiled to herself while she gentled her small son in her arms, rocking him with a steady rhythm that kept him peaceful.

"Courtney, please. You are making me dizzy!" she scolded her spinning daughter. "And it's naughty of you to ask Rahab questions when you know she can't speak. She has a terrible spring cold."

Rae's hand left her cheek to wave in front of her, brushing aside Ashley's concern. Courtney, looking suitably chastened, barreled into her aunt, hugging her legs and pressing her cheek against the soft cotton of Rae's russet skirt. Rahab was never proof against such affection and she lifted Courtney onto her lap, returning the child's generous hug.

"So sorry, Auntie Rae! I forgot!" Courtney apologized.

Rae tapped her on the nose and mouthed the words, "Naughty minx."

Courtney laughed gaily. "Did you see, Mama? She called me what Papa always does." Her smile faded and she shifted uncomfortably on Rae's lap. Her earnest question was directed at her mother. "When is Papa coming home?"

"Soon, dear."

Although Ashley answered as she always did when Courtney posed the question, Rae could not miss the longing that framed her words. Rae knew Ashley missed her husband terribly, and she loved her for it. Although she was close to all her brothers, Salem was special to Rae. He, more than Gareth or Noah, seemed to understand the ache she felt to be part of the same struggle he was engaged in. Salem never patronized her, or made light of her desire to assist the colonies in their bid for independence. In part Rae knew she had Ashley to thank for Salem's attitude. For all that she looked like a china figurine, her sister-in-law was a spirited complement to Salem's patriotic commitment. It was at Ashley's insistence that Salem had invited Rae to join them in New York nearly two years before.

Rae would have liked to believe the invitation was a way to involve her in the political drama that was part of Salem and Ashley's life, and in a minor way this had come to pass. But Rae was nothing if not honest, and she knew that at the heart of the invitation was Ashley's desire for companionship of a common mind. Ashley had found it difficult to be surrounded by so many people still clinging to the hope of reconciliation with Britain. And Rae had found it difficult to live at McClellan's Landing with her mother and father and sister—and her sister's new husband.

But she was not going to think about Troy Lawson, she admonished herself. In that part of her mind that would allow no deception, she knew they would never have suited. She only doubted herself because she had foolishly imagined herself to be in love with him, knowing all the while that he and Leah were more the thing. She could admit in her most secret thoughts that it was her pride that had been stung when Troy broke with her. Time and distance had eased love's first betrayal, and she would always thank Ashley and Salem for the welcome into their home.

"But when, Mama?" Courtney asked, pressing for a definite answer.

Rae was shaken from her reverie by her niece's plaintive question. "Sssh," she managed to get out, brushing the child's dark curls from her face. "Your mama doesn't know."

Rae's answer successfully diverted Courtney's attention. She chortled. "You sound so funny, Auntie Rae. Like ol' Jacob at the landing."

Ashley and Rae both laughed. Rae thought her gravelly excuse for a voice did indeed sound like the voice of the family's ancient retainer. She was surprised that Courtney remembered Jacob. It had been almost a year since Ashley and Salem had visited the landing.

Ashley spoke to the surprise on Rae's face. "Ol' Jacob whittled her a pull toy and she has never forgotten him. I think she spent most of the visit with him. Your mother would have been quite put out if she hadn't had Trenton to fawn over." She gave her son a small squeeze. "But he was such a handful no one seemed to mind that Courtney was amusing herself."

Rae pointed to the way Courtney was presently occupied with the cameo brooch securing the shawl over Rae's shoulders. "She is fascinated with everything around her," she rasped.

"Oh, Rae! Please don't talk! It hurts just to listen. Shall I make us another cup of tea?" Rae's horrified glance indicated that if she drank one more drop she would consign herself to Boston Harbor. Ashley smiled ruefully. "I suppose I have been overdoing it a bit. And I know drinking tea goes against all your principles, but I find that I cannot abandon my past entirely."

Rae was quick to see the shadow that passed over Ashley's features. Though Ashley tried to hide it, and was successful for the most part, there were those moments when she could not help but shudder at the thought of the life she had known in England, a life that had had very little to recommend it until the interference of one Jerusalem McClellan. Rae would have given anything to have been able to comfort her, but she knew that it was something better left to Salem. He understood more than anyone what demons chased his wife. Rae knew Ashley's brief melancholy had its roots in his absence as much as it did in her fears.

"I know. It's silly of me," Ashley said, seeing Rae's sympathetic look. "When Salem isn't here I brood. I find it hard not to think that Nigel will—"

Rae threw her a sharp look, but it was too late. Courtney's interest in the brooch had waned and she was listening intently to her mother.

"Who is Nigel, Mama?"

Ashley frowned at her daughter's inquisitiveness. "Little pitchers . . . he is my uncle, Courtney. Like Noah and Gareth are your uncles. But I do not like my Uncle Nigel."

"Why?"

"He is not a very nice man."

"Why?"

"Because he doesn't have anyone to love, I think." She could have added that Nigel Lynne, Duke of Linfield, had only ever loved one woman, his twin sister, and that his twisted obsession had brought about her death. Ashley felt regret that she had never known her mother, but she had made every effort to clear her mind of the haunting bitterness that accompanied such thoughts. Nigel's Machiavellian tendencies were better left in the past. It was only when Salem was away from her that she wondered if she were entirely safe from his plotting.

"Why?"

Rae rolled her expressive eyes at Courtney and shook her head, placing her index finger on the child's pink lips. "Enough," she whispered. "Naptime."

"Oh, Auntie Rae. Must I?"

"Yes, you must," Ashley said, standing. She walked toward the drawing room doors, shifting the sleeping bundle in her arms. "Come, Courtney. Trenton is sleeping now. He will want to have company in the nursery when he awakes."

Rae gently pushed Courtney from her lap and watched her reluctantly follow her mother up the carpeted stairs to the nursery. She waved good-bye as the girl played peek-a-boo through the rails of the banister until she was out of sight. When the trio had disappeared, Rahab leaned her head against the side of her wing chair, closing her eyes against tears that threatened her composure.

How she envied Ashley her family! It was absurd, this jealousy. Rae knew it and didn't like herself the better for it. Ashley Lynne had been the outsider, once upon a time. Five years ago Rae had not known of her existence, but when her brother had brought her home to their Virginia plantation, Rae had welcomed her, and now it seemed hard to believe there was ever a time that did not include Ashley. She had presented Robert and Charity McClellan with their first grandchild, and no one seemed at all perturbed that Courtney had arrived earlier than the wedding vows should have allowed.

Stop it! she admonished herself. That was an unworthy thought. Ashley is not the source of all this self-pity. It's this damn plaguey cold and a row of freckles you wouldn't even have if you had worn a bonnet in the first place. Rae listened to the train of her thoughts and had the good sense to wonder why the freckles bothered her so much. She was not one to be vain about her appearance, and this new concern with her looks bothered her not a little. She thought perhaps she was feeling her age.

Twenty-two. In a society where girls were married as young as fifteen, it seemed to Rae that twenty-two, soon to be twenty-three, was a very great age, indeed. Ashley had married Salem when she was nineteen, and Leah, two years Rae's junior, had wed at eighteen. Her brother Gareth's wife had been barely seventeen when she'd married him. Only Noah and Rae remained single, but, Rae reflected, Noah was hardly in danger of becoming the maiden aunt. It was unfair the way Noah was good-naturedly teased about chasing skirts while she was expected to be chased. Or was that chaste?

Her smile was wry. She had certainly been the latter. Rigidly she had controlled the ache and longing she felt for the special intimacy shared by Ashley and Salem. Some nights she would bury her head beneath her feather pillow to muffle the sound of their giggling and loving. Thank God they were mostly quiet, else Rae knew she would have had to leave a long time ago. The thought of returning to the landing and seeing, even hearing, Leah and Troy engage in such play, brought bile to her throat. She did not love Troy, but by God, she had her pride.

So sleep with your pride, m'girl. It's all you'll ever know as long as you expect every man you meet to betray you for another. Where's your courage? It's not as if you have any more sisters.

Rae knew the argument well. She had battled with it long enough. But at the moment she convinced herself to take a risk, to allow some man the chance to win her heart, she would remember there were other women who could take him away. When she realized she was spurning her suitors before they could reject her, hurting them for no other reason than that she was afraid, she held herself aloof from them all.

The irony of her name was not lost on her. She was Rahab, named for the biblical harlot at Jericho, and now called untouchable by the men who had approached her. Better that she should have been named Mary, for she was likely to remain virgin till she died. The unkindness with which she had considered this last thought brought her up short. Restlessly she moved to the large bay window and pressed her palms against the warm panes.

Outside the sun beat new life into the cold ground. There were tender green shoots in the flower boxes that lined the sills of the house across the street. Looking down, Rae saw several small buds in the box below her window. She felt unaccountably frightened for them. So much could happen. They were only ignorant plants, coaxed by the warmth of a fickle sun to aspire to color and beauty. Tonight it would be cold; she sensed it. There would be a frost and the unsuspecting buds would freeze and become nothing but fertilizer for the buds that would replace them. She wanted to protect them, perhaps bring them in for the night, but she could not help them every evening. No, it was better they learned nature's little cruelties now. She turned away, wondering if she were the only one who felt melancholy in springtime.

There was too much to risk, too much in question, this time of year. There were those moments when a spring breeze would catch her unaware. It would be cool and brisk, but thick with the fragrance of new life, and she would feel as if her heart were being squeezed with the fear of her anticipation. Springtime reminded her she was lonely, for all that she was not alone.

Ashley stood at the entrance to the drawing room, pondering the gentle slump of Rae's shoulders. It was not often Rahab could be seen looking defeated, yet Ashley sensed this was precisely how she was feeling now. Ashley knew Rae well enough to know nothing would come of questioning her mood. Rahab was a wonderful companion, but she rarely confided her innermost thoughts. She was outspoken on a variety of subjects, but Rae McClellan was not one of them.

Ashley reflected that it had not always been this way. When she had first met Rae the young girl had been vivacious and passionately involved in everything around her. The change in her mien had come on gradually, brought on first, Ashley thought, by Rae's unhappiness with her woman's role in the rebellion. She did not hide her desire to accompany her brother Noah onto the battlefield. She would gladly have taken Gareth's seat among the Virginian delegation if such a thing had been permitted. Once she had tearfully begged Salem to allow her to go with him on one of his clandestine missions for General Washington. He had refused her. With regret, it was true, but it was a firm refusal, nonetheless. She had never asked for anything again.

Salem's refusal had been especially hard to take because Rae knew that Ashley was allowed to contribute. Ashley's help was vital to Salem at formal gatherings, her crisp accent and very British mannerisms doing much to deflect suspicion away from his real purpose at the affairs. Though he sympathized with his sister he was not willing to let her take part, except in a very small manner. Ashley knew it hurt Rahab, though it was never mentioned.

But it was not only her lack of participation in the long war effort that caused the occasional slump of Rae's shoulders. Ashley remembered very well the nights when Rae had first come to them. Rahab would die rather than admit she had cried frequently during those initial months, but Ashley and Salem heard her, and introducing her to the young men in their social circle had done nothing to alleviate her sadness. For a time they thought she was recovering, then that she had merely grown indifferent. It hurt Ashley to see so much of Rae's vital spirit crushed beneath the heavy weight of her fears.

Ashley had no cure for Rae's troubled friendships with men, but she had an idea that would ease Rahab's frustration at not being able to help Salem.

"Rae, I have a favor to ask," she said, hoping Rahab would only hear the earnestness and not the prevarication.

Startled, Rae spun to face Ashley. She had not known she was not alone. Her brows lifted in question.

"I just got Courtney to sleep. She was a little cranky. I think she is coming down with a cold. No. Don't say anything. It is hardly your fault. We took shocking advantage last week of the break in the weather and now we're paying the piper. It wouldn't trouble me at all, but I received a missive from Salem earlier today. I have to deliver it this evening and I was wondering. . . well, would you mind delivering it for me? I hate to leave Courtney when she's not feeling the thing and . . ."

Rahab's dark lashes swept over her eyes to conceal the light of relief and happiness that sprang there. Not for anything did she want Ashley to know how sorry she had been feeling for herself. She nodded and mouthed her willingness to pass on her brother's message.

Ashley expelled a quiet sigh and seated herself on the edge of the divan. She waited for Rae to be seated before she tendered her explanation. "Let me see if I can answer all the questions you cannot voice," she said, a playful smile touching her lips. "The note from Salem arrived before breakfast. He was with Nathanael Greene in Georgia when he wrote it, but he says that by the time I read it he will be on his way home to us. He and the general have quite skunked the British again, picking off the outposts in both the Carolinas."

Rae smiled at the pride in Ashley's voice, hardly believing there was a time when the McClellans had doubted her loyalty to their cause. There was no doubt now; Ashley had proven herself beyond anything that had been asked of her. "The *Lydia?*"

Ashley pursed her lips together in disapproval. "Ssh! The *Lydia* met with no damage. Your brother is of no mind to lose a second ship under his command. It will be none the worse for wear when he brings it back to New York. Certainly it will be fit to join the McClellan fleet when this war is over and trading begins again."

Ashley knew how important it was to the McClellans that the war end soon. Everything Rae's parents had worked for was in danger of being lost because of the hard times. There was virtually no market for their tobacco crop, and the stud farm had been raided twice by the British, each time taking a terrible toll on the Thoroughbred stock. The McClellans were not among those who would profit monetarily from the rebellion. Salem had little interest in privateering, which was where the fortune could be won. When he secretly captained the *Lydia* it was to bombard the British outposts as he had done in the Carolinas. More often he was simply Washington's spy in New York where a large British force still resided. The pay was no more than a soldier's meager wage, and the few prizes the *Lydia* took in secret were sold back to the British to support Salem's guise as a merchant tradesman.

"Salem writes that Lord Cornwallis seems to be weary of our troops chewing at his heels. He is moving his force to

Virginia.'' Seeing Rae's concern, she hastily explained. ''Your
brother says there is no cause for alarm at this time. The British
are only in Portsmouth. Possibly they will go to Yorktown, but
Salem does not think they will head up the James toward the
landing. Cornwallis would not want to cut himself off from his
naval support. That would be the end.''

Rae nodded. She knew the area where Cornwallis's troops
were camping very well. The McClellan acres were only
slightly farther north along the bank of the James River. The
British needed to stay precisely where they were or they could
lose the support of General Clinton's forces still in New York,
or that of the troops to the south.

''You understand, of course, if the French would ever arrive
with their promise of naval guns this entire war would be ended
right and tight.''

Rae smiled at the asperity in Ashley's tone. Ashley still had
a good Britisher's wariness of the French.

''No doubt it does not suit them at this time. Oh, well . . .
Washington will manage the thing well enough without their
help. And this is what Salem writes about in the first place.
His dispatch to the general must be taken to Wolfe's Tavern
near Bowling Green. I alone can translate the code of his
message, and since I've already done so it is vital that it not
fall into enemy hands. Can you do this thing?''

Rae's slim shoulders straightened. She nodded firmly.

''Good. And your cold? You do not think it is too much?''

''I don't need a voice to be a courier,'' Rae croaked.

''How fortunate for us there is no catch phrase needed to
assure your identity. You are hardly capable of giving one
over.'' She patted Rae's forearm in a gesture that made light
of her concern. ''Poor Rahab. So much to say, and no way to
get it all out.''

Rae's bright smile said she was not offended by Ashley's
teasing, but the glint in her eyes clearly warned of retribution.

Ashley released Rae's arm and began clicking off her fingers as she covered the major points of the assignment to Rae. "First, you will go to Wolfe's this evening around eight o'clock. The tavern is patroned by a number of British regulars, Tory sympathizers, and women of a certain repute." She cleared her throat and caught Rae's eye to make certain she understood. "These women are not obvious in their profession, but they are indiscriminate in that they offer themselves to the redcoats. There will be no need to paint yourself scarlet to fit among them, but you will have to spurn any number of advances." Rae's expression was skeptical. "Don't look at me so, Rahab. Those freckles you despise are nothing more than a tease for that streak of fire in your hair. They will make you a target for every skirt pincher lifting an ale. Oh. Mayhap this is not a good idea. I should go myself. The patrons at Wolfe's know better than to bother with me."

Rae shook her head violently. "Please. I want to do this," she got out.

Ashley squashed her last doubts, taken with the animation on Rae's face. Rahab had no idea of how lovely she looked at that moment, how completely happy. "Very well. Second, you will look for Paul Kroger. He is a portly man, slightly balding, of Germanic descent, and usually can be found eating sauerbrauten at the corner table near the bar. He comes to the tavern three days each week without fail, always at the same time, to wait for a courier in the event there is a dispatch. He will wait until nine. If you are late, he will be gone. He will not be expecting you, but if you wear my plaid shawl he will know you have come on my errand. Paul is a gentleman of the first water, so do not be afraid when he invites you to take a room abovestairs. Once in the room, hand over Salem's letter, which I will baste into the hem of your skirt, and you can leave by the window. Don't worry. It leads to the sloping roof of the back porch, and from there it is the smallest of drops to the ground."

Rae's eyes widened. It was difficult to imagine her brother's permitting Ashley to engage in such intrigue. Salem was nothing if not protective of his wife.

"Salem had a great deal to say about it all in the beginning," Ashley said frankly. "But there was a need for a courier, and I convinced him the danger was minimal. Which it is. And, of course, Salem trusts Herr Kroger. Such a genial man. He's actually quite embarrassed at having to invite me to his room. His shiny pate turns bright red.

"The entire exchange won't take more than a few minutes. Herr Kroger will wait in his room until a suitable period of time has passed; then he will be on his way to Washington's camp. The affair is neatly executed under the nose of Clinton's men, and no one is the wiser. Couriers have been using Wolfe's for the passing of dispatches for nearly three years and there has never been even a suspicion of trouble."

It sounded to Rae as if the plan was almost without risk. She quelled a niggling feeling of disappointment. She had hoped for a more chancy assignment, a method of proving herself for the cause. It seemed that unless she wrenched her ankle dropping from the upper story there was no way for her to fail.

"You'll do this for me, then?" Ashley asked, giving Rae a final opportunity to back out, though she would have been shocked if Rahab had taken it.

Rae nodded happily, and unable to keep her good spirits silent, she rushed on before Ashley could stop her. "You know I will. I cannot think of anything I would rather do for you. Please, let me sew Salem's note in my skirt. I want to do this from the beginning."

Ashley's finely drawn brows raised, assessing Rae critically. Here indeed was the proof that Rahab wanted to help. Rae hated any sort of stitchery and completed her embroidery pieces only because it was expected of her. She had always been a dutiful daughter, fulfilling expectations of those things a proper young lady should list as her accomplishments. However, it was no secret among the McClellans that she would rather spend her time hunting or riding. Even the rigors of the classroom came before plying her needle.

"Of course, you may hide the note. But there is a condition. And that is that I don't hear another word from you this evening. I think you should treat your voice with more care. You never know when you will have need of it."

"I'll do anything," Rae's eyes seemed to say, pleasing Ashley greatly.

"Good. Now let us see about your manner of dress for this evening."

It was out of the question that any of Ashley's wardrobe would fit Rae. Her long and tapered limbs were not suited to the curved lushness of Ashley's figure. She loved Ashley all the better for not even suggesting rummaging through her closets. Nothing could have been more calculated to make Rahab feel ungainly and out of step with the current mode.

After much discussion and several false starts, Rae and Ashley settled on a simple shag skirt of the deepest indigo blue and a white saque that served as an overblouse. Combined with the dark watch plaid of Ashley's shawl, the outfit set off the streak of fiery copper in Rae's hair. Rae pirouetted in front of the cheval glass in her room, glancing over her shoulder as she spun, greatly pleased with the image she presented.

Ashley chuckled softly. "Do not play the harlot too well, dear sister. I would not want to explain any untoward behavior to Salem."

Rae stopped spinning, blushing at Ashley's words. In truth she did feel different, if only because of the knowledge of the kind of woman she was to portray. When her eyes returned to the glass, studying her reflection, she realized there was nothing untoward about her appearance. She looked much as she always looked. Oh, her eyes were brighter than was perhaps seemly for a young woman about to embark on something of such questionable taste. Perhaps her hair appeared a shade more red, but surely that was the influence of the clothes. And if her complexion glowed with an exceptional rosiness, it could no doubt be attributed to the latent effects of the sun. She admitted to herself that she looked nothing at all like a fallen woman, and her smile faded.

She turned on Ashley and made some quick motions about her face with her hands. Ashley had no difficulty determining what it was that Rae wanted.

"Certainly not," she said briskly. "You shan't paint your face. That is taking things a bit too far. It would not be safe for you to leave the house if you departed in such a guise. You would be accosted long before you reached the tavern. Once you are at Wolfe's you will see that I am right. All the patrons know the women for what they are. There is no need for paint or posturing attitudes. I have no doubt you will find the affair as sad as I do." Ashley sighed, shaking her head. "But there is no reason for me to refine on it so. I did not know I could be such a scold. I'll get Salem's correspondence for you to sew into the skirt."

When Ashley returned Rae was seated cross-legged on the middle of her large bed, clad only in her drawers and a thin chemise. Her bright head was bent over the skirt on her lap, and there was a slight frown of concentration on her brow as her fingers struggled with threads of the hem. Rae's sewing basket rested at her side, much of the contents strewn about the brightly patterned quilt that covered the four poster. Ashley could only admire the way Rae approached every task in her life with such single-minded determination. Once she was set upon a course of action, there was little that could be done to dissuade her from it. Ashley knew a sense of pleasure that she had been able to provide Rahab with some purpose for the time being.

Without a word she left Salem's letter on the edge of the bed and slipped out of the room. Rae would find it when she had need of it.

Rae was just repacking her sewing basket, feeling quite proud that she had managed to secure her brother's missive without Ashley's assistance, when she heard a mewling cry from the direction of the nursery. Knowing Ashley was probably taking a much needed rest, Rae shrugged into a thin robe and went to the children.

She was much astonished by the sight that greeted her. Courtney was hugging Trenton to her tiny bare chest, encouraging the babe to take her flat pink nipple in his puckered mouth. Trenton was making a vigorous protest. Without thinking of the consequences, Rae used her voice sharply. "Courtney Ann Rochelle! What in heaven's name are you doing?"

Startled by the breaking tones of her aunt's speech, Courtney nearly dropped the precarious hold she had on her young brother. Her struggling burden was almost too much for her dimpled arms. She knew she was doing something wrong because it was rare that anyone used all three of her names. "Oh, Auntie Rae," she said in a rush. "Mama's sleeping and Trenton is so hungry. You will feed him, won't you? I don't think I have any milk."

Rahab could only smile at Courtney's wide-eyed solemness. She took Trenton from his sister's arms and checked his padded bottom. He was wet as well as hungry. "I don't have any milk either, minx," she rasped as she began to change her nephew.

Courtney examined the small curves of Rae's breasts with curious eyes. "Have you tea, then?"

Rae's laughter showered the room with a trilling, husky sound. Trenton gurgled, delighted with the noise. "No, impudent miss, I do not have tea. Or coffee, if that is the bent of your next question. Only mamas of young babes have milk for their little ones. Does that satisfy you?"

Courtney supposed that it did. She struggled with her nightdress until Rahab helped her pull the material over her shoulders, then over her head.

"Go on. Get dressed. I shall help you with the—" She had fully intended to say buttons, but the word was merely a thread of sound. She tried again with no success. Her lips shaped the word, but no voice attended the action.

"Can you not speak now?" Courtney asked, distressed.

Rae shook her head and was nearly knocked to the floor as Courtney hugged her knees. "I'm so sorry, Auntie Rae."

"What are you sorry for?" Ashley asked from the doorway. She bit down a smile at the sight of her daughter, buck naked, hugging Rahab, who was only clad in a sheer robe and her underwear, while Trenton tried to scoot his powdered behind across the changing table.

"Mama!" Courtney cried, running to her mother's side and pulling Ashley into the room. Released, Rae lunged for Trenton to keep him from meeting the floor with his head. "Auntie Rae cannot speak, and it is your fault because you were sleeping."

Ashley blinked in surprise and bent to meet her daughter's flushed face. "How quickly you changed your tune. When I came in I thought it was your apology I heard."

Courtney's bright eyes shifted. "Auntie Rae cannot speak because she scolded me."

Ashley's eyes lifted over Courtney's head to where Rae was shaking her head and making dismissing motions with her hand. "Why did Rahab scold you?"

Courtney explained her dilemma the best way she could. Ashley had a hard time keeping an expressionless mien while Rae's silent laughter shook her slender body. When Courtney's story drew to a breathless halt, Ashley could do naught but hug her. Courtney had tried nothing that she had not seen her mother do hundreds of times.

"Go. Do as your auntie says and get dressed." Ashley raised her laughing eyes to Rae. "I don't know what I should do without you, Rae. I never intended when I invited you here for you to help with Courtney, and now Trenton, but I cannot imagine how I would manage without you. They are a handful."

Rae's smile said she enjoyed her place in the children's life. Fondly she handed Trenton into his mother's waiting arms and

Ashley settled into the cherrywood rocker. In a few moments he was sucking greedily at his mother's breast. Rae's heart lurched at the sight, the Madonna-like contentment on Ashley's face. Ashley glanced at Rae and caught the unmistakable yearning there. Slightly embarrassed to have seen something of Rahab's deepest secrets in her dark eyes, Ashley quickly turned her attention back to her noisy son.

"My children are such piglets," she said. "I can't think where they learned their manners."

Rae merely smiled, securing the sash of her robe.

"You really can't speak at all, can you?"

Rae shook her head regretfully.

"Oh, Rae. I can't let you go tonight. How will you manage?"

Rae's face fell, her cheeks ashen. Her eyes pleaded eloquently with Ashley.

"What am I do to with you? You beg your case as soulfully as Courtney, and everyone knows I am hardly proof against her wishes." Ashley sighed. "Very well, you may go to Wolfe's, and I pray neither of us shall regret this. But you must promise that you will drink your fill of honeyed tea between now and then. And I can't help but think a touch of spirits would soothe your throat."

Rahab agreed eagerly. She would have submitted to a mustard pack and drinking straight shots of corn liquor if it meant she could go to the tavern this evening. She did not wait for Ashley to think better of her decision, but left the nursery quickly.

She dressed in the skirt and saque, let her hair fall loosely about her shoulders, and found a pair of dark stockings and practical shoes. Carrying the shawl on one arm, she took the back stairs to the kitchen and stepped lightly around the cook and helpers, preparing her hot tea and honey.

"You gonna put a little somethin' in that tea, ain't you?" Esther wanted to know. The cook's capable hands rested militantly on her ample hips. Smudges of flour contrasted sharply against her coffee-colored skin.

Rae pointed to the honey, adding an extra dollop to appease Esther's dark gaze.

"Honey ain't gonna do nothin' but sweeten your disposition, Miss Rae. Yo want somethin' to loosen your tongue, yo try a little of my Sam's specialty. It'll scare that cold right out of your body." She laughed heartily when Rae bravely held out her steaming mug. "That's the way. Never thought you McClellans were a cowardly lot." She went to the pantry and brought back a small stoneware jug. When she uncorked it there was a shifting haze in the air, like summer heat upon the cobblestones. Rae wrinkled her nose as the alcoholic vapors were released. "Course, I always thought y'all were a might short on common sense."

Rae smiled weakly, letting Esther enjoy herself, and watched the cook fill her mug to the rim with a syrupy liquor. She stirred the mixture with some trepidation and lifted it to her nose cautiously. Amazingly, it did not smell so bad once it was mixed with the tea. She touched the cup to her lips, sipping warily. Her dark brows arched in surprise and she took a larger gulp, nodding approvingly to Esther.

"Go easy with that, Miss Rae," Esther warned. "It's got a mighty kick."

Rae thought it had a rather pleasant, warming effect. It seemed even the liberal amount Esther had added was diluted by the tea. She motioned to the cook to add some more to her mug.

Esther shook her head. "No, ma'am. Yo ain't gettin' no more." She turned her back on Rae and carried the jug back to the pantry. "Some McClellans have less sense than others," she mumbled.

Rae continued to sip at her brew and bided her time. When Esther carried herself off to the fruit cellar, Rae slipped into the pantry and made off with the jug, cautioning the giggling kitchen maids to secrecy. Once she was safely in the fragrant confines of Salem's small library, Rae made herself comfortable in the lush softness of her brother's favorite chair. Smooth leather surrounded her as she tucked her legs beneath her, curling up like a child. Smiling at her stealth, well pleased with her theft, Rae added a few drops of liquor to her mug. The drink was pleasantly warm on her tongue. She pressed her lips lightly together, then cleared her throat.

It did not hurt. She took a large swallow, added more from the jug, swallowed again, and felt a sort of numbness seize her insides. This must be the kick, she decided. It was not without its rewards, she noted as she tested her voice. She was able to say her name in a rough whisper.

Glancing at the clock on the mantelpiece, Rae saw she had less than thirty minutes before she had to leave for Wolfe's. Surely by that time, she thought, Sam's concoction should have a chance to soothe her vocal cords. Over the next half-hour Rae applied herself to the brew with the steady purposefulness that Ashley had admired earlier. She wisely controlled herself and did not repeat the large gulps that resulted in a fiery burning in the viscera and settled for small, ladylike sips. When her lips touched the final bit of liquid in her mug, only one part of her brain clearly understood there was virtually no tea diluting the alcohol.

She kicked the jug beneath her chair, straightening as she heard the handle of the library door being pulled. She schooled her welcoming smile, hoping the curve of her lips was not too silly as Ashley let herself into the room.

"I thought perhaps this is where I would find you," Ashley said, wiping her damp hands on her apron. "I've just finished giving Courtney her bath. Such a fuss she makes. Soapsuds everywhere. I can see you are ready." She pointed to the shawl, which Rahab had rather negligently tossed on the sofa. "Will it be enough for you? Perhaps you better take your pelisse. There's a sharp wind brewing this evening."

Rae turned her overly grave countenance toward the window. The sky was darkening; night still came early in spring. A sapling branch fluttered against the pane. Like an ebony skeleton, Rae thought. She brought her hand to her mouth, coughing to cover a wild urge to giggle.

Rahab was no green girl. She knew the effects of alcoholic spirits—on others. She had seen her brothers on more than one occasion stepping lively to music only they could hear, laughing boisterously at the most childish of jokes, commiserating over the ragged path of true love. Rae recognized that the rosy glow that softened her vision would lead her to trouble if her behavior was not above reproach. Her solemn eyes rested on Ashley's face and her hands pantomimed that the shawl would be sufficient.

"If you're certain. I really do appreciate this, Rae. Shall you want a bite to eat before you go?"

Rae shook her head vigorously and her smile waned. The thought of food on top of the jug brew was nearly her undoing. She stood slowly and reached for the watch plaid shawl, arranging it neatly about her shoulders. Indicating the clock, Rae showed Ashley it was time for her to leave.

"One more thing," Ashley said as she reached into her apron pocket. Rae's eyes widened as Ashley pulled out what looked like a large leather bookmark. Blinking, Rae realized it was a leather sheath, a protective covering for a finely made six-inch blade. Ashley showed Rae the knife, then slipped it back into its jacket. Its delicate edges were razor sharp. It was the work of a master craftsman. "Salem had this made for me. He despaired of the way I used to strap a pistol to my thigh for defense."

Rae chuckled as she recalled Ashley's penchant for bluffing her way through harrowing situations with an unprimed pistol. It was no wonder that Salem had given her the knife.

"I gather you know how to use this. You had a more liberal education than I. Salem had to instruct me."

Rahab nodded, lifting her skirt high as Ashley knelt to fasten the thin leather straps about her thigh. Rae had no qualms about carrying the weapon. It was as Ashley had said: Growing up as a McClellan had provided her with a liberal education. Her father felt very strongly that his daughters should be able to fend for themselves.

"I doubt you shall have any use for this. It is merely a precaution. At least, I shall feel better knowing you have it." Ashley straightened. "Please go carefully. I shall expect you long before midnight."

Rae kissed Ashley briefly on the cheek and hoped she did not smell of spirits. "I'll be fine," she rasped. "You'll see."

Before Ashley could comment on the questionable return of her voice, Rae fled the room and the house.

Chapter 2

Rae decided nothing in her twenty-two years had prepared her for what she confronted when she crossed the threshold into Wolfe's Tavern. Nothing. The part of herself that was scrupulously honest, that part dealing only in realities, admitted that if it hadn't been for the liquor she would be taking her leave at this very minute. It was not a comforting realization to know she was an honest coward.

Taking a deep breath, and immediately sorry for the action, Rae resolutely squashed her fears and pushed her way through the crowded pubroom. A variety of odors assaulted her nostrils. Among them she identified stale spirits, roasting mutton, the heavy fragrance of musk and sweat, and—oh, God—was that urine? She gave silent thanks the tavern was poorly lighted and thick with tobacco smoke so she could not see the exact nature of what she had just stepped in. She lifted her skirt a little higher, exposing a bit of ankle and calf, and shook her dainty foot. Someone laughed, but it was difficult to say whether the chuckle was directed at her plight. Rae tossed a disparaging look over her shoulder just the same. No one was going to make light of her.

As Rae slipped through the crowd, occasionally finding herself the object of some rough but essentially careless fondling, she understood why Ashley had told her not to bother painting herself as a harlot. Clearly, none but the fallen would ever step foot in Wolfe's. She shuddered to think what could have happened to Ashley's reputation if she had ever been discovered in the tavern. Rae could not help smiling at the irony of her own situation. Being seen in Wolfe's would give pause to those young bucks who thought her a cold wench.

There were several long tables in the tavern where soldiers in their cardinal-red uniforms sat shoulder to shoulder, regularly lifting their mugs as they drank to anything that caught their fancy. Interspersed about the room were booths for those who wanted relative privacy.

Not many did. Typically, the booths were crowded with officers well into their cups. One secluded enclave of lobsterbacks was entertaining two young women to a ribald adventure, equal parts speculation and fabrication. Rae's ears pinkened even though she caught only a few phrases. She smiled ruefully. She had thought she was made of sterner stuff. She cautioned herself not to gasp at the sight of one soldier burying his face in the ample bosom of his female companion. Certainly the woman did not seem to mind. The lightskirt laughed shrilly and encouraged the liberty. Her thick fingers, reminding Rae of small sausages, closed around the man's head and held him fast. No doubt he would smother in that musky caress. Rae turned away, composing her features into an expression of jaded boredom, and neatly elbowed a man who tried to pull her onto his lap.

Her slow progress to the bar was not without its reward. Rae had sufficient time to study most of the patrons and was satisfied that her contact had not yet arrived. The booth she had expected to be occupied by Herr Kroger was being used by a man who was the very antithesis of the German Ashley had described. Rae gave him only the briefest of glances. The man's casual inspection was more disconcerting than the easy fondling she had endured. Something in his disinterested gaze stripped her to the skin and found her wanting. There was nothing about him to recommend a gentleman of the first water.

"Hey, Red! You! There by the fat man!" The strident voice came from the bar area. "I'm talkin' to you, Red."

Rae did not realize she was the object of the yelling until she noticed the customer on her left was sporting three chins. No one had ever called her Red in her life. She stood on tiptoe and looked over the shoulder of the soldier in front of her, pointing to herself in question.

The barkeep nodded. "That's right, Red. It's about time you got here. Hoskins promised me help an hour ago." When Rae's immediate response was confusion, he asked, "Ain't you the serving wench Hoskins said would help out tonight?"

Rahab's first inclination was to deny knowing Hoskins. Then it occurred to her that working as a barmaid provided the easiest way to watch for Kroger. "That's right," she called back, instantly regretting the careless use of her voice. The effects of Esther's jug liquor were wearing off. Then she swayed a little on her feet as she sank back on her heels and had to amend her last thought. There was still plenty of the stuff coursing through her veins.

"Well, git over here. There's lots of work to be done and none of it without a few ales in your hand!"

Rae tried to move forward but found her path blocked by several patrons who looked less than steady on their own feet. She tapped one of them on the shoulder, pointed in the general direction of the bar, and smiled engagingly. The brawny colonial, sober or drunk, was not proof against that smile. He nudged his friends, and Rae felt as grand as Moses when a path was made for her; even grander a moment later when she was lifted and passed from one man to another until she reached the bar without her feet once touching the floor.

At journey's end she gracefully swung herself onto the counter and curtseyed regally to the crowd as if they had been her courtly bearers. The gesture won admiration and applause, and Rae felt heady as she dropped lightly to the floor.

"Looks like you know how to handle the crowd, Red," John Wolfe said gruffly. His rheumy eyes passed over Rahab from head to toe. "But you don't know a damn thing about serving, I'll wager. Yer not likely to make much, dressed as you are."

Rae nearly screamed as the owner's stubby fingers and bitten nails reached for her breasts. She sighed in relief when he only loosened the knot of her shawl. He pulled the garment from her shoulders and tossed it back to her.

"Tie that about yer waist fer an apron and loosen that blouse over yer shoulders." His chin jerked in the direction of the neckline of her saque. "You got nothin' these men haven't seen before. Probably a lot less."

Rae bit back a reply, doubting she could have voiced it anyway, and pulled at her overblouse, jerking the edges over the slender curves of her shoulders. The action was sufficient to expose the fine line of her collarbone and the high curve of her breasts. She ignored Wolfe's derisive snort when he saw the lace trim of her chemise. She supposed he thought she shouldn't have bothered with undergarments. Someone nearby whistled admiringly; someone else called impatiently for another brew. Rae felt a measure of relief knowing she was not to everyone's taste.

Wolfe looked her over again. "I suppose you'll do." He thrust a tray into her hands and quickly loaded it with a stoneware pitcher and five tankards. He pointed vaguely in the direction of one of the long tables, which was particularly rowdy. "That way. And remember, what you spill, drop, or throw at anyone comes out of your wages."

Which we have not even discussed, Rae thought. She nodded,

set her chin determinedly, and pointed her feet toward the loudest part of the room.

Jericho Smith was not particularly amused by Rae's light-hearted and flirtatious theatrics. But then nothing had much amused Jericho for some time. He was weary of everything associated with war, and he counted among the casualties the women he saw in Wolfe's Tavern. They were a sad lot, flaunting their pale skin, wiggling their hips energetically, throwing themselves prone for anyone who looked. All in aid of a few coins, which only the British soldiers could supply. Smith's own pockets were light. Hardly surprising, he thought on a short sigh. He had not taken his position as one of Washington's aides because of the pay.

Jericho twisted in his booth, settling his back against the wall so his view of the tavern was nearly unobstructed. He rested one booted leg on the bench to keep company at a distance and drank his ale slowly. His eyes never stopped searching the room and only paused occasionally on the doorway when it swung open. No one in Wolfe's ever noticed the brief disappointment set about his mouth when the object of his search failed to enter. Jericho finished his drink and raised his arm for another, grimacing only slightly when the pub's newest serving wench answered his summons. If he had to sit here, waiting for couriers who might never appear, the very least that could have been supplied him was a lightskirt more to his taste than the one hovering about his table now.

"A refill," he said carelessly to Rahab, sliding his mug to the edge of the table. His keen blue eyes swept icily over her again, finding nothing to recommend changing his opinion. The freckles sweeping the high contours of her cheeks did give him a moment's pause. They seemed at odds with the flashy copper of her thick hair and the sultry depths of her green eyes. Then she swayed on her feet, just enough so that when she caught herself, putting a hand to the small of her back, her breasts pushed forward, straining against the confines of her chemise. Jericho's lips curled derisively. "I'm hardly impressed, ma'am."

Rae followed the direction of his gaze and blushed hotly, bringing up her empty tray as if it were a shield. With courage borne of this protection, she allowed her eyes to sweep over Jericho Smith, aping the manner in which he had insolently studied her.

Even sitting as he was, Rae could tell he was a tall man, but she was neither impressed nor intimidated. All the McClellan men were virtual trees, and Rae saw nothing exceptional about the stature of this rough stranger. He had a certain lean and lazy strength, she decided critically. Like a snake before it struck. She would not let herself smile at the thought and continued her dispassionate appraisal. Rae admitted his features were not unappealing. His hair was virtually hidden by the worn tricorn he sported, but she could see evidence of its bright color in his brows and a few strands that had escaped the queue at his nape. She was not particularly partial to yellow-haired men. She thought them lacking in a certain maleness. His lashes were as heavy and dark as her own and shaded eyes that were an uncommon shade of blue, nearly the color of clear southern waters but with none of the warmth. She thought his nose a bit too bold and arrogant, his mouth indolently curved in mockery, and the set of his jaw a silent challenge.

His clothes were styled in the fashion of the colonials. He wore a plain linen shirt and neckcloth. His black coat fitted the breadth of his shoulders tightly, and Rae could see where clumsy stitches had repaired one of the split seams. A tarnished button hung loosely from one of the sleeves. His navy breeches fit snugly into the tops of his scuffed riding boots. He was no soldier, and that made him even more distasteful in her mind. His presence in Wolfe's named him a British sympathizer, and

Rae felt her stomach churn. As she was judged, so did she judge.

Rahab smiled sweetly, picking up his mug, and boldly allowed her eyes to fall to his lap where his breeches stretched tautly across his hard thighs. "I'm hardly impressed either," she rasped. She turned her back on him, well satisfied with the astonishment she had been able to bring to his placid expression. Arrogant Tory oaf!

Jericho blinked in surprise as the saucy wench gave him her back, then surprised himself with a shout of laughter and an agreeable grin. The minx gave as good as she got, and he found himself appreciative and not a little interested. He was reluctant to recall the last time he had genuinely enjoyed himself, because it meant admitting the war was exacting its price on him. He preferred to believe he was immune to the ravages that seven years of fighting and intrigue could take on his soul. These past seven years were not so different from the seven years before, or the seven years before them. At thirty-one he had more than a nodding acquaintance with adversity and ugliness. But it was not in Jericho's nature to rue what could not be changed, so he did not allow himself to dwell on the fine manor home that had been lost to him or the years he had spent at the mercy of a spiteful captain's whims. What did it matter that when he escaped Garvey's service on the *Igraine* he had not yet reached his majority? He had left that floating prison alive, and that was more than the one who had engineered his disappearance had thought him capable of.

He visibly shook himself out of bitter memory's trance and glanced about the tavern. His own inner clock had never failed him, and he knew without hearing the crier that it was nearing nine. He could not completely quell his disappointment. When he had offered to take the ailing Kroger's place this evening, it had been with the hope he would see Ashley McClellan. He knew it had been possible there might be no reason for her to come tonight, but he had allowed himself to hope, and now he chastised himself for being a fool.

He had not seen Ashley since she had given birth to Trenton, and he could not help but wish to see how she fared. Although he had talked to Salem and was assured she was doing nicely, thank you, he had a need to talk to her himself. He always felt cleansed in her unaffected presence, as well as something of a kinship with her.

Ashley Lynne McClellan, niece of the powerful Duke of Linfield, had perceived early on that much about Jericho Smith was a fraud. And it rarely bothered Smith that she knew, because he could trust her to guard his secret as dearly as if it had been her own. On occasion it frightened him, the things she suspected. He would see her look at him expectantly, willing him to share a part of himself with her and Salem, but he could never oblige her, and she seemed to understand. At least, she accepted it, never badgering him to answer the question in her eyes.

It was his accent that had given him away. Most people found nothing remarkable about Jericho Smith's lazy drawl or unrefined patterns of speech. It was generally believed he hailed from Georgia, and everyone knew the penal origins of that colony. Jericho Smith was plain folk. It was hardly a cause for embarrassment. The services that were required of Jericho did not demand that he mingle with the Tory elite or rub elbows with British commanders. Ashley alone understood the risk he would be taking if he had to do such a thing. For beneath the carefully mannered drawl were the unmistakable tones of an education rooted in an English public school. Everyone knew Jericho Smith was no fool; only Ashley suspected the extent to which this was true.

For reasons of his own, Jericho had turned his back on his country of birth and now fought for his adopted homeland. It was this kinship he shared with Ashley McClellan. And that Ashley never pressed him to explain was a result of the natural respect she had for his privacy rather than gratitude that he had once saved her from her obsessed uncle. In truth, he hoped she had forgotten the incident, because she did not deserve to be plagued by unhappy memories. He would have killed Nigel Lynne if it had been in his power or his place to do so. Such things were better left to Ashley's husband, and Jericho knew Salem McClellan was equal to the task. There were no men Jericho respected more than he did Salem. Or envied. Sometimes he did not like himself much for it.

She wasn't coming, he decided. He reached for the tankard of heady ale Rae had slipped onto his table and drank deeply. Preoccupied with thoughts of Ashley, he had missed the wench's return. A pity—he had a mind to tease her again. He shrugged and eased himself more comfortably in the booth, stretching out both legs on the bench. If Ashley wasn't coming, he was free to share the space, yet he coveted his solitude. Waving one of the serving maids over—a blousy woman who heaved her bosom with each breath—he ordered a meal. He found himself looking for the skinny wench with the sharp tongue. Perhaps he would amuse himself with her before he took his leave. He had already engaged the room, and he thought he could do worse than the slight handful she presented.

He grinned when he caught sight of her across the room. She was weaving through the crowd with considerably more skill than she had first shown. There was a fine sheen of perspiration on her face and throat, and strands of hair clung wetly to her cheeks. She was certainly earning her meager wages this evening, he thought. He wondered if she would accept continental paper money in exchange for a toss. His last coin had bought the room.

As she wove her way among the tables nearing his own, he saw her eyes dart about the room. She was discreetly taking the measure of every man in the tavern. Probably looking for a bit of sport heavier in the pockets than he was, Jericho warned himself. The thought was oddly annoying. It was only because her eyes were nearly the color of Ashley's. Of course, Ashley's were clear and guileless. This wench's were jaded. Ashley was emerald. The serving girl was green glass.

Jericho swore softly under his breath, angry at his harsh judgment. He was no diamond to Ashley's jewel. The Ashleys of the world belonged to men like Salem, men of honor and position. For him there would always be women who could not afford to discriminate, women like this young wench, who was no better than she ought to be.

His dinner arrived and he applied himself to eating the thin slices of roast mutton. A sauce of unknown origin covered two thick slices of bread, and there was a baked apple to one side. It was better fare than he was used to with the troops. He considered taking some of the meat back to the encampment, but hunger turned him against it. He drank steadily while he ate, and because he wanted to believe he retained a measure of will power, he ate slowly and therefore drank far more than was his wont. He knew he must be drinking too much because the serving wench was looking better to him all the time.

Over the rim of his pewter tankard he watched Rahab fend off the amorous attentions of an unsteady soldier. The man had coarsely jammed his hand down the front of her blouse while she was pouring his ale. She slapped it away, but the action only seemed to amuse him. He laughed loudly at her show of resistance and reached for her slender arms just above the elbow and shook her. Her breasts threatened to escape the low neckline of her saque. Twice she had managed to escape his lap, yet was being resolutely pulled back a third time. Neither the besotted soldier nor his equally drunken companion appeared to notice that she was not playing, but fighting in earnest. She had spilled most of the contents of the pitcher she still clutched in her arms, and the slippery floor made it difficult for her to get her footing each time she pushed herself upright.

Rae gasped as the gap-toothed soldier gripped her waist and brought her backside down hard against the bulge in his breeches. She felt his hot breath close to her ear and only guessed at half of the guttural crudities he muttered. She would have liked to scream at his rough handling, but had not the voice nor the hope that anyone would respond to her cries for help. Instead she twisted in his grasp and flung the pitcher at his head. It missed and connected with the hard sloping forehead of his friend. The man was stunned for a moment, yelled a harsh obscenity, and grabbed for Rahab's throat.

Rae kicked backward at her captor's shins, and he released her in time for her to elude the thick fingers hungry for her vulnerable neck. She had not the luxury of a moment's rest as she scrambled to her feet and slid out of arm's reach. Her thwarted captor stood and lunged for her. Rae agilely stepped to one side, leaving the fellow to flail at the air and fall inelegantly at her feet. Peripherally aware that she was providing a spectacle for Wolfe's regulars, and thoroughly disgusted by the knowledge, Rae tossed the heavy pitcher at the man who still desired to test the strength of her neck.

Startled, he caught it, giving Rae enough time to yank up the hem of her skirt and reach for the dagger sheathed against her thigh. The tavern became uncommonly quiet as Rae met her attacker unflinchingly. Her knife glinted like blue ice in the dull smoke of the room. The soldier paused at the intent in Rahab's eyes, yet the expectant hush that surrounded them prodded him forward. He would not be made a fool in front of his friends. He'd take the wench right here on the floor and show them all who would prick whom.

His face ruddy with anger, he slammed the pitcher against the edge of a table. It smashed easily, and he chose one of the jagged pieces of pottery as his weapon. Crouching slightly, his weight on the balls of his feet, he advanced slowly on Rahab. Without a word's passing among the spectators, a circle was cleared for the combatants. Money exchanged hands quietly as bets were tallied.

Dear God, Rae cried silently. How had she let this happen?

She should have left Wolfe's as soon as it was clear Kroger was not going to show up. Instead she had thought it would make a good story to tell Ashley if she brought home her small wage for one night of serving drinks. At the very least, she thought, she should have allowed the soldier to paw her. What difference did it make, these impersonal hands on her body? She was never going to see these people again. But a shudder had racked her as the man's cruel and calloused fingers had pinched her breast. In truth, she felt violated by the liberties that had been taken on her person during the course of this evening. She wanted to scrub her skin raw and doubted even then that she would feel clean.

Now there was nothing for it but to protect herself against a further violation, one that she did not know if she could live with. She grasped the heavy folds of her skirt in her right hand and lifted the hem away from her feet. In her left hand she held the lethal dagger and understood more clearly than her opponent the advantage left-handedness gave her in this situation. No doubt he was used to right-handed opponents. The same could be said for Rae. She knew how to protect herself, but this man could be vulnerable to a quick thrust to his blind right. Rae's major concern was quelling her own fear of the sharp and uneven shard of pottery the soldier waved in front of her. What that crude weapon could do to her face did not bear thinking about.

Rae stepped lightly on her feet, eluding the jabbing motion of the soldier's thrusts. Her eyes darted to take in the whole of the man, and she knew that if he were more her size he would be no match for her. His drunken condition made him clumsy, but also dangerously unpredictable. Rae's own bout with alcohol earlier in the evening made her more sluggish than she wished. Heaven knew, she reminded herself, if she had practiced a bit of temperance none of this would be happening.

There was a harsh gasp as the soldier's ragged weapon passed within inches of Rahab's face. Belatedly she realized it was her own protest that she heard. Her eyes glittered as she advanced on the ruddy redcoat, teasing him with the deadly point of her dagger. She dodged and feinted, jabbed and pricked. She was too quick for his leaden movements. Rahab had no intention of mortally wounding him. She wanted only to disarm and incapacitate him. But as her feet slid on the wet floor, the outcome of the combat was changed.

It was meant to be the slightest scratch on his chest. A mark that would remind him in the days to come that he should be easy with his liquor and less free with his hands. Perhaps he would even come to be amused by the light scar and learn to have a nodding respect for barmaids. That was what Rahab hoped for as she lunged forward to deliver her last thrust.

She cried out, a low, guttural sound of misery, as her feet went out from under her and she felt the point of her weapon slice flesh and snap bone. She fell against the soldier, and the weight of her combined with the driving force of her jab sent him to his knees. Rae's hand slipped from the hilt of the knife, and it was her own body that drove it fully into her attacker's chest. There was a muffled groan, then sounds of surprise and pain.

Rae reared back, dazed. She reached for the dagger and pulled it from his chest. The feel of the tempered steel sliding wetly against weaker muscle and sinew was sickening. Rae turned her head, wanting to retch. She did not see the blood blossoming darkly against the soldier's white shirt and crimson coat.

She could feel the circle of spectators closing in about her. She glanced up, and their accusing and angry faces merged as one threat against her. She could not even voice her innocence had they wanted to hear.

A hand grabbed her roughly by the arm and jerked her to her feet. It was a man. His features were distorted as if she were seeing him through a rain-spattered pane of glass. Yet she knew her eyes were peculiarly dry. She made no protest

as he dragged her through the crowd and up the narrow stairs
to the tavern's second story. He offered some explanation to
the customers bent over the body of the bleeding soldier, but
Rae did not understand his words. She allowed herself to be
pulled into a small room, lighted by a meager fire in the hearth,
and neatly pushed into a cane chair. Her head was rudely shoved
between her knees, and while she submitted to the ignominy
of this position she heard the scrape of the bolt being drawn.
She looked up questioningly, only to have a hand pressed
sharply against her nape and her face thrust again between her
knees.

"I doubt that we have much time," Jericho drawled, his
voice curiously slow given the pace of his recent actions and
the urgency of his statement.

Rae smiled giddily at the contrast. She received a less than
gentle squeeze on the back of her neck for her efforts.

"Give me the knife," he commanded. He watched Rae's
stiff fingers attempt to open their grip on her weapon. In the
end he had to pry it from her. Jericho pulled a soiled handkerchief from his pocket and wiped the blade clean. He examined
the workmanship and knew the wench had paid a neat sum for
her protection. More than likely she had stolen it. He doubted
she had bartered her body for it. He placed more value on the
dagger.

His face expressionless, Jericho lifted Rae and laid her on
the narrow bed. She made only the briefest of protests, and he
stilled it by lightly slapping her cheek. When she was perfectly
quiet he seated himself at the level of her waist and trapped
her with one arm. "If you have any thought of getting out of
this situation with your skinny neck still intact, you'll do what
I tell you. I won't ask and I won't tell you twice. Do you
understand?"

She nodded and concentrated on keeping his face from disap-
pearing. She recognized him now as the man who had studied

her so insolently. He was as cold and unfeeling as she had at
first thought, in spite of his timely rescue.

The pads of Jericho's fingers swept across the cheek he had
slapped. The action seemed to take the sting from his sharp
words. "Good. The moment you have ideas contrary to mine,
I'll leave you to test the waters yourself." His lips curved in
a hint of a smile as Rahab nodded again. "I've noticed in our
short acquaintance that you don't have much to say." Rae
opened her mouth, but he put a narrow finger to her lips. "And
it's the thing I like best about you. That, and the way you fight,
of course. Damn, but you know how to handle this piece." He
held up the dagger, examining it thoughtfully. "I'd like to meet
your instructor sometime." With no warning he tossed up Rae's
skirt and slipped the dagger in its leather sheath. "Your legs
are nice," he said conversationally, grinning as she sputtered
and tried to right her skirt. "You're a touchy thing, ain't you?
Can't figure out what you're doing in Wolfe's when you object
so violently to being petted." Rae jerked as if burnt, but Jericho
went on as though he hadn't noticed. "You must be used to
the fondling of strangers by now. Or is it only some of us you
object to?"

Rae watched him warily, wondering if she had escaped at
all. Had he only brought her to this room for his own amusement? Was she supposed to yield to him to gain his protection?
Something of her fears must have shown in her eyes, because
he laughed shortly.

"I'm not interested, ma'am. Not at the moment, anyway.
We can discuss price later. And before you get yourself all
worked up again I want you to look at this." He stretched his
left leg in front of him and withdrew a blade every bit the equal
of the one Rahab carried. He held it in front of her, permitting
her to examine it, then he lightly touched the point of it to the
hollow of her throat. He could feel her swallow hard. "Don't
ever think you can take me, because you can't. I can dispatch
a left-hander as easily as I can a right one. I can fight with my

knife in either hand. Can you say the same?'' Rahab shook her head. ''I didn't think so.'' He put the dagger away and surprised both of them by saying, ''Perhaps I'll teach you one day.''

Jericho left Rae's side briefly to listen at the door. It was difficult to tell the exact nature of the confusion and commotion below stairs. He doubted he had more than minutes before the constabulary pounded on his door. He was in no mood for a confrontation with British officers. He turned on Rae, cursing her under his breath for looking so terribly fragile and innocent on the very bed where he had hoped to take her. She had certainly put a period to that portion of the evening's entertainment.

''C'mon. On your feet. We have to get out of here. You've had as much rest as I can give you.''

Rae felt herself drawn to her feet, not by his hand, but by the compelling tone of his voice. There was something in his tone, a grudging respect perhaps, that spoke to her strength. He believed she could travel; she could believe no less.

She followed her rescuer to the window and only paused the merest of seconds before following him onto the sloping roof of the tavern's back porch. It was only after dropping to the ground, where his strong and capable hands steadied her on her feet, that it occurred to her she did not even know his name. As he led her away from the tavern she looked back once and saw two dimly lighted windows that opened above the roof. How differently things would have turned out if Kroger had appeared, she thought sadly.

''Don't look back,'' Jericho ordered, jerking her forward. ''I have to find a safe place for you. Do you have family that will hide you?''

Rae shook her head. Not for anything would she chance leading the enemy to Salem and Ashley. She couldn't let them know what she had done. God, she had killed a man this evening. Quite against her will, Rae began to shake. She sniffed inelegantly.

Jericho felt her hand tremble in his. "Don't go all missish on me now. Here, take my coat. It will help with the cold, at least." He struggled out of the jacket while Rae stood quietly, afraid to protest his suggestion for fear he would make good his threat to abandon her. He helped her slide her stiff arms into it, only too aware how pathetically lost she looked in it. "And for God's sake stop your sniffling. You laid a man low back there, and no one will be much impressed by your pretty tears and protestations. Certainly not me. But if you want to throw yourself at the mercy of the official inquiry, leave now." He waited all of three seconds for her to indicate her desire to do just that. Rae's slight spine merely stiffened. Jericho reached blindly for her hand and pulled her into an easy run beside him.

Rahab had no idea where she was. Her companion used sidestreets and alleys she had not known existed. Where there was light there were great, hulking shadows. Where light was absent there was only a penetrating darkness that frightened Rae with its intensity. She gave thanks that one of them knew where they were going.

Once Jericho realized the wench had no place to go where she could not be easily found, he knew where he would have to take her. It bothered him more than a little to use the schooner that had been set aside strictly for official use, but it sat idle now, far enough from Washington's camp that the girl would not suspect his connection with the Continental Army. He had no desire to be bartered for her freedom, knowing full well the British would be eager to forget his companion's deeds in exchange for a spy. She would be safe enough hidden along the banks of the Hudson. She could stay there until the search for her was ended, surely no more than a few days; then she could find more savory employment in another part of the city. Jericho was just feeling that he had the situation well in hand when Rae's steps faltered beside him.

He stopped. He was slightly out of breath himself so he

could appreciate that she was tired. He did not expect her collapse at his feet. "Damn," he muttered lowly, kneeling to hoist her over his shoulders. He staggered to his feet. "Not nearly the lightweight lightskirt I expected." He grimaced and adjusted Rae's unconscious form. Proceeding at a slower pace, he allowed himself a lazy smile as he considered the anger of the soldier's companions when they broke into his room and found him and the wench gone. They would feel the veriest fools that they had trusted him to keep her under guard while they fetched the regiment physician. Jericho could have told them it was a waste of their time. He was certain Rae's knife had pierced the soldier's lung. The man was not going to recover.

Jericho also knew it had been an accident, and when cooler heads prevailed the others would know it, too. But when Rae had withdrawn the bloody knife from the chest of her assailant, he did not think it prudent to wait for reason's embrace in view of the threatening stance of every man who surrounded her penitent figure. There was no telling what a crowd like that might do.

His burden groaned under the rhythmic jolting of his light steps. "Awake again, are we?" he asked genially. "Don't struggle. I'm not putting you down just so you can kiss the ground again. Consider yourself fortunate that I decided to pick you up."

Rae considered herself tortured, but there was no way to tell him so. She closed her eyes and prayed that they would reach their destination soon.

Jericho felt Rae's frame relax once more and he knew she had slipped into oblivion again. "Just a bit further, Red." He recalled the name Wolfe had given her. It was as good as any other.

He held her tightly as he slid down the embankment that led to the schooner and narrowly missed making the journey on his posterior. That would have been good for a laugh, he thought wryly. He imagined dropping her into the water and losing her forever. Jericho did not make it widely known, but he couldn't swim a stroke. His past notwithstanding, it was one more reason to hate being aboard any vessel.

Jericho wobbled slightly as he climbed aboard the schooner. Once he got his bearings he moved with a grace that belied his uneasiness. He took Rae below deck to the single cabin. The appointments of the room were not rich. Washington rarely used the craft and wished no luxury his men could not share. Still, it was a comfortable setting, probably better than anything Rae had seen recently.

Jericho was familiar with the floor plan of the cabin. There was a narrow bunk attached to one wall, three deep drawers beneath it, and several chairs neatly bolted to the floor. A storage bench sat below the single port window, its seat heavily padded for the comfort of a passenger interested in the view. There was a single desk and a stool, purely functional in design, and a walnut wardrobe and commode stood opposite the bunk. He moved easily to the bunk, dropped Rahab, then lighted several tallow candles. The flickering glow allowed him to see his companion more clearly.

Jericho Smith whistled softly, tipping back his tricorn and wiping his brow with his forearm. He did not like what he saw. He had lifted too many ales; it was the only thing that explained his part in rescuing a girl who was burning up with fever. Her condition put an end to his returning to the camp tonight. His friends would merely assume he was spending the evening in the arms of a willing wench and envy his good fortune. His brows lifted at the irony of his situation.

What Jericho knew about caring for the sick he had learned on board the prison of his youthful years and during the winter of deprivation and disease he had spent in Valley Forge. The few Indian remedies he remembered were not suited to her illness. Neither of these experiences had prepared him to help the flushed and fevered wench.

He tossed his hat on a chair and knelt by the bed. "Well, Red. I hope you have some fight left in you, 'cause you're gonna need it." He rifled the drawers beneath the bunk and came up with a nightshirt, several thick blankets, towels, and an extra set of linens for the bed. His stripping of Rae to her heated skin was as impersonal as it was efficient. He slid her into the nightshirt and pulled the hem neatly to her ankles. "There's room enough for two of you in that garment," he told her. He carefully tucked two blankets about her, then took a pitcher from the commode cupboard and went to fill it with water. He liberally doused one of the hand towels, folded it, and placed it across Rae's forehead.

Jericho stepped back to view his work. "That's it, Red. The rest is up to you." It occurred to him that he should probably have some manner of food for her. What was it the medics had told him? Starve a cold, feed a fever? Or did he have it reversed? He shook his head in disgust. How the hell had he managed to put himself in this situation? What good was he to the wench?

Oh, hell. He jammed his hat on his head and set off in the direction of a farmhouse in the area he knew to be friendly to the cause. When he returned to the schooner he had two large wafers of hardtack, plenty of dried and salted beef strips, several apples, two flasks of corn liquor, and as a special treat from the farmer's wife, a faintly warm piece of cherry cobbler. He had told them he was on the general's business and needed provisions for a few days. Though he had offered them the last of his continental notes, they had refused them. Jericho had merely sighed. Everyone seemed to know they were next to worthless.

He put everything in the storage bench except the cobbler, which he ate with rare relish while sitting at the desk. "I doubt you are in any condition to appreciate how good that was," he said, licking his fingers. There was not even the faintest of replies from the bunk, confirming Jericho's point. "What am I supposed to do with you, Red? How long have you been ill?

And what were you doing in Wolfe's feeling as poorly as you did? Earning your living, the same as every other lightskirt in the place, I'll wager.'' The absurdity of his conversation struck him and he laughed softly. ''Dear Lord, I'm talking to myself . . . and answering. You've got a strange way of twisting yourself about a man. You fight like a soldier and fall at my feet as helpless as a baby. I don't think I much like it, Red. I don't think I like it at all.''

Jericho Smith snuffed the candles, stripped to his drawers, and dropped to the floor, covering himself with the last blanket. In minutes he was asleep, his left hand resting within inches of his dagger.

At the first whimper Jericho was on his feet, crouched to pounce, his blade resting lightly in his palm. It took him longer to assess there was no danger than it had taken him to leap to his feet. ''Damn!'' he muttered, setting his weapon aside and going to his patient. ''You're on fire, Red.'' He withdrew his hand from her cheek and sat heavily beside her, his shoulders slumping. What was he supposed to do?

''Mama.''

The plaintive cry tore at Jericho Smith, and it angered him. ''I'm damn well not your mama, you stupid chit!'' he said impatiently, roughly. He immediately regretted his words, despite the fact that she had heard none of what he said. ''Hell, I'm sorry, Red. We're both out of our minds.''

Jericho moved easily about the darkened cabin. He rummaged through the bench's contents, found one of the flasks, and added the contents to the remainder of water in the pitcher. He tore one of the towels into smaller pieces and soaked the strips in the mixture. Jericho first bathed Rae's face, wiping the heated contours gently. Sweeping aside her blankets, he rolled the nightshirt to her shoulders and continued his tender ministrations on the rest of her flesh. Without light he could only make out the faint outline of her figure against the sheet, but he needed no aid to realize how neatly her curves fit the

palm of his hand beneath the damp cloth. He growled deep in
his throat at the direction of his thoughts.

"I think I liked you better when I thought you but a skinny
bit, more temper than tempting. I don't need you, and God
knows I'll be happy when you don't need me." He finished
bathing her quickly, put the nightshirt in place, and tucked her
in again. With the back of his hand he tested the temperature
of her face. It felt slightly cooler to the touch, but he washed
it again and left a freshly soaked cloth in place over her brow.

He sat with her a few minutes to make certain she was
sleeping easily, then he returned to his place on the floor. Just
moments prior to nodding off he wondered if he had wasted
good whiskey.

Thirty-six hours passed before he knew the answer. He was
on the deck of the schooner, fishing from the side, when he
heard his patient moving below. Putting aside his pole, he got
slowly to his feet and pulled his shirt from the rail where it
was drying with the rest of the newly washed clothes. He could
hear her rummaging through the drawers and wardrobe. He
threw her slightly damp garments over his shoulder and went
below.

"I think you're looking for these, Red," Jericho said from
the open doorway.

Red? It seemed familiar. As did the man leaning negligently
against the jamb. He appeared to know her. It followed he must
know her name. Rahab smiled uncertainly as she gathered the
loose neckline of her nightshirt close about her throat.

"You are a fetching little thing, but it seems rather too late
for a show of modesty. Have you forgotten who dressed you
thusly?" Jericho stepped in the cabin and dropped her clothes
on the bunk.

It seemed to Rahab that she had forgotten all manner of
things. Beginning with her own name. She did not know who

she was, let alone where she was. Every muscle in her body ached as she moved slowly toward the pile of clothes. Had this man beaten her?

"Easy, Red." Jericho swept her off her feet and put her down on the bed. "You're not steady yet, and the schooner's bobbin' a bit today. How are you feelin'? You took a nasty turn yesterday."

Of course, she thought. She had been sick. That explained the relentless pounding in her head and the infantlike weakness. It was still incredibly painful to swallow. She tried to speak, but nothing came of it. She pointed to her throat, hoping he would understand.

"Open up and let me have a peek," he ordered, grinning when she complied. She looked very much like an unfledged bird waiting for feeding time. "Good girl. You're still a bit raw. Save your voice until you feel better. I can talk for both of us."

Rae frowned. She had a vague recollection that someone else had told her to save her voice. She couldn't hold the memory and it was lost as quickly as it had come.

"Just point to where you hurt," Jericho said, thinking her in pain. Rae rolled her eyes at the impossibility of the task he set for her. Her hands swept past her entire body.

"All over. Hardly surprising, Red. You weren't fit to work the other night and you damn well know it. I can understand that you needed the coin, but I can't believe it was so important that you lent your body to be pawed when you could barely say nay."

Rae's eyes widened and her dark lashes fluttered. What sort of work had she been engaged in?

"Course I can hardly say you weren't able to defend yourself. Was he the first man you killed?"

Killed? She had killed someone? She shook her head, not crediting what this man was telling her.

Jericho misunderstood. "I thought he might not be your first, but you were so near to fainting afterward that I couldn't be sure. I'm not condemning you, Red. I know it was an accident, and I can't say the same about the men I've killed.''

Rae's mouth gaped at this last revelation. She tried to inch away from Jericho.

"Self-defense," he said matter-of-factly, eyeing her carefully. "Same as you."

Rae stilled. She believed him. She didn't understand anything that had happened to her, or was happening at this moment, but she believed this man.

Jericho's head tilted to one side as he studied Rae. His hard cerulean eyes narrowed briefly. He could not understand why most of what he'd said appeared to surprise her. She had been at Wolfe's same as he, yet she reacted as if she had not been a participant in all that had gone on. A touch of brain fever, he decided.

"Look, you still need more rest. You've been out cold for a day and a half. I'll put your things over the chairs to dry and you slide under the covers. I'll be topside if you need me. There's fresh water in the pitcher and a mug on the hook nearby." He pointed to the opposite wall. "Do you want anything now?"

Rae shook her head.

"Get some sleep. I'll check on you a little later." He paused at the door, looking back over his shoulder. "Listen, Red, forget what I said about workin' out a price. You don't have to worry about me."

Rae closed her eyes, wondering why his parting statement should make her feel the tiniest bit sad.

When Rae woke again it was dark and, she assumed, quite late. She could make out the vague shape of the stranger on the floor and heard the soft, oddly reassuring cadence of his breathing. Gingerly she stretched her limbs. Her stomach growled noisily in the relative silence of the cabin. She patted the offending portion of her anatomy and quietly slipped out of the bunk. She had taken only two steps when she felt warm fingers clutch her ankle. Her instinctive scream was smothered with her own hand as she realized who was holding her. She sat down on the edge of the bunk and he released his tight grasp.

Jericho sat up. "I'll get you something to eat," he said.

He spoke as if he had been awake for hours, Rae thought. She was certain he had been sleeping soundly. "Please," she whispered.

Her voice made him hesitate as he got to his feet. He lighted a candle and brought it close to her face. "You can talk." She nodded. "Does it hurt?"

"A bit."

Satisfied she was telling the truth, Jericho set the candle holder on the desk and rooted through the hold of the bench for food.

Rae watched the play of yellow light across his shoulders, fascinated by the rippling effect on his broad naked back. The string waistband of his drawers rested low on narrow hips. She was not quick enough to turn away when he glanced over his shoulder, and neatly caught out, she refused to deny her interest.

Jericho grinned. "Find something to impress you yet?" he asked cheekily.

Rae did not remember the exchange he was referring to. She sucked in her breath at his arrogance. "Hardly," she said, raising her chin a notch.

He chuckled appreciatively. "I suppose I deserve that," he said, turning back to get her food. "Can't say the same is still true for me. About you, I mean. You're a better-lookin' wench than I first figured."

"I'm not flattered."

"Good. Because I didn't say you were beautiful, or even comely. I merely said you were better lookin' than—"

"You first figured," she finished, mocking his country expression. That certainly put her in her place.

He thrust a small plate of food in her hands. "It ain't much."

She realized he wasn't apologizing, simply stating a fact. "Thank you."

Jericho sat cross-legged on the floor and watched Rae break off a small piece of the hardtack and press it daintily in her mouth. Her manner was curious. In this setting, with her slender legs crossed gracefully at the ankles, she gave more the appearance of a lady than a harlot. "Are you an actress?" he asked suddenly.

Rae paused before answering, giving his question careful consideration.

"No. That is, I don't think so. Might I have some water?" She thought the distraction would give her time to frame a suitable answer to the inevitable question.

Jericho stood up in a fluid movement that captured Rae's full attention. How beautiful he is when he walks, she thought. She had quite lost her concentration when he returned with the water and dropped silently to the deck.

"What do you mean you don't think so?" he probed.

Rae blinked and took a sip of her drink to wash down the dry, unleavened bread. "I'm afraid I can't remember very much, Mr.—" She looked away, a troubled half-smile forming on her lips. "See. I feel a veritable goose. I cannot even recall your name."

Jericho sighed, relieved. "Is that all? We've never been introduced. I'm Jericho Smith. And you're—?" His voice trailed off hopefully.

Rae's shoulders slumped. "I was so hoping you knew," she said wistfully.

"Meaning you don't."

She nodded. "I haven't a clue."

"Damn. Is this some whore's trick?"

"Is that what I am? A whore?"

"You tell me," he challenged grittily. "You were in Wolfe's Tavern serving drinks to a full regiment of redcoats. Smiling.

Teasing. And looking over each customer to determine the color of his coin. The only females in the place walk the streets when the pub closes.''

She put her plate and cup on the floor, her appetite gone. ''Then I suppose I must be what you say I am,'' she said slowly, meeting his eyes again. ''And I killed a man?''

''You really don't remember, do you?''

''I've told you I don't.'' Her voice cracked with tension and threatening tears.

''Don't strain yourself anymore,'' he said tiredly. In his melodic voice, he gave her a brief outline of the events at Wolfe's. ''There you have it, and here you are. It remains to be seen how we go on.''

Relief shone in Rae's eyes with his use of ''we.'' It did not sound as if he would simply desert her.

''Tomorrow's soon enough to work it out.'' Jericho reached for the candle, blew it out, and patted the hard floor as if he could shape it to his form. He pulled the blanket up to his bare shoulder and closed his eyes.

Rae cleared her throat as she drew her legs beneath her and leaned toward her roommate expectantly.

''You want something?'' he asked.

''I thought you might be more comfortable in the bunk.''

''I'm sure I would be, but where would you sleep?''

She considered his statement very odd in light of her occupation. ''Why, here of course. I imagine I must be used to sleeping with men.''

''Sleeping is not the word that comes to mind, Red,'' he said dryly.

''Oh. I see. Well, *that* isn't what I was thinking of.''

''*That* is precisely what I was thinking of.'' He turned his back to her.

''I believe you must be a gentleman,'' she said, snuggling into the feather tick.

''No, ma'am. Just discriminating.''

"Oh," she breathed softly, deeply hurt. She blinked several times to stem her tears, them simply gave in to them. They dripped silently over her freckled cheeks and when her nose filled with them she pulled both blankets over her head to smother her snuffles.

Closing his ears to her muffled sobs, Jericho cursed himself for his blunt reproach. It was as unnecessary as it was cruel. He had wanted her once, and if he was truthful, he wanted her still. But it was his very desire that drove him to push her away. He might want her, but he did not want to need her. And there was something about her that warned him it could happen. It scared the hell out of him.

In the morning Rae found Jericho on deck, leaning listlessly against the rail. His arms were folded in front of him and he appeared to be studying the scuffed toes of his boots. There was a troubled frown on his brow. She did not imagine his thoughts boded well for her. She began to turn away, loath to interrupt him.

"Don't go," he said quietly.

Rae stopped. He had not looked up. "I didn't mean to disturb you."

"I doubt you can help it," he said under his breath. Out of the corner of his eye he saw Rae stiffen and realized that not only had she heard him, but she was offended. He refused to explain. Better she remain offended. She would keep her distance. "You're feeling better this morning, I take it." He gave her the briefest of glances.

"Yes."

"Your voice is better."

"Yes."

"You're a prickly thing when your tender feelings are hurt."

"I'm surprised you credit me with emotion."

Jericho pushed away from the rail and gave her a hard look.

He would have liked it better if she did not appear so much like a schoolroom miss. Her shawl doubled as a fichu, modestly covering her shoulders. Her heavy hair had been neatly secured with the ribbon that had adorned her chemise and her face was freshly scrubbed. Hell, her freckles looked polished. "Don't pick a fight with me, Red," he said tightly. "You'll lose."

Rae swallowed, but she did not look away.

"Damn you," Jericho said after a moment. He spun on his heels and picked up the fishing pole that was lying on the deck. "I'll be back in a few hours. Then we'll talk about your future."

He was on the bank before Rae found the courage to call after him. "Please, Mr. Smith. May I come with you? I'll be quiet and I can dig for worms."

It was the mention of worms that swayed him. One eyebrow lifted lazily as he assessed the sincerity of her offer. He nodded abruptly and continued on his way, never once glancing back to see if she followed.

Rae kept her distance as she trailed Jericho along the riverbank. By accompanying him she hoped to make herself useful and give him pause about sending her away. She had no doubt the subject had been uppermost in his mind when she saw him on deck. Rae felt compelled to make him understand that until she knew her past she could not leave his protection. What would become of her? She did not think she had the stomach for whoring any longer.

Jericho left the bank for an outcropping of large rocks that had accumulated at one bend in the river. The slabs of stone had been warmed by the early morning sun and several robins and a lone whippoorwill were taking advantage of the heat. They did not even flutter as Jericho walked lightly by them. Erosion had created a natural seat of sorts on one rock and he settled there, his long legs dangling over the side well above the water.

Rae watched Jericho move among the rocks with a surefootedness she envied. She could not imagine the element in which he was out of place. While he rested comfortably in the curve of his rocky throne Rae stepped through the underbrush and walked deeper into the woods. Never asking herself if there was something a mite inconsistent about a lightskirt who knew all the best places to find slugs, she hummed softly to herself and overturned rocks and decaying logs. She plucked fat wigglies and sluggish maggots out of the rich, dark humus and dropped them into a carryall she improvised with her shawl. To the thick wrigglers she added a goodly portion of soil. "Something to play in," she told them. "While you wait your turn at the hook. No matter what some people may think, I am not without finer feelings."

Jericho appeared to be sleeping when Rae dropped beside him with her lively bounty. She was becoming accustomed to his strange ability to be ever alert, so she was not surprised when he sat up immediately and examined her bait.

He looked from the moving mound of earth on her watch plaid shawl to the serenity of Rae's expression. He handed her the roughly fashioned pole.

"Go ahead, Red. You put the crawlies on the hook. Can't stand them myself."

Rae did not believe him for a minute, but thought she recognized a peace offering of sorts in his quiet admission. She chose one energetic annelid, baited Jericho's hook, then passed the pole back to him. Without a word of thanks he dropped the line in the water. Rae watched his indolent technique with no small degree of skepticism. It was obvious he had come fishing to think, not with the intent of catching their dinner. She sat very still while Jericho returned to his resting position against the rock. The pole rested loosely in his hands and his eyes closed, but Rae knew he would be alert to any break in the peace that surrounded them.

Jericho had never known a white woman, and few white men, who could sit as motionless as Rae sat now. It was a learned skill, one he had acquired shortly after jumping ship in the colonies. Two years spent with the Seminoles in the southern colonies had not been without rewards. He had already known how to fight, but the Indians had taught him how to win. How had she come by these skills?

"Have you remembered anything?" he asked tonelessly, as if her answer were of no consequence.

"No."

Jericho permitted himself a hint of a smile at her terseness. She took her promise to be quiet seriously. He almost wished she hadn't; it would be one less thing to like about her. "I wouldn't mind if you wished to elaborate on your answer."

"No. I have not remembered anything."

"Re-ed," he warned, drawing out her name to two syllables.

"Why do you call me that?" she asked. She drew her knees up to her chest and hugged them, looking at Jericho askance.

"I heard the owner of Wolfe's call you by that name. It suits you. After all, it is the color of your hair."

Rae fingered a stray lock that brushed her forehead. She pulled it down in front of her, examining it until her eyes crossed. "Oh, surely not," she frowned, ignoring Jericho's musical laughter. "I saw myself in your shaving mirror this morning. My hair is quite brown."

Watching the sun's light accent the copper fire in her hair, brown was not a color that leaped to Jericho's mind. Auburn, perhaps. Certainly mahogany. Her hair was rich with the shades of autumn's gold and umber. "Would you prefer I call you Quite Brown?" he teased.

Rae's soft lips puckered as she blew the offending strand of hair out of her eyes. "No, I don't think so. It's odd, you know, but Red seems almost familiar. Not precisely right, but nearly. Why do you suppose that is?"

Jericho shrugged. "It's all I've ever called you. Perhaps that's why it seems right."

Not all you've ever called me, Rae could have told him. How easily he forgot harlot and whore. Enjoying the camaraderie that had sprung up between them, she decided not to correct him. "How did you come by Jericho? It seems a curious sort of name."

"Not so strange once you know I chose it for myself when everything crumbled about my head," he said flatly. The admission surprised him. He did not always share his first name, and never before had he spoken of its origins. He hesitated, then shook off the past. "No matter. It was a long time ago. I was ten."

Rae said nothing. She bit back the myriad questions that came to her, knowing he would not appreciate nor allow her probing. But he could not stop her wondering about a ten-year-old who felt compelled to rename himself, to force a memory in the manner of a punishment. "And Smith?" she asked.

There was an infinitesimal pause. "Smith is my own."

It was more than she could claim. Rae rested her cheek against her knee and studied Jericho's peaceful countenance. There was no hint of tension about his mouth, no furrow about his brow. The lashes that fanned his cheeks were so dark in contrast to the brightness of his hair they did not seem quite real. She was certain he was watching her watching him, yet by not so much as a flicker did he indicate it.

"I think you have a bite," Rae said as Jericho's pole wobbled.

Jericho cocked one eyebrow. An eyelid lifted lazily. "Appears that way." He handed her the rod. "You take it, Red. I don't care for all that thrashin' around."

Rae smiled. Jericho Smith worked hard at being lazy. Not much scratched his placid surface. She struggled halfheartedly with the line, felt it give, then pulled it in. "He got away."

"Did he take the bait?" he asked, unconcerned.

"Yes."

"Good; he'll be fatter next time around."

That philosophy would not feed them this evening, but Rae found she didn't care. She plucked another wriggler from the dirt and baited the hook. She returned the pole to Jericho's idle hands. Her fingers brushed his and she pulled back sharply. The warmth of the contact startled her. Jericho, she noticed, appeared to be unmoved.

"I have a friend named Jerusalem," Jericho said into the chasm of silence that had developed between them.

"Oh."

"I thought that a rather strange name."

"To be sure." Rae was glad he had taken the initiative to speak, but she was having difficulty responding. How could an attraction be so one-sided?

"Of course, no one calls him that. Well, hardly anyone," he added, thinking of Ashley when she was piqued with her husband. "Mostly he's called Salem."

Rae could not care less. "And mostly what are you called?"

"Smith." He grinned. "At least to my face."

"Should I—"

"Jericho's fine."

Rae understood better than Jericho would have wished. Every time she used his name she knew he would recall the walls that had crumbled and were rebuilt. He would not be destroyed again. A ten-year-old did not forgive or forget easily.

Rae continued to hug her knees, rocking slightly on the warm, smooth stone. Quite suddenly she stopped and turned the full beauty of her green eyes on him.

"Why do you suppose I became a whore?"

Jericho choked and nearly lost his grip on the fishing pole. Was there ever such a guileless harlot as she? He had not thought the two words could be linked together until he made this wench's acquaintance. "I hadn't given it any thought," he lied, gathering the precious threads of his calm. "I've no doubt you have some theory you wish to expound."

The dryness of Jericho's tone did not escape Rae. "Not if you've no wish to hear it."

He waved one hand negligently. "Pray, tell me. You may hit on some spark that will fire your memory." It was years of practice that allowed Jericho to hide the curiosity consuming him.

"I rather think I must have been sold into it," she said finally, leaning back on her elbows and stretching her legs. "My family was probably starving."

"So you put yourself on the flesh market to put food on the table."

"Something like that."

"You made the ultimate sacrifice. Virginity for venison."

"There is no need for crudity. I was only trying to say that I must have entered the profession for compelling reasons."

"I apologize, your highness."

"You're forgiven," she said grandly.

Jericho was thoughtful. "I will concede you don't talk much like any whore I've known."

"I wasn't always one, you know," she continued seriously. Silently she wondered how many of her sisters he numbered among his acquaintances. "I may have been stolen by Gypsies. Or perhaps I fled a brutal husband. Mayhap—"

"I applaud your imagination. But what does it serve? Nothing is changed."

"No, I suppose not. I had hoped—" She stopped. What was it she had hoped? That Jericho would think more kindly of her if there were some excuse for what she was? That he would be more likely to offer his protection and not desert her? It mattered naught, she decided. She would survive without him. At least she could feed herself, which was more than she could say about the fisherman at her side.

Rae sat up abruptly, pulled off her shoes, rolled her stockings in a neat ball and stuffed them into the toes of the shoes. Standing, she unhooked her skirt and dropped it to the ground, then yanked the saque over her head and tossed it in the pile. The ribbon that held her hair fluttered to her feet as she defiantly shook her head. She stood poised on the edge of the rock in her thin undergarments but a moment, her naked arms raised to the sun and sky. Then, with no more than the gentlest push of her toes, she thrust herself into the air and arced headlong into the bitingly cold river.

Damn fool chit, Jericho swore, tossing aside his pole and peering anxiously into the water. She could have broken her simple neck with a stunt like that. She didn't know how deep the water was. She didn't know if there were more rocks below. Hell, maybe she had killed herself. Then Jericho relaxed. He saw her bubbles first, then the top of her head cut the surface. He reached for his line, so that when Rae turned to look up he appeared to have been unperturbed by her reckless dive.

High above her Jericho's legs dangled. Rae wished she could pull them into the water. She knew it was a stupid thing she had done. Lord knew the water was freezing this time of year, and she had narrowly missed smashing her skull on a submerged rock bigger than anything she had been climbing on. She was fortunate it had only been her arm that scraped its edge. She didn't feel cleansed, only cold. It had been senseless to believe the water could wash away, even briefly, what she was. Scarlet to her very bones. That was her lot. She prayed for the return of her memory so it wouldn't bother her so much.

"Reckon you could put a fish on the line, Red? Seein' how you're down there and all?"

Rae sputtered, pushing wet clumps of hair out of her eyes, and glared up at Jericho. Her prayer could not be answered a moment too soon. "Get your own damn fish!" she yelled. She struck out for the bank and clambered onto the rocks. By the time she reached Jericho's perch she was shivering uncontrollably. She was glad he did not look at her. Her wet underthings were plastered to her pimply flesh and provided nothing in the way of modest protection. She crouched beside him, covering her breasts with one arm while she gathered her clothes in the other.

"Might cold, was it?" he asked pleasantly.

Rae gritted her teeth, a nearly impossible task given the way they chattered. "Invigorating is the word that comes to mind. I'm going to dress now." She turned away and headed for a more private enclosure among the outcropping.

"Red?"

She glanced over her shoulder, tapping her bare foot impatiently. Jericho's unhurried gaze swept the damp line of her long legs, the shadowed cleft of her buttocks, her slender back, and finally came to rest on the green brilliance of her eyes.

"You looked real pretty doin' that dive, but if you do somethin' that stupid in front of me again, I'll put color in your backside that will shame your hair."

Rae simply stared at him, not disbelieving he would do it, only disbelieving his audacity in saying so. Because she could think of no reply stinging enough, she thrust out her chin, sniffed derisively, and stalked off. It did not improve her temper that behind her Jericho's laughter rumbled deep in his chest.

Rae found seclusion on a large slab of stone nearer the water's edge. It was gently angled, perfect for lying on, and it had absorbed a generous amount of the sun's heat. She stretched out on the face of the rock, belly down, and nearly purred as its warmth passed into her. It seemed a wasted effort to dry her underthings separately from herself. She shifted slightly a few minutes later to take advantage of a dryer and warmer spot, but did not move again, except in the careless movements of sleep.

Jericho Smith sat hunkered on the edge of rock about ten feet above where Rae slept. He had been there for fifteen minutes, motionless, watchful, and slightly drunk on the beauty beneath him. None of it showed on his face. It was as still and fierce as one of the granite sentinels guarding this bend in the river. His lashes neatly shuttered the desire darkening his eyes. His mouth had taken on the grim, ascetic line of self-denial. He envied the rock that held Rae's body flush to it. He wanted to be under her now, feeling her restless movements as she tried to make him yield to her softer contours. He wanted to palm the curve of her buttocks, jerk her close to the hardness of his thighs, and say, "Here. This is how we fit." Perhaps he would touch his mouth to hers, show her how noses adjusted, how lips locked. His hands would cup her breasts and the budding nipples would touch the exact center of his palms. "See," he would say. "You were made to fit these hands."

But there were things he knew he would not do. He would not be particularly kind or gentle. He would not count her freckles or thread his fingers through her hair. He would not touch his lips to the backs of her knees, tug on her toes, or whisper anything of love in her ear. He envied the rock for reasons that had nothing to do with the nearness of Rae's body. He envied that stone slab because she would rise from her nap, go on her way, and the rock would be the same. That was what he wanted. To be unchanged when she was out of his life.

Jericho came to his feet as Rae stirred and was already walking away when she came fully awake.

Rae yawned, stretching sleepily. By slow degrees she became aware of her surroundings, the rhythmic splash of water against the rock, the fragrance of the budding forest behind her, and the toasty heat that had penetrated her flesh to the marrow. She shielded her eyes against the brightness of the sun and wriggled her toes, feeling perfectly content not to move more than that.

She thought her memory must be returning by slow degrees because her dreams had been so erotic they continued to fire her imagination upon waking. She could hardly credit she had been so abandoned in her affections. Some movement to her left caught her eye, and Rae sat up abruptly as the object of every one of those delicious and frightening dreams walked away from her. Jumping to her feet, she pulled on her skirt and saque, and carrying her shoes and stockings, ran after Jericho. He never stopped and she never called to him, but she was certain he slowed his pace so that she could catch him. It was as if some deeply ingrained code of values and manners would not allow him to be a complete boor.

"I'm sorry about falling asleep like that," she apologized breathlessly, treading lightly in his wake. "I only meant to shut my eyes for a few minutes."

Jericho shrugged. "You needed the rest. No harm done."

"But your fishing . . . I wasn't there to bait the hook." She noticed he had no fish on his stringer.

"The worms didn't mind. I let them go." He halted so suddenly that Rae nearly knocked him over. He gritted his teeth in frustration, working the muscles in his jaw as the smooth tips of her fingers grasped him by the waist to keep them both from toppling. Cutting off the beginnings of her apology with a brusque wave of his hand, Jericho pulled her shawl out of the top of his boot where he had stuffed it. He thrust it blindly backward and it caught Rae in her midriff. Jericho swore under his breath. "Are you all right?"

Rae did not bother to answer because he was already five paces in front of her and showed no indication that he cared one way or another. Shrugging philosophically, she shook out her shawl, tied it around her waist, and followed Jericho at a more sedate pace. It did not set well that his abruptness hurt, but Rae admitted that it did. She cautioned herself against finding him attractive when he so obviously loathed even her casual touch. Better that she should return to the city as soon as possible than stay in the care of a man so completely beyond her reach. Given her profession, Jericho Smith had already risked much for her, and Rae did not want to press his good will or her good fortune. Her shoulders slumped slightly, her walk slackened further. Perhaps she was not meant to exercise such a rational mind, she thought sadly. She was certain she had never felt so bereft in her life.

Rae only caught up to Jericho because he had stopped along the way. He was standing on the grassy bank of a narrow inlet, staring at the blue-green water and looking quite pleased with himself. She watched in astonishment, a faint smile lifting the corners of her generous mouth, as he pulled in a net from the shallow backwaters. As the net wriggled and jerked with its lively catch, it became abundantly clear to Rae why Jericho hadn't cared a fig about hooking his dinner.

"It was very shabby of you not to tell me about your trap," she admonished him lightly as she approached. He merely grinned, but Rae thought it no mere grin. His smile, mischievous and boyishly sly, brought her up short. That flash of animated humor gave his face a startling beauty, an innocent freshness that totally belied the hardships that had shaped the man. In that moment she glimpsed the unfettered youth he had been and felt her heart squeezed at the loss. She bent over his catch to hide the sudden sheen of tears in her eyes. "May I help?" she asked as he efficiently began pitching the smaller fish back into the water. He gave her a brusque nod and Rae knelt beside him, matching his quick motions. Without a word passing between them, they settled on the same two catfish for their dinner.

"Do you know how to prepare them?" Jericho asked as he lifted the net and turned toward the schooner.

Rae hesitated, thoughtful, then nodded. "Isn't it strange, but I do know. I wonder why some things are easy to remember and others, hard?" Jericho only grunted a reply that Rae decided confirmed his indifference to her plight. The remainder of the walk to the ship was silent.

On board the schooner Jericho attached the net to one of the lower rails so it fell into the water, keeping the catch fresh until they had need of them. When he straightened from his task he nearly bumped into Rae. "Dammit, Red! Must you dog my every step?" He lifted her roughly by the shoulders and set her to one side as if she were so much baggage. "Stay out of my way!" Ignoring the ashen cast to her features and the hurt darkening her eyes, Jericho strode to the bow of the schooner and gripped the rail until the knuckles of his hands whitened. He did not relax until he heard Rae moving in the cabin below.

Had there ever been such a devilish mess as this, he wondered. He wanted nothing more than he wanted Rae out of his life, yet he could not bring himself simply to abandon her. What a pathetic creature she was, knowing naught but cleaning catfish and firing a man's loins with a mere glance of her eyes. If he let her loose in the city she would be flat on her back within the hour and in prison within two. And the hell of it was that it mattered to him.

He pushed away from the rail, his mouth a grim line, and turned to face Rae as he heard her approach. His eyes covertly swept her slender figure, taking particular note of the uneven and telltale bulge in the shawl at her waistline. The minx had been busy below, he decided, and prepared himself for her pitiable arguments.

"I've decided to leave, Mr. Smith," Rae said, her chin lifting a notch. Her show of determination was undermined by a slight trembling. "You must know that I am grateful for your timely intervention," she continued with great dignity. "But I have no wish to cause you any further distress, and I cannot seem to help but do so." She pointed to her lumpy shawl. "I took a little food from the bench, and lest you think me a thief, I tidied the cabin in trade. I would have prepared your dinner, but I think I should make the most of the daylight."

His face and voice void of expression, Jericho said, "That is wise of you. These woods are not without danger at night. Between the beasts and the brigands you will have a time of it."

"Brigands?" Rae swallowed her gasp.

"There are deserters of both armies roaming these forests, Red. You'll have an easier time eluding the four-legged animals. You have taken your dagger, haven't you? You'll need it, unless you intend to spread your thighs along the way."

Rae blanched at Jericho's crudeness. "I have it," she said, patting her leg.

He nodded, apparently satisfied. "I reckon you'll want to be goin', then. Do you know your way?"

"I'll find it."

Jericho forced down a smile. "Well, Red. I wish you the best."

"Yes. You also." She stared at him a moment longer, memorizing each feature, then the whole of his face. "Well . . . good-bye."

"Good-bye, Red." Jericho watched Rae descend the gangboard and take five steps before he called to her.

Rae looked up hopefully when she heard her name. Perhaps he wasn't going to let her leave, after all. He might be ready to apologize for his callousness. She would pretend to hesitate, of course. But not so long that he might think better of his decision to invite her back. She would forgive his gruffness and promise to stay out of his way, while he would admit she wasn't such a bad companion. They would reach a pact of sorts and could begin at the business of being friends.

Jericho pricked her bubble cleanly. "Other way, Red."

Rae thought of several things she wanted to do to the man. All of them slow, none of them pleasant. The other way, indeed. She turned sharply on her heels and began walking.

Chapter 3

Rae sat huddled at the foot of a leafless oak. The tree's thick trunk provided a barrier of sorts against the intermittent gusts of a bitterly cold wind. A cluster of daffodils that had dared to show their bright yellow blossoms was now edged with icy crystals. The food she had brought along lay untouched in the lap of her skirt, while the shawl that had held it was pulled tightly across her shoulders and held in place by stiff fingers and a haphazard knot. She squeezed her eyes shut as another blast of cold air gathered force along the river and seemed to shoot right up the bank to her shelter. Had it only been this morning that she had sunned herself in nothing more than cotton undergarments?

Rae shifted uncomfortably, tucking the hem of her skirt under her feet and legs. Her foodstuffs fell unnoticed to the ground. She admitted that nothing had gone as planned since she left the schooner. She had thought she and Jericho were only a few miles from the city proper, yet she had been walking for hours and never seen any evidence that she was coming upon New

York. It occurred to her that Jericho had purposely sent her off in the wrong direction, but she could not credit him with the calculated cruelty that would play with her life. She knew she had not been walking in circles because she had been careful to follow the river's course. Now it was getting dark and this morning's penetrating heat was but a memory, hardly the stuff to keep a body warm.

She wondered what sort of beasts and brigands she could expect to encounter in this cold. Rae was now convinced she had been a fool to leave Jericho's protection before he ordered her away. Which convinced her she had but one alternative: to return to the schooner and hope that he would not toss her overboard.

Rae struggled to her feet as the wind whipped her skirt about her legs. She stepped out from behind the oak and was nearly knocked to her knees as a spindly branch thrashed her face. Pressing the back of her hand to her cheek, she felt the warm wetness of her own blood. She bit her lip to still its trembling, but her tears slipped heedlessly down her face, stinging the open wound. Blindly she pushed her way out of the undergrowth and began the long trek back to Jericho Smith.

She had only gone a hundred yards and rounded the nearest bend in the river when she spotted the schooner moored to a tree stump on the bank. Looking ghostly in the dwindling light and the shimmering of her tears, Rae thought she must be seeing it because she wanted to see it. She knuckled her eyes to clear her vision, and when the apparition remained, bobbing and rolling on the crest of the water's white waves, she scrambled down the steepest portion of the bank, finishing the hasty descent on her backside.

"I hate you, Jericho Smith!" she cried to the shadowy figure leaning against the rail of the schooner. "D'you hear? I hate you!"

"Tell me to my face, Red!" he called back, cupping his hands around his mouth so she could hear him above the rising wind. "Slip the line off the stump, hold on, and I'll pull you in."

Rae followed the mooring line to the tree stump and saw that it was pulled so taut that she had no choice but to cut it. She took out her dagger, and gripping the rope in her right hand, she slashed through it with her left. She had known once she cut the line its tension was going to pull her hard into the water, but the strength of the jolt and the bitter cold of the water nearly caused her to lose her grip. She fought to retain her tenuous hold on the rope and her dagger and succeeded in spite of Jericho's urgings that she get rid of the bloody knife or he would leave her to the fish.

Jericho dropped to his knees as Rae crumpled on the deck after he pulled her over the side. He pried her fingers from the line and impatiently tossed the dagger in the direction of the hold. He yanked her close to him, folding her in his secure and relatively dry arms, and ran his palms along the line of her slender back, assuring himself she was all in one piece.

"I hate you, Jericho," Rae whimpered against the curve of his neck.

"I know, Red."

"You followed me."

He merely nodded, pressing her shaking body closer. What could he say to her? That he had only meant to show her what a complete infant she was? It seemed unnecessarily brutal to voice his purpose now. He had never intended that she should come to any harm, yet the weather had turned cold and she had suffered for it. She could have retreated at any point and he would have been there to help her. He had rarely lost sight of her painstaking progress along the river's rough trail.

"Warm me, please. I'm so cold." Rae's fingers clung to the rough texture of his wool jacket.

"Oh, God," he muttered low against her ear. "I thought you would never come back to me."

Rae warmed to those words. "I was so afraid."

Somehow Jericho knew her fear was not of the elements but that he would not want her back. "I've got to get you below, Red. And out of these clothes. Can you walk?"

She nodded and let him help her to her feet. The deck rolled beneath them and Rae fell against Jericho, her sodden skirt wrapping around his legs. "It's the simple things I can't seem to manage," she said giddily, pushing herself away. The skirt held her fast to his side and she nearly toppled over backward.

Jericho caught her by the waist and shook his head with exaggerated patience at her bemused expression. "I reckon I'll have to carry you, infant."

He said it with such fondness that Rae could not bring herself to object. She slipped her arms about his neck and her sigh of pleasure was carried away in the wind.

"Can you manage your garments?" he asked after making certain she was steady on her feet. "I have to see to the schooner's direction, else we're liable to run aground."

Rae had been ready to tell him she could not hope to get out of her clothes on her own, but she hesitated when she realized he was needed more at the wheel and sails. "I'll be fine," she assured him. "Do what you have to do."

Jericho eyed her carefully, not quite convinced, but not really having much choice in the matter, and left the cabin. Later he estimated he had probably not even reached the bottom step before Rae simply sank to the floor.

"Little liar," he said softly as he lifted her out of the puddle that had formed around her and dropped her on the bunk. He made short work of her muddied skirt and saque, her stockings and underthings, tossing them all back in the dirty pool of water and slipping her into a nightshirt. "It's unconscionable the way you use me as a nursemaid." Rae's lips curved in a delicate smile that had nothing to do with Jericho's words and everything to do with the warming blanket he pulled around her shoulders. The teasing light in Jericho's eyes vanished when he gently washed her face and saw the extent of the scratch on her cheek. He washed the area gently and prayed it wouldn't scar.

"Hell, Red, I'm sorry," he said feelingly. "I didn't want you hurt. I would cut my own face before I'd wish this on you." But there was no response forthcoming, and Rae's slumber that evening was much more peaceful than Jericho's.

It seemed as though a redcoat cannonade rumbled through Jericho's head as he came awake. Groaning, he sat up and massaged his throbbing temples. It was hard to believe that inside his head there was so much noise and outside nothing but the cheerful call of a few birds. He stretched stiffly and washed his face at the basin that Rae had thoughtfully filled for him. He shaved quickly, not a little curious about Rae's whereabouts. He had not expected her to rise so early, not after yesterday's experience.

Jericho stepped on deck and was immediately bathed in sunshine. In his present state of mind he found nothing to glory in and merely cursed the fickleness of spring. It was as if yesterday's chilling squall had never happened. Squinting, he brought up a hand to shield his eyes and looked around for some sign of Rae. He found her kneeling at the bow rail, pulling a bucket of water over the side. She was still wearing the nightshirt and it was sticking wetly to her frame, evidence that she had been at work for some time. Hanging on the rail to dry was every stitch of clothing she owned, and Jericho couldn't imagine what she wanted with more fresh water.

"What are you doing now, Red?" he asked a trifle gruffly. It was the headache that made him so testy, he told himself, and not the sight of the damp garment hugging her curves.

Startled, Rae lifted her head jerkily. She flushed, embarrassed as she recalled Jericho's arms about her, and wondered why she should be nervous with him now. "I had to wash my things," she explained, offering a small, uncertain smile. "They were caked with mud. Now I'm going to wash my hair."

When she turned her face on him fully Jericho recoiled at the sight of her scratched cheek. He fastened his eyes at some point in the water behind her. "You have some soap?"

Rae's gaze dropped to her reflection in the bucket. Self-consciously she picked at a few strands of hair and covered the reddened weal. "I found a little in the wardrobe. You don't mind, do you?"

Did she think him a complete ogre? "No, of course I don't mind. Use anything that strikes your fancy." He hesitated. "Do you want some help?"

"Er—no ... I can manage." Before he could protest her decision Rae ducked her head into the bucket and thoroughly wet her hair. When she came up and reached blindly for the soap it was his hand that put it into hers. "Thank you." Her head bent, she began to work what passed for a lather into her hair.

Jericho watched for a while and finally gave in to the urge that seized his trembling fingers. He dropped on his haunches beside her and took the soap from her. "Let me," he commanded roughly, then more softly, "Please."

Rae was too stupified to pull away from the tug of his fingers in her hair. She nodded mutely, closing her eyes as his gentle hands massaged her scalp. Her hands fell uselessly to her side while his soaped the short tendrils of hair curling at her nape and temples. There was a curious heat building inside her, and breathing seemed more difficult now than it had when she was being dragged willy-nilly through the water. She squirmed uneasily beneath his touch.

"Am I hurting you?" Jericho asked lowly, his fingers stilling.

"No ... you're not hurting me," she denied. Not in any way that I understand, she amended silently.

Jericho's fingers stirred again and he continued to rub the lather through each silky strand, marveling that the water had not doused the fire in her hair, only darkened it. What magnificent hair for a harlot, he reminded himself critically, hoping to stem the burning building within him. It was not particularly effective, and the tension in every line of his body showed no signs of abating.

"Rinse," he said tersely. Rae leaned forward and Jericho poured the water over her head. He ignored her sputterings, drew another bucket, and rinsed her one more time. That he spilled a goodly amount of the cold river water on his shirt and breeches he didn't seem to mind. If he had known how to swim he would have leaped into the water and stayed there until his temperature cooled.

Rae flung back her wet hair and stared mutely at Jericho, a question in the dark velvet of her eyes. There was a harshness in his face that she did not understand. What had she done this time? Why did he always look at her as if he wished to throttle her? Water dripped in tiny rivulets from her hairline, past her temples, and along her pink cheeks. Her spiky lashes fluttered to stem the flow as if she were fighting tears.

"Damn you," he muttered, his eyes darkening. "I knew you'd be trouble." He leaned closer to her upturned and startled face. Her mouth was so close to his that if she touched her tongue to her own lips he would be able to taste her. "I reckon your kind can't help it."

Rae recoiled as if he had slapped her. Jumping to her feet, she stood rooted to the deck, arms akimbo, her hair in a dark fiery tangle about her face and shoulders. "How dare you! You paint me scarlet even while you want me! If I am a whore, then what are you to desire me? Are there no well-bred ladies who will honor your suit? Leave me be, Jericho Smith! You may be willing to overlook your disgust of me but I find myself unable to reciprocate!"

It was a magnificently trenchant speech, and Rae quite startled Jericho with her vehemence and vocabulary. He sat back on his heels, staring up at her flushed face and glittering eyes, and vowed that he had never known such a spirited setdown as the one he had just received. He found himself without a reply of any kind.

Determined to take advantage of Jericho's stunned silence, Rae prepared to walk away. With grave dignity she lifted her chin, quieted the breathless heaving of her chest, and stepped past his crouched figure.

"Oooooofff!" Stately carriage and dignity had its place, she supposed, but not when one had to watch out for a neglected sliver of soap on an already slick deck. Rae's arms flailed in the air in a futile attempt to right herself before she landed with an inelegant thwack on the wet deck. Droplets of water flew out from beneath her, and the cause of it all, that accursed bar of soap, sailed in an arc above the rail and landed neatly in the river.

Rae swore as she rubbed her abused posterior. Jericho's eyebrows lifted in astonishment as he struggled with a reckless urge to laugh. With great effort he tamped it down and turned away, only his bright blue eyes hinting at the humor he found in Rae's ungainly position.

Rae had no need to see his face to know what Jericho thought of her performance. She was ready to turn the force of her embarrassed anger on him when her palm touched something hard in the flesh of her buttocks, and the pain of it caused her to cry out.

When Jericho spun to face her, tears of humiliation were already burning Rae's eyes. Humor vanished. "What is it, Red? Have you hurt yourself?"

Rae could have called on some reserve of wounded pride if Jericho had ridiculed her clumsiness or berated her for being so poor spirited, but his unexpected kindness completely undid her. She buried her face in her hands and sobbed jerkily, her shoulders heaving in an aching rhythm.

Jericho first examined the shape of his nails, then studied the shifting pattern of soap bubbles on the deck, and wondered all the while at his own helplessness. He had always scoffed at men who complained they knew naught but frustration when confronted with a woman's tears. Yet he felt the very same at this moment, having no idea what was expected of him, if, indeed, she expected anything. "Hell, Red," he said finally. "If you'd just tell me what's wrong, I figure I can help." Surely it was a reasonable request, he thought, issued in a reasonable tone. He swore more eloquently when Rae only cried harder. "C'mon. It hurts to listen to you."

Any number of cutting retorts occurred to Rae, but she discovered she hadn't the breath to say any of them. She found, however, that she had voice enough to yelp loudly when Jericho sat in the puddle beside her and hauled her onto his lap. The throbbing pain in her nether parts increased sharply as she came down hard on his thighs.

"What are you tr-trying to do—kill me?" she whimpered against his chest.

"Madam," he explained patiently. "I'm trying to make some sense of your bawlin'."

"I habba plinter in my bottom," she told him, tears filling her throat and nose.

Jericho hesitated. "I beg your pardon, Red. I thought you said you had a splin—"

"Plinter in my ass! Muft I repeat ebberting?" Was the man completely lacking in any finer sensibilities?

Jericho choked on his astonishment and made a gentlemanly effort to halt his rising laughter. Rae felt the rumble in his chest as he moved against her, and before she considered the consequence of her action she pounded on him with tightly folded fists. She used every manner of vile language to heap curses on his head, and because the words sounded so ridiculous in her clogged little voice, Jericho laughed until tears shimmered in his own eyes, then scooped a handful of soapy water from the desk and neatly sprayed her gaping mouth with it. It had the desired effect. Rae sputtered into shocked silence and dared not move, fearing further retaliation. She regarded Jericho warily.

"Can't recall my ears ever burnin' like that, Red. If you're finished, I'll see what's botherin' your backside." Rae struggled in Jericho's arms when she realized his intention, but there was never any doubt who would be the victor in the uneven combat. When he sensed she had tired herself into compliance, he easily flipped her on his lap and held her captive with one leg over the back of her thighs. With the calm reserve of a seasoned physician, Jericho bunched Rae's nightshirt about her waist and examined the injured area. He needed but a moment to ascertain that he would have to remove the splinter before infection set in. He covered her again but did not release her. "Below, Red. It has to come out, and I don't figure you can manage it yourself."

Rae flamed with mortification, yet she had no recourse except to obey. "I can hardly rise if you continue to hold me," she said tartly.

"That's the spirit," Jericho teased encouragingly, lifting his leg. He chuckled as Rae scrambled out of his reach and fled to the cabin. He followed at a slower, more thoughtful pace, wondering what he had done to deserve this upheaval in his life. And worse, like it.

When he entered the cabin Rae was lying on the bunk, facing the wall, and hugging a small bolster pillow to her breast. Jericho found a valet's sewing kit in the wardrobe and chose a new needle for the operation. "I doubt you'll feel this at all," he said as he sat beside her.

"Hmmmpf."

"Humor me, Red."

It suddenly occurred to Rae that for all his easy ways, Jericho was decidedly uneasy about doing this. That thought made him seem more human, less distant, and served to relax Rae. "I shall be very brave," she assured him with a measure of mock-

ery. "But don't expect me to enjoy this. That would be painting
it a bit too rosy."

Grinning, Jericho flipped up the hem of the nightshirt and
applied himself to removing the splinter. It was deeper than he
had at first thought, and a number of painful minutes passed
before he had the thing out. To distract her while he worked,
he encouraged her to talk.

"I didn't think you would be so mean as to send me in the
wrong direction," Rae answered Jericho's query about her
aborted trek.

Clearly puzzled, he asked, "Wrong direction? Do you think
I would do that?"

"What else can I think? You said you carried me to the ship
and I cannot credit that even you could have traveled so far
with me on your back. I walked for miles and saw nothing but
river and forest. I think you meant for me to journey to Canada."

"A glance at the sun would have told you otherwise," Jericho
pointed out tersely. It bothered him no small amount that she
thought him capable of such a thing. His distraction caused him
to ply the needle with more force than was strictly necessary. He
felt worse when she barely winced, proving that she intended
to be brave, indeed.

"If you recall, the sun was not much visible during most of
my trip," she said through clenched teeth. Did he think her a
pin cushion as well as an idiot?

Jericho pulled out the splinter and dabbed at a small pooling
of blood with the hem of her nightshirt. Once the bleeding was
stopped he yanked down the shirt and told her grittily, "I moved
the schooner shortly after we came aboard. I was thinking of
your safety. Pardon me for not anticipating that you would
desire to leave."

Rae gingerly sat up and regarded Jericho skeptically. "Surely
I did not mistake your wish to be rid of me. I thought you
regretted your decision to bring me here."

Had he really been so obvious, he wondered, or was she

practiced at reading men's minds? After a moment's study Jericho looked away from Rae's frank stare and busied himself putting the needle and sewing kit away in the wardrobe. He was silent so long Rae thought he had no intention of responding.

"You are not mistaken," he finally said heavily, turning from the wardrobe to face her. "And there have been those occasions when I regretted bringing you here, but that is not to say I still regret it or that I wish you gone before you can fend for yourself. I have given the matter a great deal of thought and I have arrived at a plan that I believe we can both live with."

Rae nodded shortly, her face expressionless as she tried to hide the fear that had flashed through her at Jericho's last statement. Drawing her knees to her chest, she steeled herself to hear his plans.

"I am going to take the schooner closer to the city this evening," Jericho said, watching Rae intently. "I will go into the city—alone—and attempt to discover if the hunt for you has ended. If I believe it is safe for you to return, I have some friends who will most likely take you in." Seeing the suspicious lift of Rae's brows, he added, "There would be conditions, of course."

"Of course."

He ignored her mocking. "You will have to give up whorin' and agree to work as a servant in their home."

"Won't the mistress of the house object to my presence?" Rae asked cynically, intent upon goading him. "Mayhap she will not want me dallying with the master."

Thinking of Ashley, Jericho smiled, completely unperturbed by Rae's efforts to find fault. "She would scratch out both your eyes if you looked at her husband askance. And I doubt Salem would be much interested in you. He has everything any man could want in Ashley."

Something twisted inside Rae at the way Jericho's face softened when he spoke of this woman. No doubt his plan was prompted by a desire to see her. It galled Rae that she saw no alternative but to accept his proposal. When she spoke her voice was very cool, completely at odds with the anger sparkling in her eyes. "Then I shall be very happy to work for this paragon whose husband cannot be tempted."

Jericho laughed at Rae's stilted, nearly frozen accents. "Don't fly into the boughs. You'll do fine, Red. Just fine. I reckon there are any number of men you could tempt from fidelity's path."

"You?" Rae asked boldly. "Could I tempt you?"

"I was prepared to pay for a toss with you the other night at Wolfe's," he said, cruelly reminding them both of her profession. He steeled himself against Rae's soft gasp and the wounded look in her eyes. "Is that what you wanted to hear?"

"You know it is not," Rae said quietly, looking away from Jericho's still and watchful eyes. "But it is what I should have expected. I doubt I would have accepted you or your coin, anyway," she added, trying to regain her composure by shooting a pathetic barb in his direction. "The sooner I am away from here, the better."

A muscle twitched in Jericho's cheek. "My sentiment exactly, Red." He turned on his heel and stalked off for the upper deck. Every verbal exchange with her left a bitter taste in his mouth, he thought angrily. He was forever regretting the things he said to her, yet they were no more than truths, and they served to keep her at a manageable distance. He was no longer certain why he wanted to keep her at arm's length; perhaps for no other reason, than that he was tired of having women any man could have. "And if she were a woman for only one man?" he asked himself aloud, staring at Rae's thin white chemise where it fluttered on the rail. "Then you wouldn't deserve her, Smith. You don't deserve anyone like that." The soft conviction with which he said those words lent weight to them in his own mind, and they remained there, an invisible burden, long after he thought he had dismissed them.

Rae thought dusk would never settle on them. If she had ever passed a more uncomfortable day she was glad she could not remember it. The words they exchanged during the remainder of the morning and afternoon did not number above thirty. Silently she had gathered her clothes from the deck, and once dressed, gave Jericho his share of the meager breakfast offerings. She accepted his gruff thank you in the spirit in which it was given, turning her back on him and seeking privacy at the other end of the craft. After breakfast Jericho took the schooner farther downstream, sheltering them in the river's curve. When he took his net and pole and left to go fishing Rae did not even consider asking to go along. She occupied herself with the sewing kit, idly stitching anything that caught her fancy. She embroidered a small red rose on the collar of her nightshirt and another on the point of the schooner's mainsail. The latter was done with rather defiant strokes, plunging the needle into the muslin sail with the same relish she would have plunged it into Jericho's heart. Or so Rae told herself. Her offended pride did not permit her to examine her motives clearly when she finished the rose and found Jericho's jacket in the wardrobe and in need of some repair. She replaced the clumsy stitches on the shoulder seam with even ones that could hardly be seen and tightened two of the tarnished brass buttons.

She did not thank him for catching her in the act of biting off the thread and smoothing the material with her hands to examine her work. Embarrassed that he had seen her performing this small, wifely duty, she threw the jacket on the bunk as if it were a gauntlet, daring him to say even one word as she regally brushed past him on her way out of the cabin. She couldn't leave the small space quickly enough to suit her once he had entered. If she didn't get away from him she would do murder. At least that was the excuse she clung to.

She cooked Jericho's catch over a small fire she built on the bank. Rae did not know that he was watching from the bow of the schooner with a mixture of skepticism and astonishment.

She gave him the lion's portion of the baked fish, finding she had not the appetite to do credit to the meal. His attitude seemed to say that if she wished to starve herself he was more than willing to aid her. He ate with a gusto that made Rae want to snap that he should have caught more fish if he was so hungry.

At sunset she saw he wasted no time in removing them to a place still farther downriver. When he unerringly navigated them to a small private dock and moored them there, Rae knew this must be the place where he had first brought her. It unnerved her that somewhere close by was the tavern where she had killed a man, yet she still had no recollection of the event or her surroundings.

"Don't wander off," Jericho ordered her tersely.

"When will you be back?" Rae's question challenged him in waspish tones.

"Too soon to suit me." Jamming his tricorn on his head, he jumped the rail and was gone before Rae hurled a dinner plate at his head.

Jericho returned to the city by the same route he had left it. Twilight's indiscriminating blue-gray shadows lent him protection as he moved through alleyways and back streets. He neatly skirted a patrol of redcoats who may have felt obliged to harass him simply because he was alone. He felt no satisfaction with his maneuvering, only a sort of weariness that such stealth was so much a part of him it could no longer be considered second nature.

He paused briefly when he went by Wolfe's, the hesitation so slight that only the most careful of observers would have seen it was shock that rooted his steps for an instant.

Wolfe's was closed. Shut down by order of General Howe himself. Jericho had but a glimpse of the notice nailed to the tavern's oaken door, but he recognized the British commander's signature and stamp. Who the hell had Red killed? It had to have been someone favored by the general if he had seen fit to shut the tavern in retribution.

Jericho's pace increased as he headed toward Salem's home, keeping his head well down but alert for any other posters that would indicate that the harlot he befriended was being sought throughout the city. There were several about, and when Jericho thought he could read one without being noticed he stopped to do so. He had merely to scan it to realize neither one of them was in any danger.

The description of Rae included the phrase: "a buxom colonial wench of low morals and poor judgment." That fit any number of the women at Wolfe's that night, Jericho thought wryly, but not the chit he had undressed. She was no more than a handful. Finely sculpted, he admitted, but still no bosomy lass. Neither did she attain the height nor breadth of an Amazon. And to say her hair was red was not to describe it at all. Jericho had no doubt the dramatics of the evening had colored the accounts of the witnesses until their depiction bore little resemblance to reality.

After a hasty glance around him to be certain no one was watching, he tore down the notice, folded it, and stuffed it in his jacket pocket as he walked away. He would read it to Rae when he returned. Mayhap she would even smile at the characterization of him as a man of superior height. That was all anyone had remembered of him during his hasty ascent to the tavern's upper floor. Hunching slightly, shoulders sloping in a sluggish attitude, Jericho turned the corner, and no one who saw him would have remarked on his height at all.

When he reached Salem's house he pounded on the servants' entrance at regular intervals for several minutes before he was forced to conclude no one was home. Kicking the door in disgust, he turned away. So much for his intention to ask them to take in the wench. He would just take his chances with Salem's and Ashley's generosity and present them with their new servant tomorrow morning.

He started back to the schooner, whistling softly under his breath, well pleased that he had arrived at such a fine plan for

Rae's future. And his own, he added with a wealth of good feeling. He had been too long from camp. His compatriots would have known it had been he in the tavern the night of the killing and would understand the nature of his desertion. He wondered how long he would have to endure the ribald conjecture of the general and his aides while they took him to task. They would never believe Rae was not the woman of Amazonian proportions mentioned in the notice, nor that he had not shared her bed.

He was uncertain he believed it himself.

While Jericho was questioning the reasons for his self-imposed celibacy, Rae was sitting on the floor of the cabin, her back against the padded bench, raising a flask of whiskey to her lips. Her original reason for reaching for the flask was of no importance any longer. That niggling ache in the back of her throat, brought on by the string of curses she had laid on Jericho's head long after he was out of her hearing, had ceased to be a concern after two short swallows. Gradually a comforting warmth had erased the ache in her throat as well as the good sense to stop drinking. She was determined to extend the pleasant, numbing sensation to every part of her body that hurt, particularly her heart.

Her smile was a trifle sad. Her heart seemed peculiarly immune to the healing effects of the alcohol. What could she expect when Jericho had done naught but trample on and abuse it. "Probably doesn't credit me with one," she told the room at large. "And if the truth be known, it's most likely this brain fever that's made me so missish. I refuse to entertain any finer feelings for one Jericho Smith." Outside, water slapped at the hull of the schooner and Rae imagined it applauded her decision. She tipped the flask once more to her lips and found that her previous drink had drained it. Carelessly she dropped the empty container back into the bench and sought the other she had seen. She was distracted from her purpose by a faint rustling sound as her skirt caught beneath her and she knelt on it.

Frowning, and with the uncertain movements that spoke of her recent activity, she wrestled with the skirt as if it were a living thing and bent on thwarting her purpose.

Given Rae's condition, it took no small amount of single-mindedness to find the source of the crackling. She forgot all about her quest for the other flask as she tore at the basting stitches in her hem and found a folded piece of parchment. Wrinkled, creased, and fragile, it threatened to fall apart as she took it from its hiding place. She clumsily broke the seal, tearing the paper as she did so. The writing had been all but obliterated by the repeated washings and dunking the skirt had received. It was amazing the parchment had survived at all.

She wondered at it, wove intriguing stories about its presence in her hem, but never once hit on anything near the truth. She struggled to make out the faint, spidery handwriting by holding it over a candle flame. Not only did she find no message, visible or invisible, but she burned her thumb and one corner of the parchment. Impatient with herself and her awkwardness, she tossed the letter in the bench, promised she would show it to Jericho upon his return, and made her unsteady way to the deck for some fresh air.

Jericho's approach to the schooner was silent, but he decided he could have announced his presence with a score of whining bagpipes for all that Red took notice. He nearly tripped over her in the dark as he climbed on deck. Diverted, he noted she merely waved a hand in front of her nose, as if she were brushing aside a bothersome pest, and turned on her side. Kneeling beside her to make sure she was all right, Jericho smelled the problem before both knees touched the deck.

Knowing that he would be rid of her tomorrow, he felt he could forgive her much—even the liberal use of his small supply of spirits. Still, he considered, better not let her think he was going soft in the head. With that in mind, he filled a bucket with cold river water, and before he had second thoughts poured the contents all over Rae.

She dreamed she was drowning, and when she realized she wasn't, she came out of her nightmare bent on revenge. It only took her a moment to get her bearings. "You great, cloddish oaf!" she said as she clambered to her feet, wiping straggling wet hair out of her face. "Have you no conscience? Would you have me drown?" She advanced on him, lifting her dripping skirt out of the way of her unsteady feet, anger in every line of her sodden frame.

Jericho dropped the bucket and held out his hands, palms forward, to keep her at bay. He wondered if she could see the unholy amusement in his eyes. "Now, Red," he said placatingly. "Watch your step. You don't want to slip on the deck." Remembering that morning's accident brought a devilish grin to Jericho's lips

That grin, more than what he said, enraged Rahab. It seemed as if every one of those even white teeth was glinting in the moonlight. Never had she known such provocation. She picked up the discarded bucket by its rope handle and swung it at Jericho's head with all her might.

Rae was nothing if not accurate. If he hadn't stepped backward at the last moment he would have been lying flat out on the schooner's deck. Rae had even swung a trifle low, anticipating he would duck. Would that he had, she thought spitefully, as the force of her swing sent her spinning and allowed Jericho to grab her when her back was turned.

"Oooooofff!" she gasped as Jericho's arms came hard about her waist, squeezing the air from her lungs. The bucket flew from her hand and sailed into the opening of the hold, clattering noisily as it bounced down the stairs. "Beast! Let me go! You started this!" She twisted in his arms and repeatedly kicked backward, aiming for his shins. Her attempts to free herself and hurt him only compounded her frustration, because his arms were as secure as steel bands and he had an uncanny instinct that allowed him to anticipate her blows and avoid them.

"Give?" he prompted, with great superiority. He adjusted her again in his hold, securing her flailing arms in front of her this time. Now she could not reach behind him and pinch as was her wont. "C'mon, Red. Have done. It was only a little water."

"A little water?" she screeched. Still she writhed in his arms like a wild thing. "You may as well have tossed me overboard!"

"Don't tempt me," he gritted. This was followed by a grunt as the heel of one of her shoes finally made contact with his right instep—hard. Even through his boot it hurt like hell as Rae, glorying in her success, ground her weight mercilessly on the tender part. He bounced her in his arms, lifting her for a brief moment, and relieved the pressure. At the same time, she twisted, and with strength born of her fury, was able to release herself.

Rae staggered back, straining for balance on the shifting deck, while Jericho did the same. Jericho found his first, but remained where he was, slightly crouched and not a little wary of his opponent's next move. A moment later he questioned Rae's sanity, as she pulled up the hem of her skirt and went for her dagger. He had no idea she wore it with any regularity. Whatever else she might have forgotten, how to use her weapon obviously remained clear in her mind. Squinting, Jericho saw her advance in the pale moonlight, something feral in her eyes.

He retreated a few steps to provide an opportunity to reason with her. "Have a care, Red," he warned. "You're makin' too much of this. I meant nothin' but to wake you from your stupor."

"And I mean nothing but to wake you from yours. I am not your pet that you may toss or trample or tame as you see fit." She continued to stalk him.

"If you stop now, Red, we'll call it quits. It's clear you have no recollection of my warning to you at Wolfe's. But so help me, if you keep comin' I'll take you down, woman or no."

Rae had cornered Jericho against the rail. She stood far enough away that he could not strike but close enough that he could not doubt her aim. He had not yet reached for his own weapon. "I seem to have misplaced the bucket, but if you will drop over the side, I will consider us even." When he did not move, Rae jabbed insolently at him with her dagger. "Come, Jericho. What is a little water to someone who enjoys playing with it as much as you? Up with you. Over the side." She struck at the air again, pointing out the route he should take. She felt wonderfully malicious and hoped her smile was goading him beyond bearing.

Jericho wondered how the outcome of their battle would differ if he could swim. Would he have complied with Rae's demands to throw himself in the river? Probably not, he decided, but at least he would have had a choice. He had none now. He truly doubted it would do any good to explain he could not swim a stroke. She would not believe him, and he would be forced to disarm her anyway. And if she did believe him? Well, he was not going to allow opportunity for her to laugh at him.

"What am I to do with you?" Rae was asking rhetorically. "Can you not play the game when you are being teased? Shall I plead prettily?"

"Give me the dagger, Red," Jericho drawled in bored tones. She shook her head.

"If I take it from you, you won't like it."

"If you try, I guarantee you won't like it."

Jericho's hands were resting casually at either side of his waist on the rail. With virtually no warning, they tightened. At the same time his arms stiffened, supporting his weight as he thrust his feet up and out and sprang forward. He released the rail and for a moment he was airborne and vulnerable. If Rae had anticipated this attack and leaped out of the way he would have dropped painfully to the deck, but Jericho's charge was so stunningly swift and so visually elegant that Rae was unprepared for anything except the weight of him bearing down on her.

She made an effort to protect herself from his assault by crossing her arms in front of her. As soon as the soles of his boots touched her forearms she began reeling backward. In amazement she watched as Jericho landed lightly and gracefully on his feet while she thudded to the deck, trapped in the tangle of her soggy skirt and slips. She still gripped her dagger, but not for long. Jericho straddled her prone figure and stepped on her wrist, paralyzing her fingers so that they opened against her will. He removed his foot, and still straddling her, dropped to his knees. He had the dagger at her throat before her fingers recovered their feeling.

Breathless and furious, Rae waited for Jericho's next move. She could feel the point of the knife press lightly against the hollow of her throat. He had only to twist it ever so slightly to draw blood, or apply the smallest pressure to plunge it in.

Jericho's weight rested on his own legs rather than on Rae's stomach, but he dallied briefly with the idea of really sitting on her, just to remind her who had gotten the best of whom. "Well, Red? Give?"

Her expression every bit as mutinous as it had been when she had the upper hand, Rae shook her head. She would have scratched herself against the point of the dagger if Jericho hadn't lifted it a fraction.

"Have a care," he cautioned her, enjoying himself immensely. He tossed aside his tricorn and adjusted the fit of his jacket, taking care to keep a careful grip on the knife. "I'm a patient man, Red, and I'm prepared to wait you out. But I might as well be comfortable."

Rae would have liked to spit at him, but it would have been like spitting in the wind. At any rate, her drinking bout had dried her mouth. It was unconscionable the way he continued to best her, and it did nothing for her temperament. "What do you want from me?" she asked tightly.

"I've a mind to make you pay." As he said the words his cool blue eyes narrowed and swept her flushed face, attaching a new meaning to his demand that he was only partially aware of.

Rae felt an odd tightness in her throat that had nothing to do with the weapon pressed against her flesh. "I give," she said breathlessly, struggling a bit beneath him, hoping her hasty surrender would appease him.

He watched her for several long minutes, taking in the brightness of her eyes, the tangle of her hair, the stubborn jut of her chin. He strained to see the spray of freckles on the high curve of her cheeks that seemed so odd in light of her profession. But they appeared to be invisible now, leaving her complexion softly pale in the moon's silvery light. "So anxious of a sudden? I think it's too late for merely giving in. There are terms to be met now." He dragged the edge of the dagger gently down the exposed flesh of her chest until it rested at the neckline of her saque.

She swallowed her gasp. His intent was clear, and Rae only listened with half an ear as he threatened to slice her blouse to her waist if she did not remove it. The rest of her attention was focused on the soft, uneven pattern of his breathing, a raggedness so slight that she had to look to his broad chest for confirmation. Quickly she glanced at his face and read the clear desire in his eyes. A calmness settled over Rae, a serenity that was mocked by the thudding of her heart. "Are you certain this is what you want, Jericho?" she asked quietly, stilling beneath him.

"I'm certain. You?"

Rae's response was to reach for the hem of her saque and pull it over her head, pausing only to allow Jericho to lift the dagger. She dropped the overblouse to one side and pointed to the knife, which now rested at the lacy edge of her chemise between her breasts. "I think we can be rid of that now."

Jericho's eyes dropped to the weapon and ended up taking

in the full beauty of her breasts, immodestly concealed by her damp bodice. His hands ached to touch them, his mouth to taste them, yet he held the knife, remembering his vow to be neither gentle nor kind. He refused to yield the weapon so that she might be the one who would bend and soften while he remained unchanged by her. "You'll have to show me you can be trusted," he prevaricated in a harsh whisper.

Rae's smile was full of witchery as her hands fell on his thighs and stroked the taut material of his navy breeches as if no barrier existed. "What would you have me do?" she asked softly as her palms came precariously close to the surging evidence that he desired her. She called on her recent dreams and fantasies to guide her. Her fingers drew close, then retreated. Her teasing prompted him to make an involuntary thrust forward to follow her.

"Siren," he growled as he slipped the dagger beneath the bottom of her chemise and began nudging it upward. "Take this flimsy bit of provocation off or I swear it will be naught but a rag in a moment."

The chemise went the way of the saque, and Rae continued to watch Jericho expectantly. She knew he had seen her naked before, but somehow she also knew he had never looked at her as he did now, his eyes devouring, his body taut with the strength of his arousal. She arched beneath him, willing him to cup her breasts, touch their stiff ends with the rough pads of his fingers. He wanted to, she could see that he wanted to, yet he denied himself. There was a grim, almost pained set to his mouth.

With a swift powerful stroke, Jericho embedded Rae's dagger in the deck and unstraddled her. At first she thought he was going to leave her, or worse, toss her skirt up and simply have at her. He did neither of these things. His hands slipped beneath her naked back and lifted her until she was partially sitting up, supported as well as secured in his embrace. Her breasts flattened briefly against the coarse texture of his jacket, and she found the contrast not unpleasant. Nor was she hurt when his fingers tugged at the damp strands of hair at her nape, pulling her head back and exposing the long line of her throat. Her mouth parted slightly. Her lashes shuttered the anticipation in her eyes. There was a harshness inherent in each of his actions that could have been violent had Jericho had any less than full control. Rae was unafraid. It was only his kiss that punished.

Jericho's rough jerk brought Rae's mouth to him so that in effect she initiated the kiss, but it was he who controlled what passed between them. His mouth pressed hard on hers, a lover's stamp born of Jericho's jealousy that anyone had gone before him. His lips moved to obliterate any lingering memory she might have had of another. His tongue touched the soft under-side of her upper lip and he welcomed the shudder that swept her and passed into him. She responded to his urgency, understood something of his pain, and gave him the fullness of her mouth. Measure for measure, she returned the pressure of his lips and showed him that she wanted more as her hands slipped behind his head to make him, in part, her captive.

Her tongue swept the row of teeth she had tried to knock out of his head earlier. "I'm glad I didn't," she whispered against his mouth when he broke the kiss and sucked in air.

"Mmmm?" he asked, then showed he had little interest in her reply, because his mouth effectively cut it off. The hand that was not in her hair swept across her back, and it was then he realized how chilled she was in the cool night air. "Below," he muttered shortly. "It will be warmer."

Rae didn't know she was cold until Jericho freed her from his arms. Struck by his rather glacial composure, she hastily gathered her garments, and holding them protectively in front of her, led the way to their cabin. Jericho lighted several tallow candles; and when he turned from his task saw Rae was standing by the bunk, her bundle still raised in front of her.

One of Jericho's brows kicked up in question. "Have you

forgotten what comes next?'' he asked indifferently. ''Or are you having second thoughts?''

Both, actually, she wanted to tell him. She said nothing, however, and dropped the clothing.

The descent to the cabin had given Jericho time to evaluate his desire for Rae. He still wanted her, but she *would* come on his terms. He was through trying to erase from his mind that she was anything but a strumpet. That way lay danger. He would not give her an opening to drive her wedge. ''Get rid of your other things,'' he said, jerking his chin in her direction. He would not permit her to know what it cost him to stand across the room from her, drinking in her beauty in the candlelight, and deny himself the tenderness of a soft and giving embrace. He remained seemingly unmoved as she stepped out of her shoes and removed her stockings. There was nothing in his face to encourage her as she unfastened her skirt and pulled it off with her undergarments. He sucked in his breath when she was naked, but covered it with a curt order to get in bed. He held the vision of her, lithe and supple, bare flesh faintly luminescent in the flame and shadow, long after she had disappeared beneath the blankets.

He reached inside his jacket and withdrew the notice he had taken from town. He tossed it aside with no explanation and reached again, this time pulling out all that remained of his continental notes. He held them up so she would know what they were. ''This is so there will be no question as to the nature of what is going to happen between us.''

Rae blanched as the paper money fluttered to the desktop. It was insult heaped on injury that the notes were virtually worthless. Here was her chance to gather her affronted pride and tell him his money could be put to better use to stuff a mattress. It was too late for that, though. The ache and emptiness inside was too large to derive any satisfaction from another trenchant speech. She would fill the emptiness with him now and worry about the ache later. Rae was very much afraid she loved him. "I am not the one questioning," she reminded him quietly. And after an instant's hesitation: "Come to me."

Jericho stepped to the foot of the bed and began to strip, deft fingers working on the buttons of his shirt and breeches. He stopped once to yank off his boots and did not pause again until he was ready to join Rae in bed. He looked as if he would ask her something, but her hand reached for his, covering it, and he yielded to a force greater than himself.

"Come to me," she said again, drawing him near. When he would have brought the blankets about them, she stayed his arm. "Warm me with your body," she ordered huskily.

Jericho's groan answered her sweet sorcery and he pressed himself against her, knowing the heat and power of his own passion by the way she curved to him. Rae wrapped her arms around Jericho's neck and lifted her head, placing teasing kisses along the angular line of his jaw and the sensuous curve of his lower lip. She touched her mouth to his nose, his cheek, nuzzled his ear. Daringly the tip of her tongue peeked out to trace the curve of his lobe. "You're a beautiful man," she whispered, her breath tickling his neck. Rahab did not say the words because it was expected of her. She had no idea a tart might voice that phrase with boring regularity to even her most dog-faced clients. She said it because she meant it, and she resolutely squashed her hurt when Jericho told her in no uncertain terms to be quiet.

"I know what I am," he snapped between angry kisses that would leave marks on her shoulders and throat. "I have no need to hear it from your painted lips. There are better uses for your mouth." Then he smothered Rae's tormented gasp with his own mouth and would not allow her to dwell on the little cruelties he was determined to lash her with. He quieted her struggles and stilled her protests, and with a skill he had learned at the hands of whores, he made her pliant to his will.

His hands gave her a stormy pleasure she was certain she had never known elsewhere. They curved to her slender form, roughly familiarizing themselves with the fragile strength of her neck, the delicate roundness of her breasts, and the narrow span of her waist. If his caress was fierce, even frenzied; if his mouth covered hers with a brutal urgency, he believed it was no more than she deserved. She inflamed him by responding to his furious desire with a wild abandon that nearly undid him.

Rae sought to be his equal, giving this rushing and unrestrained delight as it was given to her. Her hands flattened on his chest and learned he was not of one plane, but smoothly rippled, especially when he sucked in his breath as her fingers drifted across his taut abdomen. Her legs tangled with his and she reveled in the masculine texture that rubbed suggestively against her own lithe softness. Her knee nudged between his legs and she arched against him, liking the insistent heat and pressure of his need flush to her skin.

She kissed his nipples and teased them with her tongue as they became erect and knew that her own swollen breasts ached for a similar touch. Jericho's hands were practiced and his demanding touch exciting, but it did not seem enough. She grew restless beneath him and sought intimacy of a more fiery nature.

Jericho was ready for her, had been for some time, yet he held back until he was certain she could take him easily. He did not question his motives as his hand slipped between their heated and perspiring bodies and touched the smooth and velvety center of her. Her thighs parted to accommodate his fingers, and her hips thrust against his palm in a rhythm he controlled. He removed his hand and knelt between her knees, slipping his hands beneath her buttocks, and lifted her to him.

Rae bucked slightly, struggling against the helplessness of her position as Jericho held her thighs fast. Jericho's palms supported the small of her back as he encouraged her to arch further. Rae's arms stretched above her head and her fingers clasped the bunk's wooden frame. Her every muscle tensed anticipating his entry.

"Jericho." Her voice was only a thread of sound, but it was what he had been waiting to hear. It was as if he uncoiled into her, his first thrust penetrating as deeply as their position allowed. Resistance, surrender, and pain took them both by surprise. He stilled in the same moment she cried out.

A heartbeat later he heard a question and an accusation in her reedy voice as she called his name. "Jericho?"

"My God," he swore softly, staring at the play of emotions crossing Rae's face, betrayal chief among them. His own features were rigid, as was everything else about him. He closed his eyes and breathed deeply, calling on a reserve of strength.

Rae's eyes fluttered shut. "I think I must not have been a whore after all."

Chapter 4

The harsh lines of Jericho's face bore witness to the truth of Rae's statement. Shock, frustration, then pain dominated his expression. His struggle to gain control was etched on his beaded brow and the whiteness about his mouth. His eyes still closed, he withdrew from Rae and wrapped himself haphazardly in a blanket, then tossed one to her and growled an order to cover herself. Jericho sat at the foot of the bed, his back flush to the wall and his knees pressed firmly to his chest as he willed his aroused body to accept that there would be no release. He thought he would come out of his skin when he felt Rae's gentle and inquiring hand on his shoulder.

"Don't touch me!" he gritted, jerking away. "Haven't you the least idea what you've done? Would you have me take you now?"

Biting her lip in mortification, Rae scrambled to the head of the bed and hugged her knees in much the same manner as Jericho. By blinking rapidly she resolutely kept the tears that glistened in her eyes from falling as she studied Jericho's huddled form and taut features from a safer distance. Though her body still trembled, anger had gradually replaced excitement. How clever of Jericho to arouse both those emotions, she thought bitterly. Fingers shaking with suppressed rage, Rae secured the blanket around her and nearly leaped from the bed. Restlessly she paced the short length of the cabin while she considered a number of things she wanted to say to Jericho when he came out of his self-pitying trance. How dare he think he was the only one hurting from what had occurred between them? What right did he have to tie her in knots, then act as if he alone knew pain? Fuming, Rae remembered how he had sprung away from her—as if she were diseased instead of virgin—then would not let her even touch him. She promised she would not let him off easily for treating her so shabbily.

"Are you goin' anywhere special, Red, or just polishin' the floor with your feet?"

Rae's agitated pacing stopped as she turned on Jericho, astonishment raising her brows and parting her lips. Just as quickly a sharp, angry breath escaped her and her eyes glittered with resentment. "Your nerve is not to be believed," she said tightly. "Now that you have recovered yourself, you find sport with me. I will not allow you to make light of this, Jericho Smith. Do you think I am lacking any sort of feeling? I reached for you because I was sharing your pain and sought to comfort and be comforted. You spurned my touch and made what happened between us seem my fault, yet it was you who left me!" Rae retrieved the paper notes on the desk and stalked to the bed, throwing them at Jericho. "Take your money! I hardly earned it!" Stiff with pride, she gave Jericho her back and stared at the far wall.

Jericho felt as if his head were spinning as he tried to make sense of her acid argument. His anticipation of her reaction fell far short of her present diatribe. He had expected weeping, even shocked quietness. Never this harangue. "Are you taking me to task because I did *not* finish what we began?" he asked, though he could scarcely credit it. "Is that the root of your vitriolic tongue?"

"Why does that shock you?" she snapped, rounding on him again. "Hadn't I the right to expect you to finish what you began?"

Jericho blinked twice, incredulous at her anger. "But you were no whore," he tried to explain. "You said so yourself. We both felt the proof of your virginity."

"What has that to do with anything? You told me that only lightskirts frequented Wolfe's, and as I was in the tavern isn't it obvious that I had at least chosen to become one? Someone had to be first!"

"But it didn't have to be me, dammit!" Jericho pushed himself away off the bed, pulling impatiently at the blanket that rested low on his hips, and came to stand in front of her. "I have no taste for inexperienced wenches, nor will I have it said that I helped you on your way to becoming a whore!"

Rae could not believe her ears. "Will you but listen to yourself?" she demanded testily. "You speak a language of contradictions. When you thought me experienced you paid me so I would not mistake the nature of your feelings for me. Do not deny that you came to me in spite of yourself. You hated the thought that I had lain with other men. Now you find that you are my first, and you can't stand that, either. How can you have it all ways, Mr. Smith?" she taunted him, thrusting her chin forward. "Shall I return to Wolfe's and gain a measure of expertise?" Surely she had not mistaken that Jericho flinched at her words. "What would you have me do?"

"What would you have me do?" Jericho returned belligerently. At his side his hands clenched into fists, his blunt nails pressed half-moons into his palms. "Was I wrong to remember you seemed to have no stomach for whorin'? I was offerin' you another choice, a second chance to decide your future, you daft chit!"

''What real choice did I have after the sheets were bloodied with my virginity?'' she pointed out, stamping her foot.

''How the hell was I supposed to know? God, I want to shake you! I was tryin' to do right by you, Red. If this is how you respond to a noble act, then you were right to pursue whoredom.''

Rae gasped. ''You? Noble?! A man who lusts after the wife of his friend?'' Seeing Jericho's stunned expression, she knew she had not mistaken his feelings for Salem's wife. Heedless of the consequences, she continued, ''Are you shocked that I have guessed it, or that I have the courage to say it? I heard the way you spoke her name. 'Everything a man could want,' '' she mocked. ''Next you will tell me you are noble because you have never acted on your carnal instincts with her, merely sniffed at her skirts.'' Rae knew she had gone too far, but there was not a word she would call back if she had it to do over. She had a need she did not understand to break Jericho's control, to provoke him as she believed she had been provoked. That was why she accepted the blow that sent her reeling backward without a murmur.

Jericho watched Rae stagger a few steps from him, then right herself with composure and dignity, her accusing green eyes never leaving his. His own face was as white as the mark made by the flat of his hand. As her cheek was suffused with color, his own turned ruddy with shame. He had never struck a woman in such a manner and never known this loss of command over his actions. His stance rigid, he waited for Rae's retaliation. Though it did not come in the expected way, it still rocked him on his heels.

''I suppose I should feel victorious that I was able to goad you,'' she said quietly. Her eyes stopped accusing him as her thoughts turned inward. ''But in truth, I feel nothing of the sort. I think I must be a very sad sort of woman to want to see you out of all patience. I thought I would be heady with power that I could fire such a response, no matter that I was hurt by it. Instead I find that I don't like myself very much for it.''

"Red . . ." Jericho interjected softly. He found himself wanting to take her into his arms, to protect them both from words that scored them. But he did not reach for her, knowing that she would reject his overture as too late and insufficient for her needs.

"Please. Don't say anything. I know I am making rather a botch of this, but I beg your indulgence." Now her eyes left his and fastened on a point beyond his shoulder. Unknown to her, the slight twist of her head gave him a full view of the mark on her cheek, the same cheek that still bore the scratches from her errant trek through the woods. Jericho felt as if she had landed a blow to his middle. Some part of him, as he listened to her go on, wondered what damage she could have wrought if her revenge had been calculating. "I am not sorry for what I said about the woman you love, but I do regret that I am not she. My experience, or lack of it, made no difference to me. It was rather a surprise, you see, because though I railed against the things you said of me, I also accepted them. But surprise or no, I wanted you. You said that you were offering me a second chance, another choice. Well, I choose whatever will make you want me. I want this night's pleasure to remember when you send me away tomorrow. I want this night's pleasure to remember when I no longer have a choice about the men who lie with me. I will remember an evening when I did have a choice, and chose you." As she said the last she faced him boldly, and only a slight glistening on the rim of her lower lashes spoke of the courage her action took.

Jericho swayed on his feet as Rae impaled him with her dark emerald gaze. Odd that he had once thought her eyes had no more sparkle or depth than green glass; that he had once thought her undeserving of nature's fine colors. He had thought then that he deserved a woman such as she appeared to be. The truth broke through his consciousness with the punch of a cannonball. "I don't deserve anyone like you," he said, breaking the weighty, expectant silence that had enveloped the cabin since Rae voiced her decision.

Rae could not doubt that he believed what he was saying; conviction framed each word and the words were said slowly, as if dragged from his inner soul. She took a step closer to him. Then another. And another. When she stood so close that she had to look up to see him, she spoke. "I do not believe that."

"It's true. You don't know me."

Rae's hands lifted and came to rest on Jericho's hips. The tips of her fingers slid between the edge of the blanket and Jericho's flushed and faintly perspiring skin. "I know what you've allowed me to know. I've come to—to know a man who wears ruthlessness as he would a hair shirt, who punishes the child he was by choosing a name meant to invoke pain each time it is heard. This is the same man who rescued a wench he had no liking for from a certain hanging, who nursed her and kept her safe, who washed her hair with profound gentleness and has caressed her with a softness in his eyes that he could not bear to bring to his hands. I think you are afraid, Jericho Smith. I think you are afraid to want anything for yourself because it may slip through your fingers." Rae released the tuck in the blanket and it fell between them revealing Jericho's stark male beauty and scorching Rae's palms with the heat of his flesh. "But know this, Jericho. It will be you who will send me away in the morning. I would not go otherwise."

"I have no use for your pity," Jericho said. He made no move to shrink from her hands or hide the state of his arousal. Instead his own hands reached for the blanket tucked carelessly at Rae's breasts.

"I don't offer it." She could feel Jericho's smooth nails touch her breasts as his fingers insinuated themselves in much the way hers had done. Her bottom lip trembled as a wave of desire swept through her, pushing her closer to Jericho. She felt an echo of her need ripple through Jericho when he glimpsed her tongue nervously wet her lower lip. "Kiss me."

Jericho's surrendering groan gave sound to the last barrier between them as Rae's covering slid to the floor. His mouth lowered to hers, and Rae accepted the kiss with a measure of thankfulness and greed. She arched against him, flinging her arms about his neck, and reveled in the feel of him pressed intimately against her. Her tongue had abandoned the line of her own lip in favor of the taste and texture of Jericho's.

"You'll show me, won't you?" she implored softly between the nibbling kisses she placed on the corners of his mouth. "You'll show me how to please you?" Her hips settled against his thighs, cradling him naturally with her slender body.

Jericho lifted Rae, sliding an arm around her back and under her knees. "You are in the wrong of it, Red," he husked in her ear as he carried her to the bunk and laid her down. "I'm thinkin' you'll be showin' me."

And she would show him, she vowed, as she drew him down till he covered her with his body. She would show him tenderness he could feel as well as see. She would show him that where she was concerned his fears were groundless. And in the event he could not put aside the ghosts that plagued him, she would have enough courage for the both of them.

She used his momentum as he came to her to turn them on the mattress. For a moment she was still, then her lips gentled on his, her breath fluttered softly against his cheek. Her hands slid down the tapering length of his back, smoothed his taut buttocks, the backs of his hard thighs. She rained kisses on his chin, his throat, across his shoulders, and along the ridged muscles of his chest.

Jericho knew ineffable pleasure at Rae's hands, and unkind, unworthy thoughts warred within him: thoughts that questioned her loving instincts and wondered if there were such a thing as a born harlot. To banish the thoughts, he followed Rae's lead, turned so they lay side by side, and applied himself to mirror Rae's caresses.

Almost against his will, he found himself doing those small, adoring things he swore he would not do. He counted the freckles on the bridge of her nose and kissed those spraying either cheek. His fingers wove through the thick auburn strands of her hair, untangling the damp strands and eliciting a wince when he tugged too hard. She retaliated by pinching his buttocks. He responded by sinking his teeth in her neck. She tickled him. He stopped her by laving her swollen nipples with the rough edge of his tongue.

It was the caress her body had demanded earlier, and her soft cry told Jericho of her satisfaction.

Moved as he had not known he could be by the telling sounds of her pleasure, Jericho continued to make forays across the slick saltiness of her skin with his mouth and hands. Her small breasts swelled and hardened against his chest, and he remembered the posters that called her a woman of Amazonian proportions. His smile was lost in the musky valley of her breasts. No Amazon, she. But still a woman whose slenderness held a supple strength and whose delicately wholesome features harbored a heart of rare bravery.

His mouth followed the curve of her ribs, liking the way she sucked in her breath when he reached the flat plane of her stomach. He kissed her navel while his hands stroked her thighs, reaching between them with an infinitely gentle probe that pleasured even as it sought proof that she was ready for him again.

She was. And this time there was no thought in Jericho's head that he render her nearly helpless as he took her. He wanted her willing, giving. God, how he wanted her.

But it was Rae who was unafraid to voice her desire. "Soon, Jericho. Please come to me." The tender sole of her foot rubbed his calf, and as her knee lifted she was opened more fully to him. Her fingertips threaded in the sunlight yellow of his hair, tugging a little desperately, a little frantically, as she signaled her need and pulled his face close to hers.

His eyes were hypnotically dark at the center, like polished black onyx, and ringed with ice blue, the color of diamond chips. Rae imagined she could see herself in those eyes; certainly she saw the reflection of her own desire. "Now. I want you inside me. Fill me as you did before. . . then stay. Don't leave me." Her palms slid down his chest, his abdomen, and rested momentarily on his narrow hips before reaching for his stiff manhood. Her hands closed around the warm and pulsing length of him and guided him to her, arching into him.

Jericho's groan of need and longing was muffled in the curve of Rae's shoulder as he thrust into her. He forced himself to be still at Rae's cry. "Have I hurt you again?" he husked.

Rae shook her head, a hint of a smile on her well-kissed lips. "You feel wonderful," she said guilelessly. Quite by accident, she tightened the warm velvet walls holding him as she adjusted to his intimate and welcome invasion. "Have I hurt you?" she asked at Jericho's murmur.

She had no idea what she had done, how good she felt surrounding him with her moist heat. Jericho did not venture a reply, merely shook his head and began to show her what her innocent movements had wrought.

In the beginning the rhythm he taught tested their patience. Rae accepted Jericho's lead, matching his slow thrusts with every rise of her hips. Hardly aware of what she was doing, she tightened about him each time his stroking took him away from her, and relaxed, opening to him, when he thrust forward. Jericho had never known anyone like her before, had never known anyone who wanted him the way this woman did.

Rae's fingers marked Jericho's back as a sense of urgency swept through them. She felt as if she were at the end of some forest trail and reaching for a branch that would swing her across a great abyss. It swung tantalizingly in front of her, daring her to take hold. In her mind's eye she saw the yawning crevice beneath her, black and bottomless, and wondered if the branch would hold. Then she didn't care any longer, and when the wind brought it to her she strained to grasp it. Each time she missed only made her want it all the more. Finally, frustrated beyond bearing by the teasing limb, she stretched, every muscle taut, and dove into the wind to take it.

"Jericho!" she called to him as she was suspended in midair, nothing to support her above the dark mouth of the abyss. Her hands flailed for purchase. "Jericho!" she cried again. She was falling with shattering speed; she could barely catch her breath. The rushing air was not cool, but hot, and Rae thought she would die as a flash of heat and light, her soul scattered and sparkling.

Then he was there, reaching out to her, and she caught his hand, and though it trembled in her own, she never doubted that he would pull her to safety. His voice soothed her. "It's all right, Red. Open your eyes. I've got you."

Rae did as she was told and looked into the black centers of Jericho's eyes, finding she had never been in any danger. She felt his hands on her buttocks, supporting and lifting her as his final thrusts brought him release. This time she soothed him, loving his power and strength even as he yielded to pleasure's end.

Jericho lay beside Rae, careful not to crush her with his weight, though in truth she would not have minded at that moment. As their breathing eased he twisted on his side, propped on one elbow, and studied Rae's flushed face and languid eyes. On impulse he brushed his mouth across her moist and softly parted lips, then lifted his head in time to be bathed in her lovely siren's smile.

"That smile heralds trouble for any man with a breath in him," Jericho said huskily, tracing its fullness with a fingertip.

"Mayhap I should not look so pleased." She attempted a bored expression, but the touch of his finger tickled, and child-like, her grin widened.

"I think I prefer the witch's smile. I am many things, but a cradle robber is not one of them." His humor faded and his eyes grew troubled. "Until this night I had never lain with an innocent."

Rae sighed, reaching up to smooth the frown lines at the corners of his eyes. Her soft palms remained on the taut planes of his cheeks. "Do not refine upon it. I have no regrets—and surely they would be mine to have. How can I regret such an introduction to womanhood? Surely you don't want me to be shamed by the pleasure you gave me?"

"No," he said slowly, grasping her wrists and pressing his lips to the center of each palm. "You were beautiful—*are* beautiful." He released her, fell on his back, and stared at the knotty pine ceiling. "I don't care much for the idea of you lyin' with other men," he told her at last. "I want you to go to the McClellans'."

"Of course."

"I won't argue ab— Of course? You mean you intended to go all along?"

"Well, yes," she said matter-of-factly. "I don't care much for the idea of lying with other men either."

"But—" He sat up abruptly, placed a stiff arm or either side of her, and stared at her face for some hint that she was lying. He found none. "But you deliberately let me think you still wanted to be a lightskirt."

"Credit me with some sense. I was not trying to appeal to your better nature. I could never have seduced you otherwise." She laughed at his incredulous expression. "I find that I can be quite without scruples in the pursuit of something I want."

Jericho's eyes widened, softened. "I've never met anyone like you, Red."

"And I've never met one such as you."

He grinned suddenly. "How can you know? You don't remember anyone in your past."

"I know that if there had been someone like you in my life, I would not have been in Wolfe's."

His grin vanished at her simple sincerity. He kissed her deeply on the mouth and felt her heartbeat quicken in response. He broke the contact abruptly and in a swift motion left the bed. Bewildered, Rae sat up and reached for him.

Jericho put a hand on her shoulder, quieting her. "I'm not leavin', Red. But it's too soon for you. I don't want to hurt you."

Rae would like to have denied that it was too soon, yet there was a certain discomfort, not precisely pain, but enough of a twinge to let her know he was probably right. She took a corner of the sheet and drew it to her breasts. "I'd like to wash," she said shyly.

The trace of a smile flitted across Jericho's mouth. "Give me a moment and I'll see to you." He cut off her objection by turning his back on her and going to the basin. Unselfconsciously he washed himself at the nightstand, then pulled on his breeches. "Just to make it more difficult to seduce me," he told her over his shoulder. He set the porcelain basin near the edge of the bed while Rae lay back, then brushed aside the sheet. With great care he bathed her thighs, wiping every trace of their combined passion from her dark triangle of hair. When he was finished he helped her into her nightshirt and kissed her closed eyelids.

"Are you crying?" he asked, tasting a salty wetness on his lips.

She sniffed. "Of course not."

"Of course not," he mocked indulgently. "What a waterworks you are." He put the basin away, gathered the blankets they had dropped on the floor, and pinched the candle. Sliding into bed beside Rae, he covered them both against the evening's chill that had begun to penetrate their senses.

"I suppose *she* never cries," Rae said a trifle wistfully.

Jericho knew instantly who *she* was and surprised himself

by feeling a little satisfied by Rae's thinly disguised jealousy. "I have no idea. What does it matter, anyway? You've quite mistaken my feelings for Ashley."

"Have I?" she probed.

But Jericho would not be drawn. "I think you will like working for the McClellans. They're fine people."

"You spoke to them, then?"

"No. They were not at home."

"Then how do you know they will hire me? Mayhap they have no positions." Rae wished she had not sounded so hopeful. She was in danger of begging Jericho to allow her to stay at the schooner.

"But I know that they do, Red. They had a young woman named Meg who looked after the children. Now *that* wench had hair of fire and a temper to match." He felt Rae flounce beside him, and he could well imagine her eyes a shade greener than they had been a moment before. " 'Course, once she set her sights on Salem's good friend Shannon, he was done for. She finagled matrimony out of that one, oh, it must have been two years ago, and Ashley hasn't replaced her."

"There you have it," Rae said certainly. "She doesn't want any help."

"Not so, Red. Her sister-in-law, Salem's sister, has been with them almost since Meg's marriage. I suppose she makes herself useful."

"Then mayhap *she* will object to my presence."

"If she does, it won't be for the reasons you imagine. I've never met her myself, though heaven knows Ashley's tried to arrange the thing often enough. Salem says he despairs of her attitude—something to do with a broken engagement. I understand she has a reputation for holding men at a distance." Jericho sighed, recalling the times he had put Ashley off about meeting Salem's sister. He had no wish for anything to cause a rift in his friendship with Salem, and attending Rahab McClellan was certain to create one. His work for Washington offered

any number of excuses, all of which Ashley accepted graciously, though he could tell she thought he was making a
grave mistake. "Anyway, if you begin to care for the children,
it will mean she will have no excuse to stay at home. She will
not thank us for it."

"Perhaps we should not upset her."

"Perhaps your presence is exactly what she needs."

Resigned, Rae curled against Jericho's back, snuggling for
warmth. "How many children are there?" she asked sleepily,
stifling a yawn with the back of her hand.

"Two. Courtney is four, I think, and Trenton is not yet one
year."

"That's nice." She yawned again and her arms settled about
Jericho's waist. "I suppose they are too young for me to cor-
rupt."

"Re-ed," he drawled in warning.

"I was only making light, Jericho."

"G'night, Red." His hands went over hers, securing them.

"Good night."

Just before he shut his eyes he thought he heard her whisper
"my love." He had to make himself believe he had imagined
it before he was able to sleep, and even then his rest was
troubled.

He woke suddenly, and for a moment recaptured the dream
he had been having. It seemed odd to him, for he rarely remembered his dreams and thought he must not have many. But this
one was still startlingly clear, and when he closed his eyes he
could still make out the rock he had been studying. Though
the slab of granite remained a stoic lookout, immovable on the
water's edge, it was not entirely immune to nature's relentless
forces. Jericho watched season after season pass, and though
he was protected by the whim of his dream, the rock altered
subtly beneath spring's lashing rains and summer's persistent
heat. In autumn decaying leaves littered the stone's obdurate

surface, and over time left an impression on its face. A hairline crack was finally etched by the inexorable cold of winter.

Jericho turned restlessly, vaguely bothered by the dream until he recalled having once envied that rock's insensitivity. When he made that connection he came bolt upright, clutching his middle as if he had been poleaxed.

"Jericho?" Rae questioned softly, placing her hand on his forearm. "Is there something wrong?" She had been on the edge of consciousness when some instinct where Jericho was concerned alerted her to his agitation. Wide awake now, she sat up.

"No. I'm fine." He swung his legs over the side of the bunk and willed himself not to flinch as Rae's hand slipped to his back. He swore he could feel her fingertips indelibly marking his skin. His breath hissed between his teeth. He would not let her have a place in his life. He *would not*.

Without the appearance of urgency, Jericho stood. "I'm hungry. Did you have anything after dinner?"

"It's the middle of the night," she reminded him unnecessarily. A frown knitted her brows and she strained to see Jericho in the darkness.

"Hunger knows nothin' of the hour," he pontificated. He picked up his jacket to find a match and flint and came across the notice he had torn down. Quickly he lighted the candle and unfolded the poster, smiling a little grimly this time at its absurdities. He handed it to Rae. "Here, I forgot about this. Do you want anything to eat?"

"No, nothing," she said absently as she looked at the notice.

Jericho rummaged through the storage bench. "I'll read that to you in a moment. I hope you can see the humor in it." He found the hardtack and broke off a piece, then shut the bench. It was too bad both flasks had been drained of whiskey, he decided; he wanted a drink more than he wanted food. He sat beside Rae on the bunk, amused by her comical expression as she studied the notice. "Don't strain yourself, Red. Let me read it to you."

Rae brushed aside his hand as he reached for it. "I am quite capable of reading the thing myself."

Jericho's brows rose skeptically and a trifle uneasily while he chewed thoughtfully on the hardtack. "Then read it to me," he challenged.

Uncertain why Jericho should doubt her, Rae read the piece carefully. "Murderess! Reward of ten pounds for the apprehension of a buxom colonial wench of low morals and poor judgment . . ." She paused, shaking her head in disbelief. "Do they mean me, d'you think?"

"Of course, they mean you. Go on."

". . . wanted for the willful killing of one of His Majesty's officers on March twenty-eighth, in Wolfe's Tavern." She looked askance at Jericho. "Your part in the affair is mentioned and a description of each of us follows, though it has been shabbily done. Have you heard enough, or must I read more?"

Jericho snatched the poster from Rae's hands and threw it aside. "Where did you learn to read?" he demanded harshly. His fingers itched to take her by the shoulders and shake the answer from her. Of a sudden so much about Red seemed clear to him, and he cursed himself for being fool enough to have been taken in.

Confused by the leashed violence in him, Rae inched away to the head of the bed. "How can I know that when I don't recall my own name? Why does it upset you so? Surely you've known women who can read before." She drew a blanket up to her shoulders as if it were a shield.

"Never any aspiring prostitutes," Jericho drawled coldly. "Those other women in Wolfe's couldn't have read more than five words on that notice between them. Doesn't it strike you odd that someone with your obvious book learnin' should decide to entertain the visiting troops on her back?"

Rae's indrawn breath was sharp. "What a vile thing to say!"

"Who *are* you, Red?"

"I don't know." Rae's back was against the wall, and though Jericho had not moved from the side of the bunk, she felt as if he were nearly on top of her.

"Who *are* you?"

"I don't know" she shouted. "I don't know ... I don't know! Why do you persist in questioning me?"

Jericho went on relentlessly. "Did you really kill that British officer?"

"You said that I did."

"Forget what I said. Did you really kill him?"

Rae buried her face in her hands. "I don't remember. I don't remember anything!"

Jericho moved swiftly, knocking Rae's hands from her face, and grasped her urgently by the chin, forcing her to look up at him. "Shall I tell you what I think? I think you have been naught but the pretty bait in a British trap!" He thrust her chin aside contemptuously, disgusted with the bewilderment she affected, and took himself off the bed to avoid throttling her.

"What trap?" she implored. "Why are you saying these things to me?"

"How well you play the role of the artless wench. Guileless. Lacking all deceit." His cerulean eyes lashed her scornfully. "Have you always been a Tory spy, or is this your first assignment? No. Don't answer. It must be your first, else you would not have been a virgin. Did they suggest that you seduce me to keep me near, or was that your own idea? And when do you plan to turn me over to them? That's why you left yesterday, isn't it? You were heading back to the British to give my location."

"But I returned to you."

"Because you couldn't find your way! How that must have stung your pride!"

Rae looked away from Jericho and drew a long, calming

breath, trying to right the world he had set on its head. "Why should the British want you? Who are you?"

"I grow weary of you playing the fool, Red. It is ill-becoming, though I admit you do it better than most female spies. None of the others like to be thought a featherhead, but it doesn't seem to bother you." When she faced him again, eyes still blank, Jericho swore harshly.

Rae held herself still, refusing to let him see how he hurt her with each accusation. "Are you as Nathan Hale was?" she asked calmly.

Jericho's reply was caustic. "How convenient that you remember him. But then, you know I am like him; you know that General Clinton would love to see me hanging from a gibbet, the same as Nathan. If I am to go that road, it damn well won't be some freckle-faced wench who springs the trap!"

Rae wished she had not mentioned Hale, for Jericho condemned her all the more for it. She remembered the name of the soldier-spy in much the same way that she recalled how to find worms and prepare catfish. "Jericho . . . please, you are wrong about me. I am not what you think. I am certain of it. What of the man you said I killed? What of the reward?"

"All a ruse to pull me in. It was a convincing fight, certainly well rehearsed, and it got my attention as you planned it should. It was my bad luck to be in the tavern that night; else you could have had one of my men."

"Even if you are correct—and it's a large if, Jericho—I still remember none of it. I am no threat to YOU. I haven't any notion where I should go to report that you are here."

"Your entreaties scarcely reach my heart, Red."

"Heart?! You have none! You puffed-up, sorry excuse for a human being!" Rae rose on her knees and smiled at Jericho contemptuously. "If I am an actress of these colonies, then surely you belong on the London stage. You have been parading around these many years, pretending to be a man." Her eyes glittered as they swept over his body, and at her side her hands shook with the force of her rage. "I'll not deny that you have perfected the trappings, but you have none of the heart and mind about you that credits a real man. Until you began your accusations I scarce understood the coward you truly are! You are so afraid that you may find something to like about me that you leap on the first excuse to put me from your life! And on the flimsiest piece of evidence—the fact that I can read! Can you not think of one reason that a would-be whore might know how to read? Can you not imagine that she comes from a family where schooling was valued only slightly less than putting food in one's belly? You turn my stomach, Jericho Smith! I'm certain when I lost my memory I lost my good sense, for if I were of one piece I would have never imagined that I could care for one such as you. You may be wanted by the British—but I, sirrah—would not have you as a gift!"

Out of breath at the end of her angry speech, Rae waited, her breasts lifting shallowly, while Jericho formed his reply. It was not long in coming, and the bitter, sneering travesty of a smile warned her before she heard the words that he thought her the most capable of liars.

"I applaud your ability to invent on the moment any number of excuses for yourself, and it is admirable the way you attack, but don't expect me to be taken in by your mendacity or stung by your nettled tongue. The only one deluded by talk of would-be whores is you, m'dear, for it's clear that you bartered yourself in order to cozy up to me. Were you told I would be more amenable to speakin' of my work in the aftermath of couplin'?"

Rae felt as if the fight had at last been driven from her. She sagged wearily against the wall, her face ashen. That he spoke of their tender lovemaking as coupling told Rae she had no chance of reasoning with him. He was prepared to think the worst of her and sever the fragile bonds that had linked them for a short time. She could not help but wonder if there was something to be said for his supposition and guesswork. True, she still remembered nothing of her past, but that did not mean

Jericho was mistaken about her presence in Wolfe's. Mayhap she had been sent there to catch a small fish in rebel waters and had unwittingly snared a shark. Rae worried her bottom lip with the edge of her teeth and stared at her folded hands, doubting herself, her motives in loving Jericho, indeed, doubting everything but that Jericho was as cold and ruthless as the predator she likened him to.

"I'll leave immediately," she told him at last. "I cannot think there is anything to be gained when my presence provokes you so." She gathered the hem of her nightshirt in one hand and scooted across the bunk, only to be brought up short as Jericho stepped forward and blocked her path.

"You will go nowhere," he said in clipped accents. "D'you suppose I am going to let you out of my sight now that I know your game? Do I really look such a fool?"

Rae tried to get around him, but he merely stepped whichever way she moved and effectively prevented her from leaving the bed. "Let me pass, Jericho. I tell you I remember nothing!" she gritted. "Does it matter who or what I am? Surely I am no threat to you while I have naught the least idea if what you say is true."

"You would say anything to leave. You still have to convince me your memory fails you."

"How do I do that?"

"That's your problem." His indifference was like a slap as he shrugged and turned his back on her, walking toward the storage bench.

Rae wondered at his actions. One moment he was blocking her path, in the next he was giving her a chance to escape. Did he think she was so fainthearted that she would not take it?

While Jericho rummaged through the bench, Rae carefully edged her way from the bed. Once her feet touched the cold deck she bounded for the door. The handle twisted easily in her grasp and she was in the companionway in a matter of seconds. Her nightshirt flapped about her legs as she took the steps two at a time and her bare feet padded almost noiselessly on the wooden stairway. In the silence of her own passage she found it difficult to credit that Jericho could be following without making it known.

But there he was, on her heels, with scarcely a winded breath to speak for his exertion. Rae had just cleared the steps when Jericho lunged and caught one of her ankles. With a cry of pained surprise Rae skidded to the deck on her hands and knees. She tried to wrest her foot away, but Jericho held her fast.

"Release me, you black-hearted cur!" she commanded. When he did not comply, but rather began to pull her inexorably toward the passageway, much like a fly being dragged against its will toward the center of a spider's web, Rae let go with a string of curses so explicit and long-winded that she hadn't any breath left to protest when Jericho flipped her over his thighs, lifted her nightshirt, and laid his hand five times sharply on her bottom. Her sobs echoed in the dark stairway and she pounded ineffectually on the steps, wishing she could get just one good lick at the man holding her down.

When he finished he yanked down her shirt, pushed her off his lap, and told her coolly that if she used language like that again he would be obliged to heat her backside with no fewer than twenty of the same. Since Jericho had thus far made good on his promises, Rae had no reason to doubt he meant this one also. Reluctantly she allowed herself to be led back into the cabin.

"Get on the bunk," he snapped, closing the door behind them. "What possessed you to make a run for it the moment my back was turned? I thought you had a modicum of sense."

Rae scrambled onto the bed and wished herself invisible as she curled against the wall. "Can you not understand that I have no wish to remain with you?"

Jericho's laugh was dull. "We're always at cross-purposes, you and I. When I wish you gone, you cling like a limpet. When I say you will remain, you wish yourself gone. I think your greatest desire is not whether you stay or go, but thwarting me. I have had enough of it. For now you will stay where you are and explain this to me.'' He reached behind him on the desk and held up the fragile, washed-out piece of parchment that Rae had tossed in the storage bench.

''What do you want to know about it?'' she asked belligerently.

Jericho sighed and dropped it on the desktop. ''Do not push me, Red. Tell me where it came from, and see if you can do it without fabrication. I am at the end of my patience where you are concerned.''

''Must you tower over me like some hulking beast? You've made it quite clear that I am no match for your strength; surely there is no reason for you to stand there glowering.''

She did not surrender easily; he'd give her that. Turning so that she could not see the faintly admiring smile that sprang to his lips, Jericho pulled out the chair from behind the desk and faced her again, straddling it. His arms embraced the ladderback frame and his chin rested on the topmost rung. ''Tell me about it, Red. And I'll know if you're lying.''

Rae's lip curled derisively. ''I don't see how. You don't know when I'm telling the truth.'' The warning light in his eyes pinned her to the wall. ''All right. I shall tell you the whole of it, but you'll wish you'd given me license to lie, for the truth is scarce worth telling.'' Without further preamble she explained where she had found the parchment and how her efforts to read its contents had been unsuccessful.

''And that's all?'' Jericho asked.

She nodded. ''I told you there was nothing to it.''

Jericho picked up the letter and studied it for several long minutes, holding it to the candlelight in much the way Rae had. ''On the contrary,'' he said at last. ''I would say there is quite a bit to be learned from this piece of work.'' He made a fist and the paper crumbled like so many ashes. Jericho brushed his palms together several times to clean them.

"Why did you do that? I thought you said something could be learned from it."

"The writing was illegible, as you said. The document's importance no longer lay with its contents, but with its existence. Are you going to pretend that you don't realize it contained your orders?"

Rae made a sound of pure frustration. "I am not pretending anything. I have no idea what that bit of nonsense in my skirt was. And if you are honest, you will admit that you don't know, either." She threw her arms out expansively. "But then, you don't require my permission to attach some foolish significance to anything that strikes you as odd. Now, if it pleases you," she added sweetly, "I wish to sleep." With that she pulled a blanket about her shoulders and lay down, facing the wall. Jericho's deep chuckle only made her grit her teeth.

Jericho blew out the candle and padded to the bunk. "Poor little spy. No stomach for interrogation." Sitting on the edge of the bed he pulled a short length of rope from his breeches. The rasping sound caught Rae's attention and he felt her stiffen beside him. Before she could guess his intention, Jericho hobbled her in her own blankets, straddled her, and drew out her wrists. She fought him with the last of her strength, landing several blows that they both knew would bruise nicely by morning, but the battle was unequal, and Rae railed as much against that as she did against the fates that had brought her to this pass.

Once her wrists were secured Jericho moved off her, letting her kick free of the blankets. "So help me, Red, if you stomp me with those feet I'll find another bit of rope in that bench and bind your ankles."

Rae quieted, but her blood continued to boil. "That's what you were doing when I ran, isn't it? You were digging in there, trying to find something to keep me at your side."

"I don't know why it surprises you," he said calmly. "You must know I am not going to release you until it is to my advantage. You've proven beyond a doubt that you cannot be trusted. As soon as I shut my eyes, you'll attempt to leave.''

Silently she cursed him for being right, then took herself to task for being so obvious about her desire to leave. "What if I promise otherwise?"

"Forget it, Red." He took another length of rope from his breeches.

"I've not kicked you," she cried, panicking. In trying to keep her feet away from him, she made her bound arms flail at him.

Jericho caught her wrists and wove the rope in his hand between her bonds. "This is too short for your feet," he explained. "Now you have a choice. I can attach your wrists to the bunk frame, or I can attach you to my wrist. Think carefully of your comfort before you decide."

"I pray that someday God will forgive me for hating you as much as I do now, Jericho Smith."

"I suppose that means your preference is the frame." In a matter of seconds he had Rae's hands raised above her head and fastened tightly to the bunk, "G'night, Red." He stretched out beside her then, one of his arms thrown carelessly about her waist. Beneath his arm the harsh rise and fall of her breathing communicated her anger. Occasionally there was a pause, followed by a brief shudder, and he knew she was struggling to control her tears. He said nothing, allowing her this moment of pride and torturing himself with the vision of her long lashes dewy with grief.

Rae had no idea that, even bound as she was, she spent a far more peaceful night than her captor.

Sunlight filtered through the water-stained port window and bathed Rae's features, softening the thrust of her chin and gentling the militant shape of her mouth so that an observer might be forgiven for thinking her face serene. But Jericho knew better, and he had not the least trouble hardening himself to the feminine wiles she practiced even as she slept. In a single, sweeping motion he cut the rope that fastened Rae to the bed, and leaving her wrists tied, went on deck.

Rae woke suddenly, though she couldn't say what it was that pulled her to awareness so quickly. At first she thought it was the strangeness of her position and she tugged stiffly at her arms, finding, somewhat to her surprise, that she could lower them in front of her. In the same moment that she realized that Jericho had at least given her a small measure of freedom, she realized he was gone. She sat up, tossing her head to push her tangled hair behind her shoulders, and struggled to pull down the hem of her shirt, which had ridden above her knees. It bothered her that Jericho must have gotten an eyeful before he left and hadn't been moved enough to grant her a little modesty.

"Damn him!" she muttered harshly.

Rae's curse did not reach her own ears, swallowed as it was by the eruption of noise on deck. There were several deep masculine voices, demanding and urgent in tone, and twice she heard Jericho's drawl weave through the conversation, bringing a measure of calm reason to the anger generated by the others. Rae ran to the door, straining to hear the nature of the confusion above her. Even when she cracked the door, the exact identity of the intruders eluded her, as did Jericho's relationship with them. There was a scuffle, and though part of Rae would have been very happy to see Jericho Smith receive a facer, she feared for her own safety should the visitors get past him.

Recalling what he had said about brigands and deserters roaming the woods, Rae looked around her for a weapon and settled on a slat from beneath the mattress. Pushing aside all caution as the voices above her grew louder and more threatening, Rae ran up the stairs to lend her assistance. At the entranceway she halted, hefted her plank as best she could in her bound hands, and prepared to bash heads.

There were three men with Jericho, none of whom Rae recognized. Two of them held Jericho by the upper arms, while the third prepared to drive a fist into his midsection. Jericho's attention was caught by Rae's appearance in the doorway, and when he looked up the others did the same.

Rae knew that she looked a sight. Her mode of dress ill became her, and her hair was matted and tangled. Surely there was murder in her eyes as she raised the slat. Still, it was unconscionable the way these three strangers stared at her, their mouths gaping in amazement and their eyebrows lifted nearly to their hairlines.

Rae shot a glance at each of them, taking their mettle. They were all tall men, though the one ready to deliver a blow to Jericho's breadbasket was the tallest and, Rae guessed, the leader. He had broad, powerful shoulders and a lithe grace that belied his stature. He was darkly handsome, with silver eyes much the color of polished steel, and for a moment he held her in her place with a gaze that delivered curiosity and relief in equal parts. Had she not been made of such strong stuff she doubted she could have torn her eyes away from the fierce-looking giant.

The other two men did not wear the same grim expression, but Rae thought they appeared less controlled than their leader, more likely to explode in hot-tempered fury at any moment. The redheaded one's animated face registered shock and disapproval, and his large eyebrows were screwed into one line above his eyes, like a small brushfire. On the other side Jericho was held firmly by a younger man, nearly as dark as the first, but plainly more volatile at this moment. His eyes fell over Rae, and she thought she saw pity, perhaps even hurt, on his attractive face before his lips tightened and his fingers squeezed Jericho's arm.

Rae crouched lightly on her bare feet, ready to ply her board with painful accuracy if one of them moved so much as an inch. "Let go of him, the both of you," she said, jerking her chin in Jericho's direction. "And you," she told the leader sharply, "you step back a few paces or I'll put your face level with your feet."

She was certain all three men were ready to oblige her, and she thought a little disdainfully that they were hardly of Jericho's stamp, for he would barely have blinked at a termagant wielding a bed slat. She lowered her board a notch and the youngest man caught sight of her bound wrists.

"Look at that!" he shouted hoarsely. "He's gone and trussed her up like she was no better than Mama's Christmas turkey."

It struck her as odd that the stranger should be distressed by Jericho's treatment, even while she did not think she cared for being compared to that particular bird. As fate would have it, there was no time to make her objection known. The leader, seeing the proof in his companion's words, vented his rage as if wounded beyond reason. His terrible guttural growl hurt Rae's ears and so startled her that she did not lower her weapon on his head until he had already landed a punishing blow to Jericho's middle.

Jericho sagged between his captors, all breath driven from his lungs, and collapsed on the deck when they dropped him to run to their friend. Rae tossed aside her slat, useless now, since it had split under the force of her blow and the hardness of a certain head, and ran to Jericho, kneeling beside him. Before she could get out a word to question his condition, a great, booming voice silenced her.

"Have you but taken leave of your senses, m'girl?" the flame-haired man wanted to know. His brawny arms came around Rae's small waist, swallowing it, and pulled her away from Jericho's side. Roughly he stood her up and twisted her to face him. His mobile features were lined with disgust. "Sure and isn't it a fine thing when a brother wants to protect his sister's virtue and gets coldcocked for his trouble."

Rae looked at the man lying facedown on the deck. He was still not awake, in spite of his friend's efforts to shake him into awareness. She glanced back at the burly Irishman, trying to make sense of his scolding, then over her shoulder at Jericho, who was sitting up now, but still having a hard time drawing a breath.

"Jericho?" she asked, confusion in each syllable. "Do you know what this man's talking about?"

" 'Fraid I do, Red," he labored, sucking in air. "That's James Shannon who's got you in his meaty hooks, and on the deck are his good friends, who happen to be two of your three brothers. Noah's sitting up. It's Salem that you laid low."

Only one name was at all familiar to her. "Salem? Salem McClellan?"

"The very same."

"But—"

"The truth is worse than anything I imagined, Red. Appears that you're Rahab McClellan, and I'm a dead man."

Chapter 5

"See here, Rae. What's the meaning of this?" Shannon turned her a trifle roughly in his arms, jouncing her around as if she were a child. "Have you gone daft? What game it is you're playing, pretendin' not to know me or your brothers?" His offended tone plainly told Rae that he considered himself the most important member of the trio. "It *is* a game yer playin', ain't it? Sure and you haven't forgotten how I dandled you on my knee when you were just a bit of a thing."

Rae tried to twist from Shannon's grasp, paying little heed to his words. "Jericho? What do you mean you are a dead man?"

"Figure it out for yourself, Red," Jericho said wearily, rubbing his middle.

Noah lifted his head sharply, eyeing Jericho narrowly. "Don't call her Red. It makes her sound like a strumpet." He glanced at his sister and took in her pale complexion, as well as her disreputable state of dress. "You have a lot to answer for, Smith. Shannon, cut Rahab's bonds, and Rae, for God's sake, if you don't want Smith tossed overboard at the first sign of Salem's wakening, you'll go below and change into something less revealing.''

Rae did not doubt the wisdom of Noah's advice, but he was still a stranger to her, and she found herself turning to Jericho for direction. Though he grimaced when she did so, thinking she had surely dug his grave with that look, he nodded quickly, giving his permission. Past her turned head Shannon and Noah exchanged troubled glances. Shrugging, as if he didn't know what to make of Rae's attitude, Shannon sliced her bonds. Rubbing her wrists to restore circulation, Rae made a quiet thank you, then hurried below. Just before she shut the cabin door she could hear Noah's cutting demand that all of Jericho's explanations be good ones.

Rae dressed quickly, alert all the while to sounds above her that might mean Jericho was suffering again at the hands of Shannon and her brothers. Brothers. It was difficult to accept that Noah and Salem were her kin when they seemed not the least familiar. She smiled faintly when she thought how she had been ready to defend Jericho from her champions. Ready to defend? Lord, she had knocked the big one silly. She hoped Salem was a tolerant sort and loved her dearly, for she had no desire to feel the flat of another man's hand on her backside.

She tidied the cabin and straightened the bunk, frowning darkly when she saw the drops of blood on the sheets. Had Shannon said they were protecting her virtue? At the moment, only she and Jericho and the Lord knew they were too late for that. What a muddle everything had become, she thought disgustedly as she arranged the blankets over the stain. She could not even think clearly. At this moment she had no idea whether she regretted all that had happened or if it was perhaps the best adventure of her life. Certainly it was the *only* adventure she remembered, she reminded herself with a sigh.

Eyes closed, she massaged her temples, trying to recall what she knew about herself from what little Jericho had said. She was the sister Salem despaired of, the one with the broken engagement, the one who kept men at a distance. Well, Jericho Smith had put a period to that. Now Salem really had good reason to despair and would not thank any of them for it. And Ashley? The thought of her sister-in-law caused Rae's shoulders to sag dispiritedly. Here was the woman Jericho, if not loving her, at least cared for deeply. Jericho had told her that Ashley had tried to introduce them to Salem's sister. How odd, to have heard herself talked about and not even realized it was she. Keep thinking along those lines, m'girl, and your brain will turn to soup.

There were a number of footsteps in the passageway that interrupted Rae from her disjointed thoughts. She sat down on the edge of the bunk, changed her mind when she considered that she might look too comfortable there for her brothers' tastes, and chose the window seat instead. She was steadying the racing of her heart when there was a brisk knock at the door.

"Are you decent, Rahab?"

Rae recognized it was Noah who wanted to know. "Yes. You may come in."

Jericho was escorted in on the arms of Noah and Salem. Shannon followed, shutting the door behind him and leaning against it. Rae supposed he was doing it in aid of blocking Jericho's escape, but she doubted Jericho was considering such an action. His shuttered expression made it impossible to tell what his thoughts were, and Rae could not help but wonder how much he regretted coming to her aid in the first place.

Noah sat with Jericho on the bunk, while Salem leaned casually against the desk, his hands folded in front of him. Rae had carefully avoided Salem's eyes since he had entered the room, but now he spoke to her and she could not put off the confrontation a moment longer.

"Rae, I don't know whether to hug you or beat you," he said. His silvery eyes took in the whole of her, then softened when he saw her confusion. "For the moment, I shall do neither. Jericho says you don't know any of us. Is that true?"

Rae wished that it weren't. Surely she hadn't mistaken the fondness in Salem's expression as his eyes swept over her. She wanted to wrap herself in that warmth, but worried that it would be unseemly for her to act on her feelings. She bit her lip and maintained shy contact. "I know who you are—now—but I don't remember any of you. I'm sorry about clobbering you. I didn't know what to think when I came on deck."

Salem rubbed the back of his head and grinned ruefully. "It's no more than I taught you to do. I suppose it was inevitable that someday you should demonstrate your skill on my noggin." His smile faded. "Except for the memory loss, Rae, are you feeling well?"

"Yes, I'm fine. I gather you think Jericho treated me shabbily, but you are in the wrong of it there." She ignored the startled lift of Jericho's head. "He thought I was a spy, with orders to betray him, so he had no choice but to keep me at his side."

"Why would you think that, Smith?" Noah demanded.

"Because she could read," Jericho said lowly.

"Of course she can read, you simple son of—" Shannon cut himself off and looked at Rae apologetically. "Sorry, Rae. I forgot myself."

Rae brushed aside his concern airly. "Don't fret. Jericho's heard worse than that from my own lips." She blushed when she recalled what he had done about it, and it took no small amount of willpower not to touch her offended parts. She broke away from Salem's speculative gaze by putting forth her own questions. "I'm very much afraid I understand virtually nothing of what has happened to me. Indeed, I cannot recollect a thing of my personal life prior to waking on this schooner. How did I come to be in Wolfe's? Were we so badly in need of the ready that you sent me to work in that flesh market?" It was difficult to say who was most distressed by her last statement, though Jericho choked the loudest. "It is hard to credit, because Jericho thought so highly of you, and he didn't like the idea at all that I was a lightskirt. He was going to arrange for me to work for you, providing you didn't mind a harlot in your employ. But then, I am your sister, so it is doubtful whether you would have wanted to hire me at all, since you could scarce afford it. It's all rather confusing, don't you think?"

Shannon's face was ruddy with embarrassment, Noah looked as if his eyes would fall out of his head, Jericho appeared to wish the schooner would sink, and Salem glanced overhead, seeking a higher guidance.

Rae looked from man to man and feigned a cough, hiding her satisfied smile behind the back of her hand. Her dizzy speech had not been without its rewards. Her champions looked less as though they wished to stretch Jericho's neck and more as though they pitied him for having spent several days in the sole company of a cork-brained female.

Salem lowered his eyes, and after a shrewd glance at Rahab, spoke to Jericho. "I'm certain you can appreciate that as much as I'd like to shake her, Rae's still my sister and deserving of my protection. Perhaps you would care to explain why she thinks she is a lightskirt."

Jericho knew Salem too well not to understand that the invitation he issued was no less than a command. Jericho had used the same tone on any number of occasions, but in this cabin their roles had been reversed. He was answerable to his friend now, and though he wished to give a good account of himself and preserve the friendship, he would not permit himself to deny what had happened with Rahab. She seemed bent on covering the things he had done to her, but Jericho had never hid behind a woman's skirts and he refused to begin now. Neither was he going to allow Rae to be cast as blameless merely because she was a McClellan. It smacked of noblesse oblige, and that he would not tolerate.

"What other construction would you put on a serving wench

in Wolfe's who answered to 'Red' and played the crowd as if she were trodding the boards?" he asked simply.

Shannon looked as if he might smash the faint smile hovering about Jericho's lips, but Salem stayed him with a wave of his hand. "You were serving drinks, Rae? Why?"

"I don't have any idea. I thought you would supply the answer."

Noah spoke up. "I think questioning her is useless, Salem. She's nearly as blank as a babe. Now, don't go huffy on me, Rae. You know it's true."

"Noah is one for the truth," Jericho explained to Rae. "When he's not a soldier, your brother is a barrister."

"Oh." She looked at Noah curiously, wondering why she hadn't known without being told. Out of patience with herself, her eyes dropped to her folded hands. Rae felt all adrift. She wished she was not sitting alone on the bench with so much space on either side of her. There was nothing to grip, nothing for support, and she seemed to float aimlessly, waiting to attach herself with the tenaciousness of a barnacle to any outstretched hand or a fragment of conversation she could recall and understand.

Without meaning to, Rae's forlorn expression made Salem's voice unnecessarily sharp. "Do you mean to say, Smith, that Rae never explained herself?"

"She never had the opportunity. When there was a moment to tender explanations, your sister couldn't remember any. Surely you're aware of the manner in which we left the tavern."

"I killed a man," Rae said, tears thick in her throat. "If Jericho had not come to my rescue, I would be hanging by now. It is not right that you treat him with such contempt, not unless you are sorry that he aided me."

Jericho would have moved to Rae's side, but Salem was quicker. Rae's brother sat beside her and pulled her into his embrace. Rae went so naturally, as if by instinct, that Jericho began to understand that a special bond existed between them, one so strong that it could not be erased by Rae's loss of memory. Though nothing showed on his face, Jericho's insides ached as if something had been torn from him. Salem held Rae as surely as the sun held the earth, offering warmth in his arms and light in his tender smile. Jericho looked away, studying the toe of his scuffed boot and praying that his suffering would be short-lived. He had always known he had nothing to offer a decent woman, hadn't he? Hell, he hadn't even been much of a catch when he thought she was a whore.

Salem's chin was resting on the top of Rae's head and his hand stroked her back while she sobbed quietly into the folds of his linen shirt. His soft voice soothed her, repeating those universal phrases of assurance until she quieted. When she was calm, he turned his attention back to Jericho. "There is still much in the way of explanation for you to offer, Smith, but Rae has reminded me that you did see to her safety when she needed you most. For that I thank you."

Jericho squirmed. Salem's gratitude was more difficult to accept than his anger. He brushed at a piece of lint on his dark breeches and shrugged indifferently. "I was glad to do it—I think."

Rae gave him a watery smile. "You're very kind to say so, but I was not a gracious guest, and well you know it." She glanced at Salem. "I was rather ill in the beginning, and Jericho took care of me."

"God, Rae! Hadn't you and Ashley the sense between you not to behave so foolishly?" His spurt of exasperated anger was lost on Rahab; she was looking at him blankly again. "You don't remember any of it, do you?"

"What has Ashley to do with this?" Jericho asked. Almost immediately he wished he hadn't put forward the question. Rae's glance was sharp and knowing, and he realized she still misunderstood his feelings for Salem's wife.

Salem sighed heavily. "Noah, you tell all. You won't make a botch of it." In truth, he hadn't forgiven Ashley for her part in the scheme, and he had no wish to air his personal grievances in front of the others.

Noah stood and paced the room slowly as he talked, using the persuasive voice he usually reserved for the courtroom. Rae listened attentively, hoping to hear something that would trigger her memory, but the things Noah told them remained unfamiliar, and she was better able to imagine their happening to someone else than to herself.

She formed a hazy picture of Ashley, harried and anxious, small hands twisting nervously when the crier announced the midnight hour and there was no sign of her. Rae learned that her sister-in-law had not fretted long before she took action. Ashley had sent a trusted servant to Wolfe's, and he had been able to identify Rahab as the barmaid the authorities were searching for. Even at the risk of exposing Salem's Loyalist standing for the sham it was, Ashley had traveled secretly to Washington's camp, hoping to enlist the aid of Noah in discovering Rae's whereabouts.

"Until she met Herr Kroger in the camp, she hadn't a clue about your rescuer," Noah told Rae. "Kroger explained that Smith had offered to take his place at Wolfe's." Here Noah gave Jericho a hard, contemptuous glance. "Of course, we realized she was with you. We were foolish enough to be relieved. Ashley swore you would keep Rae safe until everything calmed." Noah leaned back against the desk, his thumbs hooked in the waistband of his breeches. A self-deriding sneer changed the shape of his full mouth. "More fools we. For the first twenty-four hours we told ourselves it was wise of you to stay away. At thirty-six we wondered that you hadn't seen fit to let us know that she was safe. At forty-eight—"

"At forty-eight I came home," Salem interjected. His words fell heavily in the room and required no elaboration.

A half-smile replaced Noah's sneer. "Patience is not a virtue Jerusalem holds in much regard, and I don't think he credited you with as much restraint around Rahab as Ashley did."

Rae's face flushed and she dared not look around her, but Jericho continued to study his boots, unmoved and unaffected. Only the taut planes of his face and a certain grimness about his mouth revealed that Noah's insight stung.

"Salem remembered the schooner, but when we arrived, it was gone. That did not necessarily ease anyone's mind."

"I moved it to keep her safe."

Her. Rae shuddered at Jericho's impersonal reference. She was no longer Red, not even Rae. Merely her. Her insides knotted. If there were ties to be severed, then she would sever them. She interrupted as Noah would have asked Jericho another question and began to detail the events since she had come to the schooner. The version she offered her brothers and Shannon was highly condensed and infinitely amusing. Jericho was portrayed as the complete gentleman, long-suffering and indulgent, as he dealt with the feather-brained strumpet who had some skill with a dagger and a penchant for colorful language.

"So you see," she finished. "We would have had a rather boring time of it if we had found the message in my skirt at the beginning. Jericho would have understood all and that would have been that. I realize it would have saved much in the way of grief if I had not lost my memory, but Jericho contrived as best he could. I regret that I did not act more wisely when I went to Wolfe's, and certainly I did not want to kill the officer, but I cannot change what has already occurred. Can you forgive me for setting you all to worry?"

Salem squeezed Rae's shoulders gently. "As long as you have not come to any harm, then all is forgiven." His words encompassed Jericho as well as Rahab, and he felt his sister relax slightly in his embrace. Curious, that. Why was she so determined to protect Jericho Smith? Did gratitude explain it, or perhaps something else, something deeper? "Noah and Shannon have to return to Washington's camp. Smith, the general is expecting you, too. I think you can anticipate a bitter tongue-lashing for not reporting your whereabouts—if he doesn't have you taken out and shot." Rae gasped. "I was kidding, Rahab. Smith is highly respected for the work he does. And he has as many lives as a cat. There's no cause to think he can't call on one of them this time."

"I wasn't worried," she lied. "Will I be returning home with you? What about the authorities?"

"The British are looking for a barmaid, not my sister. You will be safe at home with Ashley and the children."

"I gather that means I won't be permitted to carry any more messages."

Noah laughed. "I always told Salem you weren't anyone's fool." Some imp made Rae stick out her tongue at her brother, which caused Noah to smile broadly. "You haven't forgotten all, Rae. You spent most of your childhood pointing that weapon at me."

"Sure, and it's good to know she's the same colleen she always was," Shannon said heartily.

Neither Salem nor Noah was certain that was completely true, but they guarded their thoughts. Rae was not up to a brutal confrontation, and Jericho could withstand it. And if they were honest, neither was certain he wanted to hear the truth.

"I should like to talk to your sister—alone," Jericho said. His tone was a little belligerent, not at all appropriate to a man asking a favor.

Salem was ready to deny him, but Rahab squeezed his hand and he relented. "A few minutes. I have to get her back soon. Ashley has worried herself sick."

"I understand." He waited until he and Rae were alone, then he left the bed to sit beside her on the bench. He frowned when she edged away from him. "Why did you do it? Why pretend as if this has all been a lark? You excused my vile behavior and never mentioned what happened here. Your brothers are not stripling lads. They know what happens between a man and a woman."

"Would you have me tell them that I demanded you lie with

me?'' she asked sharply. ''I will not shame them with the knowledge that their sister is but a whore, after all.''

''I see,'' he said, sighing. She seemed determined to punish herself. ''Then you were not acting on some misguided notion that you were protecting me.''

''Protecting you?'' she scoffed. ''From what?''

''Salem and Noah still see you through a sibling's eyes. They would not credit your story that you seduced me.'' Jericho was not certain he believed it himself, nor was he happy that she took all the responsibility for what had happened between them. He had provoked her, treating her like she was a strumpet until she had acted on it. Then, in bed, she had been like no woman he had known, loving him with a completeness that frightened him because it threatened to intrude upon his well-ordered life. ''Your brothers would demand that I marry you.''

''Do you think you are the only one who would chafe at the bonds of marriage? Mayhap I was protecting myself from such a pass. I am certain we would not suit. Think on it. We rarely spent more than a few hours together before there was some sort of argument. You never made a secret of your dislike for me.''

''I never disliked you.'' He could not bring himself to admit that he was afraid of her, of what she could do to him if she realized his vulnerability. Jericho reached for her hand, but she pulled away. Stung, he got to his feet and stared out the window, pretending great interest in the antics of a mother rabbit and her brood on the edge of the wood. ''If there should be a reason later on,'' he said heavily, ''that you should have need of my name, I hope you will not hesitate to contact me.''

Rae's eyes widened and her hand flew to her mouth. Here was something she had not considered. ''A child! I had not thought!''

Jericho's expression softened as he looked down at her. ''Of course you hadn't.''

''A child!'' Her thoughts flew ahead to the inevitable disappointment of her brothers, the wedding under fire, the pity on the faces of the guests as their eyes settled on the bride's rounded middle. "Oh, it would be too awful," she said, never thinking of the construction Jericho would put on her words.

To Jericho it was the final proof that Rae wanted nothing to do with him. It was easy for him to believe, since it was no more than he had expected once he'd realized the truth of her identity. "I agree," he said coldly. "Still, should it happen, I will not have my offspring labeled bastard. There are too many in this world now, and the course their lives run is unsteady, at best. You must promise that you will seek me out, else I will tell Salem and Noah the whole of it now, and we will be married, child or no."

In that moment Rae knew Jericho Smith was a bastard, and she ached for him, nearly wept for him, but in the end held to her decision to put him from her life. It mattered not at all about his birth; what mattered was that he not be coerced into a marriage that was fated to make him unhappy and bitter. "I promise," she said quietly. "Though I doubt I have conceived. After all, it was only the once."

Jericho snorted. "I'm certain you can talk to any number of chits who were trotted down the aisle, bellies burgeoning, repeating that bit of nonsense up until the moment they said 'I do.' Ashley among them," he finished brutally.

"You mean Salem and Ashley . . ." she faltered, not knowing what to make of Salem's hypocrisy. "It doesn't seem right that Salem should have been so suspicious and angry with you. He is not in a position to cast stones."

"I don't think I would tell him that, if I were you. He and Ashley have made a success of their marriage. He is more likely to recommend the thing than dwell on how it came about."

Rae's hands twisted in her lap. "There is nothing to say, then. I will keep silent unless I needs must speak of it. Marriage is not for either of us."

"As you say. We would not suit."

"Well ..." She wished she had some witty truism that would end this painful conversation, something glib that would wrap it all up neatly. Her throat felt thick and achy, but her eyes remained dry.

Jericho shifted on his feet. "Well, I reckon this is good-bye." Eloquent to the end, aren't you, Smith. Who would guess at the age of eight you could quote from the Bard's most famous works? "The quality of mercy is not strained. . . ."

Rae smiled faintly. "I reckon it is," she mocked softly.

At the door to the cabin Jericho paused, his knuckles nearly white on the handle. He glanced over his shoulder. "I was wonderin', Red. If you get your memory back, think you'll still remember any of these last few days?"

Rae froze, afraid any careless move would shatter her fragile hold on her emotions. He had called her Red. It was almost her undoing. "If there is no child, does it really matter?"

Jericho turned his head and spoke to the door. A muscle twitched in his cheek. "No, I suppose it doesn't." He left the cabin then, before Rae saw his shoulders heave once in despair.

Twenty minutes after Jericho's departure, Salem returned to the cabin. "Are you ready to go?"

Rae nodded, smiling, not understanding that her brother knew her too well to believe in the brittle curve of her lips. "Have the others left?"

"A few minutes ago. There were some things we still needed to discuss with Smith." Seeing her bewilderment he explained. "Not all about you, Rae. There is a war on, you know, and Smith is an able and much needed commander. Here, he gave me this to return to you." He held out the dagger in its leather sheath.

"I don't think I want it. Anyway, didn't I hear Noah say it belonged to Ashley?"

"It does, but I doubt that she'll want it." He tossed it carelessly on the bed. "Too painful a reminder for everyone. Let's be on our way. Even the children have been fractious with missing you.''

Rahab tried to respond to the forced lightness in Salem's voice by forming a picture of her niece and nephew in her mind. She had no idea how much it would hurt when she met them and found she had drawn it all wrong.

Rae lay on her back in the open field and blinked several times at the brightness of the cobalt sky before shielding her eyes with her forearm. In response to a cool breeze from the river, high grass rippled on all sides, and the corner of Rae's mouth lifted in a sleepy smile as it tickled her bare arms and ankles. She stretched lazily and sucked in the fragrant September air. Indian summer had come to McClellan's Landing, and Rae had fallen victim to its warm promise, seeking a moment's respite from her family's watchful eyes.

They meant well, of course, but it had been six months since she left Jericho Smith and four since she'd returned to Virginia with Ashley and the children, and Rae was weary of being hovered over as if she were some unfledged chick. Salem had helped her see the funny side of all the familial concern, but he was no longer around to offer any aid. On Washington's orders, he had abandoned his pose as a British supporter, sent his family back to the relative safety of the landing, and taken his place as one of thousands of regular soldiers waiting for a battle that would end the war.

Rae wrote to him often, newsy and humorous little missives that inadequately described the state of her own mind, if they mentioned it at all. Though she wished they wouldn't, she knew her mother and Ashley kept Salem and Noah aware of her progress, or lack of it, in recapturing her memory. Rae saw nothing to be gained by informing them of every odd bit she would suddenly remember, especially if they were sharing it with Jericho. She did not want him to know how it was breaking her, this struggle to clear the shadows from her past. She did not want him to suspect that a day rarely passed when she did not wish she were back in the schooner on the Hudson, in the company of a man who thought she was no better than she ought to be.

She supposed she should have realized that it would be easier to be without her memory in the company of Jericho than in the presence of her family, but when she'd left the schooner it hadn't occurred to her. It was a matter of expectations, she decided a few weeks later. Jericho's expectations were shockingly low or nonexistent, and he only had the flimsiest guidelines on which to base her actions.

Not so her family. They all had their own ideas about the sort of person she was—daughter, sister, aunt, friend. Rae realized there existed among the members of her family a collective memory that could be called on to chronicle many of the events of her life. In the beginning it had only been Salem and Ashley who, in the course of an easy dinner conversation, would mention something about the landing or the children, even something about Rae's parents, and catch themselves, looking to Rae expectantly to see if she knew what they were talking about. Almost always they felt obliged to explain themselves when her stare remained blank or confused, and she hated the disappointed glances that were exchanged when no one thought she would notice. And now those patient, somehow sad glances were multiplied beyond Rae's bearing at the landing. With a frequency that alarmed all who cared for her, she found subtle ways to exclude herself from family gatherings.

A faint frown crossed Rae's face as the sunlight's path was blocked momentarily, leaving her in cool shadows. She sighed softly, not bothering to remove her forearm from her eyes. It was too much to hope that a cloud could be blamed for disturbing her worship of warmth and solitude.

"Charity thought I might find you here," Ashley said, drop-

ping into the grass beside Rae. She was too fearful of being
turned away to ask Rahab for permission to join her. Pretending
to be unperturbed by Rae's less than welcoming air, Ashley
smoothed the folds of her gold skirt about her legs and drank
in the view of the landing that the grassy knoll afforded her.

Thousands of acres of fertile, rich Virginia soil surrounded
the McClellan homestead. The house seemed to be part of the
land, as if it had been planted there rather than built, and
indeed, the McClellans tended it as if it were a living thing.
The sweeping verandas were an open invitation to travelers,
who could catch a teasing glimpse of the red brick mansion
through a break in the trees along the river. The windows, their
white shutters thrown open, winked in the sunlight and sent
a sparkling greeting to passersby. The landing was the very
antithesis of the fortresslike home Ashley had known on the
Linfield estate. Her glance rested thoughtfully on her sister-in-
law. Rahab was lucky to have grown up in such a loving
environment; no matter that she couldn't quite appreciate it at
the moment.

"I might have known Mother would see me," Rae answered
resignedly. "I can't seem to escape her eagle eye. Was she
always so astute?"

Ashley smiled. "Always with the ones she loves." She hesitated. "You used to call her Mama."

"That is what Leah told me. And Gareth, when he came
from Williamsport to visit. And his wife. But I can't bring
myself to say it now. It isn't comfortable. Does it hurt her very
much?"

There was nothing to be gained by lying. "Yes, it hurts
Charity. And Robert, when you call him Father instead of Papa.
But they are trying to understand, so they practice patience and
love you all the more."

Rae lifted her forearm a tad so that she could see Ashley.
Salem's wife was much different from how Rahab had first
imagined her. She admitted she had not wanted to like Ashley,

because Jericho thought so highly of her, even loved her, but there had been no help for it. She was very hard not to like. It was depressing, really. Ashley was quick-witted, lovely to look at, talented at the spinet and with a needle, a loving and patient mother, unfailingly gracious and even-tempered with everyone but Salem. Rae suspected that this last small failing was because Ashley loved her husband to distraction. Rae could hardly fault her for that. "Do you know," she said at last, "that sometimes I wish they would not be so quick to treat me as if I were a bit of crystal. The children are the most natural around me, as if it doesn't matter that I can't recall the time Trenton spit up on my favorite ballgown or when Courtney played peek-a-boo beneath my skirts."

"Perhaps it's because Courtney and Trenton don't remember much of those things, either," Ashley suggested. "When it comes to memory, you may even be younger than they are. You shared only a short past with the children. The rest of us are not so content to build a friendship on your recent memories."

"Then why doesn't someone just knock me over the head with a—"

"Bed slat?"

"Exactly. Perhaps it would raise some recollection."

"More likely it would raise a nasty lump," Ashley said dryly. "From the beginning the doctors have told us that you will recover in your own way, in your own time."

Rae snorted. "I don't think they know what they're talking about. Aren't they the same men who proposed no one mention any remotely disturbing events in my past? Until I cornered you for an explanation I thought I must have been the only child in the world who had not shed a tear over a skinned knee, a broken dolly, or the loss of a pet. I would never have known I had been engaged to Troy if Jericho hadn't said something about it before he knew who I was. I waited for someone to bring it up to me. In the end I had to beg you to tell me the whole of the story. You were so afraid it would stir some sort of regret or sadness.''

''Yet you didn't feel a thing.''

''Not personally. Don't you see? It was as if it happened to another person. I cannot even imagine having loved Troy. He is such a perfect complement for Leah that I think we would never have suited.''

''It's true that they deal well together, but you were very hurt at the time it happened. You found it difficult to take the attentions of any suitor seriously after that. If it hadn't been for your loss of memory, I doubt you would have let Jericho Smith within an arm's length of you.''

Rae cast her arm aside completely and stared narrowly at Ashley. ''What makes you think I did?'' she asked sharply.

''Credit me with some sense, Rae. I am not one of your brothers, who believe your story because they want to believe it, even need to believe it. I have not the least doubt that if Jericho had known who you were his treatment of you would have been naught but impeccable. And if you had understood you were not any man's bit of muslin you would have given him a set down that would have driven that lazy smile from his face.''

Rae wished Ashley had not mentioned Jericho's rather indolent grin. She had been trying for months to forget what it looked like. ''So?'' she asked a trifle belligerently.

''So I think that you and Jericho acted as circumstances permitted you to act.''

''Meaning?''

''Meaning that if you had been less fortunate you would be carrying Jericho's child at this moment,'' Ashley said bluntly.

Less fortunate. Rae's eyes closed briefly. No, she thought, Ashley was in the wrong there. She was less fortunate because she was not carrying his babe. When she opened her eyes they glistened wetly. ''What do you know of it? You got pregnant so you could force my brother to marry you!''

The flat of Ashley's hand met Rae's cheek with surprising force. Stunned for a moment, Rae could only stare at Ashley, then tears flooded her vision and Ashley's flushed face blurred. Rae started to bury her face in her hands, miserable that she had been so hateful to someone who had shown her every kindness, but Ashley reached for her, gently drawing her wrists away, and moved so that Rae could rest her head on her lap. Ashley stroked the streak of fire in Rae's hair, while the younger woman cried out her grief.

"It's all right, darling," Ashley said in quiet, soothing tones. "You've been strong for so long, it's all right to cry now. You've been aching forever, it seems." Rahab had been hurting in silence since Salem had taken her from Jericho's side. Ashley had watched her try to resume a life she no longer understood, make polite conversation with people she was supposed to know, but didn't, and pick up the threads of memories she wasn't certain she cared about. It had been painful to see Rahab attend an evening social and watch her withdraw into herself as the night wore on. She was frightened of saying the wrong thing, of calling someone by the wrong name, of thinking she knew someone she had never met before in her life. Salem and Ashley had known at that moment that they had to get Rae out of New York and back to the landing. It was the veriest coincidence that General Washington's needs had matched their own. Thus Rae would never know she had been the reason for their returning to Virginia with such haste.

Coming home had not provided the healing balm Ashley and Salem had hoped it would. Of a certainty there was support and an abundance of love, but no one had foreseen that Rae would feel out of place. Rather than being comforted by so much attention and good intentions, it seemed as if Rahab were in danger of being smothered by the weight of the cotton-wool wrapping.

Ashley gave Rae a bit of the hem of her skirt so she could dry her eyes. "I don't have a handkerchief," she explained.

"Invariably I use my husband's sleeve. It's shocking to think that while he's gone I shall have to make do with my own linen." Rae's watery smile lifted Ashley's heart. She continued to stroke Rae's hair, the gentle pressure assuring Rae there was no hurry for her to move. "It's true that I was carrying Courtney before I married your brother," she explained. "But—"

"There's no need to—"

"There's every need. I was saying that I never forced your brother into marriage. Did someone tell you that I had?"

Rae shook her head. "Jericho mentioned something to me—about its only taking the once—" She sniffed as her cheeks warmed, and her fingers plucked at a bit of Ashley's gold skirt. "You know what I mean—and that it had happened to you and Salem. I made up the part about you forcing Salem's hand."

"You're sorry, aren't you, that you're not going to have Jericho's babe?"

"Does it make me so very bad, do you think?" Rae asked plaintively. An errant tear slipped from her eye and splattered noiselessly on the back of her hand. "I wouldn't have demanded that he marry me. But to have his child, a boy with his bright yellow hair or his funny smile, or a girl with cerulean eyes and thick lashes, well, that would have been lovely."

Ashley could have pointed out that the child might have taken after Rahab, but she didn't think that news would have been welcomed. Rae still had not the least sense that her looks were striking and vibrant when she became animated. If men of her acquaintance called her cold, it was because they had glimpsed her smile and despaired when it was not turned on them. "I don't think that wanting Jericho's child makes you bad. Does he know that you love him?"

Rae's breath caught. She considered lying about her feelings, but suspected Ashley would have none of it. "I never told him that I did."

"Then he doesn't know. Is that the way you want it?"

"Yes . . . no . . . I can't say. We said good-bye."

There was a smile in Ashley's voice and in her eyes. "And you can't say hello again, is that it? What rubbish!"

"Perhaps," Rae shrugged. "It doesn't matter much anyway. He can't have many good memories of me. I was nothing but trouble to him, and he would spare you no detail in the telling of the misery I caused."

The conviction with which Rae spoke warned Ashley that any statement to the contrary would not be heard. Ashley thought of the letter she had just received from Salem lying on the cherry wood desk in their room. The contents of that letter were the main reason Ashley had sought Rae out. Salem had penned the letter some three weeks earlier, and it frightened Ashley that because the delivery had been slow, she and Rae could have spent the last minutes talking about a dead man.

Jericho, Salem had written, was known of late by a different moniker than the preferred Smith. The troops were given to calling him Saint Smith, not because he acted like one, but because they figured it was only a matter of time before he joined them.

At the same moment that Rae was being encouraged to talk about the days—and nights—she had spent with Jericho on the schooner, Jericho was belly down at the edge of a cropping of trees taking the measure of General Lord Cornwallis's troops camped along the York River. Inadequately camouflaged by the sparse growth about him, Jericho had had to dig a small trench he could lie in while gathering the information Washington needed. His shirt clung to him, damp with his sweat, and his wool jacket was hot, heavy, and smelling like something had wandered up a sleeve and died. His breeches and stockings were soiled from the crawling and digging he had done; his boots felt as if they had all the earth from his trench in them. He was uncomfortable and cramped, weary and cross. And he had dirt under his fingernails. He examined his hands in distaste and swore under his breath. God, he hated dirt in his nails.

Grimacing, he decided Tom Paine had surely been right when he wrote, "These are the times that try men's souls."

Jericho ignored the urge to clean his nails and struggled instead to unfold a small piece of foolscap so he could begin drawing the earthworks and trenches as the redcoats were laying them out. His sketches were meticulous in detail, and while he drew he forgot his miserable position, the danger, and the unrelenting heat. If he felt anything at that time it was satisfaction in knowing that the cherry-red troops all around him were ripe for the picking. Cornwallis had chosen a poor location to dig in. Even by taking up two posts, one in York and one on the opposite bank in Gloucester, his army's back was set firmly to the sea. Normally this was a favored position for the English, since they had the mightiest naval power in the world, but not this time, Jericho thought a trifle smugly. This time they would find themselves cut off from their navy by the French, who were on their way from the West Indies, led by Admiral de Grasse.

At least, Jericho hoped that was the case. He was as impatient as General Washington and eight thousand other men for news that the French navy was finally going to lend its support. There were already able French commanders leading troops on land, and Comte de Rochambeau, certain his countrymen would arrive in time to blockade Cornwallis, had put up $20,000 from his own war chest to pay the uneasy patriot troops who could easily be driven to mutiny by their poverty. Washington had gambled on de Grasse's support a few weeks earlier and had left New York to take on Cornwallis.

Jericho continued to sketch, wondering if Rahab knew how close he was to her now. Not that she would care, he assured himself. She would be more interested to know that Salem and Noah traveled with Washington and that Shannon remained in New York with a few thousand colonial regulars to keep Clinton from suspecting the main force was moving 415 miles to the south. Rae and her family would know soon enough what was happening. In a matter of days the population around Yorktown was going to swell dramatically with militia and sailors. Washington planned to make his headquarters in Williamsburg, not far from the McClellans' plantation. The army's presence would not be a secret for long. It was clear from the line of trenches Cornwallis was laying down that he anticipated a heavy and bloody confrontation with the Continental Army.

Jericho carefully folded the map he had made, took off his tricorn, and slipped the paper into his hat's special lining. Too many spies had been caught with plans in their shoes. Jericho joked that if he were going to hang, at least he had used his head. Gallows humor, the men called it. Saint Smith, they called him. Smiling hollowly as the sun beat down on the bright beacon of his hair, Jericho jammed his hat on his head and lay motionless in the trench, resigned to spending the remaining eight hours of daylight in his earthen coffin, until night made it safe to travel.

Saint Smith, he repeated to himself grimly, turning on his back. He closed his eyes and folded his hands on his chest as if testing out the length and breadth of his casket. He hoped death was more comfortable, and he shifted restlessly in response to his morbid thoughts. He supposed it was an improvement on his state of mind that he even recognized his thoughts as morbid. Of late he had played a dangerous game of tag with death, too many times to count. The general had finally demanded to know what he was doing, giving Jericho the severest dressing down he had had since he was a stripling youth.

Jericho could not recall what excuses he had made for his careless behavior. Whatever he had said had not approached the truth, because Jericho was not certain he understood that elusive element himself. He knew that his lack of caution, devising risk-filled assignments that only he was reckless enough to take, had begun after he'd said good-bye to Rae. But what he didn't know was why, and more often than not, he avoided thinking about it. Now was no exception. He told himself he needed rest more than introspection, and placing a hand on the musket by his side, he cleared his mind by envisioning the placid surface of a glassy pond. In no time at all he was asleep.

Jericho could not exercise the same control over his sleeping thoughts as he could over his waking ones. It was only a matter of time before the smooth surface of the water developed a few ripples in it, and only a little longer before the ripples took on the shape of a face that was dearer to him than was his conscious desire.

The eyes formed first, alive, deeply green, beckoning him with their teasing, vixen slant. Dark lashes fluttered playfully, mocking a harlot's advances. The slender line of her nose, faintly tilted on the end, took shape next, followed by a familiar sprinkling of freckles that outlined the arch of her cheeks and disappeared into the soft threads of mahogany hair at her temples. She was breathing softly, her dewy lips slightly parted, and Jericho could just make out the pearly edge of her teeth where the tip of her tongue rested nervously. Jericho smiled at the uncertain tilt of her head, the question inherent in her posture, as she returned his steady regard. He did not feel so powerless, knowing she was as off balance as he in the face of their attraction.

He reached for her hand, drawing her from the pool of water. She stepped forward lightly, skin glistening wetly, droplets of water sparkling on her white throat like a choker of perfectly matched diamonds. Her long, tapered fingers gripped his wrist for support as she was pulled inexorably into the safety of his embrace. And that was when Jericho admitted, at least in his dreams, that he loved Rae McClellan. If he had not loved her so well, there would have been nothing safe about the circle of his arms.

He held her slender torso close to his chest, and though her small breasts flattened, he could still feel the hard coral tips of her nipples. As her arms wound about his neck his own hands fell to her buttocks and urged her closer, cradling her in his thighs. They rocked on their feet, mouths fusing in a kiss that was only a sweet prelude to the union desired by their bodies. The tips of Rae's nails caressed his shoulders and followed the light mat of hair on his chest until it led her to the source of his arousal. Without warning her nails scratched him as they traced the path and Jericho growled low, putting some space between them.

"Sheathe your damn claws," he told her harshly, not sure he liked this wildness in Rae. It seemed calculated and hard.

At first there was no response, then a rough voice laughed. "Did you hear that, Dugan? He thinks he's got a cat by the tail!"

"Aye, Zach, but wot kind of cat?" The tip of Dugan's bayonet rested precariously close to Jericho's swollen manhood. He nudged his prey with more gentleness than he had when he had scraped the sharp weapon across Smith's chest. "Oi'd say our spy 'as been dreaming of a loidy cat. Cor, and it's rare I seen such a stiff piece wot could pleasure every camp follower we got."

Jericho's dream had vanished, forgotten now as he was presented with a complication he would have liked to avoid. A frisson of fear ran down his spine. Though he did not show it, he was alert to the smallest movements of the two men who stood over him, and if he didn't have much hope of getting the better of them, he wasn't ready to give up, either. It was difficult not to tighten his fingers on the musket, especially with a bayonet poised at his privates. It must have been some kind of dream that had put him in such a state and kept him from hearing the advance of the two redcoats. A narrow glance at their cloddish boots told Jericho they had not been especially quiet as they crept up on him.

Zach stood at Jericho's feet and leaned carelessly on the butt of his musket, a simple smile splitting his clean-shaven face.

Clearly he was enjoying himself at the expense of the Yankee Doodle. Jericho did not discount him as a threat, but the more dangerous of the two was the man who was prepared to spear him. It was not merely the fatal aim of the bayonet that worried Jericho, but the fact that he was certain he had met Dugan before. And the encounter was not one Dugan was likely to forget, since he had left it the scarred loser. Jericho's shaded blue eyes followed Dugan's thick legs upward, rested briefly on the red coat that did not fit comfortably about Dugan's paunchy middle, and studied the bulky shoulders that had not yet turned to fat. Not by a flicker of his lashes did Jericho allow Dugan to know he was being inspected, yet something gave him away perhaps a quickening of his heartbeat, when he saw Dugan was missing the lobe of his left ear.

Dugan poked him in the thigh. "Looks like we woke 'im from 'is nap," he told Zach. "Get on your feet, man. 'Ands on your 'ead. Oi'd as lief run you through 'ere, but there are orders for spies to 'ang. An example for the men, don't you know."

Jericho thought then that Dugan did not recognize him, or he would never have been allowed to stand. He came to his feet slowly, almost lazily, careful to give no indication that his fingers itched to reach for the musket or the knife in his boot. "Reckon you fellows caught me out fairly," he drawled, not looking too keenly at Dugan. It had been fifteen years since he had seen him, and then Jericho hadn't been much above fifteen himself. Still, Dugan was not the forgiving sort, certainly not when he had been bested in front of his shipmates by a mere lad with more good looks than good sense.

"It seems a shame, it does," Zach was saying, "to have to take him back to camp when he's already dug his own grave here. What's your name?" He grinned, as if sharing something hugely funny. "Just so we can set up a proper marker in case we change our minds."

Jericho felt his blood run cold as Dugan answered in his

place. "D'you mean you don't recognize 'im from the circulars, Zach?" he scoffed, never taking his eyes from his captive. " 'E's wanted as a spy, our friend is. Been causin' grief for our troops up and down the coast, 'specially these last few months. Oi'd thought you'd know from the color of 'is 'air. It's been too long, Smith. Did you think Oi'd forget your pretty face? Oi'ad a mind it was you in the bushes when Oi spied your yellow 'air. You shouldn't 'ave taken off your 'at. Like as not Oi'd never 'ave seen you." His eyes darted over Jericho's face and beads of sweat formed on his upper lip and forehead, betraying his nervousness as his anger continued to mount. "You knew me right off, didn't you? Thought Oi'd never let you up. 'Ad a mind not to, o' course, but then Oi pictured you swinging from a gibbet, and damn, if that didn't look good to me."

Zach's eyebrows rose, not quite believing his good fortune. "Smith? Jericho Smith? That's who we've got, then?"

"The very one. Ain't that right, Jericho?" Dugan poked Jericho with his weapon again and smiled malevolently. "Or do you prefer Geoffrey Hunter-Smythe? As I recall, there was a time you swore that was your name."

"I think I swore I was the Earl of Stanhope, too," Jericho said easily, as if there was no pain in remembering what he wished to forget. "No one believed that, either."

Zach whistled under his breath. "Here, what's this he's saying, Dugan? We've got ourselves a doodle spy who's a bloody lord to boot?"

"Don't start marching in the parade now," Dugan warned him impatiently. "This bloke's no more quality than we are, though he can spin you a pretty tale. We've still got to get 'im back to camp, and 'e's quick as a bead of mercury. 'E's the one wot took my ear all those years ago. 'E don't fight fair."

"Let's put the question to Zach," Jericho said, pretending to ignore Dugan for the moment. "Was an ear too much to take from a man who wanted to bugger me? Has he abandoned young sailors in favor of drummer boys these days?'' Jericho's words were calculated to cause confusion, and they succeeded beyond his hopes.

Zach's musket fell to the ground as surprise brought him up sharply, while Dugan forgot caution and lunged at his captive. Jericho sprang aside and grabbed the musket, using the force of Dugan's leap to throw him to the ground and wrest the weapon from him. Zach was bending to recover his musket, opening his mouth at the same time to shout a warning to the camp below, when Jericho clubbed him on the side of the head. He toppled soundlessly to the ground, a narrow streak of blood forming at his temple. Jericho spun as he heard Dugan get clumsily to his feet and try to tackle him. He eluded the heavier man easily, but he feared their noise in the brush would alert more redcoats. He tossed the musket out of Dugan's reach and went for his knife.

''You've slowed a bit,'' Jericho taunted him. ''There was a time when you could have nearly had my ear ... and a lot more besides.''

''You were a snotty young pup fifteen years ago,'' Dugan breathed heavily, touching his missing lobe. ''You 'aven't changed.'' He studied Jericho's stance, trying to anticipate his moves, and in his mind's eye he saw the slender youth Jericho had been, dancing before him, eluding him with lightning steps, making a fool of him in front of his mates, who knew why he wanted the lad. No one really cared that he wanted the boy in his bunk; their thinking was that if he could get Jericho, he could have him. The humiliation had come when he had tried to corner his quarry. He had jumped ship not long after that, made a life for himself as a waterfront pimp in London until he had been given the choice of joining the forces in America or spending time in Newgate. In all those years he had never been certain what had happened to the boy who had once sworn he was the heir to Stanhope—until now.

As Jericho and Dugan drew wary circles in the undergrowth,

Jericho maneuvered his opponent closer to the trench. Uppermost in Jericho's mind was to end the confrontation quickly. Every second delayed meant someone on the fringes of the camp was more likely to glance toward the grassy parapet and see him. He fanned his weapon in front of him, pushing Dugan backward until he teetered on the edge of the trench. Dugan's arms flapped uselessly as he tried to right himself, and Jericho took advantage of his soft, unprotected middle by landing a kick there that drove the breath from Dugan's lungs.

Loose dirt flew from the trench as Dugan's body filled the space with a heavy thud. Before he could recover Jericho jumped on top of him, straddling his huge belly, and held his knife to Dugan's throat. He hesitated while Dugan blinked helplessly, too stunned to scream for help.

"Awww, what the hell," Jericho muttered, and rather than giving Dugan the steely edge of his knife, he surprised them both by roundhousing his empty fist on the vulnerable area above his scarred ear. Dugan blinked once more, than his dazed eyes closed and his head drifted to the side. "I'm gettin' too damn soft," Jericho told himself as he put away the knife. With swift, economical motions, he stripped both men to the uniforms they were born in, covered himself in what he thought would fit best from each man, took the best musket among them, and broke the other two, then buried the remaining clothes. Slipping the map into an inside pocket in his red coat, he said a fond farewell to his discarded tricorn and tossed it deep into the woods. "Certainly these are the times . . ."

Whistling softly to himself, Jericho Smith left the edge of the woods and moved freely among the lobsterbacks in Cornwallis's camp. He inspected the earthworks and trenches, observed some of the units drilling, and even availed himself of a little food from the mess. He was still able to leave the camp unnoticed some thirty minutes before two soldiers strode buck naked from the forest and demanded to see Cornwallis himself.

While Dugan and Zach were relating their tale and wrestling with their embarrassment, Jericho found himself in a similarly awkward position. He had waited too long to shed the incriminating red coat, and now three militiamen were marching him triumphantly into the Marquis de Lafayette's headquarters not far from the Cornwallis camp. They had been quick; he'd give them that. He hadn't known they were following his route until they had leaped on him from behind, relieved him of his new musket and knife, and upbraided him mercilessly for thinking he could not be seen in a uniform that was a marksman's dream and a soldier's nightmare. His explanation fell on deaf ears, and though part of him was relieved the men did not believe his outrageous adventure, it was nonetheless damn humiliating.

Still, the humor of the situation struck him when he was brought to Lafayette's tent. Jericho had met Washington's trusted major general not long after he had arrived in the colonies. Lafayette was hardly unaware of Jericho's service these last seven years. The young French commander took one look at him trapped neatly between three Yankee ruffians and laughed uproariously.

"Come," he commanded, smiling hugely. "Sit. I must hear zee way of it. Zee general will want to know how it is we captured zis infamous spy. Zen we shall see about zee hanging."

Chapter 6

" 'Zen,' he says, 'we shall see about zeeee hanging.' " Jericho finished, smiling ruefully at the man across the table. He lifted his tankard of ale to toast the absent marquess, then drank deeply. "I can tell you, Gareth, I wanted to crawl away with my tail between my legs." Jericho supposed the Raleigh Tavern had heard stranger confessions from the planters who had stayed there while Virginia's General Assembly was in session. Of course, it had been a while since the Raleigh had been privy to such stories. Governor Jefferson had made Richmond the capital two years ago. Richmond was a prudent choice, safe and central, as Jefferson said, but it was Williamsburg that had accommodated the beginnings of a revolution. That counted for something with Jericho Smith.

Gareth McClellan laughed, appreciating Jericho's ability to see something funny in his capture. He was certain Lafayette had made the most of Smith's embarrassment. "I should like to have seen it. It is not every day our side captures such a notorious spy."

Jericho groaned. "I'd hoped that when I told you the tale you'd be less likely to make sport of me. It appears I misjudged my man."

Gareth was unrepentant. He shrugged his broad shoulders and leaned back in his chair, stretching long, muscular legs in front of him. Gareth was a larger man than either his older or younger brother, but he carried himself with a certain grace and dignity that did much to assure others he was at least likely to weigh the choices before he resorted to fisticuffs. It was not particularly comforting once one was looking up at him with dusty breeches and loose teeth, but Gareth's reputation for giving some thought before he landed his blows made him a more favored opponent than Salem or Noah. The outcome did not differ for those who chose to brazen it out, but it was some condolence to know that Gareth allowed a few moments for escape.

"Now that you're a free man, so to speak," Gareth said, "what are you doing in Williamsburg?"

"I may have escaped Lafayette, but the general always has some need of me. I've just been at his headquarters. You know Cornwallis is hemmed in."

"I've heard there are as many French in the harbor as in all Paris."

"A slight exaggeration," Jericho grinned. "Our forces are digging the trenches and fixing the cannon and mortars in place. When everything has been made ready, the bombardment will begin."

"Noah? Salem? Are they well?"

"When last I left them. Regretting you're not with them?" Jericho guessed shrewdly.

Gareth's dark brows raised slightly as his mouth pursed to one side in a grimace of acknowledgment. "I suppose that is the way of it. There was a tacit agreement among us that one son would remain behind to assist our parents and sisters. Since

I was already in the assembly, Noah and Salem gave me the short straw.''

Jericho did not suppose there were many who viewed staying behind as the short straw. ''You go out to the landing often?'' He hoped the question sounded casual.

''Almost every day. I've always been responsible for the stud.''

Jericho noticed Gareth did not look particularly amused as he anticipated the next inquiry. If he ever became interested in another woman, Jericho vowed she would not have a brother to her credit. ''How is your family, then?''

''Darlene is fine. We're expecting our first child in November.''

Jericho was genuinely pleased for Gareth and his wife. ''I'm happy for you. And your parents?''

''Healthy and in fine spirits. Both are confident Salem and Noah will be home soon. It's been too long since they've visited.''

''You aren't going to make this easy for me, are you?'' Jericho observed.

Gareth pretended ignorance. ''Make what easy?''

''Dammit!'' he swore, more loudly than he intended. The tavern quieted and a number of heads turned in their direction. Jericho sighed and made an effort to relax. ''All right. How is Rahab?'' His tongue tripped over the unfamiliarity of saying her name aloud. In his mind she was still Red.

Gareth leaned forward in his chair and spoke with deadly earnest. ''You know, Smith, if I had been there the morning Salem and Noah found Rae, I would have thrown you in the Hudson. Maybe, just maybe, after I heard her story I would have fished you out again, but I can tell you I would have given the matter some serious thought.''

''I would have expected as much. You can ask your brothers—I didn't fight them.''

Satisfied that Jericho understood how he felt about the treatment of his sister, Gareth resumed his easy posture. It was odd, he thought, how simply Smith accepted the censure. Gareth had pegged him as a harder, colder man, unwilling to accept when he was in the wrong. "Rae is doing much better. She's here in Williamsburg now, staying with Darlene and me. In theory she's supposed to be keeping an eye on my wife before she delivers. Mostly she encourages Darlene's excesses. Did you know Rae's recovered most of her memory?"

Jericho didn't know, because he hadn't asked either Salem or Noah and they had not volunteered information of late. "I hadn't known. That's good news." But does she still remember me, he wanted to scream. Yet he remained quiet, and nothing in his expression gave away his inner turmoil.

"We think so," Gareth agreed. "It began to return to her only a few weeks ago. Rae said she and Ashley had a conversation that helped her. I don't understand it myself, but she seems to be the Rae we all recall. I can tell you, her brain fever frightened us a lot more than anyone let on."

Jericho made appropriate noises of understanding and motioned to the barmaid for another ale. He felt very much in need of more drink. It was incredible to him that he could not voice his question. In his mind he rephrased it, tested it, and still held his silence. He asked himself why it mattered that she should remember him and dismissed the thought quickly, more frightened of the answer than he had been of Dugan's bayonet. It did not sit well that Rae had rightly named him a coward.

Goaded by that thought, he found the words tripping out. "Does she remember—" he began, but was cut off when Gareth's attention was caught by something at the door to the tavern. A prickle of heat flushed Jericho's nape. He knew who it was before he glanced over his shoulder.

Rae stood in the entranceway, a slender silhouette against the brightness of the light at her back. She was wearing a mobcap on her head that hid the splendor of her hair and gave her the appearance of a milkmaid. When she stepped into the tavern her plain red skirt swished about her legs, and Jericho thought her wooden clogs seemed too heavy for her feet. He wondered what sort of work she had been doing before she came in search of Gareth. He imagined her engaged in a succession of chores: churning butter, scrubbing kettles, making beds. He wished he had not thought of her in a bedroom. His eyes turned distant, shuttered, as he sought to hide the bent of his mind. He had no idea how unapproachable he looked when his gaze finally met Rae's.

"Over here," Gareth called to his sister.

Rae's wide smile as she neared the table was a thing of refreshing beauty, yet Jericho felt his stomach coil as he realized it was only vaguely intended for him. A muscle twitched in his cheek as he willed her to greet him with something more than the polite regard reserved for friends of her brothers. He stood along with Gareth when she reached their table.

Rae motioned them to sit down with a breezy wave of her hand. "I apologize for interrupting your coze, Gareth, but Darlene says you would want to know that Fielding stopped by the house to say he is on his way to Yorktown."

Gareth sighed. "It's no more than I expected. He's been making noises about leaving for a few days now. I suppose I can manage without him at the landing for a while." He explained to Jericho. "Fielding is the best groom we have."

Jericho was staring at Rae, only half listening to Gareth. "What? Oh. Well, if it's in my power I shall see that he gets back to your employment in one piece."

Rae's attention turned from her brother to Jericho. "That's most kind of you, sir. Bill Fielding is nearly without equal when it comes to gentling the horses." She dipped a small curtsy as Jericho gave her a puzzled frown. "Forgive Gareth, but he sometimes forgets his manners. I'm Rahab McClellan, Gareth's sister." She looked at Jericho expectantly.

Jericho stood again, gave Rae a curt bow, and wondered if

anyone in the Raleigh knew he was dying inside. When he straightened his face was hard, pale, and his speech was stilted, the soft drawl noticeably absent. "Jericho Smith, Miss McClellan ... and as much as I would like the pleasure of your company, I have to be going. Gareth. Miss McClellan." He tipped his hat and turned on his heel. Before he reached the tavern door he heard Rae clearly say, "What an odd sort of man, Gareth." Jericho's eyes closed briefly in pain and he hurried into the steet as if a company of redcoats was at his heels.

Rae sank into the chair vacated by Jericho as soon as he was gone. Freckles stood out sharply on a face that now rivaled Jericho's for paleness. She could not meet her brother's speculative gaze.

"What was that in aid of, Rae?" he asked gently.

Rae shrugged, unable to move words past the lump in her throat. Her eyes glistened wetly, while in her head she chanted her refusal to shed tears. In spite of that, her chin wobbled.

"Let's go," Gareth said quietly, reaching across the table to touch Rae's wrist.

Rae accepted her brother's suggestion without demur. Once they were in the street she breathed deeply and fought for composure. She felt Gareth's incredibly large and infinitely gentle hand at her elbow.

"Are you all right?"

She nodded. "I need but a moment."

Gareth allowed her more than that. They walked slowly along Duke of Gloucester Street toward Gareth's town home in silence. Rae was hardly aware of the fragrance of fresh bread as they passed the baker's shop, or the spark and glow coming from the forge. She missed the shy wave from the boy sweeping the stoop in front of the apothecary. Her senses were too dulled from her encounter with Jericho to take in smells and sounds, and she could not have said by what route they finally reached Gareth's house.

Darlene was picking herbs in the garden when she saw her husband's approach. She straightened quickly, smoothed the linen overblouse that inadequately hid her burgeoning middle, and pretended she had only been inspecting the flowering shadbush and jonquils. She hid the herbs stealthily in her apron pocket as Gareth and Rae stopped in front of the white picket gate at the entrance to the yard. Darlene hurried to the brick walk to greet them before Gareth could give her a scold for not lying abed. She was secretly amused by his peculiar notion that she had become incapable of doing even the simplest tasks once her belly had begun to swell.

All thoughts of receiving a scold fled as she caught sight of Rae's expressionless face and her husband's look of concern. She doubted it was Fielding's desertion that had created this distress. Arms akimbo and looking rather militant in spite of her small stature and obvious pregnancy, Darlene addressed them both, blocking their path to the house. "What has happened? I scarce recall ever seeing such dark looks."

Rae sighed and shook her head, impatient with her own black mood. "Oh, Darlene, you may well ask. It is naught but foolishness, I assure you. Isn't that right, Gareth?"

Gareth did not answer her, but spoke instead to Darlene. "Jericho Smith was sharing my table when Rahab delivered Fielding's message."

Darlene's small hands went to her cheeks as her mouth formed a silent O. "That must have been quite a shock for you, Rae."

"I think you've understated it nicely," Gareth said. "She pretended not to know him at all."

"Oh, Rae, you didn't!"

"I'm afraid I did. He looked so . . . forbidding. I couldn't . . . I was . . ."

Darlene grasped the situation immediately as Rae foundered for words to express her confusion and hurt. She took Rae's hand and pulled her toward the front door. "Come. A spot of something warm to drink is just what you need, then you shall tell us the whole of it. I'll have Betty prepare the very thing and bring it to the library.''

Recognizing Darlene would brook no argument, Rae allowed herself to be led to Gareth's small library and settled comfortably in the leather chair usually reserved for her brother. ''There's nothing very much to tell,'' she said when she had a cup of sassafras tea thrust into her hands. Darlene and Gareth shared the divan opposite her, but Rae found her gaze drifting to the haphazard arrangement of books on the shelves behind them. ''I pretended not to know him because I thought it would put him at his ease. He was not at all pleased to see me. I doubt you can realize how embarrassing it is for him to be reminded that he thought me a spy and a . . . well, you know what he thought. What we both thought. I had only hoped to spare him and myself the pain of recollection.''

Gareth's gentle and knowing eyes scanned Rae's face. ''I had no idea that you carried tender feelings for Smith.'' He was not certain how he felt about it. He had always respected Jericho Smith, and the unsettling business on the schooner had not really changed his opinion. In spite of what he had told Smith in the Raleigh, Gareth did not put the blame for what had happened entirely at Jericho's feet. But Smith as the recipient of Rahab's tender feelings was something else again. Jericho had never struck Gareth as a man who welcomed affection.

At Rae's blush, Darlene interjected, ''I believe it is more than tender feelings, isn't it, Rahab? Have you loved him all these long months?''

Rae nodded. ''I had not meant to, you understand. Please don't tell Mama and Papa. They would be so distressed, because they know, as I do, that nothing can come of it. Jericho will never return my feelings.''

Gareth was inclined to agree with his sister. Jericho had ever shown himself to be a loner, shunning holiday celebrations at the landing in spite of the many invitations Charity McClellan had extended via Salem over the years. It was not until the incident with Rahab that Gareth realized Jericho had never even met the McClellan womenfolk. Oh, he was briefly acquainted with Darlene and knew Ashley better, had even saved her life years ago, but they were McClellans by marriage, not birth. Jericho had so studiously avoided joining the McClellans at the landing that Gareth suspected he did not want to be drawn into familial attachments.

"What makes you so certain?" Darlene asked.

"Intrepid Mr. Smith is not so brave when it comes to affairs of the heart, I fear." She smiled weakly, attempting to make light of it. "And I think what he is capable of giving has already been given to another. There is nothing for it but that I learn to accept I am naught but a source of embarrassment to him. Well, perhaps not any longer, now that he thinks I don't recall what happened in New York." She finished her tea quickly, eager to avoid too many probing questions. Gareth looked as if he wanted a few delicate matters cleared, and Rae was not in the mood for lengthy and complicated prevarications. "Excuse me, please. I think I'll go to my room for a while. I have a slight headache."

Neither Darlene nor Gareth objected to her leaving, but she caught the worried glances they exchanged as she stood. Stooopid, she told herself. It had been stupid to feign a headache when she had only to say that she wanted to be alone with her thoughts. Her clogs thumped noisily to the polished hardwood floor as she kicked them off and threw herself onto the bed. The snowy white canopy that topped the four poster billowed soundlessly, and the fringe bobbed and swayed in the wake of her breezy anger.

Rae thought she had seen the last of the frowning exchanges once she had begun to recover her memory. Because everything did not come back to her at once, she imagined her memory was like the sum total of the patches in a quilt. Her mind gathered the pieces one at a time, and they were fitted together in a way that was much to Rae's liking: the pattern was deceptively simple, and each bit of fabric was rich with detailed work. It seemed to her that she had learned to manage her unruly thoughts and impulses in a way that was acceptable for a woman with her mostly conventional upbringing. Indeed, until the evening she had entered Wolfe's Tavern, it seemed to Rae that her life had been unexceptional. Dull was the other description that came to her when her mood was unkind.

There were some events she still could not remember clearly. When she forced herself to think on them she invariably triggered a violent headache. Her recollection of the fight in Wolfe's was one of those things; an evening years ago when she had pointed a musket at two intruders at the landing was another. She and Ashley were the only ones who did not find it odd that there had been no attendant headache when she remembered her broken engagement. It had done much to relieve her sister and Troy that Rae bore them no ill feelings.

Rae turned on her back and considered going downstairs to tell Darlene and Gareth her headache was more heartache. She decided against it, fearing that they did not already expect as much, it would do little to ease their worry. Worse, perhaps they would think they should do something about it. She could imagine few things more dreadful than Gareth's telling Jericho that she had lied this afternoon. That Jericho might hear she loved him did not bear thinking about.

Rae yawned sleepily and her eyes fluttered closed. A nap seemed the most sensible escape from her unhappy thoughts. Later, when Darlene came to her room to get her for dinner, Rae's slumber was so obviously peaceful that Darlene slipped quietly from the chamber without disturbing her.

On October 9th the skies were clear, the sun bright, and Jericho remembered he had squinted watching General Washington hold a match to the cannon that began the patriots' volley on the British earthworks.

Only five days had passed, and here he was squinting again, this time to find his direction in the dark and keep the rain from shielding his vision. He knew the men all around him were having the same difficulty as they moved silently toward the British redoubt that was their goal, but the thought hardly comforted him.

Neither did the fact that their commander, Colonel Alexander Hamilton, had ordered them to strike the stronghold with their guns unloaded. What faced them then was a pitched battle, with only bayonets, and the brief advantage of surprise.

Jericho glanced around, looking for Noah among the men close at hand, and cursed softly when he couldn't find him. He wished Noah had elected to miss this maneuver and had remained in camp with Salem. There was no other man in the present company with whom Jericho had more than a nodding acquaintance. It was the way he preferred it. Since Breed's Hill he had done everything he could to avoid fighting beside men he had come to know well. It was his way of insulating himself against the carnage.

Jericho had one last thought for Noah before he heard the command to storm the redoubt. His voice joined the terrible, charging cry of the Americans as they raced for the stronghold, and then his concentration was directed solely on the bloody confrontation at hand.

The fighting was fevered. The British soon rallied from their startled confusion and met their enemy at close quarters with fixed bayonets. Jericho, like all the men on both sides, hardened himself to the fact that in order to survive he must wound or kill, and wielded his bayonet with unerring accuracy.

At the outset of this mission Jericho had known he wanted to survive it. The man the others called Saint Smith had ceased to exist. Jericho's reckless disregard for his life had ended when he had seen Rahab in the Raleigh. Even though he had tried to prepare himself for the news that she was lost to him, it had still stunned him that she could have forgotten. The depth of his hurt brought home the truth, and it was then he realized he had been given a second chance with her. He could approach her later with no fear that she would be repelled by his past ill treatment of her. And no redcoat was going to take the opportunity away from him.

The man beside Jericho had fallen to his knees, and Jericho's blood chilled when he glanced down and saw it was Noah. Out of the corner of his eye he caught the glint of a bayonet poised to strike Noah's chest. With his own weapon he pushed the bayonet upward so it thrust harmlessly in the air and at the same time kicked Noah squarely in the shoulder so he rolled out of the way. Before he could strike again or regain his balance, Jericho was attacked on his blind side.

A bayonet's sharp point pierced his thigh, was withdrawn quickly, and stabbed into him again at another angle. This time when it was withdrawn his blood mixed with the blood of the victims before him. Jericho swore gutturally with the pain of the wound and swung the butt of his musket down and backward to club his attacker in the belly. The sound of harshly expelled breath behind him let him know his aim was true. Jericho wavered slightly on his feet as his leg threatened to give way and earth crumbled beneath him. Rain diluted the blood that stained his breeches in an ever widening patch, and crimson droplets struck the toes of his boots. Vaguely he realized Noah was on his feet again and capably defending himself against another advance.

That was all right, then. Noah was uninjured. It seemed very important to know that as he lost consciousness.

"Am I dreaming?" Jericho asked haltingly. His throat was dry and his tongue cleaved to the roof of his mouth. "Is it over?" A curious hush had descended all around him, and he struggled to his elbows to find the cause of it. It was no longer night, and he was no longer in the field of battle. A gentle hand on his shoulder attempted to get him to lie down again, but he would have none of it. On all sides of him lay other wounded, each straining in turn to hear something so sweet that they shared Jericho's belief they were dreaming.

In the distance, beyond the expectant silence of the camp, a British drummer boy beat out the call to parley. Cornwallis was ready to talk about the terms of surrender.

"For you it is, Mr. Smith," Rae said quietly. "Soon, perhaps, for everyone. Now lie back. You are in no condition to enter into the negotiations."

Jericho's vision cleared at the edges and he found himself staring into Rahab's serene green eyes. "You? What are—" His question was interrupted as Rae touched a wet cloth to his parched lips and bathed his fevered face. She held a flask of water to his lips and encouraged him to take some drink, then pulled it away before he had his fill.

"You may have more when you've shown you can hold that down." She lowered Jericho's head to the ground and slipped her arm from beneath him.

"What are you doing here? This is no place for a woman."

"What nonsense, Mr. Smith," she said briskly, dismissing the subject. "Anyway, I shan't be here for long. I only arrived this morning with Gareth. Noah and Salem have requested that we take you to the landing, where you can get proper care. Given the condition of that dreadful limb of yours, it seems one of their better ideas."

"Noah is well? He wasn't hurt?"

Rae blinked hard at the sudden welling of tears and busied herself folding the bandages in her lap. "He is unharmed, at much cost to yourself. He says you saved his life."

Jericho was uncomfortable with Rae's gratitude, and in his foggy state of mind he could not think why she called him Mr. Smith. His aching leg throbbed with unrelenting regularity and made it difficult for him to think. "I recall a very painful ride on Noah's shoulders. It must have been he who brought me back last night, so we are quite even."

"It was not last night," Rae corrected him. "It was three days ago, and Noah will not feel his debt has ended until you are well again. Gareth is bringing a litter to carry you to the wagon. Then we are leaving for the landing. Mama has had a room prepared for you and there will be no getting out of it. You can wipe that mutinous look right off your face." Seeing that he was in no mood to oblige her, Rae put her bandages to one side and picked up the animal-skin flask again, tipping it against his lips as she raised his head slightly.

Jericho cursed at how easily she kept him from speaking his wishes and drank deeply. When he finished he would tell her that he refused to go. If Cornwallis was going to surrender he wanted to witness it, and what the McClellans wanted for him be damned.

Rae lowered Jericho's head once more and wiped the corner of his lips where the water had spilled when he had passed out again. She lifted the damp cloth to her own eyes and impatiently wiped away the tears that blurred her vision.

Noah had warned her not to come when he had gone to Gareth for help in moving their friend. Jericho was badly injured, and there was nothing in her experience that would prepare her for the hundreds of wounded men she would see in the camp. But she was not a piece of fluff, Rae had told her brothers, and she was not one to faint at the sight of blood. Now, looking around her at the men laid out in even rows on the ground, she was not so certain. It tore at her that she was inadequate to the task of helping them all. Glancing at Jericho's still face one more time, assured by the shallow breaths he took, Rae left her bandages and flask behind and hurried from the area.

Salem caught her by the shoulders and steadied her as she barreled into him. Beside him Noah and Gareth carried the litter. "Are you all right, Rae?"

She nodded. "Please, let's get him from here quickly. There are so many who need . . . I had not thought . . . Is there nothing we can do for them?"

Salem pulled Rae close and hugged her fiercely. "Most are not as seriously injured as Jericho." He did not say that those who had been were already dead, but Rae understood it, nonetheless. "Many will not come because they want to see the surrender march. Did you hear the drums?"

"Yes. Jericho heard them also. He wants to stay."

"He would," Noah put in grimly. "The trouble is it could take days before the terms are hammered out, and by then—"

"Noah!" Gareth growled sharply, seeing Rahab's pale face. "That's quite enough. Rahab, you will wait over by the wagon while we put Jericho on the litter. You were right when you said we must move him quickly."

Two days later, as Jericho continued to fight for his life in a sunlit bedchamber at the landing, the garrison from York marched in orderly units between rows of sharply turned-out French troops and proud, but not so neatly uniformed, patriots. They laid down their arms while their drummers played, "The World Turned Upside Down," and speculation was rampant among the troops on both sides that perhaps this was indeed the end of it all.

Unaware of what was taking place some miles away, Rae sat in a chair beside Jericho's bed and read and reread the same passage from the first of Tom Paine's *Crisis* papers: "What we obtain too cheap, we esteem too lightly: It is dearness only that gives everything its value."

Surely Jericho Smith had paid dearly indeed. Must his suffering know no end? The thought was a hollow echo in her head as she recalled the grave pronouncement of the doctor who had come at her father's request earlier in the day. Jericho's life might be won at the cost of his leg. Rae knew it was what her father had suspected when he sent a servant for the doctor, but Rae had yet to come to terms with it. She remembered Jericho's easy grace, his agile movements as he climbed, walked, or ran. Would he hate them for saving his life each time he took an ungainly step, or would it be enough that he could walk at all?

Rae came out of her reverie, startled to feel a hand on her arm. She looked up to see her sister's concerned face.

"I think it's time you rested," Leah said quietly. An ash-blond braid circled her head like a golden halo. Her complexion was smooth, her features delicate.

Rae shook her head. "If Jericho wakes and sees you, he will surely think he has met one of the Maker's angels."

Leah's whisper became a bit louder and more earnest. "He'll feel a sight worse if he wakes and sees you. The devil's hand-maiden, if ever there was one. You need to be in your own bed, and if you won't go willingly it's only a matter of time before ol' Jacob and Papa are carrying you out."

There was more than a little truth to Leah's heated speech. Rae had been feeling light-headed, and the last time Jericho had moved restlessly, trying to tear the bandages from his thigh, she had not been able to restrain him herself. Luckily Charity had been in the hallway and had helped her, but her mother's entreaties that she needed to leave the sickroom were not enough for Rae. Apparently Charity had called for reinforcements. If she ignored Leah, then Ashley would be sent. Her mother was not above sending in Darlene, who was now staying with them until her child was born.

The landing was nothing if not accommodating as the children began to return home. Gareth was already here with his wife, and everyone expected that Salem and Noah would return soon. Sighing, Rae got to her feet and left Leah alone with Jericho. She was not proof against them all, and no doubt Charity would use them to secure rest for her daughter.

There was no change in Jericho's condition when Leah was relieved by Ashley some hours later. "I've just given him a small dose of laudanum with his drink," she told Ashley. "His eyes were glazed with pain, though he tried to talk in spite of it. I could not make out a thing he said. Do you think he'll lose his leg?''

"I will continue to pray it does not happen," Ashley said, sadness dulling her eyes. "Go on. I'll call if I need help." Jericho's stillness disturbed her and brought back uneasy memories of the time when Salem had been nearly as ill. She understood Rae's adamant fight to stay by his side when it was apparent to all she had no energy left.

When Jericho woke it was dark. A single candle had been lit on the bedside table and it created diffuse shadows on the wall. Someone, he could not make out who, moved from the chair on his left and hovered over him. A cool hand touched his heated brow, and when it would have been removed he stayed it with a surprisingly firm grip.

"No . . . more . . . la-laud . . ." he rasped, unable to complete the word as the heat and pain in his leg seemed to shoot up his spine to his brain. Unintentionally he squeezed the wrist he held more tightly.

Rae stilled her urge to cry out as her fingers went numb and her flesh was bruised. "But the pain. You need it for the pain."

He shook his head wildly. "Lisss—sen to me." Thank God it was Rae and not the other one. Leah had drowned out his words with gibberish she supposed to be soothing, and had forced laudanum down his throat. Rae would understand him. She knew him better than anyone. Or she had. Did it matter anymore, he wondered as he struggled for coherency. His thoughts leapfrogged out of control while his free hand beat a tattoo into the soft mattress. "Poultice. In—deee—an . . ."

"What? In the what?" Rae bent her ear closer to his mouth and her voice was harsh with frustration. "I can't understand—"

Jericho repeated himself, his voice the merest thread of

sound. "Indian. Black . . . mud . . . pack . . . herbs. Don' wan' to lose my leg . . . Unner-stan?"

She understood the last part only too well. It was the first part of his message she was having difficulty with. "I won't let anyone touch your leg. What sort of herbs? What must I do?"

"Goo' girl," he slurred. "Knew you . . . unner-stan." His brow furrowed beneath Rae's hand as he concentrated to carefully pronounce the things he required. Rae repeated each item in turn, and the brief release of pressure about her wrist was the manner in which he told her she had heard correctly.

It was a strange combination of things Jericho had requested, Rae thought, but the poultice they had been using on his leg had failed to draw out the poison. The doctor had told them it was too late for that sort of remedy and Charity had abandoned it. Now Jericho was begging for another. Had he any idea what he was asking for?

Rae hesitated only long enough to shake out her fingers as Jericho released her hand. She was out the door in a flurry of skirts and down the grand staircase so quickly that her feet barely touched every second step. The house was eerily quiet, at odds with Rae's frantic, driven activity. In the kitchen she laid a small fire in the hearth and set a copper kettle over it to warm. Taking a lantern from the wall, she lighted it, then grabbed a wooden bucket and headed for her mother's garden. She scooped handfuls of fertile Virginia soil into the bucket and ran to the pump to mix it with just enough water to make a thick black plaster. From the garden she plucked the herbs Jericho had asked for and dropped them into her pocket. A trip to the nearby woods was necessary to gather the remaining plants and bark scrapings. When she returned to the kitchen she was out of breath, but triumphant.

The mud sizzled as she poured it into the hot copper pot. She stirred it a few times and left it to bubble on its own while she attended to the greenery in her pocket. The plants she had collected were laid out on a butcher block table, and she took the stem or leaf, sometimes the root, as Jericho had specified, and ground them together in a mortar. Wrinkling her nose at the smell of the ingredients, Rae scraped the pestle so none of the medicine was lost. From the pantry she took a piece of cheesecloth and laid it flat on the table, then spooned some of the hot mud plaster on top of it. She added the green, malodorous paste from the mortar and kneaded the mixture as if it were bread dough, blowing on her fingers occasionally to ease the burning. When she was certain the herbs had spread to every part of the mud, she gathered the corners of the cheesecloth, tied them, and carried her precious bundle to Jericho's bedchamber.

In the short time she had been gone he had thrown off his bedcovers, and his nightshirt had ridden up to his hips. Remembering that modesty had never been his strong suit, Rae merely shook her head and covered him, except for his injury. Knowing it was bound to be painful, she pressed the cheesecloth pack as lightly as she could to the wound. Still, his body jerked in response.

"Rahab, what are you about?" her mother demanded from the doorway. Charity was dressed in a sky-blue robe only slightly lighter than the color of her eyes. Her coffee-colored hair was twisted in a loose braid that hung over her left shoulder, and a ruffled cap sat slightly askew on her head. Behind her Robert peered into the room, his hands braced on either side of the door frame. He was much taller than his wife, darker, and though his deep green eyes were known to sparkle with good humor, this was not the way of it now. Robert positively glowered over Charity's head. "We heard you moving about," Charity continued as she stepped into the bedchamber. "We couldn't imagine . . ."

Rae did not think her father's dark looks were because he had been awakened from a sound sleep. No doubt he did not like the idea of his unmarried daughter wrestling with a masculine leg when there were servants who could be called to do this work. "Mama. Papa. I've made another poultice for Mr. Smith."

"We can smell it," Robert said bluntly, pushing away from the door. He carried himself with a certain regal stature that called attention to his height rather than his limp. He followed Charity's lead and stopped beside the bed, watching Rae's sure fingers as she kept the steaming poultice in place over Jericho's wound. His expression softened as he realized the uselessness of scolding her for not ringing for help. He could hardly fault her self-reliance when he had brought her up to have just that. "I've not smelled anything like it before. What is in it?"

Rae told him.

"Where did you learn to make such a thing?"

"Mr. Smith told me how to do it. Indian, I think he said it was."

Robert nodded. "Salem once mentioned to me that he thought Smith had spent some time with Indians. How did he find the strength to speak of it?"

"It was difficult for him, to be sure. But he seemed to know he is in danger of losing his leg and he begged me to help him, Papa. I couldn't refuse him."

"I would be more shocked if you had." Robert rolled up the sleeve of his maroon dressing gown. "Here, let me hold that for a while. I know what it is to fear losing a limb. I want to help. You and your mother can prepare more poultices."

"Perhaps I should wake a few of the servants," Rae suggested.

Robert looked appalled. "What? And let it be said I don't have the stamina of my daughter? Fie on you, girl! Take yourself and your mother off to the kitchen."

Throughout the night the trio worked tirelessly, and by morning their efforts began to show the first signs of being rewarded. The inflammation surrounding the wound had lessened considerably, and Jericho's breathing was no longer labored. Shortly after daybreak Ashley and Leah shooed all three of them from the room and continued what they had begun. By noon Jericho's fever was broken, there was a hint of healthy pink skin around the two stab wounds, and his thigh was no longer hot to the touch.

A servant was again dispatched for the doctor, and when he arrived at dusk, carrying the saws to remove the leg in his black satchel, he declared the change nothing less than a wonderwork. Until then Rae had been afraid to hope, but at the physician's words her heart leapt and thudded joyfully in her breast. Because the doctor announced his good news while the family was seated at the dinner table, there was no concealing from them the light of love that flooded her eyes.

Rae's secret, which had been guarded by Ashley, Darlene, and Gareth was out. Cheeks flaming, Rae lowered her eyes to her empty plate and her hands twisted the linen napkin in her lap. There was an uncomfortable silence that lasted until Charity extended an invitation to the physician to dine with them. Rae sighed gratefully as the spell was broken and voices clamored for someone to please pass the sweet potatoes, the glazed biscuits, the sausages. As food was handed around the table Rae took her fair share, mindful that while her family had entered into a spirited dinner conversation, there were watchful eyes all around her ready to place some significance on her appetite or lack of it.

Shortly after the doctor excused himself, Rahab did the same. She smiled inwardly as she shut the double doors to the dining room behind her and her father demanded of everyone at once: "Why didn't you tell me that was the way of it?"

Rae did not wait to hear the replies and hurried instead to Jericho's room, relieving the young housemaid who cared for him while the family was at dinner. "You can go, Damali. Tildy is keeping your dinner warm in the kitchen."

"I don't mind stayin', Miss Rae. You might need some help gettin' him to eat." She pointed to the tray on the nightstand that held a bowl of broth with some fresh chunks of bread floating in it.

"I'm sure I can manage," Rae told her. "At least, I think I can," she added to herself once Damali was gone. Rahab had never particularly enjoyed this part of caring for a sick patient. Her brothers, on those occasions when they had been laid low, had resented their weakness and hated being spoon fed like small children. Invariably they had tried to wrest the spoon from her, and the entire affair had become a very messy business indeed. She eyed the bowl of bread and broth as if it were her enemy.

"Reckon it'll attack, do you think?"

Startled, Rae turned toward the bed. Jericho was looking suspiciously alert for someone who was supposed to be sleeping comfortably, according to the doctor. "Hmmpf. How long have you been awake?"

"Only since you came in."

"Oh." She had not suspected she would feel ill at ease in his presence, and she was impatient with herself. The lazy regard in his bright eyes was disconcerting, and she was not certain it was appropriate in a man who had recently been at death's door. "How do you feel?" she asked briskly, ignoring the heat in her cheeks.

"I feel like hell."

"Please. Your language, Mr. Smith. Is there something I can get for you? Some laudanum, perhaps?"

Jericho blinked widely and nearly choked on his surprise. *His* language? She was admonishing him for saying hell when she had near burned his ears with verbiage more suited to the lowlife skulking along the wharfs? How could she not remember that he had heated her bottom for the offense she had given?

"Are you all right, Mr. Smith?" Rae asked, a perfect study of concern and impartial solicitude. "You looked decidedly peaked for a moment." She turned away after he assured her he was recovered and hid her satisfied smile as she bent over the tray. As long as she kept the upper hand there was no chance of his further bruising her heart. He would be gone soon enough and would never have to know the nature of her feelings for him. "Can you eat something? Or would you prefer to rest some more? You've never told me if you want the laudanum."

"No laudanum," he said quickly. "I'd like somethin' to eat, Miss McClellan, if you'd be so kind."

"Of course." Rae helped him sit up, plumping the pillows beneath him. Mindful of his leg and the poultice that rested there, she sat on the very edge of the bed while she spoon fed him the broth.

Jericho could not help but grin as Rae concentrated on lifting the spoon from the bowl to his mouth. The tip of her pink tongue peeped out at the corner of her lips, evidence that she took this task seriously.

"You find something amusing, Mr. Smith?" she asked tartly.

Jericho denied it. "It may have escaped your notice, miss, but it is my leg that's injured, not my arms."

He was still an odious man, she thought. He teased her with that unhurried smile while butter wouldn't melt in his mouth. She did not protest when he took the bowl from the tray and lifted it to his lips, sipping the broth in a mannerly fashion. Over the rim of the small bowl his eyes laughed at her.

"There," he said after the first few sips. "D'you see how easy that is?" He returned the bowl to the tray. "That's all I have room for now."

Rae put the tray aside. "Then you should be sleeping. You are far from well yet. If you expect to use your leg again you'll be sensible and let me give you some laudanum so the pain doesn't make you restless." She began to get up, but Jericho stayed her hand. Unfortunately he held the wrist that he had bruised the evening before, and Rae could not hide her wince.

Jericho released her as if scalded, cursing himself for touching her at all. It was easy to forget she was a gently reared lady who would not approve of virtual strangers handling her with familiarity. "Beggin' your pardon, miss. I didn't mean to take liberties."

Now it was Rae who nearly choked. What a hypocrite he was, playing the gentleman when he knew very well that once he had touched a lot more of her than her wrist. Her breasts swelled involuntarily in response to the drift of her thoughts. "I have a slight tenderness on my wrist," she explained coolly.

Something clicked in Jericho's mind. "Let me see."

"Why ever would you—"

"Let me see."

Implacable. That's what he was. Relentless when he was in pursuit of something. "Oh, very well. Though why it should concern you . . ." She pulled back the sleeve of her blouse and waved her discolored wrist in front of him.

Though she hid it quckly again, Jericho had seen enough. He blanched. "I did that, didn't I?"

Rae shrugged and got to her feet. "I assure you it's not worth a moment's worry. Anyway, if you hadn't, I would have doped you, and then you couldn't have given me the recipe for the poultice."

"Still, I would rather not have hurt you, Red."

Rae's eyes widened and her slender body tensed. It was as if her breathing had stopped, and she wondered how Jericho could help but notice the effect of his words on her. "What did you call me?" she asked when she was sure an unsteady voice would not betray her.

Jericho had not noticed Rae's reaction because he was busy kicking himself for having let the nickname slip. "Red," he answered inadequately, wondering how he would pull his posterior from the fire this time.

"You must have misunderstood someone," she said evenly and coldly. "My family calls me Rae. And I have not given you leave to address me so casually." There, that should put him squarely in his place.

Until this moment Jericho had never considered that he might not like Rahab McClellan once he got to know her. But he had to think on it now. Red had upbraided him with spirited abandon, yet she had never made him feel as if he had just crawled out from under a rock. Rahab, however, with a flick of one dark eyebrow and a voice that would ice the Caribbean, held with more propriety than suited Jericho.

"Your pardon again, Miss McClellan," he said stiffly. "I wasn't thinking clearly. Red doesn't suit you at all."

But it does! It does! "Of course it doesn't," was what she said. She got up from the bed.

"I think I'll take that laudanum now." Jericho rearranged his own pillows and slid gingerly down the bed, careful not to dislodge the poultice. He pulled the sheet about his neck, and after swallowing his medicine he turned his face away from Rahab and shut his eyes.

Rae stared at his averted head for several long minutes, then turned on her heel, a shudder rippling her shoulders, and ran from the room for the privacy of her own chamber.

A cool, early November breeze ruffled Rae's hair as she crossed the yard from the stables to the house. Beside her Courtney chattered amiably, stopping only to blow tunelessly on the instrument Jericho had whittled for her. Courtney was in perpetual delight since her beloved Papa and Uncle Noah had returned to the landing. Ashley said dryly that there were more men in her camp than in Washington's. Certainly the little girl had twisted every adult male heart about her finger.

"It's a fine thing, isn't it, Auntie Rae?" she said, holding the instrument up for Rae's inspection. "I think Uncle Jericho must be a better whistler than even ol' Jacob."

"I don't know about that, but it is a most excellent thing," Rae agreed. Uncle Jericho indeed. One would think the man was a member of the family the way he was fawned over. Oh,

Rae, these thoughts are not worthy of you. "And it has a name. It's called a pipe."

Courtney's steps halted as she examined the instrument again. "Does the 'bacco go in these holes then?"

Rae smiled reluctantly. "No, that's a different sort of pipe. One for smoking. Yours is for music."

Courtney thrust the pipe into Rae's hands. "Make music."

"It's been a long time since . . . oh, very well. There is no need to go all sad-faced on me." She blew softly into the end of the pipe, warming up first, then managing a credible rendition of "Yankee Doodle." Courtney's clapping, off beat but appreciative, encouraged her to play through it again until another set of hands, louder and more rhythmic, joined her niece's clapping. She stopped abruptly, straightening, and faced Jericho, who was leaning casually against one of the veranda supports, looking very fit in a pair of Salem's buff britches, white linen shirt, and a navy jacket of Noah's. It was useless to attempt any sort of hauteur, because she had already hidden the pipe behind her back as a child might do when neatly caught with both hands in the cookie jar.

Courtney, plainly oblivious of her aunt's embarrassment, demanded more music.

"Yes, Miss McClellan, play something else for us."

Rae gave the pipe back to Courtney. "I was only playing for my niece, Mr. Smith. I had no idea you were there. Should you be outside? It's a trifle cold today."

Jericho ignored Rae and spoke to Courtney. "Tildy says she has a warm tart with your name on it, minx. But only if you hurry." When Rae made to follow the little girl, Jericho pushed away from the white pillar and blocked her path. "Let her go. I want to talk to you . . . Red."

Rae lifted her chin a notch. "I believe we had this conversation some weeks ago. I can make allowances that you may have forgotten; you were quite ill at the time. But I still have not given you leave—"

"Cut line, Red," Jericho said, emphasizing her name deliberately. "You are the one who has difficulty rememberin'—and forgettin'." His cerulean eyes bore into her startled ones. After a moment he took pity on her and his face softened. "Come, let's walk a bit. Your mother says there is nothing wrong with a 'modicum of exercise,' as she phrased it. And your father has lent me his cane." He twirled the ebony stick with a flourish.

Rae allowed herself to be turned away from the house and lend her support to Jericho as he hobbled down the steps. Her insides were roiling, and she found refuge by ignoring the myriad questions that plagued her, and by making inconsequential conversation. Maybe she had only imagined the knowing look in his eyes. "Papa doesn't use the cane often. He hates calling attention to his infirmity."

"I can sympathize, but for the time bein' there is nothing for it. What causes your father's limp? Gout?" For himself Jericho was quite content to let the confrontation ride a while longer. Two things had kept him from addressing it earlier: the fact that Rae had often managed to avoid him while he was convalescing in his chamber, and that while he was bedridden escape was all too easy for her. He had waited this long; he could wait a little longer.

Rae flashed a small smile. "Don't ever say you suspected that. He would be most put out. No, he was shot in the leg years ago. And no, it wasn't during the war with the French and Indians. It was Ashley's uncle who did the thing."

"The Duke of Linfield."

"Yes. Oh, but of course, you know that. You helped her when Nigel sent someone here to abduct her. It seems as if you are a guardian angel for the McClellans. First Ashley, then Noah. Salem says you are the very man to have in a fray."

"What a convenient memory you possess, Red. Or are you goin' to protest you still don't recall Wolfe's?" When she didn't reply, Jericho pointed with his cane to the summerhouse. "Let's have a seat over there."

"Perhaps we should return to the—"

"Over there," he said imperturably.

"But your leg—"

"There."

Rae gritted her teeth and stayed at Jericho's side until he had mounted the few steps to the open, airy floor of the summerhouse. Once he had chosen his seat on one of the benches that lined the octagonal structure, she took a place on the opposite side.

"I would not have thought you would be so skittish about sitting close to me," he said affably.

Rae did not mince her words. "How long have you known the truth, and who told you?"

Jericho gave her one of his infuriatingly calm smiles. "Now, that is more like it, Red. Do you recall the evenin' you flew out of my room because—well, actually I don't know why you flew out—"

"Go on. I remember."

"Leah saw you go and came to me demandin' an explanation. She had no qualms about takin' a sick man to task when she thought I had done somethin' to her sister. You McClellans do tend to rally round, don't you?"

Rae's foot tapped impatiently.

"In a rather incoherent fashion I explained the problem to her, and she simply gaped at me like I'd gone daft. Perhaps you didn't like being called Red, she said, because no one would like being reminded that she had thought herself a strumpet. Naturally, this was a source of confusion to me, since you'd led me to believe you remembered none of it. The next day I heard the whole of it from Gareth."

Rae was very still. "The whole of it?" Oh, surely Gareth hadn't said she loved this overbearing man!

Jericho nodded. "The whole. You pretended not to know me because you imagined you presented an embarrassment to me. I thought about that for a long time, and do you know, I concluded that given the same circumstances I would act exactly in the same manner.''

"Now, why doesn't that surprise me?" she asked mockingly.

Bless her biting little tongue. "The point is, that is scarcely the confession of a man who looks upon his honest mistakes with shame."

Rae looked away from him, eyes lowered. "And what of my mistakes? I threw myself at you, practically begged you to—to—" Words failed her as she thought of her brazen behavior. "If you imagine I would act in precisely the same manner, you are sadly out of it there."

"I doubt the matter will arise, Red. I am hardly likely to mistake you for a lightskirt again. And the intimacy that we shared, surely that is between us? Your brothers may suspect, but they cannot know with any certainty. Contrary to what you think, they would not believe ill of you. The blame would have been laid at my door, and not so wrongly, either. I was not the innocent, Red. I could have refused your invitation."

Rae's lips twisted in an ironic smile. "I think I am supposed to voice that last statement."

Jericho shrugged and absently traced a long, smooth squiggle on the floor with the tip of his cane. "Perhaps." He hesitated, the tracing stopped, then resumed, but this time its movement was deliberate. "I don't see why we can't be civil to one another. Friends, as it were. Doesn't your family find it odd that you rarely left my side when I was ill and haven't come near me since I began to recover?"

"That's not true," Rae gasped. "I'm here with you now." Jericho shot her a look that made her ashamed of her shabby retort. "I doubt anyone has remarked on it."

"Mayhap not to you, but I can tell you they suspect me of gross misconduct, although what anyone thinks I did to you from my sickbed I can't begin to imagine." He leaned back, looking at her through a fan of dark lashes, wondering if she could detect his lie. Take it easy, he warned himself. And slow.

The Strategy for the Assault on Rahab McClellan's Heart had changed in light of the fact that she knew him, but the goal remained the same. Jericho sensed it was a toss-up as to who was frightened the more. "It would do much to ease my situation here if you did not treat me as a leper."

"That's doing it up a bit too brown. My family is in your debt, and well you know it. Still, I suppose there is no reason we can't be civil, though that is not precisely our history." She twisted the frog clasp on her riding jacket. "There is something I would like to clear with you. . ."

"Go on."

"You mentioned Wolfe's as if I should remember it. In truth, I don't. It is the cause of severe headaches when I think on it. There are a few other incidents like that, but they don't concern you. I would prefer it if we don't refine on what happened in the tavern."

"It is not a subject I find pleasant to discuss, either," he assured her. "Is that it?"

Rae shook her head. "Did—did Gareth say anything else to you?"

"Of what nature? You'll have to be more specific. Gareth and I have talked of many things."

"It's of no import. Foolishness on my part, really." The clasp nearly fell off in her fingers.

Jericho's eyes narrowed suspiciously on her stomach. "Red, you never carried my child did you?"

Rae stood, mouth gaping. "How could you think . . . ? That would hardly be of no import! And don't call me Red!"

"There is an inconsistency here," Jericho drawled, a teasing smile in his voice, in his eyes. She was a beauty in all her ruffled pride. "Everyone is quick to point out to me that Red makes you sound like a strumpet, yet, unless I have forgotten my Bible, isn't Rahab the name of a harlot? Do you see my confusion?"

"Ooooooh!" Her hands rested on her slim hips in frustration.

"Salem and Gareth gave me that name when I was born, and they can hardly be held accountable since they were only ten and eight at the time. I'm certain you were born knowing what a harlot was, but they were not!"

"But your parents," he interjected, struggling not to laugh aloud.

"My mother nearly died giving birth to me and Papa was too distraught to realize what the boys were calling me. By the time Mama recovered, the name had stuck. Why do you think they are forever calling me Rae? And before you split the stitches in your leg, shaking it with your ill-timed glee, let me remind you that the reason you no doubt recall Rahab the harlot, is because the Lord's guiding hand made certain she escaped Jericho. Think on that, Mr. Smith."

Jericho watched her leave, her shoulders and spine stiff as she marched back to the house. He shook his head, an admiring smile lifting the corners of his well-shaped mouth. God, he had missed his fiery Red!

"Solemn and Oswell were on that ranch when I was a boy, and how this family has held it together since they have only you and now at the time," Ty said. "You went out, knowing what a risk it was, but you came back."

"For your brains," he suggested, struggling not to break down.

"That is their nerve and giving brains for you, boys, and too damn dumb to read it? What the boys were calling me, but the time Marie discovered the nerve and stuff. Why do you think they are forever holding on? Stay? You'd always split the will you bought me with a will? I'll lose the truth and my brains had to be a will because they couldn't you're done. If this is real, it is because they'd put a stubborn will in exchange for the control but the Think, or that Mr. Smith.

Before Marie would not leave her mother and stay with an ex son and for you the house. He shook his head, admitting that being put above all his wife and of mouth, you, he had raised his first wife."

Chapter 7

"Damn and blast!" Rae's heartfelt sentiment was intended for her ears alone, but Lazurus heard his mistress's distress and tossed his head from side to side, snorting in agreement. Rae grasped her mount's black mane, steadying him and herself while she hopped on one foot beside him, trying to dislodge a stone that had slipped through a tear in the sole of her boot.

"We make a fine pair, don't we, Lazurus? Both of us in need of new shoes and sweeter dispositions, I'll wager." The offending bit of rock fell back to the dusty road. She patted Lazurus's flank affectionately and began walking, limping slightly when she touched down on the tender portion of her foot. Beside her, the horse favored his left foreleg where he had taken a pebble that refused Rae's best attempt at removal.

Jericho could not quite curb his grin as he came upon them, limping in unison along the rutted road. He reined in his mount, a spirited bay mare that danced in front of Lazurus as if mocking his gimpy gait, and leaned forward in his saddle.

"Athena is as ill-mannered as her rider, Lazurus. They are

both gloating over our misfortune. Pay them no mind.'' Rae encouraged her horse to keep going while Jericho held Athena to an ambling walk beside them.

"What happened?" Jericho asked, undaunted by Rae's cheek. Since the confrontation in the summerhouse not yet one week ago, she had thawed noticeably in her attitude toward him. At least she did not retreat from a room when he happened to come upon her, and Noah once timed them at twelve minutes before Jericho pushed Rae into the boughs with his provocation. That had brought a smile to the rest of the McClellans, and a scowl to Rae's finely cut mouth when she realized she had been the evening's entertainment. But the most important realization—that Jericho's provoking was all in aid of securing her heart—went right by her.

From his superior height Jericho looked down on Rae, thinking that the sort of provocation she needed at the moment required his mouth hot on hers. She always looked in need of kissing.

Her black velvet riding hat sat at an odd angle on the crown of her auburn hair and the feather accent dipped and waved as she limped along. He had a desire to pluck the jaunty creation, toss it to one side, and loose the braid that coiled so primly on her head. His fingers would tangle in the waves, trapping her, forcing her to quiet as he tilted her face upward and accepted the invitation on her parted lips.

"Did you hear a word I said?" Rae demanded with a touch of impatience. She glanced up a second too late to see the arrested expression on Jericho's face.

Jericho shook himself out of his reverie. "You said something about Lazurus catching a stone. I didn't get it all."

"Hmmpf. I thought I was talking to the air. Shall I repeat myself or is it enough, do you think?"

Yes, her mouth really did look in need of kissing. It was pursed comically to one side in Rae's version of exasperation. Jericho blinked. "It's enough. Have you been walking long?"

"Not above thirty minutes. Lazurus and I went farther from the house than was my original intention. It is such a lovely day for riding—"

"Or walking."

"That too. I expect we'll have a snowfall before long. Have you noticed how it grows colder each day? Winter will be upon us before we know it."

"Red, why are you talking about the weather?"

Rae thought about that a moment. "I suppose because I am not in the mood to be needled and I know you have a particular fondness for that pastime."

"You know, I admire that honest streak in you that makes you speak your mind. If I promise not to be objectionable, will you ride with me? Athena can carry us both." He showed her by moving back in the saddle and making a place for her to sit. Jericho would have been surprised if Rae hadn't studied him a bit skeptically before she took his proffered hand. There was a certain caution about her that had not been evident on the schooner. He could barely blame her for cultivating a little circumspection around him.

Athena pranced a bit as Rae settled herself in front of Jericho. The fit was tighter than she'd imagined it would be, especially when his arms came around her waist to take up the reins in both hands. Her hip was trapped in the cradle of his, and it was very hard to sit without leaning back into his encircling arm and shoulder. This closeness confused her, equal parts security and danger. She was sure she was ill-prepared for this assault on her senses. "I don't think this is—"

"Hush. You're up here now. Let it rest."

His voice was very close to her ear and his breath brushed a stray stand of hair past her lobe. Unconsciously she lifted her shoulder to rub the spot that he had tickled and glanced back self-consciously to see if he had noticed. She thought it was probably a mistake, because it put her lips in very close proximity to his, and she knew a swift desire to have that mouth on hers.

"Rae?"

"Mmmm?"

"Would I be being objectionable if I kissed you?"

"Only if you didn't."

Rae was not certain what she expected, but it was not the whisper of his mouth across her own, more a promise of a kiss than a kiss itself. She leaned into him, following as his head lifted, and this time she initiated the sweet brush of their lips. Her mouth parted invitingly, touched him once, twice, then lost contact as Athena grew restless beneath them. She felt Jericho's legs tighten on the horse to still her movements. Rae smiled nervously and her tongue wet her lower lip. "Mayhap this is not a good idea."

With a mouth like she had it was always a good idea. But what he said was, "Slip your arms around my neck."

No doubt it was another mistake to obey the husky command in his voice, and she would have cause later to wonder at her sanity, but for now there was naught else she wanted in the world. Rae's arms circled his neck, and if Athena had reared up on her hind legs Rae thought there would be no dislodging Jericho from the firmness of her embrace. Jericho's mouth now made good on its promise, tasting the fullness of what Rae offered. His tongue slipped along the edge of her teeth and traced the soft underside of her lip, and when he pressed harder, nudging her teeth apart, Rae eagerly accepted his charged hunger.

Neither of them could have said where that kiss might have taken them had it not been interrupted. Jericho liked to think he would not have ravished her in the road. Rae liked to think he might have at least considered it. But the intervention of a dusty stranger and his nag made their thoughts rhetorical as they pulled guiltily apart. Neither of them knew when he had come upon them or how long he had been staring at them.

Rae did not particularly care for the looks of the stranger. It was difficult to tell height while he was mounted, but she thought him shorter than herself and possessed of a braggadocio manner that she often found in men who had nothing at all to boast of. He completely ignored her, which did nothing to win her favor, and addressed Jericho, a sly smile on his lips and a gutter wink in his dark eyes that made his apology ring false.

"Beggin' yer pardon, sir. But I didn't see you till I took the bend. Then I says, 'Well, Sam Judge'—that's what I call myself—'Well, Sam Judge,' says I, 'mayhap they won't take no notice of you if you go quietly on by.' But Berry here . . .'' He patted his animal on the neck and the nag tossed her head in agitation. Sam Judge rolled his eyes as if he didn't know what to make of the horse's skittishness, while Rae thought personally the horse was well within her rights. "Berry here ain't known for goin' silently about, and she's the one what ought to beg your pardon."

Rae did not have to turn around to know that Jericho had taken the full measure of the man in front of them and that his eyes would be glacial. That was why the warmth of his reply startled her. "Then we'll accept her apology. Where are you headin', Sam Judge?"

"That's jest the thing. I don't rightly know. I'm lookin' fer a place called McClellan's Landing. I've got a packet here fer a Miz Ashley Lynne, but folks I asked in Norfolk says they only know Ashley McClellan and directed me this way. Had to ferry the river and hire me this nag to git this fer."

"I'm Ashley McClellan," Rae said calmly. "Lynne is my maiden name."

Jericho nearly groaned aloud. Had he really thought she was learning caution? Oh well, in for a penny, in for a pound. "I'm Jerusalem McClellan," he said easily, surreptitiously squeezing Rae's waist to remain quiet and let him handle this. "Ashley is my wife."

"Hear that, Berry? The one you thought was a doxy is the

wife. Jest shows you can't be too quick to sit in judgment. Oh, but it's good to see a marriage what ain't ended after the vows been said.''

Rae stiffened. He had called her a doxy! If Jericho didn't smash his face she was going to—as soon as she found a way out of his steel embrace. Sam Judge's insolent gaze was all over her, and Jericho wasn't lifting a finger to poke the blighter's eyes out.

''You said you have a packet?'' Jericho prompted.

''That I do.'' He unfastened two buttons on his jacket, reached inside his vest and pulled out a rather thick packet wrapped in oilcloth and bound neatly with twine. Sam Judge turned it over so they could see there was also a seal and that it remained unbroken. ''So there's no doubtin' Sam Judge's honesty,'' he said, kicking Berry forward and delivering the goods into Rae's lap.

Her fingers gripped the edges tightly and willed Jericho to loose her arms so she could bat Sam Judge over the head with it. Jericho had even taken his foot from the stirrup and trapped her ankles beneath his calf. He knew she wanted to get one good kick in before the stranger departed. She supposed they must look very cozy to Sam Judge.

Gritting her teeth, Rae smiled sweetly. ''Thank you kindly, Mr. Judge. Would you like to come to the landing for some refreshment?'' My brothers will put your eyes out. ''I imagine you've had a tiring trip.'' And I'll stomp all over your dirty grin. ''Most couriers bring our mail by way of the river. It's an easier journey.'' Then we'll ask questions about why you're sniffing around our home with packages for Ashley.

''That's your home over there?'' he asked, pointing to the east wing of the house that was the only part visible from the road.

''My parents' home,'' Jericho answered for Rae. ''Will you have that refreshment? Perhaps a reply will be necessary and you can carry it back for my wife?''

Sam Judge was looking distinctly uncomfortable, and Rae mentally applauded Jericho's inventiveness. They really did need to bring Judge in so they could question him, though how they would keep it from Ashley she didn't know.

Judge pretended to give the cast of the sky a great deal of thought before he replied. "I'd like that refreshment, o' course, and I'd like to oblige you with yer reply, but it looks like a storm's brewing over yonder. Wouldn't be surprised if it snowed a might. Berry and me don't want to be caught in that."

Rae wondered what he would have done if the weather had not been so accommodating. There were some ominous-looking clouds in the northwest. "Are you certain? We can put you up for the night."

"Don't want to get snowed in, Mrs. McClellan." He kicked Berry hard in the flanks and turned her. "Nice bit of luck, chancin' upon the two of you this way. Saved Berry's agin' legs." He tipped his dusty tricorn to each of them in turn. "Hope I've been the bearer of good news." He gave Berry another nudge and she picked up her pace. His voice trailed off as he continued to talk to his animal. "Nice folks, ain't they, Berry? Don't know when I last seen a wife that kissed like a . . ."

"Oooooh!" Rae struggled in Jericho's arms.

"Stop it! Don't listen to him. We have to get back to the house. Will your horse find his own way?"

"Of course, but he's hurt. I hate to leave him to make his own way back. Go on, boy. Go on, Lazurus." She leaned over, slapped him on the rump, and watched him go. "Oooah! Why didn't you run him through?"

Jericho gave Athena a light kick. "Lazurus?"

"No. Sam Judge!"

"Oh, we're back to him? And what should I have used to do the deed? I know it's gauche of me to have left the house without my dress sword, but there it is. I would have my knife, but your mother frowns on me carryin' a weapon all the time.''

"Do not make light of me, Jericho Smith! You know what that man was!''

Jericho gave Rae a small shake. "Exactly. Which is why I was not goin' to try to take him while I had your safety to think of. I consider myself lucky to be alive as it is. Did you see the piece he was carrying in his breeches? Loaded too, I'll wager, and ready to cut me down once he had a clear shot. It was you he wanted, or rather Ashley. I don't doubt he would have taken you, if he thought he could have got you away from me."

"Then you weren't trying to keep me from landing him a facer? You were using me as a shield!''

"A bit of both, I'm afraid. Not very chivalrous, but undeniably true. And your own fault, I might add. What possessed you to tell him you were Ashley?"

"Because I wanted to see that packet before Ashley saw it. Only her uncle would have the audacity to send her something after all these years and still refuse to recognize her marriage. That it was addressed to Ashley Lynne was a deliberate cut, and I will not have her hurt again. My family has suffered aplenty at that man's hands! Anyway,'' she said, calming herself, "you did not have to say you were Salem.''

"What? And ruin Ashley's rep after you announced Lynne was your maiden name? Who exactly was it she was supposed to be kissing if not her husband?''

Rae frowned deeply. "I take your point. Oh, Jericho, what are we going to do?''

Jericho reined in Athena at the summerhouse. "Let's have a look at that packet before we go in the house. I don't want Ashley accidently coming upon us.'' He helped Rae down, then dismounted himself, favoring his injured leg only the slightest degree. He gave Athena a nudge in the direction of the stables.

Unlike the last time they had been in the summerhouse, Jericho and Rae did not choose opposite sides. Rae sat close at Jericho's side, huddled for warmth. A brisk wind had kicked up, and the sky was gray now as the dark clouds Sam Judge had seen moved toward them with surprising speed. The feather in Rae's hat tickled her cheek once too often, and she tore the thing off impatiently. Jericho took the packet from her lap and examined the seal.

"Recognize it?" he asked, lifting it for her inspection.

An elaborately scrolled L was at the center of the seal and on its perimeter was a Latin inscription Rae could not read. "It's the Lynne seal," she said. "Ashley showed it to me once. She told me what those words mean. I've forgotten now."

"Vestiga nulla retrosum. It means no returning footsteps. Fitting, don't you think? Nigel never turns back."

Rae's head snapped up, her coiled braid lost its moorings, and her hands fell slowly to her lap. She looked at him shrewdly. "This is not the time, but be warned, Jericho, I *will* discover how it is you can read Latin. Heavens! You're more a mystery than a certain lightskirt who could read the King's English."

"Don't refine on it, Rae," he said tersely. "Are those the words Ashley told you?"

"Yes. It's the Lynne seal."

Jericho took off the twine and broke the seal. Inside the oilcloth were a number of letters, all individually sealed. Jericho hesitated. "Should we?"

"Absolutely." She took the first one from the pile and cracked the seal. "You take the next," she told him as she unfolded the vellum. She began to read in silence while Jericho opened another missive. Minutes later she folded it again and set it down, her hands trembling, her face pale. She looked askance at Jericho. He had just finished reading, and a muscle leaped in his clenched jaw. "He's obsessed with having her back at Linfield, isn't he?" she asked in a choked little voice. "He writes over and over for her to return to her home."

"There were some very ugly threats scattered among those pleas in the letter I read. Yours?"

She nodded. "His mind isn't right. It can't be. Some of the things he said he would do . . ."

Jericho picked up another letter, ripped it open, and scanned the contents. He would not let Rae touch them again, but his impassive face told her that each was like the one she'd first read. In the end he gathered them up and wrapped the oilcloth about them, slipping the twine around the packet. "They date from as long as two years ago to as recently as ten weeks ago. There are threats against the children, Courtney first, and later Trenton is mentioned."

"Dear God!"

"Rae, he must have been getting reports on Ashley while she and Salem were in New York. There are some threats directed at you, also." Jericho's fist slammed into the bench. "Dammit! Why didn't your brother have something done about Nigel Lynne five years ago?"

"I believe he tried, Jericho," Rae said quietly. Her chest felt tight as she thought how much Jericho must love Ashley. He had to know that Salem did everything in his power to protect his wife, but for Jericho it still wasn't enough. "There were few recourses available to Salem. Have you forgotten there has been war these last years?"

"Pray, do not be stupid."

"Then, pray, what would you have done? Sent someone to kill him as he has sent people here?"

"No. I would have seen to the matter myself."

Rae had guessed as much. "Which is precisely what Ashley would not permit! Did you know my father suspects she is really the owner of the Linfield holdings? Papa thinks Nigel was disinherited, but Ashley will have none of it! She wants nothing to do with her uncle, and that includes not letting her husband within striking distance of him. He is a dangerous man, Jericho. We are all safer here, and that is why Ashley would never let Salem go to England and finish it."

Jericho's knuckles whitened on the packet. "Rae, listen to me. I know what you say is true, but these letters are something else again. These threats to you and the children cannot be dismissed. I have some assurance that you might, just might, be able to defend yourself. But what of Courtney and Trenton?"

Rae clutched Jericho's arm. It was only the thickness of his riding coat that prevented her nails from scoring him. "Don't speak of that! I tell you we are safe at the landing!"

He knew she wanted to believe it was true. He wished to God it were. "I'm going to bury this packet out here. I refuse to take it into the house. I cannot conceive of the place where it cannot be stumbled upon. If Salem demands to see the evidence, though I doubt that he will, he can see it here."

Rae agreed numbly. "Whatever you think best." She leaned back, shutting her eyes while Jericho stepped to the back of the summerhouse and vaulted gracefully over the rail, dropping to the ground out of view of the house. It was not long before he was back and pulling Rae to her feet.

"The ground was hard. God, I hate dirt under my nails."

Rae's giggle was a little hysterical.

"Rae?" He had her in his arms in the next moment. She was shaking. "You're so cold." He rubbed her back, her upper arms. Finally he simply drew her icy hands under his coat and held her. "It's all right. Everything's going to be fine. I promise."

She hugged him, resting her cheek against his smooth linen shirt. "Why has the duke sent the letters now? Why after all this time?" Jericho did not have any answers for her, and she drew back a little, looking up at the grim expression in his eyes, the hint of whiteness about his mouth. "That man—Sam Judge—do you really believe he would have killed you, or rather Salem?"

"To get to Ashley he would have. I'd admit he did not seem

the sort of man the duke would send to do the deed, but surely you're not doubting the man was no courier.''

"I wish we had been able to draw him back to the house. We could have ended it. I can't help but wonder what he would have done if he hadn't met us?''

"What I would have done in his place: delivered the package into Ashley's hands, then when y'all attacked with your questions, I would have sworn on the McClellan family Bible I'd never heard of the duke of Linfield. Eventually you would have let me go, no matter what your suspicions.''

Rae shivered, realizing he was right.

"Come. Let's go back to the house. I'll talk to your father and brothers after dinner.''

Jericho's task of talking to the McClellan men alone was a difficult one. The men did not necessarily linger over a glass of wine in the absence of the women. Without Rae's assistance, Jericho doubted he could have managed. He admired the way she practically herded her mother and sisters into another room for an impromptu musicale. He kept the men at the dining table with a hard stare and the tiniest shake of his head. Gareth was the most difficult, since he was wont to follow his very pregnant wife everywhere.

Robert had a teasing smile for Gareth, then poured himself a glass of port and slid the decanter toward Salem. "What's this about, Smith?'' It occurred to him that perhaps Jericho was going to make his intentions toward Rahab formally known. It was odd that he would do it in front of the entire family, but the idea did not displease Robert.

"It's the Duke of Linfield, sir. He's sent a warning.''

Robert choked. Salem's hand remained poised over the decanter. Gareth and Noah were looking extremely thin-lipped. Only Leah's husband, Troy Lawson, did not at first understand the import of Jericho's words. He sat forward at the table, his lean face grave, and kept his counsel while listening carefully to the others.

"What sort of warning?" Salem asked sharply.

Jericho explained the events of a few hours before, and when he finished a heavy silence permeated the room.

I once promised Ashley I would not resort to Nigel's methods, but I can see no alternative left to me," Salem said tightly. "There is only one reason he sent those letters and that is to taunt us. To let us know that when we thought Ashley safe, she was not. And now Courtney and Trenton."

"And Rahab," Jericho added with quiet force.

"*And* my sister," Salem went on, as if Jericho had not spoken, "who doesn't have the sense to realize the danger of saying she is my wife. We will forever be looking over our shoulders until the duke is dead. There is nothing for it but that I go to Linfield and end this."

"No." Jericho's voice joined the others, and the sharp sound brought Salem's head up. He was not used to being gainsaid.

"What do you propose?" Silence greeted his question and he smiled a trifle bitterly. "Exactly. I am willing to entertain better suggestions, but I doubt there are any."

"You cannot seriously suppose you will have access to the duke," Troy said calmly. "Once he saw you, your life would be forfeit. Robert has no more chance than you of succeeding. Gareth or Noah might have the opportunity to get near him, for they are strangers to Nigel. But they have the look of McClellans, and you say the duke is shrewd, so I think he would find them out. It is not cowardice that keeps me from volunteering my services, but simply a lack of the skill and cunning this piece of work requires." He paused, looking thoughtfully at his folded hands. "I understand from what I have heard that there is no legal recourse open to you. It appears the duke is too canny to be caught in a scheme to bring him to these shores." He glanced around and saw there was agreement from the others. "Therefore, it seems to me the reasonable thing is to employ someone who can put pressure on the duke, or, if need be, put a period to his existence."

Salem had listened carefully to Troy's analysis. There was no faulting his logic, but Salem did not want to put the fate of his enemy in the hands of another. "It would be folly to send a stranger to do what I should have done long ago. There is no one I trust to see to the matter."

"No one?" Jericho asked mildly. There was the merest hint of a smile on his lips. He looked relaxed, without the aura of tension the others projected. He had pushed his chair away from the table and his long legs were stretched in front of him, casually crossed at the ankles. His long-fingered, capable hands were folded loosely in his lap, and his clear blue eyes held the spark of some subtle purpose.

"You?" Salem was incredulous and took no pains to hide it.

"Why not?" Jericho drawled softly. "The British will not mount another offensive until spring of next year, if one comes at all. By then I will have returned. My leg is no longer a concern, and I'm unattached." Forgive me, Rae, for having said the last. "Troy mentioned skill and cunnin'. Is there anyone here who says I haven't an ample supply of both? I thought not. What say, Salem? Reckon I could hobnob with a toff like the Duke of Linfield?"

Salem could not help it. The tension that had been squeezing his chest and gut released itself in a spurt of laughter. The others soon joined, while Jericho merely grinned good-naturedly and let their nervous humor run its course. Salem wiped a tear from his eye and took a sip of his port to steady himself. "Forgive me, Smith. Your offer is generous and appreciated," he said seriously. "In so many ways you are exactly the man I could trust with a matter of such personal importance, but I fear that while you have great skill and cunning and courage as I have not witnessed in many others, the duke would identify you as a Yankee in a minute and be on his guard."

"A minute is all I need." Jericho saw his grim observation had the effect of sobering everyone.

"But you have to see him first. Years ago I was able to gain access to him through his interest in horseflesh. I doubt he would again be so accommodating to another Yankee buyer."

"You realize you're only makin' the case stronger against your goin'. I have notions about seein' the duke that are a lot less troublesome than tryin' to pretend an interest in his stud."

Guessing that Jericho had it in his mind that he would waylay the duke, Salem discouraged the idea immediately. "He does not travel without an entourage of servants who are loyal to him, Smith, and Linfield is a fortress."

Jericho chuckled. "I'm not interested in takin' him on the road. It's too dangerous. And do you think I have intentions of scalin' his damn walls when the doors are open to his friends?"

"You are not his friend," Robert pointed out.

"No. But I could be."

Robert coughed uneasily. "I'll be blunt, Jericho. The duke is much taken with his station in life. He has no interest in associating himself with someone beyond the pale. A Yankee, even if you professed a Tory's sympathies, would hardly be welcomed in his circle. Your wardrobe could easily be fixed, but your manner of speech would set you apart instantly. And in his eyes it would set you beneath him."

"Is that what's troublin' y'all? What a fuss over nothin'."

"It is hardly nothing, Jericho," Salem replied. "You could never be counted among the duke's friends. Believe me, that is not something to regret."

"But if I could?" He asked the question casually, hiding from everyone that he was in earnest.

"If you could? Then yes, God help me, I would take up your offer."

"Reckon that's what I've been waitin' to hear. If y'all will excuse me one minute, I have to fetch somethin'." He was gone less than that, and he grinned at the puzzled faces still circling the table when he shut the door behind him again. In his hands he carried two books from Robert's precious collection in the library. One was Plutarch's Lives, the other a specially bound volume of writings by Rousseau. Neither was in English, but in their original Greek and French. Jericho opened the Plutarch tome first and began to read at random, first in Greek, then translating, in impeccable English that did not leave one syllable wanting full expression. Holding up his hand to halt their excited curiosity, he did the same with the Rousseau work.

"I regret my French is not what it used to be. Rochambeau and Lafayette both found it eminently understandable, but lacking heart. You know the French; no one can speak their language as well as they can. Greek is not so difficult, but my Latin is better. My tutor was a pedant, and he had a petty scholar's love for the nominative and the dative. My command of the mother tongue is the issue here. Would the duke find something offensive with my speech?"

No one spoke for a long moment. Finally Salem said, "Smith, you sound like a pompous ass."

Jericho smiled widely. "I imagine that means ol' Nigel will attach himself to me like scum on a pond."

"Hell, yes. Who are you, Jericho Smith?"

His smile faded. "Is it important?" he asked quietly, a warning look in his eyes.

Robert spoke for everyone. "No. We know your mettle, and your past is your own affair."

"Good. Perhaps someday. . . but not now." He laid Rousseau and Plutarch aside. "I think it is time for us to plan our strategy. First, I must secure passage. . ."

Rahab thought her heart would stop beating when she heard the handle on the door to the music room twist. Her father walked in first and immediately went to the spinet. Much to Rae's surprise, he sat down beside Leah on the stool and joined in the singing in his endearingly off-key voice. No worry there, she thought. Troy and Noah came in next, carrying some light refreshment to ease all the parched throats. Gareth dropped his bulk beside Darlene and inquired about her health. Ashley had her legs propped on a green velvet ottoman, and Salem nudged them aside when he sat there, leaning back against the arm of her chair and reaching for her hand. He seemed the very definition of contentment.

"I'd like to have a word with you, Rae."

Rae was startled to find Jericho standing at her back. Never would she become accustomed to his manner of sneaking up on a person. She looked around quickly and saw no one paying them any attention. His voice had been no more than a whisper in her ear. "Of course."

"A walk?" he invited.

She nodded. "I'll get my cloak." Rae caught her mother's eye and motioned she was leaving. Charity smiled serenely and never missed her turn to join the round they were singing. Rae slipped out the door, blissfully unaware of how soon her departure would alter the room's atmosphere.

Jericho helped Rae slip into her pelisse. "You'll probably want this." He handed her a rabbit-fur muff and took Salem's cape from the cloakroom for himself. "I don't think he'd begrudge me this, d'you?"

Rae's smile was a little nervous. "No. He wouldn't mind."

Jericho shrugged into the heavy wool cloak, and taking Rae's elbow, escorted her to the veranda.

Without a word, they paused on the uppermost step and absorbed the sight that greeted them. It had begun to snow, soft furry flakes that captured the moon's silver light and spangled the ground before they vanished in a glittery flash. The earth sparkled as though all of heaven's stars had fallen upon it. Each melting flake had a hundred more to take its place.

It was actually warmer now than it had been a few hours before, and Rae slipped back her hood to catch the snow in her hair and feel it on her face as they walked. Automatically she started toward the summerhouse, but Jericho turned her toward the river and she did not resist.

"I had not credited you with so much patience, Rae," Jericho observed quietly, taking his fill of her glittering hair and soft profile turned skyward. He envied every flake that kissed her cheek and brushed her lips.

"I'm learning."

They walked in silence for nearly a hundred yards. Behind them the manor house glowed warmly from within, scattering its protective light for a short distance beyond the circular drive. Ahead of them lay one of the plantation's docking points and the James River. Noise was muted here by the water's unhurried flow; occasionally something jumped or moved in the trees on their left, but mostly there was a lovely blanket of quiet, a serenity Jericho and Rae were loath to break.

"I seem to remember a bench around here," Jericho said. "Care to be my guide?"

Rae led him a little farther along the path's gentle slope, then veered nearer the grove of stately pines. The bench was sheltered by a canopy of pine boughs, and a break in the trees provided them with an unobstructed view of the river. It was easy to imagine they were watching nature's play through a window at the landing.

Jericho sat beside Rae but leaned forward, elbows on his knees, chin resting on his fists. "I didn't expect it would be this hard, Red. To tell you, I mean." His private name for her slipped out without his being aware of it. "I've explained everything to Robert and your brothers. Do you know, Troy has a fair head on his shoulders. It's no wonder you—"

"That's long in the past and not what you want to talk about," she chided. "Or at least it's not what I want to talk about. What has been decided about the duke? Am I the only one to know? Is that why you brought me out here?" There was an end to her patience, and Rae had just reached it.

"I brought you out here because I want to tell you things

I've told none of the others, not your father, not your brothers. I want to explain to you why I am the one going to Linfield.''

Part of Rae's mind registered that Jericho was talking differently. The drawl was absent, and there was a certain clipped purpose to his words. But those changes only received a vague recognition, it was the content of his speech that made her hands ice in the rabbit-fur muff.

''No!'' It was a cry of pain as well as denial. Words slipped from her mouth before she knew what she was saying. ''I knew you loved her, of course, but I had thought . . . oh, I don't know what I thought!''

Jericho had straightened, turning on Rae as she spoke, clearly incredulous. But she was not looking at him; her eyes were tightly closed in further refusal. He gave her shoulders a gentle shake and she pulled from him sharply. His hands dropped uselessly to his side. ''What's this nonsense? Who is it I'm supposed to love?'' His fingers snapped as he hit upon the gist of her thoughts. ''Ashley.'' He said her name more loudly than he intended.

''Yes.''

His voice dropped. ''Is that what you really think?''

''Yes.''

''I see. And if I said it was you I loved . . .''

''*If* you said it I would be hard-pressed to believe you.''

''Why is that?''

''Because if you loved me, you would not go to Linfield.''

Jericho sighed. ''I have often thought that love should not be bound by such conditions. Apparently, it is a matter on which we disagree.''

''Apparently,'' she mocked bitterly.

''Then you are not interested in alternative explanations?''

''No. I want to hear none of it.''

Jericho felt defeated. He had never thought Rae would misinterpret his going to Linfield as further proof that he loved Ashley. Perhaps there had been a time when she would have been justified in believing that, but no longer. She did not want to hear that it was she herself who had prompted his suggestion, that, and the fact that Jericho thought he was the only one among them with a chance of succeeding. Nothing less than those reasons could have made him volunteer for a journey to England that meant an ocean voyage. The thought of the trip that confronted him was sufficient to make his palms sweat, in spite of the cold.

"Rae," he tried again. "If you would but listen to me you would understand that it is—"

"Do you imagine your reasons are important to me?" she scoffed. "Do you think it matters why you are choosing suicide when there is nothing I can do to prevent it? Is there? Is there something I can say that will keep you from going?"

"No."

"Then I trust you take my point."

In Jericho's mind there was nothing he was in danger of losing that he had already not lost. "I'll damn well take more than that, Red!"

Jericho gave Rae no chance of escaping. His arms blocked her on either side and then they closed around her, pulling her tight in a hard embrace that gave no quarter. Rae doubled her fists and pushed at his stomach, but the muff softened the blow and it had no effect other than to trap her arms between them. Her mouth opened to hurl a curse at him, but Jericho made certain no sound came out.

His mouth was hard on hers, punishing. He ground the sensitive underside of her lips against teeth that had closed sharply against his invasion. He jerked her once in his arms, tugging at her hair to lift her face. When her lips parted again his tongue swept her mouth in a savage foreplay that frightened Rae with its brutal intensity. She bit his tongue, and when he pulled back sharply she drew a deep breath, prepared to rend the air with a scream that would be heard miles away in Williamsburg.

Jericho was quicker. His head lowered and bit her lower lip.

He hadn't done it hard, it was more of a nip really, and somehow tender, given the response he could have made. Rae went very still in his arms; then Jericho's mouth touched her lips again, a nibble, this time and the gentleness kept her quiet. His mouth moved over her still unresponsive lips, tasting and teasing, denying the fierce hunger that had driven him moments earlier, that was with him even now. He touched the corner of her mouth flicking it with his tongue, and he felt a small shudder pass through her. Encouraged, he kissed her cheeks, her closed lids. His mouth slipped along the line of her slender throat and nestled in the curve of her shoulder.

"What are you doing to me?" she asked on a hushed breath as he pulled her to her feet. "What is it you want?"

His head lifted and his mouth hovered above hers. "You . . . only you."

His words, not his mouth, touched Rae's lips, but it felt like the sweetest kiss she had ever known. When Jericho banished the distance that separated them, Rae's lips answered the gentle probe of his mouth and savored the heady, intimate pleasure.

Rae's response lightened Jericho's heart. He was certain she would listen to him now, and perhaps if she could not agree with him, she would still promise to wait for him. That was all he really wanted, her word that she would not bind herself to another while he was gone.

"Red? I lo—" In the same moment he was wondering why she was preparing to scream, Jericho felt a great weight descend upon his head. His vision blurred, his knees buckled, and the last thing he saw was a gloved hand covering Rae's mouth so that her scream had no sound. No sound at all.

Rae fought wildly against the wiry strength of the man who held her, but she could not escape his grasp. Two men stood in front of her, impassively watching her struggle with her captor. Another bent over Jericho, satisfying himself and his companions that there would be no resistance from that quarter. The features of the men she could see were obscured by shadow.

They all wore tricorns tipped forward on their heads. But the identity of the man who held her was never a mystery. His size, the peculiar smell of clothes long in need of washing, and a sly chuckle in her ear, warned Rae it was Sam Judge who kept her pinned flush to his body.

Kicking behind her, Rae at last landed a painful blow to his shin. Judge's hand slipped from her mouth, and because she saw it was useless to scream for Jericho, she cried out for her brothers. "Saaa—luuumm! Nooo—"

One of the men in front of her shoved a dirty, greasy rag into her mouth. Rae tried to push it out, but a scarf was tied roughly around her head to keep the gag in place. Her hair tangled painfully in the knot at the back of her head, and in short order the muff was flung aside and her hands were bound with a small length of rope.

Sam Judge still held her tightly by the waist, and when he spoke to his companions Rae felt some satisfaction that he was out of breath. "Didn't Sam Judge tell you it was them what was sittin' there as pretty as you please?"

"Aye, you did, Sam," said the man leaning over Jericho. "Heard him call her Ashley as clear as a bell, and she be yellin' for him now like she think we kilt him."

"Sure, I did. Jest the way I told you we would be fools not to do something about the papers we found aboard the *Marion*. Didn't Sam Judge also say that privateerin' would pay sooner or later?"

"You said that, too, Sam," one of them replied good-naturedly. "Didn't expect our fortune in quite this way, though."

"Yeah," said the third. "I never thought our bounty would be this beauty. But we still have to collect on her. Reckon that duke fellow will pay the ransom?"

Rae's eyes shot from man to man, thoroughly confused by their conversation. That they had been sent by Nigel Lynne no longer seemed clear. Privateers, they called themselves. Rae called them pirates.

"He'll pay," Sam Judge said certainly. "Wasn't he goin' to pay that limey bloke you shot to bring her to him?" He shrugged. "Why should he care who has her as long as he gets her in the end? For a fair price, too, says I. C'mon, let's get her in the skiff." One of the men grabbed Rae by her ankles while Sam slipped his arms beneath her shoulders. Rae renewed her struggle and received naught but bruises from her effort.

"What about this one?"

Sam paused, grunting low when Rae, panicking that they might kill Jericho, slammed her head backward into his chest. "Jest a moment. Drop her legs, Wendell, and help her stand."

Wendell? Rae thought giddily as she was allowed to stand. What sort of name was that for a pirate?

"Now give her a good clip," Sam Judge said, still holding her arms.

Obviously it was a fine name for a scurvy bastard, Rae decided as Wendell's fist gave her a powerful chuck on the chin.

Rae slumped in Sam's arms. "God, she's a pain in the arse. Jest like the rest of her sex. Now, about her husband. We'll take him, I think. He looks like he can pull his weight on board, and after that scuffle with the *Marion* an extra hand won't be amiss."

"There was nothing in that bloke's things that said anything about money for this 'un," Wendell pointed out. "And he could be a troublemaker."

"How much trouble is he goin' to cause while we got her?" Sam asked, hoisting Rae's limp form over his shoulder. "Oh, hell, I don't care, do what you want. Jest as soon kill him as look at him."

Wendell shrugged, picking up Rae's muff. "Jud. Hank. Bring him along. Sam's right about needing the extra man."

Jud and Hank lifted Jericho between them and followed the others to the skiff that was hidden a few hundred feet downstream. The snowfall was heavier now and their tracks were covered in minutes of their passing. The boat rocked as they settled in, and there was no gentle handling for Rae and certainly none for Jericho. Both of them were deposited like so much baggage between seats on the skiff as Sam pushed away from the bank.

"Take off his cloak, Jud, and give it a pitch over in them rocks. And Wendell, git yer nose out of that damn furry thing and toss it out. It'll give their parents somethin' to think about when they come up missin'. Plenty of time will be lost while they drag the river."

By the time the landing's bell and cannon sounded the alarm, calling servants and neighbors to join the search, the party of pirates and captives was well on its way to the safety of their ship.

Chapter 8

Jericho came to awareness by slow degrees. First there was the unrelenting pounding of his head that made him wish he were still unconscious. Next he noticed one side of his face was resting against something soft and fragrant. Rae's scent, he thought groggily. She always smelled as fresh as sunlight after a summer rain. He smiled sleepily and nestled closer, but the movement only increased the thundering in his head, and he groaned. There were fingers stroking his temple, tracing his hairline, and they stilled abruptly at the sound.

"Jericho?" It was a whispered uncertainty, as if she were loath to wake him, but could not help herself.

"Mmmmm." It was the best he could do.

The fingers brushed his cheek, then continued to thread in his hair. "I was so afraid they'd killed you."

He was very much afraid they had. There was something about his present situation that was very dreamlike. "Did they hurt you?"

Rae was glad for the inky darkness that kept him from seeing what was surely a magnificent bruise on her cheek and chin. Her wrists were raw from where she had worked free of the binding ropes, and her mouth still tasted like the cloth that had gagged her. By morning she hoped the swelling would be gone.

"No." She felt his shoulders relax, and tears welled in her eyes. He could not even lift his head, and still his first concern was for her. She sniffed.

"Are you crying, Red?"

"No."

He smiled weakly. What a dreadful little liar she was. "Do you know where we are?"

She shook her head then realized it hardly communicated anything to Jericho. "No. I mean I know we're on a ship. But I don't know where. They blindfolded me," she invented so he wouldn't know she had been unconscious when they brought her on board. "They took us down river on a skiff, then put us here. We haven't been here long; they're just getting ready to set sail."

Jericho moaned and tried to sit up, but Rae's soft hands stopped him. "We have to get—"

"No," she told him sharply. "There is nothing we can do now. A guard is in the companionway, the door is locked, and there are no portholes in this room. There is nothing that can be used as a weapon, in fact, I think we are the only things in here. It would appear we are deep in the belly of the ship. I don't doubt it will be difficult to know when daylight is upon the rest of the world."

"God!" This was his worst nightmare. Jericho's hands trembled and his tongue touched a salty bead of perspiration on his upper lip. Beneath him the ship heaved as the anchor was finally lifted and the sails caught wind. He clutched Rae's skirt and his eyes squeezed shut.

Rae sensed Jericho's panic and grew fearful herself. "What is it, Jericho? What's wrong?"

"Hold me, Red." His voice shook.

It startled Rae that he should sound so young, so pathetically like a child awakened in the middle of the night from a bad dream. She did not hesitate to provide whatever reassurance he required. Even though she was cold, she slipped out of her pelisse and covered him, wondering when his cape had disappeared. Bending forward, she hugged him, sliding her hands along his back in soothing strokes. Her lips rested very near his ear and she whispered that she was there, holding him forever, if need be.

The ship rolled in an even rhythm that reminded her of the sleepy movements of a rocking chair. She placed a tender kiss on Jericho's temple. His soft hair tickled her lips, and she smiled. Yellow hair as fine as a babe's, she thought, and a voice as pure as youth. For the moment she was the mother, he the child. She didn't mind at all.

When Jericho woke again it was the memory of his panic and not the thrumming in his head that caused him discomfort. In truth, he held to the opinion the injury to his head was not worth a comment. He had some difficulty in sitting up, because Rahab was slumped over him, deeply asleep. Gingerly he moved her and saw to her comfort, reddening to the roots of his hair when he realized she had given up her pelisse for him. She snuggled into the fur-lined cape, and he was satisfied he had done as well as he could by her.

He had no idea if it was day or night, though he suspected it was still the latter. The guard in the companionway was now in possession of a lantern. A thin stream of yellow light illuminated the outline of the door to their prison, as well as a few narrow cracks in the wall. It was sufficient for Jericho's eyes to adjust and allow him to see Rae's profile. Quietly, so as not to alert the guard, Jericho paced off the room and found it to be tiny beyond his imaginings. He estimated the length at eight feet and the width a toe under seven. He leaned against a wall until he was able to breathe without struggling, and his heart resumed a normal rhythm.

Slowly he raised his hand and knew a little relief when only the tips of his fingers touched the ceiling. That, then, was something to be thankful for. The room was as grim as Rae had described. The plankings were solid, the beams tight. No weapons to be had there. Jericho noticed there was not a chamber pot or even a loose bed of straw. It bothered him no small amount that there was no modest way of relieving oneself, but Rahab would be mortified, and that bothered him even more.

He blamed himself bitterly for falling so easily into Nigel Lynne's trap. He had never considered that Sam Judge might be lurking on the McClellan property after delivering the duke's packet. Admit it, Smith, if you had thought it, you still would not have believed he could take you so easily. But then you forgot what being in Red's arms did to your upperworks. Hell, it was hardly fair to lay any of their grave predicament at Rahab's feet. She was bearing the strain of their capture far better than he.

"Come to bed, Jericho."

He had to smile. She sounded so wifely, and he heard her pat the unyielding floorboards as if making a soft spot for him in a feather tick. He levered himself away from the wall and hunkered beside her. "Are you certain this is proper?" he asked with teasing solemnity.

"Quite certain. Listen:

Since in a bed a man and maid
May bundle and be chaste,
It doth no good to burn up wood;
It is a needless waste."

Jericho nearly gave a shout of laughter. Rae was dear beyond words. He could think of no one, man or woman, who could take the heaviness from his shoulders as simply as she did. "Never say your papa quoted that broadside while you dandled on his knee."

"Papa? Heavens no!" Rae pretended shock. "It was Mama.

She was raised in New England, you know, and believes that thrift will bring one closer to the angels.''

He chuckled. "Then by all means, let us bundle." He slid beneath the pelisse as Rae lifted it for him. Rae curled into him, resting her head on the curve of his shoulder, and wrapped one arm about his chest.

For some time Jericho merely relished the closeness, wishing the circumstances differed. "I'm sorry this happened, Red," he said after a while.

She nodded. "I know."

"I don't have a plan for removing us from this situation."

"It's only been hours. We'll think of something."

"We," she had said, and Jericho warmed to that. "It is Judge who took us, isn't it?"

"Yes. And three others. Of course, there are many more men aboard this vessel. How long before we reach England?"

"Six weeks, if they take the northern course and use the Westerlies to their advantage. Did they mention the duke?"

"It's the strangest thing, Jericho, but I don't think they are in Nigel's employ." Rae recounted the conversation she had heard. "What do you make of it?"

Jericho's face remained impassive as he thought. "I think they've stumbled upon something they would better be rid of. It sounds as if the duke's man was on board the *Marion* when it was raided by Judge and his crew. Somehow they discovered Ashley was worth money. It explains why Sam Judge so easily accepted you were your sister-in-law. That was the one thing I couldn't understand. If the duke had hired him, Judge would have had a description of her."

"I never thought of that."

"Your brothers and I did. We thought he might be no more than a messenger, after all. I caught the briefest glimpse of him after I was felled, and I remember thinking how foolish I had been. What did they use to clobber me?"

"The butt of a pistol."

"Why did they bring me?"

She shivered. "I don't know. They dragged me away," she lied again. "I don't know their reasoning. Perhaps Nigel wanted Salem also."

"Nigel wants Salem dead. I don't know why I'm not."

"Please don't talk that way. You're frightening me."

He stroked her hair. It had come loose from its pins and hung freely about her neck and shoulders. "There are certain things we have to face, none of them pleasant. I'd rather we spoke of them now, in the event we are separated. Do you understand me, Red?"

"Yes."

"It is unlikely that Nigel will pay a ransom for you, and we know he won't for me. But it is no good telling Sam Judge that; our lives would be ended here and Ashley and Salem would be in danger once again. Our best hope for safety lies in letting Sam and his men believe in their mistake. In addition, we must make them understand that Nigel will not part with his blunt if you are harmed in any way." Jericho stressed the last so Rahab could not doubt his meaning.

"I know. I have thought on it, too. If they touch me . . ." She cringed, unable to finish her thought aloud.

"Listen! Sam Judge is possessed of a shrewd and canny mind. I think he will agree you are not to be hurt."

Rae thought of her disfigured cheek, but remained silent. She knew that Jericho would do all that was in his power to protect her.

"For now our task is to survive this voyage," he said calmly. "Once we reach English shores, then mayhap there is a chance of escape. If none exists, we will make our own. We are survivors, you and I."

Rae thought he was; she was not certain about herself. Desperate for assurance, she moved restlessly against him. He seemed to understand her need, for his arms tightened around her and his fingers in her hair softly stroked her nape.

"Love me, Jericho."

Since the thought had been in his own mind, he was not startled by her request. Lying with her now seemed the most natural affirmation that they were alive and bound to each other. It would mock their fears; it would be an act of defiance in the face of their despair. He hesitated. For him, at least, it would also be an act of great love. Though she used the word, he doubted its truth. He did not want her to turn to him for any reason less than love. "Why?"

His question startled Rae. She turned, lifting her head, and strained to see his face in the darkness. "I did not ask 'why' when you turned to me for comfort," she said. "I simply gave it."

His breath caught. His panic was only hours old, and he remembered every moment of it with painful clarity. He strove for calm. "Can you not see this is different? You are not asking only to be held."

"I was asking you to love me," she whispered. A bitter ache in her throat made it difficult to talk. "Just love me. Can it be so hard for you to pretend?"

Jericho's eyes widened as he realized she had misunderstood. Still holding her in his embrace, he turned her so that she lay partially beneath him. His face was very close to hers. "Pretend, Rae? It is not pretend at all." He thought he heard her give a tiny gasp, then his mouth touched hers and another sort of sound, a sound of pleasure, was what he heard.

His fingers stroked her face, relearning its lines in the dark. "What is this?" he asked roughly when he touched her swollen cheek.

"I tripped when I was getting in the skiff. It is nothing."

He kissed the bruised area very gently, butterfly wings brushing her face. Soft kisses traced the slender column of her neck. Rae's fingers wound in Jericho's hair, holding her to him as she felt his hands on her breasts. The barrier of their clothes was a frustration which had to be borne. In spite of their need, neither was unaware of the possibility that they might be intruded upon. The thought that their time was so precious heightened their desire.

Rae lifted her skirts for Jericho as his knee nudged her thighs. His hand slipped beneath her pantalettes and rolled them downward, his palm hot on her abdomen and hip, and finally on the soft triangle of hair at her thighs.

Rae's fingers fumbled with the buttons on Jericho's breeches, and her hands slipped beneath the material to touch him. He whispered something in her ear that she could not make out, but sounded like encouragement, as her hand closed around him. The kiss he centered on her mouth was hot and bruising, and Rae accepted it greedily, finding pleasure in his fevered desire for her.

She felt his fingers slip between her thighs, his touch there more gentle than his mouth, and her hips rolled slightly as she tried to center his hand where it seemed her need for him was the greatest. Her breath hissed as the pressure of his manipulation increased, and rather than tamping the fire that burned her loins, merely fed it.

She broke from his kiss only to whisper throatily against his lips, "Come to me. I need you."

He did not require proof beyond the velvet moistness of her body, but that she spoke of her mind's desire was precious to him. He turned on his back and pulled her over him. The pelisse slid to the floor. He brought her knees forward so she straddled him and her skirts fell about her legs. "Come to me," he said. Rae was at first bemused by this position, but as Jericho guided her hand back to his stiff member, she understood his intention.

Jericho wished he could see her face as she opened to him, taking him fully into her. He imagined her surprise, her pleasure, her green eyes darkening with emotion. He knew her face would be flushed, her cheeks so pink that the sprinkling of freckles would have all but disappeared. And after a moment her mouth would curve in a siren's smile. She would start to move.

Rahab leaned forward and Jericho's hands palmed her buttocks, caressing them as she clasped him tightly within her. Hesitantly she lifted, then fell, full of wonder at the control she could exercise in this play. She rose again, more confidently, and at Jericho's husky urgings she caught the rhythm that would bind their hearts and minds as one.

Urgency trapped them both, finally driving their movements to a frenetic pace. Jericho's fingers were hard on the backs of Rae's silky thighs. Rae's hands clutched at his shoulders. She arched away from him, her spine thrown into an arc of tension, the long curve of her throat exposed as the first shudder shook her body. Glittery sensation rippled through her.

Jericho wished it might last, that the demons might be kept at bay a while longer, but as he gave himself up to the pleasure that coursed through his flesh and sinew, he knew that the hard reality he and Rae shared was only minutes away.

Replete and drowsy, Rae rested her head against Jericho's shoulder. She could still feel him inside her, a not unpleasant feeling, and she wondered at the path of his seed, if perhaps this time she would conceive. Where once she would have welcomed having his child, it frightened her now. Their hold on life was too tenuous to be complicated by a third life. She could not bear to think she might soon carry a life she could never take in her arms.

Trying not to betray her tension, she pulled away from Jericho and righted her clothes. Jericho sat up and adjusted his breeches. "Do not say you regret this, even if you do," he told her quietly. "I could better face Sam Judge right now than your recriminations."

"I was not going to say anything of the sort. I am not ashamed. Are you?"

He reached for her, found her hand and brought it to his lips. "No. I am human, and rather than offer it as an excuse, I find that in moments like those just past, I revel in it."

She could not help but smile and brought his hand up to feel it.

"Red, you must believe I love you."

She would have given anything to have heard that while they were at the landing, certainly when they were on the schooner. Now the precariousness of their situation made it seem a confession under duress. "You don't have to say that," she admonished him gently. "I have quite grown used to the idea of loving you without having it returned. It is enough for now that you care for me, and I know you do."

"No. It is not enough. Caring is a paltry thing compared to what I feel." The words rose from Jericho's soul, but they still could not convey the struggle he had had to first admit them to himself. He had thought himself incapable of anything so fine and exquisite as love, when, in truth, he had only been frightened of it. It felt as if he had been on his own forever, needing no one and wanting to need no one, and had come to live his life as if things should never be different.

There were those he counted as his friends, but none he counted as necessary to his happiness. Before Rae he had never thought of happiness. His childhood years had been erased by staggering treachery, and his consuming goal was life, at whatever cost to his pride or the rules of conduct that marked his upbringing. In America he had had life and had set his sights on liberty. To cleanse himself of years of servitude and degradation, he had fought for himself and others toward that moral purpose. But pursuing happiness? That seemed more a whimsical touch of Jefferson's pen than a goal to which Jericho could aspire.

Until Rae. She made him happy. He wondered if he could say that to her. Would she understand? Would it make a difference?

Rae's hands touched Jericho's face. Her fingers were her eyes in the darkness of their prison and they studied him, finding the firm thrust of his jaw, the resolute set of his mouth. There was tension in the taut planes of his cheek and a muscle jumped beneath the soft pads of her fingers. But most astonishing was the hint of something wet on his lashes.

Her fingers paused there, not quite believing the evidence of his tears.

Jericho shuddered, expelling a breath he had not known he was holding, as Rae launched herself into his arms and rained kisses over his face, his shuttered eyes, his damp cheeks.

"Oh, Red, you make me happy."

The last flicker of doubt that he loved her vanished. She accepted his words as the tribute they were intended to be. When she tasted his smile in response to her ceaseless kissing she smiled herself, quite happily too, and rested her face against his neck and shoulder, content to hold and be held in this newfound security.

"Jericho?"

"Mmmm?"

"I did not mean to be cruel when I said those things about comforting you."

"I know." His chest paused in its normal rise and fall as he came to a decision. "I want to explain about that."

She put a finger to his lips. "No, I did not bring it up again to wrest answers from you."

He nipped her finger. "Still, I want to tell you. It is part of what I wanted to tell you at the landing, the reason I volunteered to go to Linfield."

"Oh." She felt shame that her ill-founded jealousy had stopped him and perhaps delivered them to this pass.

"Are you blaming yourself for something?"

"No."

Her denial came too quickly to be believed, but Jericho let it go. What he had to say would soon take her mind from it. For himself it was not at all difficult to lose the train of other thoughts as he remembered Stanhope, magnificent and stately with gray stone turrets that aspired for a place among the clouds and rooms that held priceless treasures on their walls and on their floors.

So he told her, opening himself to her as he had to no other, and, as always, it began with Stanhope. . . .

There were one hundred twelve rooms, one hundred thirteen if one counted the dungeon. Geoffrey knew because when he had first grasped the concept of numbers beyond ten he had taken his father by the hand and demanded they count them all. To the servants' surprise, Thomas Hunter-Smythe, sixth Earl of Stanhope, gravely followed his young son to every corner of the house and marked a numeral on the door of each room they passed with a piece of chalk. Then, in honor of his son's inquisitiveness, he had refused to allow the housekeeper or any of her staff to polish the markings away. It endeared him to his son, if not to the people whose job it was to keep Stanhope gleaming with brooms and beeswax.

Geoffrey counted everything. There were one hundred fifty-two leaded windows, including twelve of stained glass in the chapel, eight round ones in each of the two turrets, and two odd hexagonal ones on either side of the double-door entrance. There were none in the dungeon. There were seven pieces of artwork on the walls that he liked, and sixty-four that he did not. His father would not let him chalk any of them. Thank God, said the servants, the earl was not entirely gone in the upperworks.

There were four hundred twenty-three books in the library, sixteen jade and porcelain figurines beyond his reach in the music room; fifty chairs could be seated around the table in the banquet room, and there were two silver-handled pistols in a teak case in his father's study. Counting everything was not merely whimsy to Geoffrey. Somehow it made the whole of Stanhope, the estate that would someday be his, less over-whelming to his young mind. He could not conceive of how it could ever belong to him, but the earl said it was so, and Geoffrey saw no cause to disagree. The servants merely shook their heads, wondering what the earl was thinking, promising to make his by-blow his heir.

Geoffrey did not live with his father at Stanhope. He lived with his mother in Wibbery, at the end of a shady lane in a two-story cottage with boxwood hedges and a flower garden. Most of the time it did not bother Geoff that he did not live with the earl, because he could visit as he wished, but he saw that it made his mother sad. She was always most beautiful when Thomas came to visit. "Elise," he would say as she opened the door for him and she would fall into his arms, laughing as if she had forgotten their sad parting of a day, a week, or even months before. Her hair was like cornsilk, her eyes the violet-blue of forget-me-nots, and her smile always greeted him. She never cried until after he was gone.

Geoffrey was always welcome at Stanhope, unless the earl's wife was in residence. Everyone, especially the earl, agreed it was better for all that Lady Helen found London and her London lovers more to her taste than country life. There was rarely a scene, except when she once happened to spy the earl's brat, as she called him. It was the first time Geoffrey heard the word bastard.

Not long after that he was sent away to school, and there he heard the word frequently. He fought bloody battles in defense of a title he did not have and a label he did. He bore the thrashings of the headmaster stoically, counting every stroke of the birch with concentrated effort. He hated that he had brought shame to his mother and father by his behavior, for he knew from his mother's letters that they were always informed of his latest unruliness. Sometimes he wondered if he had shamed them by his birth. Gradually he withdrew into himself and could ignore the taunts and curious eyes of the other boys. He possessed a quick and clever mind and learned to channel his bewildered anger into his studies. He read voraciously, took tutoring when it was available to advance himself, and approached every assignment as if his life depended upon mastering it.

Late in the summer of his tenth year he received two letters, several weeks apart, that turned his world around.

The first was authored jointly by his mother and father, and Geoffrey could see the different handwritings, his mother's fine and neat, his father's bold and sprawling, vying for equal space on the vellum. He knew they had been happy when they had written their missive. With a wisdom that belied his years, he knew they had been in love and laughing with it.

First there was sad news, or rather it was supposed to be sad, but Geoffrey could not find it in his young heart to grieve for the death of Lady Helen. He had never forgiven her for calling him a bastard. Following the paragraph that briefly detailed Lady Helen's passing, the earl wrote that he and Elise were going to be married. There would be a scandal, of course, because he was not hypocritical enough to observe a year's mourning. He was posting the banns, and they were coming to get him as soon as they were married.

Geoffrey held the letter close to his chest, later slept with it under his lumpy pillow, and carried it on his person until it fell apart. His name, the letter had said, would be entered in the family Bible as Geoffrey Hunter-Smythe, and someday he would be the seventh Earl of Stanhope. He didn't give a fig for the title, but that he was no longer the bastard Geoffrey Adams was reason enough for whoops of joy that could be heard all along the school's corridors.

The weeks went by more slowly than he had thought possible as he waited for the arrival of his mother and father. What came instead was a letter.

Spidery, imperfect handwriting introduced the author of this epistle as his father's cousin, Charles Newbrough. He had the regrettable duty to inform Geoffrey that his parents were dead, the victims of a carriage accident on their way to see Geoffrey.

It had happened six days earlier, and Geoffrey experienced a rage that he had not been sent for. It did not seem possible that his parents had been days in their graves, and not only had he not felt their passing, he had not been allowed to see them. Bitter tears splotched the ink, and he crumbled the parchment in his fists without reading the whole of it.

The following day a carriage arrived for him, and he met Charles Newbrough in the headmaster's study. Newbrough was younger than Geoffrey thought his father's cousin should be, and for his insolence in speaking up when he hadn't been given leave to do so, Geoff received a sharp box on his ears from the headmaster. The cousin was then introduced to Geoffrey as the seventh earl of Stanhope. Still grieving for his parents, Geoff had no reaction to this usurpation of his title, if he even noticed it then. He was whisked away from the school with his belongings crated and packed on top of the coach. He bore it all in silence, regarding his cousin's dissolute and bored visage with a discourteous stare. Geoff did not care at all for Charles Newbrough's face: His eyes were small and set wide apart, and the space between them was filled with a beak more suited to a hawk. He was dressed in somber clothes and wore a black armband on his coat sleeve. Geoffrey couldn't help but think it was for show.

In front of the headmaster Charles Newbrough had been somewhat solicitous of Geoffrey's feelings in the recounting of the accident that had killed his parents. In the coach his pretense of amiability was abandoned. Geoffrey was coldly informed that as his parents had never married, he was still naught but a bastard, and an orphan besides. There was no will left by either of his parents; the estate was entailed, so its title fell to the closest legitimate male heir, and that was that. The cottage Geoffrey had grown up in belonged to the estate, and his mother's things had been sold so she might not have the final ignominy of a pauper's grave. Geoffrey was, in short, a penniless bastard orphan.

Geoff remembered leaping from his padded seat as the coach rocked along the road and launching himself at his cousin. Lies! It was all lies! If his parents had been killed on their way to get him, then they had already married. He had a letter to prove it. Charles Newbrough had paled then, demanding to see the letter, and it was only then that Geoff remembered how, in not being able to part with it, he had caused its destruction. Charles threw Geoffrey off him as if he were naught but a speck of dirt.

Until then Geoff had thought his destination was Stanhope. Now he looked at his cousin through eyes that had the last of the shutters removed and understood Newbrough would not be planning to have him anywhere around. It was then that he learned he was going to sea, and to make certain he did not protest too vociferously, Charles Newbrough knocked his young cousin senseless.

Service on the *Igraine* under the command of Liam Garvey might have been the dream of some young boy already hardened to London street life; for Geoff it was no less than five years of unrelieved hell. Not that he did not become hardened quickly. By his twelfth year he had finally lost count of something: the number of times the captain had threatened to use him as a whore. He worked himself to near exhaustion during the day, doing every thankless task assigned to him. At night, at Garvey's whim, he was dragged into the captain's cabin to wait in terror until the impotent captain admitted defeat. He knew better than to speak of the captain's failure lest Garvey make good on his threat to pass him to every other sailor on the *Igraine*. He became Garvey's whore in fiction, if not in fact.

At fourteen he understood fully what that title had meant and the protection it had afforded him. It was then that Garvey found a softer, more pliable youth for his needs, and let Jericho, as Geoff called himself now, fend for himself among the men. By the time he was sixteen he had crippled one man, taken Dugan's ear, and eventually killed another—all because they thought him fair game for their play. For the last he would have hanged had a man's life been worth more on their ship than it was. As it was, he took thirty strokes from the cat and was left to rot in the vessel's dark hold.

He grew to a curious sort of manhood on board the *Igraine*. Physically he filled out and upward, taking on the hard flesh and muscle of a man, and the scars of the dangerous work and punishment. Emotionally he was much a child, with a child's impenetrable barriers erected against further hurt. His bright and clever mind became as dull as tarnished brass from ill-use.

He probably would have died in the hold but for the fire that had threatened to damage the *Igraine's* precious cargo of silks. Fire was every seaman's worst fear, but it brought Jericho's release from the brig, because they needed all hands to fight the blaze. When it was over, no one remembered to order him back. Three days later, in Savannah, he jumped ship.

He survived in the beginning because he learned to steal and was good at it more often than not. When he was seventeen he indentured himself to a planter north of Savannah for the price of four books he stole from Richard Dunna's home. His term of service was seven years—he stayed three because that was how long it took him to read every book in Dunna's library. He began in the fields, working alongside slaves and others like him, but Dunna was curious about a youth who would steal books, and he took Jericho out of the fields after a few months. Jericho worked in the main house, proved himself quick with the accounts, and ate better than he had in years. He was given access to the library, and it was a rare evening that Dunna did not find him, deep asleep with an open book in his hand in the library's loft. When Dunna saw Jericho return the last volume to its place, he knew he was seeing the last of the gravely quiet young man. In the years he had known Jericho, he could not remember hearing above two hundred words come from his lips.

Jericho left Savannah and went south, drifted into spending

almost two years with a tribe of Seminoles in Spanish-held Florida, and learned how to move among people again. He traveled north, aimlessly at first, then heard of a group of men known as the Sons of Liberty. At last he acquired a purpose.

"Oh, my dearest love," Rae cried out softly. Throughout Jericho's recital she had remained silent, giving him respect as well as lending her strength.

Jericho felt the tightness in his chest ease by slow degrees. He was her "dearest love," not her "poor love." "I was afraid," he said carefully, "that it would make a difference."

"It does."

His chest squeezed again.

"If anything, I love you more."

He turned his face to place a kiss in her soft hair. "Thank you for that. God, I love you."

When he said it like that Rae wondered that she had ever doubted the depth of his feelings. They were quiet for a long while. The ship rolled steadily beneath them, and unknown to either, the pearl gray of dawn was lighting the eastern sky.

Rae's voice was drowsy. "You've never doubted that your parents married."

"Never. If Father said he would marry Mother before he came for me, then that is what he did. It was his way."

"Did you ever think about trying to claim Stanhope?"

"The idea consumed me when I was ten, but it was gradually beat out of me. I took the name Jericho so I would never completely forget what had been done. But now? No, I don't think about it much. Anyway, I've heard rumors over the years from people who know of Charles Newbrough. He is naught but a wastrel and a gambler. I doubt there is much left of Stanhope to be reclaimed. In truth, that bothers me most. He wanted it so badly, but didn't know how to care for it."

"Then Stanhope never played a part in the plans you and my family discussed for the Duke of Linfield."

"Not directly, no. Your father was going to supply me with money and clothes. I was going to supply well-mannered arrogance."

Rae could not help but smile. "I can believe that."

"I came by it honestly," he told her, giving her shoulders a light squeeze. "My father, from as early as I can remember, brought me up to believe I was Stanhope's heir. It rather clings."

"I don't know about that. You gave an awfully good impression of a soft-spoken Georgia boy."

"Thank you, ma'am. Now why don't you—"

Jericho had been about to advise Rae to get a little more sleep, but Sam Judge's arrival put an end to that. As the door opened Jericho got to his feet and held out a hand, helping Rae to hers.

Sam Judge's lantern preceded him into the room, swinging from his outstretched hand. "Well," he said, grinning with satisfaction, "you two don't look any the worse for your travels. Didn't I say, Jud, that they'd be fine down here?"

"You said it, Sam."

The yellow light illuminated the bruise on Rae's cheek, and Sam stepped closer to examine it. "Appears Wendell hit you a might harder than was needed."

Jericho's hand tightened on Rae's waist when he saw her face clearly. His eyes were accusing. "You said you fell."

Caught in her lie, Rae did not respond. Sam answered for her. "Suppose she thought you might take the room apart if you knew the truth. Isn't that so, ma'am?"

Rae nodded.

"See? She was only tryin' to make things easier on you."

Jericho turned his attention back to Judge, and his ice-blue eyes bore into the shorter man. "You know if she is harmed, her uncle won't give you a sixpence for her."

Sam stepped back and lowered his lantern, effectively lessening the impact of Jericho's stare. "Suspected as much," he shrugged. "Told the others the very same thing not above an hour ago. That's why we're goin' to give your wife better accommodations and see that she's well taken care of. Now that we're safely out to sea there's no longer a concern that you'll decide to leave us. As for her face, it'll heal by the time we reach London." He looked at Jericho shrewdly. "Whether or not she receives any other discipline is entirely up to yourself, but I can promise the next bruise won't show unless she lifts her skirts."

Rae's fingers intertwined with the ones Jericho was inadvertently digging into her side. "Please don't worry," she soothed. "I'll not do anything amiss."

Sam Judge chortled. "That's good of you, Miz McClellan. That'll save your husband from gettin' a few stripes on his back."

Rae looked at Jericho in bewilderment. "I don't understand."

"He's saying that if you behave yourself, I won't be flogged, and that if I do what I'm told, you won't be hurt. Is that the way of it, Judge?"

"That's the way of it," Sam Judge agreed. "Knew you was a bright 'un." He turned to Jud, who was leaning against the door frame. "Didn't I say that he was a bright 'un, Jud?"

"You said it. Are we going to take them up now?"

"In a minute. First, a test. Jest to make sure they understand." He jerked his chin in Jericho's direction. "You, McClellan. You're goin' to be working side by side with us on deck. Have you ever been part of crew before?"

"Yes."

"Good. Then you know the importance of obeyin' orders, isn't that so?"

"Yes."

"If I tell you to ready the mizzenmast sail, you'll do that." Jericho nodded.

"Say: Yes, sir."

Jericho knew no one on board called Sam Judge sir, but he complied. "Yes, sir."

Sam grinned at Rae's discomfort. "Your wife is having a bit of trouble with your willingness to comply. You'll have to take her in hand."

"My wife is doing just fine," Jericho said coldly. "What else would you have me do now that I've called you sir? Shall I kneel before you? Kiss your hand, perhaps? Would you have me howl at the moon or stand on my head? That is what this test is about, is it not? You want me to prove that I'll follow your orders to save my wife from injury."

Behind Sam, Jud was grinning at the way Jericho had taken the sport from Sam's play. If the man was willing to abandon his pride and do anything, it was hardly any fun to mock him.

Jericho's words gave Sam a moment's pause also; then he said coolly, "I've a mind to see your wife's teats, McClellan. Unfasten her blouse."

Rae felt Jericho's refusal in every limb of his body, and she blanched herself at Sam Judge's crudity and cunning, but Jericho had already taught her the importance of taking the sting from their captor's amusement. She removed Jericho's hand from her side and took a small step forward so that he could reach the hooks at her back. Before she lost her nerve she lifted her hair out of Jericho's way and held herself proudly, chin raised and eyes defiantly centered on Sam Judge's startled face.

"Cows have teats, Mr. Judge," she said calmly. "I have breasts." She could feel Jericho's fingers trembling as he undid the first four hooks. Her hair fell over her shoulder as she lowered her arms and eased the bodice down. Rae's chemise offered scant protection from the eyes that studied her, but she began to lower the straps anyway. The high curves of her breasts shone softly in the lantern light, and the chemise outlined the erect tips of her nipples. Before Jericho could help her lower her undergarment the few inches necessary to completely expose herself, Sam Judge halted her.

"Cover yourself, woman. You have as little pride as yer man. Never seen the likes of it in all my days. You ever seen it, Jud?"

Jud, whose eyes were still on Rae's breasts, said that no, he'd never seen the like.

Jericho quickly helped Rae right her clothes, then picked up her discarded pelisse and drew it about her shoulders. He did not make the mistake of thinking she trembled from the cold, and he held her flush to his body, his chin resting lightly against her silky hair. "Are we quits?" he asked his captors.

"Aye, we're quits," Judge said. "If your wife wasn't worth a fortune to us, I'd even have a mind to let her go. Her spunk is bound to cause trouble. Only a matter of time."

"If it is only the money that is your concern, then ransom us to our family. My parents will pay for our safe return."

"With what?" he scoffed. "Tobacco? Continental notes that aren't worth a diddly? Whatever the McClellans have, the Duke of Linfield has more. That's what his man said, and he had Wendell's pistol at his head to encourage the truth."

"Then the duke did not hire you?"

"We ain't for hire, are we, Jud?"

"No," Jud said. "We go our own way.

"This time your path leads to Hades," Rae said softly. "My uncle is not a man who deals fairly with people. You will have a difficult time spending your fortune in Newgate."

"Let us worry about that," Judge said. "The man we met when we took the *Marion* said the duke would reward us for seeing you safely to Linfield. Harrity, his name was. Tried to save his simple soul when it was obvious he didn't have anythin' worth takin'. Traded you instead. O' course, he thought we'd let him share in the fortune. But that Wendell, whether it's his fist or a pistol, he don't have light touch. The few brains Harrity had, well, it wasn't pretty, ma'am." He grinned when Rae shivered. "It appears that you and your husband understand the rules a little better than Harrity. As long as either of you don't do anythin' foolish, we'll be obliged to treat you squarely."

"We understand," Jericho said flatly.

"I thought that was the way of it. Jud and I will escort your wife to her cabin. It's not much, but it's better than this hole. For her own safety, she won't be allowed on deck. Most of my men I can trust to leave her alone, but it's a long voyage, and there's no sense takin' chances by paradin' her around. After she's settled, someone will take you up. You'll work side by side with the rest of us and you won't be seein' any more of her. Leastways, not until we're docked in London."

"How will I know that she is all right?"

"You'll know it because I'll tell you. It's my cabin she'll be sharin'," he added with a sly wink at Jericho. "Would you look at that, Jud. She's fainted. Now don't that beat all?"

Jericho caught Rae's limp form against him. "There was no need to make it sound as if you intended to rape her," he gritted.

"How do you know I won't?"

"Because . . ." He paused and glanced at Jud, then back to Sam, a warning in his eyes. "Do you really want me to say?" Jericho had seen the way Judge had looked at Rae when she started to undress, with more loathing than interest. He had seen the same look in his captain's eyes when some waterfront wench had settled herself on his lap and pressed her musky bosom against his chest.

Judge was distinctly uncomfortable. Clearly his bravado and innuendo were a way of saving face in front of the men he commanded. They had as little idea about his preferences as Rae.

"Because if you touched her, I would kill you," Jericho said, allowing Judge an out while communicating that he knew the real reason Rae was safe. Jericho knew he had now made a powerful and guarded enemy.

Sam's chest puffed, but he continued to watch Jericho through narrowed eyes. "Guess that's the chance I'll have to take. Ain't that right, Jud?"

"Right, Sam. And I always thought you were a lucky devil."

Sam nodded and he pointed to Rae. "Carry her up to the cabin."

Rae was coming out of her faint when Jud reached for her. "It's all right," she said. "I can walk."

Jericho bent his head and whispered in her ear. "He won't harm you. Trust me."

She nodded, not understanding, but simply believing in Jericho. Rae gave his hand a tender squeeze, more worried that when they left he would be alone in the dark than concerned for anything that awaited her. She looked back once to reassure herself before Sam Judge closed the door on Jericho's beloved face.

She was led up four narrow flights of steps, more like ladders than stairs, and taken to a small cabin that had even fewer appointments than the room she had shared with Jericho on the schooner. There was an unmade bunk on one wall, a trunk at its base, and a commode. Everything, including the twelve square panes of glass at the cabin's front, was grimy with dust. With a gruff command to make herself comfortable, she was left alone. When the door was locked behind her, Rae sank to the floor and wept.

Rae tallied the days that passed by scoring the head of the bunk with her thumbnail. The ship's relentless rolling beneath her feet was a constant reminder that her fate remained unchanged. Of Jericho she knew next to nothing. Her captor spoke little, except to hurl ugly, hateful taunts at her. Rae ignored him because she knew her apparent unconcern frustrated him.

Sam Judge left her alone almost immediately upon rising each dawn. He would roll up the hammock he had anchored to the cabin walls and toss it into the trunk. She rarely saw him again until late at night when he pulled it out and strung it up. By then she was well under the covers, dressed in a woolen nightshirt he had thrown in her direction the very first evening. Rae did not fully understand what kept Sam Judge from her bed, but she was grateful for it. She even became used to the gravelly snore that meant he was deeply asleep.

She cleaned and tidied the cabin daily, as if the routine gave her purpose. Mindful that she must not allow herself to become weakened during her confinement, Rae ate the two meals brought to her each day and paced the cabin for hours on end. Once a week a tub filled with seawater was dragged into her room, and she was permitted to bathe and wash her hair. Mostly she thought she would go mad for want of the fresh air and sunshine that was not filtered through water-stained glass.

In the main, her meals were brought to Rae by men who treated her with a modicum of respect. There were those occasional comments about envying their leader his good fortune, and Rae did nothing to disavow them of their notion. If sharing Sam Judge's cabin protected her in some manner from the others, then she was not going to do anything to lift the scales from their eyes.

She wondered about her family, and once found the temerity to tell Sam Judge that the McClellans were probably in pursuit of his ship. That was when she discovered what had happened to Jericho's cape, and that her family no doubt thought they were drowned. It was not sympathy for her grief that drove Judge from the cabin that evening, but the fact that Rae's hiccuping sobs made it impossible for him to sleep. The following day he told her that if she disturbed him likewise again he'd introduce her husband to the cat. She never cried after that.

Jericho found it as difficult as Rae to obey Judge's petty dictates, but he never openly expressed his belligerence. He went about his work without speaking, his thoughts filled continuously with Rae and escape. He came to realize that many of the men who held them had been made desperate by the poverty the war had visited upon them. They had become privateers in hopes of recouping their losses and clung to Judge's belief that in Ashley McClellan they had at last found their fortune. Jericho knew they were beyond reason. Those who had never been driven by poverty were motivated by greed. They had stepped outside the law once too often to think it had any power over them.

In the beginning there were taunts about Jericho's inability to protect his wife from Sam Judge, but he pretended he didn't hear. When the men had a lottery to see who would claim Rahab if Judge tired of her, Jericho cast his own name into the pot and walked away. No one knew quite what to make of that, and the ribald comments ceased within his hearing not long after. Jericho worked tirelessly, could not be drawn into a fight, and eventually commanded the grudging respect of some of the crew for his skill at having bested them at their game. If circumstances had been different, some said, he would have been welcomed aboard as a partner rather than a prisoner. Jericho did not find their speculation amusing, for he always felt himself within a hair's breadth of killing any one of their number. But thinking of Rae, he always refrained.

So thirty-six days passed, most of them uneventful. It was on the thirty-seventh day, when Jericho looked down from his perch on the mainmast yardarm and saw Rahab being dragged onto the deck, her wrists bound tightly behind her, that he doubted he could control himself any longer.

Chapter 9

Rae stumbled as she was forced on deck. The sunlight blinded her, but she could not shield her eyes, and strands of her loose hair were whipped carelessly about her face in the salty breeze. She licked her dry lips and fought down a scream as Wendell grabbed her roughly from behind.

She struggled uselessly in his iron grasp, looking about wildly for Jericho. In the moment before Wendell jerked her head around she thought she spied Jericho's bright yellow hair high above her. The thought of him on the slick rigging made her feel sick at her stomach. She had always tried *not* to imagine what sort of work he did for Sam Judge. "Take your hands off me," she gritted. "Or I swear I'll do more than scratch your face."

For the first time since she had come topside, the crew looked away from her and took note of Wendell's bloody jaw and neck. Four neat parallel scratches marked his ruddy complexion and disappeared into his neck cloth.

Sam Judge motioned to two men. "Miller. Davis. Take her. Hank, take Wendell and put him at the mast. Get the cat."

Judge was quickly obeyed. Rae was pulled away from Wendell, and each of her arms was locked securely in the hold of Miller and Davis. Startled by Judge's command, she watched in confusion as Wendell was bound to the mast, and out of the corner of her eye she saw Jericho descending like lightning toward her.

Jericho nearly flew down the rigging and leaped to the deck, landing lightly on his feet and startling the men around him. He broke through the gathering and strode over to where Rae was being held.

God, it had been too long. It took all his willpower to keep from taking her in his arms. "Have you been harmed?" he asked tersely, his eyes hungrily running over Rae's unnaturally pale face. Her dark eyes seemed too large, almost bruised with violet shadows beneath her lower lashes. Her hair was darker than he remembered, without the flash of fire in it, and it blew about the slender stem of her neck and across her eyes. He wanted to touch the tips of his fingers to her cheek and ask where her freckles had gone. Even winter's cold sunlight was better than none at all, and he knew that of the two of them, he was the more fortunate.

Rae found herself leaning forward, a posture that clearly spoke of her desire to be held in familiar arms. She was pulled back abruptly. "No," she said, tossing back her head so that her hair fell away from her eyes. "I haven't been harmed. Wendell tried to—to—"

Judge interrupted her. "Wendell thought your wife was hungry for somethin' besides her mornin' meal," he said bluntly. " 'Course, he tells the story a bit differently. I heard her screaming like a banshee and interrupted them. Wendell will be punished for it."

"Then why are my wife's wrists bound?"

"Because she was going to scratch his eyes out. Then mine."

He put his index finger in the neck of his shirt and drew it down, revealing several bloody tracks like those Wendell sported. "Didn't Sam Judge say her spunk would be trouble? Only a matter of time. Said it, didn't I?"

Jericho nodded wearily. "Let her go. She's not going to attack anyone now."

Judge ignored him and motioned to Hank, who was standing at Wendell's back with the whip. "Give him ten. Eyes front! Everyone! The next man who forgets that the wench here is in my care until her uncle pays will get thirty! Begin!"

Jericho turned around to watch the flogging and used his body to block Rae's view. Wendell's broad back had been bared, and the cat whispered cruelly in the air before it marked his flesh. The leather thongs were dipped in a bucket of salt water before each stroke, making every cut sting painfully while preventing infection. A pattern of thin crimson lines emerged on Wendell's white back, crisscrossing as Hank swung the whip from two angles. After six strokes Wendell cried out, a tortured rasping sound that raised the flesh on Rae's arms. At eight strokes he screamed once, then was strangely silent for the last two strikes, except for a pathetic whimper. Though it seemed an eternity to those watching, the punishment did not last above five minutes.

Sam Judge gave the next order. "Cut him down and give him the whip. McClellan, take his place."

Jericho was the only man aboard not surprised by the command. He had known as soon as he saw the scratches on Sam Judge that he would be expected to take Rae's place beneath the cat. Jericho also understood that his punishment was in part a payment for Sam's keeping Rae in his protection. Jericho had never had any illusions that eventually he would have to pay for knowing Sam's secret.

"Twenty strokes, Wendell," Sam said, as Jericho stripped off his shirt.

Rae screamed at Sam Judge. "No! He didn't do anything!"

"But you did," was the calm reply. "You attacked me and one of my men."

"I was defending myself!"

"Wendell says you bargained with your body for the opportunity to be let out of the cabin, then turned on him."

"That's a lie! A lie! You heard me! I wanted nothing from him." She kicked at the men on either side of her, trying to escape them. They might have been bronze bookends for all the good it did her. "I didn't mean to hurt you, I went a little mad! Please let him go!"

Sam Judge looked at Rae impassively. "Twenty-one."

"What? Oh, no!" Tears glistened in her eyes and dampened her lashes. "Don't do this."

"Twenty-two."

Rae quieted, hating herself for begging and only bringing more grief to Jericho. She bit back a sob.

Jericho tossed his shirt at one of the men. "She doesn't need to see this," he told Sam. "You've made your point."

"Twenty-three. And she stays right here."

Jericho heard Rae breathe in sharply as she struggled for control. Without looking back he walked to the mast, slick with Wendell's sweat, and allowed himself to be bound.

"Do you want a gag?" Hank asked.

Jericho nodded and clamped his teeth around the wadded cloth Hank shoved in his mouth. Not for anything did he want Rae to hear him scream. He turned his face toward her to show her he could bear it, and because she was his strength. Her eyes were sad, haunted, and her bottom lip was slightly red and swollen because she had bitten it hard to keep from crying out to him.

"Begin!"

Wendell snapped the cat across Jericho's back viciously. His own condition was not so weak that he could not ply the whip with the devastating force of bitter revenge. Because Jericho's gag kept him from shouting his pain, Wendell flayed him all the harder.

Rae's face blurred as Jericho's eyes watered. Don't let me cry, he begged silently. His legs shook under the force of each blow after ten, and at fifteen he thought his knees would buckle. Blood trickled down his back. He glanced at the bucket where Wendell was dipping the cat and saw the water had turned a reddish hue. Jericho's knuckles whitened as they pulled on the ropes that bound him to the mast. At twenty he tasted blood in his mouth where he had bitten his tongue in spite of the gag. At twenty-two he saw Rae leaning forward again, and a nod from Sam Judge to release her.

Immediately after the last stroke fell he was cut down and Rae was there to support him, lending her shoulders to his arm. Jericho threw the gag in the bucket and held Rahab in an embrace that was not as strong as he would have wished.

"Touchin', ain't it?" Sam Judge asked scornfully. "Everyone back to work. Miller. Take the missus below. You can loose her wrists once she's in the cabin. I think she's sheathed her claws."

Rae left Jericho's arm reluctantly, but she did not move far. Miller hovered at her side. "Will you be all right?" she whispered.

He nodded. "You?"

"Yes. I . . . I won't do anything again. I promise. No matter what happens."

"Don't say that. This is not your fault, Red. You keep on giving anyone who bothers you hell. I can bear it."

But she couldn't. Not after what she had just witnessed. Rae gave him a watery smile that did not reach her eyes and left with Miller before she embarrassed them both with her tears.

Rahab was repairing the hem of her skirt when a scuffle in the companionway alerted her to some trouble outside her door.

Before she could rise from the bunk the door was flung open and Jericho was pushed inside. Then the door was shut and locked again. There was pounding on the other side, and Rae looked at Jericho in question.

"They're fixing some bolts to the door. Sam's orders. You and I are to remain here until Nigel pays the ransom."

"We're in London, then?" she asked in a flat voice.

"No. The coast. Flying a Dutch flag. We arrived sometime last night. Sam's got us neatly hidden in a smugglers' cove, and as long as the smugglers don't object, the ship is safe from the authorities."

A curious feeling of relief passed through Rae now that they were at their journey's end. She could no longer muster the emotion to be frightened. Six days had passed since Jericho had had his back flayed. It might well have been six months, for all that she had felt alive during that time.

Rae nodded briefly as she bent her head over her stitching. Jericho watched her for several minutes, wondering at her silence, her apathy. She had barely spared him a glance since he had come in, while his own eyes had skimmed every line of her body. He could not recall having seen her beaten before, and it was playing hell with his own confidence that they could somehow escape the ship. Her shoulders sloped forward as she worked, but the posture was more of defeat than concentration. He sat beside her, and she pricked her finger as his nearness made her flinch.

"Why do you move away from me?" he asked.

Rae sucked on the pad of her finger and shrugged, never once glancing in his direction. She made a few more careless stitches and bit off the thread, then she smoothed the skirt absently and drew it over her bare legs and ankles. She slipped the needle back into Sam Judge's minuscule sewing kit and gasped when Jericho pulled the box from her hands, flinging it across the room.

"Forget that thing!" he said roughly when she made a move to get it. "Stay here and talk to me. Look at me!"

She glared at him. "What would you have me say?"

"Tell me what's wrong. Have I grown another head? Do I smell? Have I done something to give you disgust of me?"

Rahab shook her head.

"Then what's wrong? I thought it a great piece of luck that Judge consigned me here rather than in the hold."

"Don't you see? If he put you in here, it only means that he knows escape is hopeless."

"What I see is that sharing this cabin with him has made you as foolish as he. How can you be the same woman who faced a redcoat with naught but a dagger and cloak of courage?"

"I don't remember that woman, Jericho," she sighed. "Perhaps I am not meant to. That I could kill a man has never seemed real to me."

Jericho took Rae by the shoulders and gave her a light shake. "Killing him was an accident, but facing him was something else again. Now you are not even alone, and you have given in. Is this what fear has done to you?"

"I'm not afraid," she said sincerely. "I am weary of it all. I want to go to sleep and never wake up." Her eyes searched his face. "They'll kill you, you know. If the duke doesn't pay, and we know he won't, they'll kill you and rape me. Sam told me. He said he would watch and make certain I lived while they used me. I want to die before then."

Jericho's head reeled at her words. "When did he tell you this?" he demanded harshly.

Rae looked confused. "When? Why he has told me from the very first. Night after night. Though I pretended not to hear, he knew that I did, and never relented."

"Bastard."

She shrugged again. "I could stand it until . . ."

"Until?"

"Until he said that you told the others you despised me for

causing your punishment. You told them after I was returned to the cabin that I should have let Wendell have me. After all, I never fussed about Sam taking me. But Sam never touched me. I thought you knew that. So why did you say those things?''

''I never did. Oh, Red. Don't you see, Sam used your own guilt to cloud your reason? I never blamed you for the lashes Judge delivered. You did that to yourself. Sam saw an opening and drove in a wedge before you knew what happened. He's been torturing you for weeks, trying to break you as if you were some damned spirited filly. Has he succeeded, Red? Has he?''

''I don't know.''

It was not the response Jericho wanted to hear. ''Maybe this will help you make up your mind.'' He let go of her shoulders, jerked off his boots, and reached deep inside them. From one he extracted a knife and held up the tarnished blade for her inspection. ''I've been carrying this piece around for nearly a sennight now, and I have the blisters to prove it.'' He tossed it on her lap and pulled out another dagger, this one of wood. ''I used the first to whittle this one. No soft pine here, but hard wood, varnished, and stiletto sharp. No one but you knows I have them.''

''But . . . how?''

''Didn't I say I was a good thief? And I know more tricks with a piece of good wood than making a child's whistle for your niece. Do you see that I've never given up hope that we'll be free of this place, Red?'' He took the dagger from her lap where she was fingering it lightly. In a lightninglike flash of movement, which Rae had come to expect of Jericho, but to which she would never become accustomed, she found herself flat on her back on the bunk with the sharp tips of both daggers pressing against the vulnerable column of her neck. One of Jericho's legs held her thighs immobile, and her hands had somehow been trapped beneath her back.

Jericho felt Rae's heart fluttering wildly in her breast, and it gave him hope that she was not so ready to die as she had said. "Listen to me carefully, Red. This is no game I'm playing. If you want to die, I'll kill you myself rather than let Sam's men have you. You can choose which hand does the deed. Left holds the wooden dagger. Right, the steel one. Your neck won't know the difference, and though you don't recall, I told you once before, when I held you thusly in Wolfe's, that I am adept with either hand. It will be as painless as death can be under any circumstances. But do not think I shall be quick to join you. I value life more dearly than you do. After I dispatch you as per your request, I am going to use these tools to loosen the window frames. I am going to punch them out and lower myself over the side. God only knows how I'm going to get ashore, because I can't swim; I was rather counting on you to help, but if you're dead . . ."

A series of emotions flitted across Rae's face as Jericho spoke to her: anger, hurt, fear, and hatred. But in the end a faint smile tugged at the corners of her mouth, and she said the first thing that came to her mind. "I didn't know you couldn't swim."

"Not one stroke."

"That means you would drown."

"Probably."

"You need me, then."

Jericho slid the daggers beneath the bolster at Rae's head. "I shall always need you." His head lowered and his mouth closed over hers hungrily. There was a punishment for her in his brutal kiss as well as raw need, and Rae felt anger and desire warring within him. His mouth savaged hers, but Rae had no fear that his intention was anything other than to show how much he loved her. She matched the grinding pressure, arching into him and freeing her hands. They closed around his back, and through his thin shirt she could feel the rough edge of his healing wounds. Her fingers hesitated.

"Go ahead," he said hoarsely. "Touch them. They no longer

hurt. It always looks worse than it feels—except when they're being laid. That hurts like hell.''

She remembered only too well. Her palms ran across his back in a soft caress. ''I'm so sorry,'' she whispered against his mouth. ''So sorry that I believed the things Judge told me. I don't want to die.''

His kiss was gentle this time, infinitely loving, deeply caring. He tasted blood on her inner lip. ''God, I hurt you.''

Rae touched a finger to his mouth, and there was a smile in her dark eyes. ''A rather late show of remorse in someone who was holding two daggers to my throat a few minutes ago. Would you have killed me?''

''Men have begged me to kill them when they lay dying on the battlefield, Red. I couldn't then, not even when there was nothing but certain death facing them. I couldn't have taken your life when there is still so much that we don't know about our future.''

''You were terribly convincing.''

''I was meant to be convincing. Kiss me.''

''Shouldn't we be prying away the windows?''

''In the middle of the morning?'' he asked innocently, as if the thought had never occurred to him. ''Someone's liable to see us leave. We have to wait for night. Now kiss me.''

''In the middle of the morning? Someone's liable to—''

''There's a bolt on this side of the door also. I'm certain Sam must have used it before.'' She nodded that he had. ''Well, I closed it. It's been forty-two days by my reckoning since we made love.''

· Rae glanced overhead at the thumbnail scoring on the bunk frame. ''Forty-three.''

''Shut up, Red,'' he said huskily.

Rae's hands touched the taut planes of Jericho's cheeks and drew his face close to hers. She tilted her head but a few degrees to bring her lips to his. So sweet, she thought. Her tongue whispered across his parted lips, skimmed his teeth, then took pleasure in the heady taste of his full kiss.

Rae wondered if they dared remove their clothes. She wanted the freedom of touching Jericho's tautly muscled flesh unhampered by their garments. It was not enough to slip her fingers beneath his shirt. The soft linen trapped her hands, teasing the fingers that caught in the folds. Did he suspect that she wanted his naked arms to enfold her or that she desired the warm dampness of his mouth on her breasts?

The feel of Jericho's warm breath on the whorl of her ear sent sparks of delicious heat down her back. As if he knew she was burning, he touched his tongue to her lobe. The act was deceiving, for rather than tamping the heat, it fanned the flames. Then his teeth gingerly nipped her, and sparks of fire and ice shot through her again. She made a soft sound of pleasure and wanting against the throbbing cord in his neck. She heard its echo in her ear and felt it in the tightening of his fingers in her hair.

"Your hair is darker," he said, pressing a kiss in the soft mahogany strands.

She touched her hair self-consciously, thinking he did not find it attractive. "Is it?" she asked uncertainly.

"Red," he chastised gently. "It was only an observation, not a criticism."

"Oh." Embarrassed, her hand fluttered to Jericho's shoulder. "I've never liked the way I look," she admitted a trifle breathlessly. Jericho was kissing her brow and the baby-fine hair at her temples.

"Why?" He shifted, propping himself on one elbow to study her face.

"I suppose because I always wanted to look like my sister."

"Leah? Too pale."

"Then Salem brought Ashley home, and I thought she was everything that was beautiful."

"Too dark."

Rahab raised a skeptical eyebrow. "You're a sweet liar."

"I'm not. From almost the beginning I thought you were a sassy-looking wench. You held my interest even when I railed against it. I like everything I see. Your eyes." He bent down and touched his lips to her lids, closing her amused and sparkling eyes. "Your nose." She smiled faintly as he kissed its tip. "Chin. Not too bony. Don't think I'd like a bony chin." He saw it was trembling suspiciously as she tried to suppress her laughter. "Your neck. I like your neck. No. I love your neck. It's so achingly fragile, so smooth, like lily petals. And it tastes better than your mother's ginger snaps."

"Praise indeed," she said dryly. "Since I saw you eat above a dozen of them one evening." Then her laughter bubbled to the surface as Jericho buried his face against the column of her throat, nuzzling her like a kitten. Make that a tomcat, she amended. "That tickles."

Jericho was unperturbed. Her laughter was like innocence, and she made him feel pure and unsullied, as if nothing painful had ever happened to him. "That sound is precious. I think it must spice your lips, because they're nearly as tasty as your throat." He silenced her protest easily by teasing the corners of her mouth. "But, Red . . ."

"Mmmm?"

"I miss your freckles like hell."

"Beast."

"I mean it. Someday you and I are going to find a sylvan spot by a glassy little pond. You'll give me a swimming lesson, and afterwards we'll dry on the bank wearing nothing but sunshine, and I'll kiss every freckle as it appears."

"But, Jericho. I would get them all over."

He continued to look at her straight-faced; then his lazy libertine smile asserted itself. "I hope so, Red. Lord, do I hope so!"

Rahab hugged him. "Don't ever stop loving me, Jericho Smith."

"Couldn't."

She believed him. He had struggled with his feelings for too long to have them be transient. She tugged at his shirt. "Let's take this off."

Jericho obliged; then, without waiting for her encouragement, he took off his stockings and breeches. Rae stole little glances at him while she removed her own clothes, fascinated by the lithe strength of his body. He was sitting on the edge of the bunk, and when his breeches joined the pile of their discarded clothes, Rae sat up on her knees, slightly behind him, and drew her arms about his chest. The curve of her cheek rested against his shoulder blade, and she could hear the thudding of his heart as her hands explored the smooth planes of his chest and abdomen. When her hands teased the length of his thighs and discovered how ready he was for her she smiled a little wickedly and whispered something brazen in his ear.

Jericho blinked, not believing what he heard. He grabbed her wrists and twisted in her embrace, bearing her down to the mattress. His laughter rumbled deep in his chest when he saw she was red to the roots of her hair, embarrassed by her own temerity. "Say that to my face. Never mind. Show me."

She did. As the color receded from Rae's face, Jericho allowed her to roll him over and pin him to the rumpled sheets. Her hands and mouth explored his body, intrigued by the male scent of him. She aroused his nipples with the tip of her tongue and slid her body along his length, pressing her swollen breasts to flesh that seemed unyielding but that would ripple suddenly when she found a particularly sensitive spot.

Rae's hands slipped over his sleek skin. Her lips followed, seeking his arousal, taunting him as no woman ever had. Rae's confidence swelled as Jericho sucked in his breath as she pleasured him. Her nails lightly scored the tight backs of his thighs; his buttocks. Her hair fell like a dark, secretive veil about her face. The soft ends curled, light and airy against his flesh, alluring and tempting.

"Red . . ." There was a warning in Jericho's tone, a gritty signal that said his control was precarious at best. His eyes were almost black as she lifted her head. "Come here."

Rae reveled in the sound, the watchfulness of his obsidian gaze, her own heart beating arhythmically in response. "But—"

"Here." His finger tapped his mouth.

Rae abandoned her posture and fell gladly into his outstretched arms, greedily taking the loving, hungry kiss he offered. Jericho's calloused fingers traced her shoulders and the tender skin of her inner arm and drew a spiral path that ended at the hardened tips of her coral nipples. She blossomed beneath his careful nurturing, filling his palms and later his mouth. Jericho's knee nudged her thighs apart and she yielded, her dark eyes brilliant as she anticipated where his hand would fall. He brushed the silky curve of her mound, fingers dipping, stroking the moist source of her pleasure.

Jericho watched in fascination as Rae's head fell back, her throat arching. Her mouth parted briefly on a tight little sound that was at once a release and an indrawing of air. Her legs tangled in his. The heel of her foot nudged the back of Jericho's leg. There was a pause in the sinuous movement as she accepted his entry, adjusting to his deep thrust and responding to his rhythm. Words of wanting caught in her throat, but Jericho saw and urged her to speak them. She buried her face in his shoulder and whispered on a ragged thread of sound that she loved him, loved his loving, loved the way he filled her and felt inside her.

Her words sent them both over the edge. Tension that had pulled them as taut as wind-filled sails gave way, shuddered its release, and left them feeling as if they had survived a tempest's fury. Their breathing slowed, and their perspiring bodies exchanged a warm, damp heat while they listened to the sound of their hearts finding a normal rhythm. The ship rocked listlessly in the smugglers' cove, and briefly they felt like babes in a cradle.

There was nothing either wanted to say that was not communicated by the closeness of their bodies, the gentle touch of his hand on her shoulder, his head at her breast, her fingers in his yellow hair. Reluctantly Jericho left Rae's side, placing a promising kiss on her lips. He dressed in silence by the edge of the bunk, then helped Rae with her clothes and fasteners. Rae smoothed the blankets and sat down again, but Jericho sat on the floor at her feet and rested his back against her legs.

"Do you really have a plan?" she asked.

"Of sorts," he replied honestly. "I meant what I said about going through the glass and over the side. The shore is not so far, and the cove seems to have quiet water. If you can help me reach safe ground, then we only have to find a hiding place until Judge gives up on us. London is a few days' hard walking from here, but we could lose ourselves in that town. We'll send for Salem to come for you."

Rae calculated the amount of time that would pass before her family received the message and the time it would take for the *Lydia* to reach London. "It will be almost three months before anyone arrives. How will we live?"

"I'll find employment. Don't worry, we won't starve."

Rae said nothing. In truth, she found it difficult not to worry because Jericho's plan did little to ease her mind. It was too simple for her to put much faith in. "Has Sam sent word to the duke?"

"Two men left a few minutes before I was brought down here. There should be news of his decision by tomorrow morning. You and I will be gone by then. We'll never know if Nigel agrees to pay the ransom."

Rahab hoped Jericho was right. She stroked the back of his head, deep in her own thoughts of what their future contained. "Jericho?"

"Hmmm?"

"I don't want you to think ill of me for suggesting this when it seems the world is tumbling in upon us, but if we arrive safely in London, do you suppose we might be married?" She rushed on as she felt the cords in his neck stiffen. "I know it sounds a foolish request, but I can't like the idea of living as husband and wife while we wait for Salem. It is no good saying that what happened this morning won't happen again, because I know it will. I want it to, and you know how determined I can be about some things. But if we continue to love each other there is the chance that I will soon be with child, and I haven't forgotten what you said about bastards. I should love above almost all things to have your child, Jericho, but I would have us marry." Having presented her case, she came to a breathless halt.

"Are you quite through?"

She nodded, biting her lower lip.

"I wish you would not steal my thunder, but I suppose you can't help yourself. I was going to wait until we were on the road to London. Will you marry me, Red?" Shock kept her silent, and Jericho twisted his head to look up at her. "Am I to take the gaping posture of your mouth as your assent or as an indication that you wish to be fed?"

Rae's mouth closed abruptly and one tiny sound emerged. "Wretch."

"That is hardly an answer."

"Yes! Yes! I'll marry you." Her arms circled his neck from behind and she nearly choked him in her enthusiasm.

Jericho accepted her embrace, then drew her down to his lap. They sat in contented silence for a very long time, just holding each other, Rae's head resting on his shoulder, and if their clasp was perhaps a little desperate, the expressions on their faces were serene.

Jericho smiled to himself when he realized she had fallen asleep. He liked the idea that she had found peace and comfort in the shelter of his arms. Her face was thinner than he remembered, her lashes like dark smudges against pale cheeks. She looked too fragile to have held him so tightly such a short time ago, and it occurred to him that perhaps his need for her had blinded him to her exhaustion. It was apparent to him now that she had not eaten adequately nor slept decently for days.

"I'm going to care for you from now on." Love welled in him as he touched his lips to her hair, and the depth of his emotion struck him as a fine and wondrous thing. "This is forever, Red," he whispered. "Forever."

It took some careful maneuvering to get Rae onto the bunk again, but Jericho managed the thing without waking her. After he covered her with a blanket he took the steel dagger from beneath the bolster and began to examine the wooden window frames to see if his spontaneous idea could be turned into a reality. The blade slid along the edge of the glass and he noted with a large measure of satisfaction that loosening the frames and removing the panes would be a simple task. Certainly it was less noisy than knocking them out, and the frames themselves could be dismantled easily. He rifled the chest at the foot of the bunk and found enough materials to make a rope of sorts that would see them safely to the water. Getting out of the cabin was the least of their problems, he thought. Getting to the shore was another matter entirely, and in truth, it frightened him. He glanced at Rae's heavy skirt and tried to imagine how she would keep herself afloat while helping him. There was nothing for it but that she leave her heavy articles of clothing behind. He did not know if they could survive the frigid temperatures of the water or if they could survive on land without adequate protection, but he doubted they could survive at all on board Judge's ship.

At dusk Wendell brought their dinner. Rae blinked sleepily, waking when she heard the harsh scrape of the bolts being released. Wendell kicked the door viciously, waiting for Jericho to unlock the door from the inside. When it was done Jericho went to Rae's side, lending her his support as she sat up and looked warily at Wendell. In the unguarded moment between sleep and wakefulness he saw how frightened she was, and he longed to slip his dagger between Wendell's ribs.

Wendell sneered at the menace in Jericho's eyes and set the tray on the floor. Straightening, he said, "Sam says to eat hearty."

"What is the word from the duke?"

"None yet. Don't expect to hear afore morning. Getting a might anxious, are we?"

Jericho did not deign to reply. He picked up the tray and placed it on his lap, ignoring Wendell completely while pretending interest in the dinner. Sam apparently was in a celebrating frame of mind, for their meal included fresh chicken, biscuits with gravy, and wine. No doubt Sam anticipated that Nigel Lynne would agree to the ransom demands. Jericho lost his appetite even as the odor of the warm food reached his nostrils. He knew it for what it most likely was: his last meal.

Wendell saw that Jericho could not be provoked, and Rae avoided his taunting, superior look. Muttering an oath, he left the cabin and threw the bolts with more force than was necessary.

"I hate that man," Rae said after his retreating steps could be heard in the companionway. She yawned and stretched her arms and back. "I'm sorry I slept so long. I can't imagine why."

"That's not so difficult to understand," Jericho said, forcing a smile for her benefit. "You're exhausted. And it would please me greatly if you ate. You'll need your strength if you're to drag me to shore."

One brow kicked up as Rae reached for a chicken leg. "Not one stroke?"

"Not one. I haven't the slightest idea how to go about staying afloat."

"Your very proper education had a regrettable lapse, it seems. I learned to swim nearly as soon as I learned to walk.

Papa was afraid one of us would wander into the river, and he taught us each in turn. You'll be pleased to know I'm a strong swimmer, at least as good as my brothers. Aren't you going to eat?''

He shook his head, his stomach churning. "I'm afraid I'll sink," he said lightly.

Rae licked her fingers and dabbed at the gravy with the hard biscuit. "You won't. Lock the door and take off your breeches." She took the tray and set it on her lap.

Jericho blinked owlishly. "Red, I don't think this is—"

"Oh, piffle. Your mind shows a singular lack of imagination. I wasn't referring to that."

"Remind me to expand your vocabulary," he said dryly, rising to his feet. "There are other words for *that.*" He pushed the bolt and took off his breeches. He looked at them and her in bewilderment. "Now what?"

Rae giggled at his expression, then took a quick gulp of wine to school her features. "I'm going to teach you a trick that Papa showed us. Make a knot in each leg of your breeches. Go on. I've not gone daft." She sipped on her wine, not caring for its peculiar bitterness, but too thirsty to complain. She'd never had wine from a tin cup before, and a dirty one at that. Jericho held up the breeches for her inspection. "That's good. Now fill them with air."

"And how should I do that?" he demanded.

"Gather the waistband close, put it to your mouth, and blow."

"Red . . ."

"Do it."

Jericho did and was visibly surprised when the breeches ballooned a little, holding the trapped air. As soon as he quit blowing, they sagged.

"You've got to hold the waistband tightly once they're filled with air," she told him. "Do you want your wine? I've an uncommon thirst."

"No, you drink it. But what is this in aid of?"

"To help you float, silly. I admit it works better in the water, but you'll see that for yourself. You can rest one of your arms between the legs while keeping the waist closed, and the air inside will keep you afloat."

Jericho looked at the limp breeches skeptically. "Why am I not confident this can work?" he asked conversationally.

"It will work. I promise. I'll be holding you anyway, but this will make you a little lighter in the water and easier for me to pull. And if I should lose my grasp on you, you won't sink while I'm trying to recover it."

"Perhaps we could simply fight our way off this ship," he suggested. "At least there would be some dignity in that."

"I doubt there is any dignity in dying that way," she said tartly. "If you remember to keep air in your chest, you'll float well enough without me. When you go under water, don't panic. You'll rise enough to snatch another big breath. Let the tide take you in."

"There are rocks before we get to shore."

Rae covered her mouth to stifle a yawn. "I suppose I've not yet awakened," she apologized. She finished Jericho's wine, hoping the bracing bite of the spirits would rouse her. "You said something about rocks?"

"Yes. There are rocks before we get to shore."

"Then I suppose we may get batted about a bit. . . ." She laughed. "Try saying that. Batted about a bit— batted abou—" Rae put a hand to her head. "I'm sorry. I don't know what's . . . I feel so dizzy of a sudden." The tray on her lap slid to the floor before she could catch it. The noise of it clattering to the deck seemed uncommonly loud to her ears.

Jericho snatched the cup of wine from Rae's hand and sniffed it suspiciously. The faint odor in the cup confirmed his thoughts. "The bastards," he cursed, tossing the cup aside. He took Rae by the shoulders and gave her a shake. Her head wobbled loosely and her eyes were unfocused.

"Jericho? Waass wrong wif me?" she slurred. "So tired."

"You've been drugged," he said tersely.

For a brief moment she was alert to this dangerous complication. "You muss go. Leave here."

"I'm not leaving you."

"You musses. Promise me. You can get help." Her voice trailed off to a whisper.

He didn't want to hear what she was saying. "C'mon, Red. You've got to stay awake."

"Can't." Her heavy lids closed, and if he hadn't been supporting her she would have dropped back to the mattress.

"You have to." He knew she could not hear him, for she had gone completely limp in his arms. Her head lolled unsteadily on his shoulder. Perhaps if she had not finished both cups of wine he could have kept her awake, but the double dose defeated him. He realized they were both meant to be drowsy now, harmless and impotent. Sam Judge was not taking any chances that they would get away from him.

Jericho laid Rahab down, then sat for several minutes with his elbows on his knees, head in his hands. She had told him to leave, but he didn't know if he could do that. What if he couldn't get to shore, to say nothing of finding help? Who had she thought he could summon? But if he did not make the attempt, what could he do for her here? With the answer to his last question thundering through his head, Jericho moved to the chest and began pulling out the items that would make his safety line to the water. Damn, but he hoped Rae was right about his breeches holding him up.

Nigel Lynne, Duke of Linfield, was unamused by the scratching at his library door. His coffee-colored eyes narrowed on the cards in his hand and his finely molded mouth thinned. Without glancing at the door or his three companions, he bid the servant enter.

"What is it, Stephens?" he asked coldly when the head of the household staff showed his grave face.

"Begging your pardon, your grace," Stephens said stiffly, not flinching in the face of the duke's displeasure. He was used to his employer's remote and chilly countenance. "There are two men here to see you."

"It may have escaped your attention, but there are three men seeing me now." His companions chuckled, and the duke smiled wryly. He snapped a card on the table. "I believe this is mine," he said, gathering the trick. "Afraid you're going to lose the wager, Lesley."

Lord Lesley merely smiled and helped himself to another glass of scotch from the decanter at his side. He lifted the glass to his lips in a mocking salute to the duke's astonishing run of luck. "It's only some blunt."

"Yes, but I've got prime bay mare riding on this," Charles Newbrough put in. His nostrils flared suddenly as his face became troubled, and his nose looked even more hawkish than usual.

"You should know better than to wager horseflesh when dealing with Nigel," Lord Evans said calmly, laying out his next card. "It brings out his acquisitive nature. Ain't that right, Nigel?"

"Quite," the duke agreed. He frowned. "Was there something else, Stephens? I thought you knew a dismissal when you heard it."

Stephens coughed. "These men say it's important business, your grace. They refuse to leave until they speak to you."

"Who are they?" Nigel drawled in bored accents, watching the play on the table carefully.

"They are called Davis and Miller. They appear to be colonials."

"I think they're calling themselves Americans now," Newbrough said, pulling at the teal-blue sleeve of his velvet jacket. "Unkempt lot, all of them."

"Keep that card in there, Richard," Nigel said pleasantly, "or I'll have three witnesses as to why I put a ball through your chest." He turned to his manservant. "Have they stated their business?"

"Something to do with a Mr. Harrity, your grace. They said you would know what they meant."

"Indeed, I do. Show them in." He tossed his last three cards on the table, faceup.

"Here, what's this?" Newbrough demanded, blanching when he saw the cards were winners. "You've got to play them out."

"Never mind the wager," Nigel said sharply. "Your stud at Stanhope is safe for the time being. I'll forfeit."

"Oh. Well, that's all right then."

"I thought it might be."

Lesley and Evans were more interested in the cause of Nigel's forfeit than they were in their funds. The faintly bored look in their eyes had vanished as their curiosity was piqued. Both men were in their early thirties, nearly a decade younger than Nigel Lynne, but they had gambled, wenched, and drunk with the duke for more years than they had not and couldn't remember when he had ever let business interfere with his pleasures.

"Who are these men?" Evans asked, pouring a drink for himself. "And who is Harrity?"

Lesley stroked his fair face thoughtfully. "Yes, Nigel. Do give over. What dealings do you have with American rabble?"

Nigel leaned back in his chair. "Harrity is the man I hired to bring back my errant ward." No one, not even his closest friends, knew that Ashley Lynne was his niece. The duke himself did not accept the blood tie and had chosen to raise her as a distant illegitimate relative. He did not want anyone to know that his beloved twin sister, who had died birthing Ashley, had had an affair with a man so far below her station. Even now, more than twenty years after the fact, the thought of his sister's defiance in light of his wishes to see her contract a suitable marriage had the ability to enrage him. Only a certain whiteness about his mouth gave away his feelings, and it vanished quickly.

"Your ward?" Newbrough asked, gathering the cards and shuffling them negligently. "You mean the chit you were going to marry off to old Bosworth? Seems I remember an invitation to the wedding. Sorry business, that. Pretty thing, as I recall. Never much for joining your romps here at Linfield, though."

A muscle jumped in the duke's hollow cheek. "Indeed," he said, calmly enough. "She took it into her head that Bosworth was too old for her."

Lesley chuckled. "She may have been in the right of it there, Nigel. Bosworth's been dead for years, you know."

"And his estate was inherited by some third cousin," the duke reminded him. "It should have been Ashley's." Though he did not say it, each man understood that Nigel would have managed to acquire the lands for himself.

"Just so," Evans said. "She went to the colonies, isn't that right?"

"Yes. And now, with Cornwallis's surrender at—where the devil was it?"

"Yorktown," Lesley supplied.

"Yes, Yorktown. Lord North is doing everything in his power to persuade our king it's all over. If George listens it will be nothing less than a miracle. Still, I thought the time was right to bring Ashley home. I wonder what is keeping our visitors?"

"No doubt your man is bathing them first," Newbrough offered.

He was not far off the mark, because Stephens had refused entry to Davis and Miller before they made some effort at being presentable. Neither man had ever met anyone quite like the unyielding butler and found themselves tucking in their shirts, slicking back their unruly hair, and shaking off their road dust. They wished Sam Judge had come himself on this business.

They had never seen anything so imposing or forbidding as Linfield House, but then they had not yet met its owner.

"This is a private matter," Davis said, after they had been taken to the library and introduced to the duke. Hat in hand, he shifted his weight uneasily from one foot to the other. He did not expect to be listened to, and he felt a swelling of power as Nigel agreed and excused himself from his friends.

In the study Nigel turned on the two men, eyeing them with contempt. "You have news from Harrity, I believe."

Davis's chest contracted abruptly at the spearing glance the duke gave him. The only eyes he had seen that cold had belonged to a reptile. "Harrity's dead," he replied shortly.

Nigel looked thoughtful. "Then what are you about?"

Miller spoke up. "Before he died he spoke at length of his business with you."

"So?"

"We've brought Ashley Lynne to you."

Nigel appeared unmoved, but then only he could feel the pounding of his heart. "Have you?" he asked carefully.

"For a price," Davis added. He named the sum Sam had told him to demand and noted with satisfaction that the duke did not blink. Sam Judge surely was on to something this time.

"You'll forgive me if I am somewhat skeptical, shall we say, of your claim. You will have to produce my ward before I'm going to part with that much of the ready."

Davis's weight shifted again. "We don't have her here; but she's safe enough, and will remain that way if you agree to the payment."

"I see." Nigel leaned against the mantelpiece and toyed with a jade figurine. His casual air belied the alertness of his eyes. "Mayhap you will tell me how you came to have my ward."

Davis explained the attack on the *Marion* and how it had led to the abduction of the people he knew as Ashley and Salem at McClellan's Landing.

"You have Salem," he mused. "That is something I had not requested of Harrity, but certainly an unexpected . . . bonus. I won't pay anything for his safe release, you understand."

"Sam Judge didn't think you would, but he said you may be interested in his *unsafe* release, if you get my meaning. The man is her husband, after all, and liable to raise a stink about what's happened."

Nigel flicked at a loose thread on his jacket. Colonials were so crude, he thought distastefully. Savages, all of them. "Let us say I am appreciative of my ward's safe return, and to show my gratefulness I will add five hundred pounds to the sum you named. Do you take my meaning?"

Miller and Davis nodded in unison.

"Now describe my ward to me."

"Dark hair, white skin," Davis said. "Green eyes that kind of spit at you when she's riled. Which was most of the time she was on board. Tiny gal." Davis never gave a thought to the fact that all women of his acquaintance and most men were shorter than he. "Slender thing. Not much to her but spunk."

Nigel nodded. "She has a birthmark that I told Harrity to look for so there would be no mistaking her. Do you know of it?"

Davis nearly blanched. What birthmark? he wondered. Had Harrity ever said anything about it? Then he remembered what Jud had told him Sam had done when Ashley and Salem were still in the hold. "On her breast," he said with more conviction than he felt. He ignored Miller's look of surprise, concentrating on Nigel's face. Apparently he had guessed correctly. Damn Sam for not telling them. "Sam Judge made certain himself. Done it real proper, too," he added quickly, relieved when he saw the muscle in the duke's cheek relax.

"Good." He took a small key from his vest pocket and went to the desk, opened the middle drawer, and flipped a hidden spring. "In the event it should enter your mind to simply rob me, let me assure you that what I am giving you now is the limit of my resources at hand.'' He gave Miller a small pouch filled with gold sovereigns. ''This is merely a show of good-will.''

Miller opened the bag and could not keep his astonishment from showing. At his side, Davis was similarly impressed, but strove not to let it be seen.

Nigel had anticipated that they would look into the pouch and regarded them as one might a maggot. They were so far beneath him that he could not be insulted by their behavior. ''I wish to have Ashley brought here. When can it be done?''

''When can you arrange for payment?''

''Tomorrow.''

''She will be here tomorrow evening.'' Miller and Davis left the room, the gold sovereigns clinking slightly as Miller bounced the pouch in his hand.

Nigel stayed in the study until he was certain Stephens had shown them the door, then he went to join his friends. On the way he saw Stephens. ''Prepare Ashley's bedchamber. My ward is returning home tomorrow.''

''Very good, your grace.'' For a moment there was despair on his face as he wondered what manner of little cruelties the duke planned to practice on poor Miss Ashley. He glanced along the long, dark hallway, made sure no one had seen his show of concern, then went to inform the head housekeeper of the news.

Chapter 10

Rae tried to lift her head but found the simple movement more than she could manage. Her cheek lay against something cool and unyielding, and her head tapped it with painful regularity. Her lids felt heavy, much too heavy to open, and beneath them her eyes were grainy, as if filled with sand from her desert-dry mouth. Even the effort to wet her lips came to naught. Her pelisse covered her shoulders, and she wished she had the strength to pull the hood over her head to protect it from the jolting ride.

Though she found it difficult to move, her mind was oddly clear. She recognized the subdued voices around her as belonging to Sam Judge, Davis, and Wendell. She realized she was no longer on board the ship, but that she had been transferred to a carriage, and not a well-sprung conveyance, either. Each rut in the road jolted her spine and punished her pounding temples. Occasionally a soft moan escaped her lips, but no one heard, or if they heard, paid no attention.

Rae could not measure the passing of time. She had no idea

if it had been hours or days since she had last seen Jericho. In her mind she had memories, as fleeting as a firefly's light, of Jericho moving purposefully about the cabin, of him tossing something snakelike out the windows. She recalled someone shaking her, loud and angry voices demanding answers from her, but she had been unable to speak, or even make sense of their urgency.

Later there had been rough hands on her body, holding her up and forcing her to drink more bitter-tasting wine. She had spit it in someone's face. Sam's? A sharp slap to her cheek and a thumb and finger on her nose had made her take the rest of it. Her pelisse had been thrown about her shoulders, more as an afterthought, not because there had been any concern that she might freeze once she was taken outside. The bitter, bracing air had been her undoing. One deep breath and she fell limply to the deck. It was the last thing she remembered.

She tried to concentrate on the conversation around her now, but kept drifting in and out of consciousness. The little that she heard and understood made her wish she had heard nothing at all.

"You think he's dead, then?" Davis asked.

" 'Course he's dead," Sam Judge said. "Leastways for our purposes he is. And don't let on any different to that duke fellow. I aim to collect every bit of the money coming to us, so you would do well to keep your mouth shut. How far are we from Linfield?"

Davis peered out the coach window and studied the wooded landscape. "Another five miles and I reckon we'll be at the front gate."

Sam nodded, satisfied. "Tell Miller to pull this rig over."

Davis and Wendell exchanged puzzled glances.

"You don't think we was gonna march her up to the front door, do ye? Tell Miller to stop the rig. We'll leave her here, get our blunt, and escort the duke to the area. Then we're off. I'm not givin' him a chance to change his mind."

The carriage lurched to a sudden stop as Davis relayed Sam's orders. Rahab struggled listlessly as she was pulled from the coach, but the men only laughed at her poor attempts. She was as effective as a spitting kitten.

Wendell threw her over his shoulders, and Rae's empty stomach heaved at his roughness. She was carried from the edge of the road to a place several hundred feet into the woods. Sam pointed out where he wanted her and Wendell dropped her heavily to the ground. Judge unwound a length of rope he had been carrying at his waist and bound Rae's hands, then tied them to the base of a tree. Her shoulder and head rested uncomfortably against the trunk, and she shivered uncontrollably as cold air seeped through her cloak.

It was on the edge of her tongue to beg them not to leave her, but her pride and a good measure of fear asserted itself. She realized that alone she was safer than if either Wendell or Davis was made to stay with her. It was a case of better the devil you *didn't* know.

For a few minutes after the three men left the woods it seemed to Rae that the woods were eerily quiet. Then, over the chattering of her teeth, she began to hear sounds of the night animals prowling the area in search of prey. She felt her skin crawl over numb flesh. Her last thought before she slipped into oblivion was of what manner of beasts might be found in English woods.

They ran about on cloven feet, she decided, and thrashed noisily through the underbrush. Their talons were long and sharp and their breath was hot. Caught in their trap as she was, there was no place to hide, and she imagined she huddled closer to the tree for protection.

"Bring me the torch," Nigel demanded sharply of a servant. His large, powerful hand was grasping Rae's chin, forcing her face upward. Her eyes opened long enough to stare at him with fear, and then there was a clumsy rushing nearby, and finally the area was bathed in yellow light. Nigel thrust Rae's face away from him and knew a burning rage. His voice, however, caught none of the emotion coursing through him. ''This is not she. This is not my ward.'' He straightened and began walking toward the road.

The servant looked at the girl's pale face, her nearly blue lips, and her frozen posture. She could barely hold her head up and her wrists looked raw. Poor thing, he thought. If she was part of the scheme to separate the duke from his money, her friends had treated her most shabbily, and if she was innocent, then she had been treated abominably. Left in these woods, she would freeze to death. Before his courage failed him, he ran after his employer. ''Your pardon, your grace, but what's to be done with the girl?'' The torch shook slightly in his hand.

The duke never paused in his deliberate and angry stride. ''Take care of it.''

The footman stopped in his tracks as Nigel continued to where his horse was being held for him by one of the grooms. He watched the duke mount, still the horse's restless prancing, and turn it sharply toward Linfield. Slowly, mulling over the duke's curt orders, the footman retraced his steps back to Rae's side.

Nigel whipped his horse to a full gallop that never eased until he reached the Linfield stables. Grooms took care of the horse while Nigel strode to the house, his quirt beating a tattoo against his thigh. He tossed his cape at Stephens when he came through the door and went immediately to his study where he poured himself three fingers of scotch. He downed it and was pouring another when the scratching at the door distracted him. ''What is it?''

Stephens stepped inside the study. ''I've come to inquire about Miss Ashley, your grace. Is someone attending to her?''

''My ward is not coming. It was some Gypsy wench those men sought to foist on me.''

''I see.'' Stephens slipped out of the room as the duke lifted his glass.

Nigel stared broodingly at the fire laid in the hearth. His thin mouth curled derisively. Sam Judge thought to make a fool of him, but he intended to have the last laugh in the fool American's scheme. It was bound to give the man something to think about when his carriage was held up by three highwaymen and he was relieved of all the blunt and jewels he had just received. Nigel wished he could see the man's face when he returned to his ship, without anything to show for his work, and tried to explain this night's events to his crew. If his men did not accuse him of holding out on them and mutiny, the naval authorities would have Judge's ship in tow by morning. Lord Lesley had eagerly agreed to follow Miller and Davis back to their ship to find its location, and it was Evans who fancied himself a highwayman.

"Always wanted to rob a coach," he had told the others. "Must be the greatest lark. Rather like Robin Hood in this case."

Once Evans had put forth his plan, there was no keeping Lesley and Newbrough from joining. Nigel had found he rather liked the idea of getting back his ward without straining his resources. Now he was glad for their foresight. No one, certainly not a colonial savage, made a fool of the Duke of Linfield.

Laughing and good-humored voices signaled the return of the nobles-turned-highwaymen. All three men were dressed in coarse black breeches and capes they had borrowed from Nigel's servants for this occasion. Pistols were tucked neatly in their waistbands, and they wore black gloves, tricorns, and scarves over the lower halves of their faces.

Nigel's brow merely rose a notch at the peculiar picture they made as they entered his study. He could imagine all three showing up at the next masked ball in such a guise. "A successful venture?" he asked dryly, as they deposited several pouches of money and jewelry on the divan.

Lesley pulled down his scarf and sailed his hat jauntily across the room. It skidded along the smooth marble top of the mantelpiece and dropped, as if by design, on the fireplace poker. "Most successful," Lesley grinned. "May take it up as a hobby. Astonishingly good fun. They were quite put out that anyone would rob *them*. Put up some resistance, too. Messy business, that. Evans had to wound one of them before they gave over. How is your ward, Nigel? Annoying of them to leave her in the woods. We probably should have killed the lot of them. One would think they didn't trust you."

Nigel handed the decanter of spirits to Newbrough and went to stand by the mantel as his friends made themselves comfortable. "It was not my ward they had." Newbrough sputtered on the first swallow of liquor. "Not your ward? You said they described her to you. Who—"

"I have no idea," Nigel drawled. "She has only a surface resemblance to Ashley. No doubt she was part of their plan."

"Did she say so?" Evans asked.

"Think she would admit it?" Newbrough scoffed, looking down his great nose at Evans.

Lord Evans shrugged. "Nigel knows how to make a chit talk. Ain't that right, Nigel? Where is she? Bring her in and we'll discover what she knows."

"Forget the chit. She was near dead when we found her. I doubt she can speak of anything now." A hard glance at each of his friends told them what he had not said, and an uneasy silence blanketed the room.

In the kitchen of the great house there was a wealth of uneasiness, but not one moment of silence. Everyone had an opinion about what should be done with the girl the footman had brought there. Mrs. Timms, the cook, made it known that she wanted no part of the goings-on. The girl was bound to be nothing but trouble. The kitchen boys knew better than to gainsay the cook, else their ears would suffer a certain boxing. The housekeeper, who had made it her life's work never to agree with anything Mrs. Timms said, decided it was their Christian duty to see to the girl. Hadn't his grace said to take care of her? The footman coughed, but thought the wiser course was to remain silent. One of the upstairs maids sided with the housekeeper, and a kitchen servant declared her soft in the head. Sides were drawn, and the dispute was gathering alarming volume when Stephens entered and demanded to know the nature of the argument.

As the servants stepped aside, Rahab was revealed to him. She was slumped in a straight-backed chair, dangerously close to toppling forward on the table. "Who is she?" he asked, coming forward. He made as if to touch her, then drew back. There was no telling what sort of illness she might have, though she appeared to be suffering from no more than the bad effects of the cold.

"She's the one those ruffians said was Miss Ashley," the footman explained. "The duke said I should take care of her."

Stephen's wintry and disapproving expression remained unchanged, but he knew very well what it was the duke had meant. He wondered if they dared allow the chit to remain in the house. Of course, it was doubtful that the duke would ever notice her. Nigel Lynne knew only those servants who held positions of responsibility in his house, and this girl would be far beneath his inspection. The duke had called her a Gypsy, but Stephens could see this clearly was not the case. "She is nothing at all like Miss Ashley." he said, submitting Rahab to a sweeping glance.

"That's the truth," Mrs. Timms said. "And she has about as much business as that one in my kitchen. What am I supposed to do with her? She can hardly hold her head up, and she's dripping all over the floor now."

Rae's cape and clothes that had been stiff from the cold and damp ground were indeed thawing, and the ring of water at her feet was simply one more reason Mrs. Timms wanted her gone.

"Provided the girl is willing and free of disease, have you

work for her, Mrs. Ritchie?'' Stephens asked the housekeeper. He ignored the cook's disgruntled snort.

"You dismissed Betty not above a week ago,'' she reminded him. ''I've been short staffed since. Of course there's work for the lass. Nancy can train her.''

Nancy bobbed her assent, and one of the kitchen girls repeated that she had gone daft. Before there was any hair pulling, Stephens held up his hand and addressed the footman and Nancy. ''She shall have Betty's bed. You can take her there. She may have one night here. If she cannot work in the morning, then she's to go. There is not one of you with enough time to tend to a sick girl.''

Mrs. Timms gave the housekeeper a triumphant glance, for there was, in her estimation, no chance that the girl would be able to work. She was clearly in danger of expiring before the night was over. Mrs. Ritchie glared at the cook and dared her to speak her uncharitable thoughts aloud. She would have the girl polishing silver at dawn's light if she had to tie her in a chair to keep her upright.

The footman and Nancy ignored the battle of wills that raged over their heads and pulled Rahab to her feet, supporting her between them, and took leave of the kitchen.

"Did his grace really say we should take her in, Jack?'' Nancy asked as they struggled to mount the narrow, dark passageway to the servants' sleeping quarters. ''Or were you just being tenderhearted?''

Jack blushed under Nancy's gentle teasing. ''I couldn't leave her there, Nance. She was a pathetic sight, I can tell you, and his nibs didn't give her a second thought once he saw she wasn't Miss Ashley.''

"Hush, Jack. You musn't speak so. Someone might hear, and you'd be dismissed without a character. Then what would become of us?'' Her dark curls bounced saucily about her face. ''I'll not marry you if you don't have employment, for there is no life in being poor.''

Jack held his tongue, because she was right about someone's hearing them, and about the fact that there was no future for them if he was released from the duke's service. He grunted as Rahab slipped in his hold and nearly carried them all down the stairs.

"Let me put her on my shoulders." He stooped low and hefted Rae. She moaned softly.

"Have you hurt her, Jack?"

"No," he panted, taking the steps quickly.

"Well, be careful." Nancy passed him at the landing and ran ahead to open the door to the room she had shared with the unfortunate Betty. She lighted a tallow candle and turned down the covers on the thin straw-filled mattress. "Over here, Jack. Be quick. Help me get her cape off. Oooh, did you ever see such a thing?" she asked as her fingers touched the soft fur lining of the pelisse. "It's like something a grand lady would own. How do you suppose she came by it?"

Jack was not one for speculation. "Don't know," he said shortly, lowering Rahab to the mattress. "But tell her to keep it here, if she doesn't want to answer a lot of Cook's questions."

At that moment Rahab stirred. "Jack, look! She's waking up." Nancy sat beside Rae, touching the back of her hand to Rae's forehead. "Don't say a word, deary. You're safe. I'm Nancy, and this here is my Jack. We're going to be mar—"

"Nancy," Jack admonished. "I doubt she wants every detail. You're at Linfield, miss, and Stephens says you might stay if you can work on the morrow."

Rae blinked, puzzlement in the line of her dark brows as they came together above her clouded eyes. "Linfield? Then Nigel paid the ransom?"

Nancy's mouth gaped in astonishment. "Jack?" she whispered. "Did you hear? She called his grace by his Christian name. What can she be thinking of? Who are you?"

"Did the duke pay the ransom?" Rae demanded again as

her teeth began to chatter wildly. She massaged the chafed skin on her wrists. "So—so cold. The ransom? Did he—"

There was very little the servants at Linfield did not know about the duke's dealings, but they were never discussed with anyone outside the household. The rule was set down by Stephens, not the duke, and it was strictly enforced. Jack looked at Rae warily, wondering what he should tell her. After all, she was nearly a member of the staff, and it seemed she knew things neither he nor Nancy could guess. "There was a ransom paid, but it was stolen back. Your friends were chased off without a farthing."

"Not my friends," Rae said, pulling the blanket up to her chin. "I can't keep my eyes open. Drugged my wine." Her speech slurred at the last, but her companions were able to make it out.

"Drugged!" Nancy cried, appalled at this bit of unseemly behavior and not a little intrigued. "Do you think she's telling the truth?"

"Does it matter? Take care to get her out of her wet things, and I'll see if I can't use a bit of guile on Mrs. Timms to get her something hot to drink. She looks as if she could use with a bit of warmth." Jack left the room without looking squarely at Nancy, afraid she would see how much he regretted bringing the girl into the house. He was beginning to believe the cook's pronouncement that she would be nothing but trouble.

Nancy crooned softly to Rahab as she undressed her. "Here, what's this?" she demanded, arms akimbo as she saw an unfamiliar protrusion beneath Rae's slip. Nancy carefully lifted the material and stared, openmouthed, at the wooden dagger strapped to Rae's thigh. "Well, I never! This isn't the colonies, m'girl, and we don't have to fend off savages at every turn. You've spent too much time in the company of pirates and their ilk, poor thing." Nancy shuddered delicately as she relieved Rae of her weapon. Having no place to put it, she slid it beneath Rae's mattress. "Out of sight, out of mind." She stripped Rae of the rest of her clothes and managed to get her into a clean nightdress.

There was still a debate raging belowstairs when she went to see what was keeping the warm drink from reaching her patient. She thought it best to keep the dagger a secret, so while Jack cajoled Mrs. Timms, Nancy made off with a cup of freshly brewed tea.

It was not a simple task to get Rae to drink the stuff, for in her confused state she imagined it was poisoned also. It was well after midnight when Nancy was able to go to her own bed, but by then she was a firm believer in Rae's garbled tale.

It was still dark when Nancy shook Rae awake. "It's time you were up, m'girl. If you want to stay here, you'll have to show Stephens you can do the work."

Rae turned groggily on her side and received a sharp slap on her posterior.

"Up with you. I'll help what I can, but you have to get out of bed."

Much against her will, Rae felt herself being pulled to her feet. She swayed unsteadily and stared stupidly at the soft chocolate eyes that peered anxiously into her face. A button nose screwed up in front of her and a pair of full, cherry-red lips pursed in impatience. Rae giggled at the face and yelped when she was pinched on her upper arm.

Nancy stamped her foot. "There's no time for that, m'girl. We've got to get you dressed, for there's work to be done. I've put out your clothes, but don't expect I'll do the same every day. I'm hardly in your service. Can you manage, do you think, or are you still feeling the drugs those brigands gave you?"

Rae's eyes widened. "How did you know?"

"You told me often enough last night. You don't remember, do you? Of course not, poor thing. Don't fret; it will stay with me and Jack unless you want Stephens to know."

"Jack?"

"If you're going to ask a lot of questions, then you may as well be dressing at the same time," Nancy said pointedly. "There's water in the basin over there. It's cold, mind you, but just what you need to clear your head."

Rae moved sluggishly to the basin and dunked her face full in the cold water, holding on to the stand for support. Behind her she could hear Nancy's gasp, but when she reached for a towel one was put in her hand. She dried her face and throat briskly, rolled up her sleeves, and scrubbed the rest of her while keeping the nightdress on. Nancy would have been horrified if she had taken it off to wash. It was not a common practice to clean oneself while naked, and the maid would have thought Rae a doxy if she had tried it. After her hasty washing, Rae discovered she felt much more the thing.

"Who is Jack?" she asked as she began changing her clothes.

"My intended. He's the one what brought you here from the woods."

"Oh, I remember that. He was very gentle, I think."

"That's my Jack," Nancy said happily. "He's a footman now, but don't think he'll be that forever. Someday he'll be head of all staff, mark my words."

"And Stephens?"

"He's in charge now. He's the one who said you could stay. I'm Nancy Wright."

"I remember."

That pleased Nancy, and she beamed. "You'll be working under Mrs. Ritchie's keen eye. She's the housekeeper, and she's hard but fair. She stood up to the cook last night and is giving you a chance. Don't cross her, or you'll be out on your ear as Betty was."

Rae didn't think she could take in much more. Betty's story would have to wait, though Nancy appeared eager to tell all. "Am I really at Linfield, then?"

"Of course."

"How strange. I never thought . . ." Her voice trailed off as she twisted to fasten her skirt. "Does the duke know I am here?"

"I think so, though why it should matter to you I can't suppose. He told my Jack to take care of you. What's wrong? You're pale of a sudden." Nancy helped Rae sit down on the edge of the bed. "You're very lucky to be alive after the trick that was played on him. The duke is not one to suffer fools. Anyone can see you're not Miss Ashley."

"Almost anyone," Rae said tersely. "If Sam Judge had known, I wouldn't be here at all." Nancy's bewildered face stopped Rae from explaining further. "Never mind." She pulled on thick black stockings and slid on her own shoes. "You said I was to begin work. What would you have me do?"

Nancy eyed Rae shrewdly as she straightened. It was clear she was not ready for any strenuous labor, but she was a game one, Nancy would give her that. "There's fires to be laid. Come. I'll show you what's to be done." At the door she paused. "What's your name? I can't keep calling you poor thing."

"Rahab." When Nancy continued to look at her expectantly, she added, "Smith. Rahab Smith."

"What an odd sort of name."

"Yes." But one I hope will be mine someday, she said silently. Her eyes closed briefly, as if in prayer. Jericho, where are you?

Jericho was wondering much the same about Rahab. He remembered calling out her name in his sleep, and he wondered if the old crofter whose cottage he shared had heard him. He didn't like to think he had disturbed the man's sleep when he had been shown every kindness by the farmer. He owed his life to the gnarled little man who had dragged him from the water and offered hospitality with virtually no questions asked. Drew Goodfellow was a man deserving of his name, and Jericho gave his thanks again that he had been found by one such as he.

It had taken nearly twenty-four hours for him to recover from his dunking in the cold seawater, and Drew watched over him like a nervous mother protecting the runt of her brood.

Now Drew stepped away from the hearth and placed a bowl of hot gruel on the table in front of Jericho. "Eat that."

Jericho smiled to himself, half expecting Goodfellow to spoonfeed him. Dutifully he began eating.

"Your friends were surprised by the authorities this morning," Drew said as he sat on a three-legged stool beside Jericho. He placed his knobby cane on his lap and rolled it back and forth across his thighs, working his arthritic fingers to some measure of nimbleness. "The ship and crew were taken away. I watched from the hill."

And the damp air had nearly crippled his hands, Jericho thought, but he knew better than to mention it. "Hardly my friends, Drew. I can't say I'm sorry for them."

"I thought that might be the way of it."

"Did you see many of the crew?"

"Most all of them."

"Was there a woman among them?"

Drew's silver brows shot up in surprise. "A woman? None that I saw. These eyes aren't what they used to be, but there was no woman on board. Is she the one you been crying out for in your sleep? Rahab, I think you called her."

"Strange, I usually call her Red."

Drew chuckled. "Hell, you must have said that more than a hundred times the first night. I thought you were calling out a sailor's warning. Never thought it was a woman."

"I have to find her, Drew." Jericho pushed the bowl away from him. "She's in danger. I left her on the ship because I couldn't take her with me, but now I don't know what's happened to her.''

"They made a thorough search. They were customs men, and there aren't many hiding places they don't know. She definitely was not aboard when they towed that vessel out of the cove. I'd like to know how the customs men happened upon that place. There's many a smuggler around here asking himself the same question. Not much happens in these parts that they don't know about.''

Jericho imagined Drew had been a fair smuggler in his own right at one time. He probably still kept his hand in, scouting the area for a small share of the prizes. He said as much.

"Aye, I watch out for my friends. Good lads, all of them. And they take care of old Drew, now that I can't sail anymore. I'm not ashamed of my work.''

"I'm glad you still have a sharp eye, Drew, else you wouldn't have seen me floundering in the water.''

"You were a sight!'' Drew said, not unkindly. "Thrashing about like a windmill with one arm and holding on to those breeches for all you were worth with the other.''

"Those breeches kept me afloat for quite a while. Red taught me that trick.''

"Well, she should have taught you to take off your boots. They nearly pulled you under.''

"I don't suppose she thought I would be stupid enough to wear them.'' His fingers threaded through his yellow hair absently. "I wonder what has become of her.'' He refused to allow himself to imagine the worst, so even to his own ears he sounded unworried. The tension was in the long line of his legs stretched beneath the table. "I suppose I shall have to start at Linfield.''

Drew Goodfellow stopped rolling his cane. "Linfield? Why there?''

"It's a complicated tale, Drew.''

"Do you think I can't ken it?''

Jericho laughed, making his decision to trust the old man. There was nothing to be lost, and perhaps something to be gained by sharing the story. Drew's face was thoughtful as Jericho unraveled the threads of his life and intertwined them with Rae's, but beyond a grunt every now and again to show he was listening, Drew gave nothing away. Twice during Jericho's recital he poured them tea laced liberally with some fine French spirits, courtesy of his smuggler friends. When Jericho finished, Drew swallowed the last of his brew and set his cup down firmly.

"Seems to me you're starting off in the wrong direction, son," he said at last.

"What do you mean?"

"It's not Linfield, but Stanhope that should be your destination."

"Stanhope? But why? Rahab isn't there."

"No. But your inheritance is, and with it your entry into the duke's circle. How else will you see Rahab?"

"There must be some way."

"You say that because you've never been to Linfield. If the duke is holding her against her will as you suspect, then you won't be able to reach her. Even as one of the duke's guests it will be difficult for you to find her. The house is a labyrinth of rooms."

"You are familiar with Linfield?"

"I've made deliveries there twice, years ago. Most of us around here have had dealings with the duke, but he's a bad 'un. Plays both ends against the middle. Turned us in to the customs men once when he thought he wasn't getting his share of the bounty. I couldn't prove it, of course, but I know it was him. He was hailed as a hero among his peers, and we near starved that winter. As I said, that was years ago. He's out of smuggling now, and good riddance, I say." Drew looked at Jericho sharply. "If you want to find out if your lady's safe, mayhap my associates can make inquiries."

"1 want to go along," Jericho said stubbornly.

"I think you're being a mite foolish, but have it your way," Drew shrugged. "I still think you should be considering Stanhope."

Jericho gave Goodfellow one of his easy smiles. "Oh, I'm not putting that aside. There is something appealing about going to Stanhope."

Rae adjusted the mobcap on her head and tucked a few loose strands of hair beneath it. She bent over the hearth in the dining room and poked at the fire until it flared again, then added a few pieces of wood. Servants were setting covered dishes on the sideboard and the fragrant smell of warm food made Rae's mouth water and her stomach growl. She had been up nearly four hours and hadn't yet had her own breakfast. She glanced at the feast that was being laid out and wondered what the penalty would be for stealing a hot roll or a bit of bacon. Imagining that the duke would cut off her hands quelled her appetite for the moment, and she hurried from the room just as Nigel and his three guests were entering. Feeling faint from lack of food and the thought that the duke might recognize her as the girl he had seen in the woods, Rae braced herself against the doorjamb, head lowered, and waited for them to pass.

She thought she had escaped as beneath their notice and was ready to flee down the hall when the last man through the door stopped beside her and picked up her chin, forcing her to lift her face. She stared at him without expression in her eyes, not daring to pull away or show insolence as he inspected her with careless regard. His nostrils flared slightly as his eyes fell to the level of Rae's thumping heart and the rise and fall of her breasts. He dropped her chin and sauntered into the room.

Rae quickly shut the door to the dining room with herself safely in the hallway. For a moment she could not move, and from inside the room she could hear the man who had held her say, "Really, Nigel, you have some of the most comely wenches in the Isles serving you. Why is it that you never have them warming your bed?"

"I always thought your tastes were rather plebian, Newbrough," Nigel said, dismissing the subject.

Rahab pushed away from the door and for a moment she found it difficult to breathe. Newbrough! It did not seem possible! Could it really be Jericho's cousin inside that room? Rae shivered when she thought of the way he had held her, looking down his hawkish nose at her, and the spark of interest she had seen in his face, particularly in his wide-set eyes. She would do well to stay out of his way. While the duke saw his female help as only that, at least one of his guests thought them no better than warm bricks in a cold bed.

"We do not listen at doors here at Linfield," a disapproving voice said in Rahab's ear.

Her hand flew to her throat but did not cover her surprised gasp in time. The man towering over her had to be Stephens, and there was nothing for it but that she apologize. "I'm sorry," she said quickly, bobbing slightly. "I wasn't really listening, not intentionally anyway, but one of the duke's guests frightened me and—"

"Your regrets would have been sufficient," Stephens said dryly. "Come away from the door, girl, unless you want everyone to know your business."

Rae stepped further into the hall and mumbled another apology that was nearly drowned out by the rumbling in her stomach.

"Now what is this about one of the duke's guests?" Stephens felt it incumbent upon his position to protect his staff from the unwanted attentions of the quality, if indeed, they were unwanted.

"He touched me," Rae said, flushing. It sounded inadequate to her own ears. Stephens would think her a fool.

"How?"

"He made me lift my face for his inspection. I thought he would check my teeth as if I were some mare at auction."

"That will be quite enough," Stephens snapped. "You may go to the kitchen now and have your breakfast. There are some matters you and I will discuss concerning your employment later today."

Realizing she was being dismissed, Rae gave Stephens a quick curtsy and hurried toward the kitchen. Behind her, Stephens stared at her retreating form thoughtfully, wondering what it was about this chit that should remind him of a certain colonial sea captain who had come to Linfield years ago. In the end he dismissed it from his mind, putting it down to her regrettable accent.

After eating breakfast under the sharp eye of Mrs. Timms, Rae followed Nancy about the house and learned more about her position. She gave Nancy's chattering half her attention while she thought of her upcoming meeting with Stephens. In her mind she formed the sort of questions she expected him to ask of her and tried to think of answers that would placate him.

She already knew she did not want to be dismissed from Linfield. Rae was confident she could leave anytime she wanted to, but if she went away now she did not know how Jericho would find her. Even as she thought his name, she resolutely pushed it aside. She was dangerously close to weeping each time she recalled his escaping the ship and risking his life to bring help. She felt she owed it to him to stay in one place, rather than striking out on her own.

As long as the duke did not know her identity, she believed she was safer at Linfield than she would be anywhere else. It occurred to her that if she was careful she might even discover Nigel's next move against Ashley. That would be the time to leave, and not one moment before.

Stephens cornered her in the late afternoon when she was dusting the library shelves. The duke and his companions were out riding, and Rae was humming to herself as she went about her work, knowing for the present she was out of harm's way.

"Come down from there, girl," Stephens said, pointing to Rae's position on the ladder.

Rae hurried down and fidgeted with her feather duster as she stood before Stephens. "You wanted to see me?"

"I can see you well enough. I want to talk to you."

"That's what I meant."

"Then say what you mean, girl. No, don't start apologizing, else this interview will never be at a close. Now tell me how you came to be with those men who claimed to have Miss Ashley. And tell me truly. I will not suffer liars among my staff."

Rae chose her words carefully. "I was abducted from my home nearly eight weeks ago. Those men thought I was Miss Ashley."

"Why would they think that?"

"I told them I was, you see."

"I am afraid I do not see. Explain yourself more clearly."

"I live at McClellan's Landing, sir. I've worked there nearly all my life. Miss Ashley lives there, too, with her husband. When some strangers came to the plantation and began asking about her, I feared for her, because once before someone had tried to take her away. She has always been kindness itself to me, sir, so I didn't want any harm to come to her. She loves living at the landing, and she even confided in me that she never wanted to return here. Her confidence was dear to me, so I told them I was she—and here I am." Rae was certain Stephens could detect no lie, because she had told none. "What's to become of me, sir?"

Stephens's mouth softened a bit. He could not find fault with Rae's story, and he admired her for her loyalty to her employer. "That is entirely up to you. What sort of position did you have in the colonies?"

"I was Miss Ashley's personal maid."

"Really?" An eyebrow arched in disbelief. The chit was giving herself airs.

Rae blushed. "Well, not her maid precisely."

"Pray, then. What precisely were your duties?"

"I did much the same as I'm doing here. Dusting, laying the fires, polishing. I looked after her children, made candles and butter, dressed hair. A little of everything, I suppose."

"Indeed. The Americans have no sense of station, do they?"

Rae bit her lip to keep from laughing at the butler's offended sense of what was correct. "I'm sure I wouldn't know. Though I admit things seem a bit different here."

"I hope so," Stephens said dryly. "Regarding what is to become of you, you may have employment here as long as you prove satisfactory. The circumstances of your birth and your arrival cannot be helped. You will conduct yourself in such a fashion as befitting one of Mrs. Ritchie's staff. You will not be making candles, dressing hair, or, God forbid, playing nanny to any children. Your wages will be six pounds per annum, and you will have one Saturday and one Sunday off per month, though not in the same week. You will keep yourself out of his grace's path, for he cannot help but be offended by your speech. If you value your employment here, you will not mention your association with Miss Ashley to anyone. The duke forbids anyone to speak of her."

"But she's such a fine lady," Rae protested, thinking Stephens would find it strange if she did not.

"It is no lady that would take flight with a Yankee trader. And that is my final word on the subject."

"But—"

"My final word. I will not make allowances for your pert tongue again." Stephens turned his back on the astonished Rae and left the room.

Later that night Rae slipped beneath the cool sheets of her bed, her body in a limp state of exhaustion, but her mind spinning restlessly. Jericho was in her every thought, and she lacked the strength as well as the desire to erase his image from behind her closed lids. She wished she had not been so drugged that she could not even assure herself that he had made it safely to shore. She smiled weakly, remembering his whispered talk about a swimming lesson in a sylvan setting. How she wished they were in that spot now!

The little boy in him that demanded that everything should be counted would number each tiny freckle on her sun-drenched skin with his mouth. He would start at her forehead, brush her nose and cheeks, pay particular attention to the gentle slope of shoulders. His lips would pay homage to her breasts and slide past the taut plane of her abdomen. He was a thorough rogue, for he would inspect her navel, kissing it just to make sure nothing had escaped his notice. Then he would tease her by going to her ankles, knowing all the while that she desired his mouth elsewhere, and he would turn her slender calves in his hands, stroking them with his palms and getting a sense of their fine curves. His lips would touch her knees, and he would probably ask her a series of silly questions about the tiny scars there. She would have to concentrate on her answers; it was so difficult to talk when he kept kissing the soft inner flesh of her thighs. But if she did not answer him he would stop, and that was worse than anything she could imagine.

So she would tell him that once she had fallen from the top of the apple tree that Salem had dared her to climb, and he would press a smile to the crescent-moon scar. Then he would touch another, and she would say that was from tripping over her own feet as she ran to keep up with her older brothers when they were doing their very best to be rid of her. That would make him laugh, and the sound of it would ripple through her like a warm breeze through her hair. She would be so encouraged that she would offer to show him the barely discernible mark on her hip. It had been made when her horse had failed to clear a fence and she fell on a loose stone. Jericho would have to look closely to see, and mayhap his kisses would cover a lot of territory so he could not fail to miss it.

He would nip her gently on her hip, teasing her with his teeth and tongue, and then his mouth would draw ever nearer to the little bud of sensation at the apex of her thighs, moist with her body's musky honey.

A sob of pure longing shook Rahab and she clutched her pillow to her breast.

"Rahab?" Nancy called her name softly from the other bed. "What is it? Are you ill?"

Rae sobbed into the pillow, unable to answer, and after a moment she heard Nancy slide out of her bed, then felt her gentle hand on her shoulder. "Rahab? Please tell me what is the matter."

"I—I miss my f—family. And J—Jericho."

"Aah," Nancy said wisely. "Of course you do. You're sick at heart for your home." She continued to pat Rae's back. "Tell me about Jericho. Is it as grand a place as Linfield?"

Rae gave her a watery giggle and sniffled loudly. "It's not a place. Jericho is the name of the man I love."

"Oh, I'm sorry."

"You couldn't know."

"No, I mean I'm sorry you've been separated from him. How you must hurt! I don't know what I'd do if I was to be taken from my Jack. Like as not I'd drown in my own tears, just as you're doing. Go on, have a good cry."

Rae did. Several minutes went by before Nancy gave her a handkerchief and she blew noisily into it. "Thank you. I feel better now—I think."

"A cry always helps a bit. Does your man know what's happened to you—about the pirates and all?"

"Yes. He knows, and I'm certain he's doing everything he can to find me, but I miss him so."

"Listen, I have an idea! When we next get a day off together, we'll go to the village and post a letter with a ship bound for the colonies,'' Nancy assumed Jericho was still overseas, and Rae did nothing to right the record, but there was something she had to straighten out.

"It's the United States of America."

"What? Oh, you mean the colonies. Yes, well I'm certain the letter will find him no matter how we address it."

Rae was so astonished by Nancy's response that she didn't know whether to laugh or cry. Seven years of fighting and none of it had ever touched this girl. Rae bit back a stinging reply, realizing it was hardly Nancy's fault she knew so little of what had touched nearly one-third of Rae's life. "I could write my family," she said after a little thought. "Perhaps they could arrange passage."

"That's very expensive," Nancy said gently, trying not to stab at Rae's hopes.

Rae nodded without further comment. She sat up and made a place beside her for Nancy. "May I confide in you?"

"Of course you can. We'll be fast friends, you and I. And don't worry that I gossip. I can't abide it."

Rae hoped Nancy could not see her smile in the darkness. She imagined this was going straight from her mouth to Jack's ear, but she needed to speak to someone more sympathetic than the butler, even if she could only talk in partial truths. Quietly she related the same story she had told Stephens that afternoon, while Nancy listened raptly. "Tell me why the duke forbids anyone to speak of Miss Ashley," she said when she finished.

"She disobeyed him," Nancy explained simply. "He arranged a most enviable marriage for her. She would have had position and title and wealth nearly the equal of the duke's, and she refused to wed Lord Bosworth. She shamed the duke. I know you think Miss Ashley is a fine lady, but she is naught but a by-blow. She was fortunate to have the duke as her guardian."

Rae sighed. Nancy was nothing if not loyal. Poor Ashley.

No one understood what her life here had been like. "Do all the servants feel as you do?"

"Why yes." Nancy's voice lowered confidentially. "That is to say, there are some who think the duke is something of a libertine, and not all approve of his licentious behavior, but regarding his ward, he acted as a saint. No one will fault him there."

Rae held her tongue. Surely there was no more certain way to lose her position than to speak ill of the duke. She would not forget that. Carefully she said, "Do you not think it odd that the duke would want to take her away from her husband and her children and the new life she has made for herself?"

"Who can say if it is odd?" Nancy shrugged. "Quality is a source of amazement to me. I've heard Mrs. Timms say that the duke doesn't recognize Miss Ashley's marriage. I don't pretend to understand or judge. Like when I found that horrible weapon fastened to your leg. I didn't judge you harshly for that, even though I thought it the strangest thing."

"What are you talking about? What weapon?"

"The dagger. Didn't you know it was there?"

"No. Jericho must have done that."

Nancy, for all her saucy ways, had never allowed any man to see more than a bit of ankle. "Oh my."

"Where is it now?" she asked, pretending not to hear Nancy's startled accents. "You haven't thrown it away, have you?"

"No. It's under the mattress." Nancy scooted off the bed and lifted the padding enough to find the dagger. "Here it is." She gave it to Rae. "Never say you're going to wear it!"

"Jericho meant for me to have it, so of course I will."

"But there are no savages here!"

Rae laughed without humor, recalling the way Newbrough had looked at her. "Are there not?" she asked softly, running her finger along the wooden edge. "I wish I were so certain."

* * *

Rae wore the dagger in spite of the fact that Newbrough left a few days after Nancy had given it to her. She never had occasion to see him again. Lesley and Evans departed a week before Christmas for their own estates, and Rae settled into the routine of her new way of life. She was up before dawn and busy well into the evening. If she had been able to go outside more often her day would not have been much different than those she had known at the landing. The other servants warmed to her once they saw she was willing to do her share and more. Even Mrs. Timms thawed when she realized Rahab was not going to cause a stir in the household. Indeed, it seemed the duke did not know of her existence.

Christmas at Linfield was not an especially festive occasion. Rae shared a syllabub that Mrs. Timms had specially prepared with the household staff and watched the great yule log burn in the dining room fireplace while Stephens gravely thanked the employees on behalf of the duke for their splendid service. That night she cried herself to sleep, and Nancy was kind enough to pretend she hadn't heard.

Shortly after the New Year the duke left for London on business. There was nothing to indicate to Rae that his business had anything to do with Ashley, so she tried to enjoy his absence. She thought Mrs. Ritchie's particular standards would relax with the duke gone, but if anything, the housekeeper became more demanding. ''She's forever afraid his grace will come back before he's due,'' Nancy confided in her, ''so she doesn't dare let herself be open to criticism.'' Rae smiled ruefully and continued to polish the brass candlesticks for the third time in two weeks.

Rae was in the kitchen eating her breakfast when the striking of pots and pans beyond the door announced the tinker had come to call. He shook snow off his stooped shoulders and feet as he stood in the doorway. Mrs. Timms was already giving him the sharp edge of her tongue for tramping snow that far into her kitchen. He merely grinned, which deepened the creases about his mouth and eyes.

Rae felt sorry for him when she saw him struggle to take off his gloves and move his stiff fingers. He glanced about the kitchen with no more than a stranger's curious interest, until his eyes fell on Rae's face. It was the briefest of pauses, so that Rae thought she might have imagined the surprise in his arrested look. In the next moment he was ignoring her and sidling closer to the hearth to warm his hands.

While Mrs. Timms was pulling out the pots that needed mending and some of the other servants were gathering around the door to see the wares the tinker had in his cart outside, Rae prepared a steaming cup of tea for the man.

"Here, you must have something to warm you. You can hardly work while you're frozen through." She thrust the cup into his hands beneath the disapproving eye of the cook.

"Your smile's enough to warm any man, Red."

Rae blinked, uncertain she had heard correctly.

"Enough of your blarney, old man," Mrs. Timms scolded. "The girl doesn't need her head turned by the likes of you."

"As if I could," he snorted. "She most likely has a feller. Don't you, Red?"

Rahab nodded slowly, but before she could say his name the tinker clutched his heart. "Aaah! It's fair to breakin', it is. Crumblin' as easy as Jericho's walls."

Rae's eyes widened further, and she slipped her hands into her pockets so no one would see how they trembled.

"Go on with you, tinker," Mrs. Timms said sharply. "Have you come to work or prattle? Drink your tea and leave the girl alone. Rahab, there's no use for idle hands here."

"Mightn't I see the tinker's wares?"

Mrs. Timms softened under the appeal in Rae's face. "All right," she said gruffly. "A few minutes, no more."

Chapter 11

Jericho crossed his arms in front of him and patted his shoulders to keep warm. Occasionally he stepped in place or gave a little hop to make certain he could feel his feet. The trees blocked most of the biting wind, but what got through seemed to go right up his cape. The woolen muffler about his face made it possible to breathe the dry, icy air.

The rattle and clatter of pots made him cock his head toward the approach of the cart. It was about time! He stepped out of the woods and hurried to the edge of the road. Drew slowed the cart just enough for him to hop on.

"Well?" There was a very large question in the one word.

Drew gave the reins to Jericho and he slipped his hands beneath his armpits so his fingers would not ache. "She's there."

"How do you know?"

"Damnedest thing, son. She's one of the servants. She was sitting there in the kitchen, pretty as you please, when I walked in. Every bit the woman you described to me, so I knew her right off. I can tell you, it was a shock to see her there.''

Jericho gave the reins a jerk and stopped the cart. ''If she was in the kitchen then why isn't she with you now? What was to prevent her from leaving?''

''Keep moving. She's not coming with us, so there's no use turning around.''

''The hell you say.''

''She's got a mind of her own, that one. I believe you mentioned it yourself a couple or three times. Now, let's move along, or I swear I'll clobber you with one of those damn clanging pots.''

Jericho snapped the ribbons, muttering a few choice words that nearly heated the air around them. ''Tell me the whole of it.''

''I was able to talk to her for a little while before that snippety cook yanked Red away. It seems the duke does not know she is underfoot.'' He described what Rahab had related to him of her arrival at the house. ''Her main worry these past weeks has not been herself, but you. She wondered why you took so long to make your presence known.''

''You explained, didn't you?''

''I told her it was my fault. That I was sick and you damn well couldn't be loosed from my side.''

''Considering all you had done for me, it was small repayment.'' It also had been an agony of waiting, but Jericho did not mention it. Drew knew it right enough. ''Did she understand?''

Drew chuckled. ''I think her word was noble. Her eyes got all soft and teary and she kissed this old leathery cheek. You don't mind if I fall a little in love with her, do you?''

''I mind like hell!'' Jericho said flatly, then grinned under his muffler. ''So why isn't she here now?'' The smile had vanished, and beneath his gloves Jericho's knuckles were white.

''She says she is safe enough where she is, and there is no reason why you can't follow the plan you began with her brothers. She wants to stay at Linfield and see if she can't uncover something that will be in aid of protecting Ashley from the duke.''

Jericho groaned. ''I swear to you, Drew, she's over my knee the minute I lay eyes on her again. What nonsense is she plotting? She's taken leave of her senses!''

''She would not be moved,'' Drew said firmly. ''She insists you go about your business.''

''How does she think I will come up with the blunt? She knows that her father was going to see that my expenses were covered.'' Drew coughed and cleared his throat at the same time. Jericho glanced sideways and saw his companion was looking a trifle discomfited. ''Out with it, man. What did you say to her?''

''I believe I must have mentioned Stanhope.''

''You believe?''

''All right. I told her flat-out that you had a plan to recover your inheritance.''

''It was your plan,'' Jericho said dryly.

''Don't split hairs. She thought it was an admirable idea.''

''She would. Didn't I mention she has cotton batting where most other people have brains?''

''You're too hard on her, son. She's a plucky thing, a regular out-and-outer.''

''She's daft. Whatever they say, love is not blind, just lacking all reason.''

Drew's face crinkled in a deep smile. ''I suppose this means we're going to Stanhope.''

Jericho rolled his eyes and sighed. ''Aye, Drew Goodfellow, I suppose it does.''

Rae hugged herself, fairly dancing about her small room as she dressed for bed. Jericho was alive! For the first time she admitted to herself that she had been afraid he was not. She should never have entertained the thought, even at the back of her mind. He was alive, and finally she felt that way, too!

"Is it the full moon, do you think?" Nancy asked.

"What?" Rae stopped spinning and reentered the present.

"I wondered if it was the full moon that's made you all silly this evening."

Rae's smile was beatific. "I daresay it is. Isn't it wonderful?"

Nancy yawned and pulled the covers up to her chin. "So you say. Be a dear and put out the candle." She turned on her side as the room darkened.

Rae stood at the small attic window for a long time, bathed in moonlight, staring out at the great expanse of the Linfield lands. Jericho had been there today, hiding somewhere in the orchard and hazelwood, and she had never known until an old tinker called her Red. She laughed softly to herself. Had she expected her skin to tingle when he was within a half-mile of her? Yes, that's what she had expected. Love made her feel as if every one of her senses stretched far beyond the boundaries of Linfield. She fell asleep that night with a sweet smile dimpling her cheek and a sigh on her parted lips.

Rahab succeeded in springing the lock on the duke's desk after two weeks of concentrated effort wherein she dusted, polished, and swept the study ten times. Mrs. Ritchie was heard to remark that never had she had a girl with more sense of her duty than Rahab Smith. A quick search of the contents showed nothing more remarkable than a few bills of sale and invitations to dine and party with, in Rae's estimation, what must have been a full third of England's finest names. It was shocking, she thought, that Nigel Lynne was considered such an eligible match for a young girl to make. She admitted that he had rather an arresting countenance, very masculine yet finely etched. Still, he had cruel eyes. Those she remembered well, and she wondered that others did not see the more sinister side of him.

Rahab left the desk exactly as she found it, carefully wiping away her finger smudges and polishing the brass plate around the lock until it glistened and the scratches she had made were invisible. Even so, when the duke returned a day later she held her breath, waiting for the axe to fall. When it did not she congratulated herself on her stealth and ceased jumping at shadows.

"You'll never credit what I just heard," Nancy, who still maintained she never gossiped, whispered to Rae.

They were sitting at the dining room table, deftly polishing a mountain of silver utensils. Rae was wishing the Lynnes had chosen a less intricate pattern that did not hold tarnish in every crevice. "What did you hear?" she whispered back, mocking Nancy's self-important air.

"I should make you beg for being such a tease, but this is too delicious to be put off. The Earl of Stanhope was stopped by highwaymen not more than a fortnight past. I can't think of anyone more deserving to be ordered to stand and deliver. Oh, now, look what you've done!" she exclaimed as the spoons in Rae's lap clattered to the floor. "What a noise!"

Both girls bent to pick them up, Rae apologizing for her clumsiness.

"How did you hear this?" Rae asked, beginning to polish once more.

"From my Jack, who got it from one of the grooms at Stanhope who was riding with the earl when it happened. The way I hear it the earl was white from fear and nearly fainted dead away. That should teach him a thing or two about what it's like to be singled out and picked on," she said smartly.

"You too?" Rae's question was full of grim fury.

"Of course me, and every other young thing in skirts. He thinks because we're in service we don't have anything to say in the matter. I didn't know he was here long enough to bother you. You should have said something."

"I did. To Stephens."

"That was a good thing. He'll keep an eye out for you if

the earl returns. Now that Betty's gone, it'll be hard on all of us."

"So that's why she was dismissed. I often wondered. But surely she spoke out against the earl."

"What could she have said? She hopped in his bed easily enough when he crooked his little finger, not that she could have done much to put him off. Anyway, she wasn't dismissed for that, only for having the bad luck to end up carrying his bastard."

"Poor girl," Rae said sadly. "I hope the earl had his entire fortune on his person that night." Because Jericho is more deserving of it, she added to herself.

Rae's fierceness made Nancy laugh. "If only it were so. I understand the highwaymen left the earl stripped of his jewelry and his dignity. It will be some time before we see him around here, I think."

Rae offered no comment and continued polishing, a serenely satisfied smile on her face.

The first Saturday in February the weather broke, and Nancy wheedled Jack until he agreed to escort Rahab and her to town. It was well over an hour's brisk walk to Hemmings, and Rae basked in the clean, sharp air every step of the way. She walked a little ahead of Nancy and Jack, allowing them a little time to themselves. She carried a large straw basket in the crook of her arm and a list of items that Mrs. Ritchie had asked her to purchase in her apron pocket. Beside it rested Rae's letter to her parents, a letter very long on loving regards and dreadfully short on details. It couldn't be helped, she supposed, for she would not take the risk that her missive might, just might, fall into the wrong hands. She tapped the letter lightly, making certain for the tenth time that it was safe. Nancy promised her that Jack would help her post it. She seemed to think he knew where to take it.

Hemmings was not a town, but a cozy little hamlet tucked between river and wood. It sported a livery, a hostelry called Blackamore's, a smithy, two small dress establishments, a milliner and wigmaker's, a barber dentist, and several other tradesmen's shops. The houses were prevailingly Tudor in design, with flat arches and dark wood-panel accents on their clean white walls. The snow-covered rooftops fairly gleamed as the sun beat down on them, and Rae found herself glancing overhead to avoid the precariously positioned icicles threatening to drop.

The first order of business was Rae's letter, and she did not relax until she saw Jack hand it over to the captain of a small merchant ship. It cost Rae most of her first quarter's wages to send the thing, and even at that price the captain could not guarantee delivery. He reminded Jack that there was little more being done than talking of peace. Normal trade had not yet resumed, and the best he could do was pass the letter on to a Frog friend of his who dealt with the Americans. Rae had to be satisfied with that.

A little of the day's brightness vanished for Rae, but she put on a good face for Nancy who cheerily insisted that everything would turn out right enough. Jack proved to be fainthearted about attending Nancy in the milliner's and left the women alone to discuss lace and ribbons with the owner. Neither of them bought more than thread and a length of hair ribbon, but they pretended that they were grand ladies and that nothing had caught their fancy. It was more pleasant than reminding each other that they hadn't enough money between them to purchase even one *chapeau*.

They came out of the shop giggling. "A *chapeau*, indeed," Nancy snorted while trying to catch her breath. "She doesn't know a *chapeau* from a chateau." They both thought of the owner wearing a house on her head and burst into fresh laughter. "La, but that was fun!" Nancy dabbed at her eyes, then pulled at Rae's arm, dragging her into the dressmaker's.

It was just going on noon when they finished purchasing the items on Mrs. Ritchie's list and Nancy suggested they meet Jack at Blackamore's for lunch. The inn was nearly vacant when they walked in, and Nancy chose a table off the main room. Rae set her basket by her chair on the polished oak floor and draped her pelisse on a hook near the hearth, then warmed her hands in front of the fire. Jack came in a few minutes later and the hosteler took their order. They had timed their arrival nicely, for their meal had hardly been served when there was a flurry of activity caused by the passengers of the afternoon coach.

Rae paid them no mind, as her back was to the window and the adjoining room, but Nancy's head bobbed around as she tried to glimpse everyone alighting from the carriage, making a game of where they had been and where they were bound.

"If you wanted to see them all you should have chosen the main room, love," Jack said patiently.

"Oh, hush." Nancy tapped Jack's wrist lightly with the back of her spoon. Her eyes narrowed on someone coming through the inn's door. "Now where did he come from? He wasn't on the coach."

"I'm sure I don't know. And stop staring, Nancy. There's no mistaking he's quality and liable to take you to task for your saucy smile."

Nancy lowered her eyes so demurely that Rae had to laugh. None of the trio saw the stranger's arrested posture as he glanced in their direction.

"I'll have a table in that room," Jericho told the hosteler. "Near the fire." He found it remarkable that he was able to get the words out. Red! He could hardly believe she was here! His eyes wandered hungrily over her straight, narrow back and the curling length of hair tied at her nape with a shiny blue ribbon. God, he wanted to touch that hair. Perhaps he could hold off wringing her neck long enough to do that, or better still, he would strangle her with it.

Nothing of his wayward thoughts showed on his face as he followed the innkeeper into the room. While the owner poured him an ale, he hung his great cape and tricorn beside Rae's pelisse, then took his seat, facing Rae now. He leaned back in his chair, stretching his legs and folding his arms in front of him. And waited.

An indolent smile lifted the corners of his mouth, and his hooded cerulean eyes slid over Rae's face as it raised, suffused first with color, then went ashen with shock, and finally contorted in a fit of choking. Jericho merely shook his head as the soup she had been spooning to her lips went sputtering across the table. She was, as always, providing a delightful spectacle.

He bit back his laughter as her male companion clapped her soundly on the back to help her recover her breath and nearly sent her bosom into her soup bowl. Rae reached for the bowl to steady it, fumbled, and the contents poured over the front of her gray day dress. Jericho supposed the dress was a loan from the other woman at the table, because it did not fit Rae very well, being rather a shade too form fitting, especially now with the broth soaking through in an ever widening circle. If one made allowances for the bits of carrot and onion and beef, it was not an unappealing sight as the damp cloth clung tenaciously to the curves of her breasts, in spite of her best efforts to pull it away. Only when he realized the soup must be burning her did his smile fade and spur him to action. He came to his feet in one leaping movement, and grabbing his tankard of ale, he poured the frothy contents all over the front of Rae's gown.

Nancy and Jack exchanged looks of absolute astonishment as Rae stood, straightening to her full regal height, faced the lord squarely, and demanded to know if he had cow dung between his ears. Nancy blinked twice. Surely she had not seen a glimmer of a smile on the young lord's lips. No, it was not there now, and how could it be when Rahab was giving him a set down that made Nancy's ears burn?

"What was that in aid of, you simple-minded jackanapes?" Rae asked hotly. "Is your own wardrobe so extensive that you give no thought to ruining mine, or is it that you don't know the proper way to dispose of your libation?"

"I thought the spilled soup was burning you," Jericho said calmly. "It appears I mistook the situation."

"It appears so! The soup was lukewarm at best, indeed, a few degrees cooler than the drink you poured over me. And the soup would have stayed in the bowl had you not been staring so rudely! Now look what you have done! This poor dress is not even mine!"

"Don't worry about the dress," Nancy said hurriedly, eager to placate both parties. "We can scrub out the stain."

Rae hardly heard Nancy's entreaty, because Jericho's eyes were taking her at her word, examining her thoroughly to see what he had done. Her breath caught in her throat as his long, slender fingers reached up to pluck a bit of carrot from her bodice and his thumb unerringly brushed her nipple.

"You seem to have a veritable garden on your . . . person," he said, wicked teasing in his eyes. "Innkeeper!" His imperious voice brought the owner running. "Do you have a room this lady may have while she makes repairs on her gown? Something with a good fire, I think, so she may dry it also. And a bed, that she might rest while she waits."

"Aye, m'lord."

Jericho nodded in satisfaction. "Good. Then show her to it. Add it to my bill."

"Very good, m'lord. This way, miss." Rae brushed past Jericho with her head held high and followed the innkeeper to the second floor. He showed her to a bedroom at the end of the hall with small windows on two sides and a meager fire in the grate. He stoked it for her before he went for a tub that she might use to rinse her dress.

Rae was in her underthings, dabbing at the stain on the white linen front, when Nancy came in.

"You forgot your pelisse and basket," she said, laying them on the bed. "His lordship asked me to bring them to you. Where is the dress?"

Rae pointed to the tub.

"Have you no sense, girl? Why are you soaking the entire thing? It will be hours before it's dry enough for you to wear home."

"Oh, I hadn't thought of that," Rae lied, forcing a frown to her lips. "What a scatterbrain I am."

"Hmmph! I should say!" Nancy flounced on the bed, testing the mattress. "Mmm. Not so bad. What possessed you to speak in such a sharp manner to his lordship? You were fortunate he didn't take a crop to your shoulders!"

"*He* was fortunate I did not pour something over *his* head!"

"Lord, you frighten me when you talk so! I think you really mean it."

"I do."

Nancy pressed her hands to her cheeks and shook her head in disbelief. "I think he made allowances because it's obvious you're a foreigner, otherwise—" She made a cutting motion with her index finger across her throat. "Off with your head."

Rae snorted. "And you insist this is a civilized country." She finished scrubbing at the stain on her linen bodice. "Nancy, there's no need for you to stay with me. Go on and spend the afternoon with Jack. You don't really want to leave for Linfield yet, do you? I'll meet you in front of the milliner's in a few hours, then we can walk home together. I don't want to spoil your day."

Nancy pretended reluctance, but she knew in her heart that she wanted time alone with her Jack. "If you're certain you don't mind?"

"I don't. Truly."

Nancy scooted off the bed, then impulsively gave Rae a squeeze. "You're a dear heart!"

Rae laughed as Nancy quit the room in a flurry of skirts and excited anticipation.

When the door opened again Rae was on her knees, bent over the tub and scrubbing furiously at her dress. She did not turn around, for she knew who it was. "I've a good mind to make you wash this! Was there ever such a mess?"

Jericho bolted the door and leaned one shoulder against it, studying the curve of Rae's back and buttocks appreciatively. "That was quite a display you put on below for your friends, but I admit I find this private display more to my liking."

"Cretin."

He chuckled. "What a waspish tongue. Have you no respect for your betters?"

Rae glanced over her shoulder, one brow raised in mockery. "Point them out to me first."

Jericho pushed away from the door and hunkered down beside her. His natty buff riding breeches pulled tautly over his thighs and the sleeve of his black velvet jacket brushed Rae's bare forearm. "Impertinent wench. Come, give us a kiss."

"Us? My, you do take your new role seriously." She examined the dress, found the stain had been removed, and began wringing it out, ignoring the playful growl of impatience in Jericho's throat. "But tell me, m'lord. What of my role? Am I at your mercy then? Naught but a diverting pleasure to ease your jaded boredom?"

"How well you know my mind."

She looked at him pointedly. "And other parts of you too, I'll wager." Just as he made to grasp her waist she slipped away, leaving Jericho clutching at air while she laid the wet gown over the back of a chair. She took her time arranging it so it would dry evenly by the fire and unwittingly gave Jericho a comely vision of her lithe form in slender silhouette. She just happened to glance in his direction in time to see the look of serious intent in his eyes as he bore down on her. Rae gave a little shriek and blocked his path by putting the chair between them.

"Have a care m'lord," she warned him. "If you take me to your bed I won't allow you to escape it so easily. I'll pluck out your heart and make it my own."

"You already have it, wench. I thought to take yours in fair exchange."

Rae stepped out from behind the chair and pulled the ribbon from her hair. She gave her head a sprightly toss and her hair fell loosely about her back and shoulders. She dangled the blue ribbon at the end of her finger above her breast. "Then take it, m'lord."

Nothing loath, Jericho smiled his wicked smile, the one that lighted his eyes with sensual promise, and stepped forward, taking the ribbon from Rae. He slipped it beneath her hair and wound it around her neck, pulling on both ends until she perforce had to close the gap between them.

When there remained but a hair's breadth separation, Jericho abandoned his hold on the ribbon and clutched Rae in his arms. He knew a deep satisfaction when her arms slipped around his back in a like embrace.

His mouth settled in her hair near her ear and he breathed in her fresh fragrance as he whispered how much he had missed her.

"No more than I have longed for you," Rae murmured against the hollow of his throat.

Jericho's lips touched Rae's face in four places before they finally settled on her mouth, giving her a deep, hungry kiss that brought her arching toward him and forced her on tiptoes. Her breasts flattened against his chest, and she could feel the buttons of his jacket marking her skin, every bit the brand of his mouth on hers.

They stood in the center of the room, bodies intertwined for a long time, reveling in the simplest of touches that heightened their desire while reaffirming that this pleasure was not a dream.

Rae's hands slipped beneath the tails of Jericho's superfine jacket and cupped the taut curve of his buttocks, pulling him toward her so that she might be held in the masculine cradle of his thighs. She slid her body sinuously against him, delighting in the contours that fit against her so well.

Jericho's fingers were far from idle, threading through the soft texture of Rae's hair and teasing the sensitive back of her neck. His thumb traced the column of her spine and sent a shiver of pure sensation through her that shook him as well. His hand slipped between them, urging the straps of her chemise downward over her shoulders and lifting her breasts free of the thin material. For a moment he did nothing but look, holding her a little back from him. His darkening eyes alone were enough to cause Rae's nipples to harden, and his smile maddened her even as it made her heart thud erratically.

She could barely breathe as one of his hands cupped the underside of her breast and the thumb flicked across the coral tip. His other hand supported her shoulders as his head slowly lowered and her head fell back, raising her breast to his mouth. A startled cry, more a whimpered rush of air, broke free of Rae's throat as Jericho took the budding end in his teeth and gave a gentle tug. Strings of hot desire pulled at her fingers, curling them in his bright yellow hair and holding him to her while his tongue laved her sensitive flesh.

She felt a wave of disappointment when his mouth lifted, but it vanished as he sought her other breast and repeated his loving ministrations. She rocked in his arms as her toes seemed to lose purchase on the floor, and she thought she would fall. But his arm was there, waiting for her, first beneath her thighs, then sliding to the back of her knees. She was lifted in the air and held there, close to his chest, while her arms circled his neck and her mouth planted kisses on his cheeks and jaw and finally on his finely carved mouth.

She loved the taste of him, the sweet-salty taste of his skin, the faintly bitter taste of ale on his tongue. Her teeth nibbled at his lower lip until a soft groaning sound in his throat made her pull away.

Jericho rolled with her onto the bed and the mattress and ropes sighed heavily with their combined weight and the force of their tumble. The sound made Rae laugh, and Jericho pressed his lips to her neck so that he might feel her delight. Her joy at unexpected things drenched him with happiness.

"Jericho?"

"Mmmm?" His mouth was still against her throat and her voice tickled him.

"We've barely said good day; no, in point of fact we've yet to say good day, and here I am about to be ravished. Shouldn't we talk?"

He raised his head so that it hovered above her. "Good day." He punctuated each word with a kiss.

"I mean it, Mr. Smith."

"Sssh! M'lord to you, Miss Saucebox."

Rae evaded Jericho's next buss so that his lips landed on the cord in her neck. It didn't bother him at all and he nuzzled her quite contentedly, refusing to be put off by this late show of propriety. Rae tried to lift his shoulders, but it was quite useless. "Jericho. Please listen to me, I'm afraid we've gone about this all wrong. I don't want to fall into your arms like some demirep."

"Why? I don't mind."

His hands were on her bare breasts again, and Rae found it difficult to concentrate, especially when she wanted to make love as urgently as he. Still, there were some things that had to be said. She only had a glimmer of an idea of what he had been doing these weeks past, and she wanted to know all before she had to return to Linfield. "Please stop a moment and let me think."

Jericho's hands quieted on her breasts, but he did not remove them. "Red, I know you are full of curiosity, but the time to ask questions is before or after, not during. Since we've already passed before and this is during, that leaves us with after. I would be pleased if you would observe these simple rules of etiquette and have done. We're going to have a fight, you and I, one that's bang up to the mark, once we get around to talking, and I'd rather save it for after.'' Barely drawing in air, he kissed her soundly. Her arms stole around his neck and he broke the kiss. "What would you rather do?''

When he kissed her like that Rae's answer was easy. Talking could definitely wait until after.

Jericho sat up and Rae helped him out of his closely fitting jacket. She smiled to herself when he hung it neatly on the bedpost. He had a reputation to maintain, one that did not include wrinkled and disreputable coats with loose buttons and torn sleeves. He saw the direction of her gaze and grinned, then tossed his shirt on the floor as if to say to hell with it. Rae slipped out of her shoes, stockings, and undergarments and threw them with abandon toward his fallen shirt. She made a seductive show of ridding herself of her dagger and delighted in his lusty regard. The rest of Jericho's clothes joined the pile, and he slipped beneath the sheets that Rae held open for him.

They snuggled and teased and warmed each other with the palms of their hands and the soles of their feet.

"Mr. Franklin's stove provides but a spark of heat compared to you, Red.''

"Jericho, if that was your idea of a romantic compliment, you are sadly mistaken.''

Laughter rumbled deep in his chest, which Rae caught as it trembled on his lips. Her thighs parted and she reached for him, guiding his entry, a little in awe of what her body accepted, nay demanded, in fulfillment. His thrust was slow, and once he was in her completely he was still. Above her his eyes taunted her, watching her carefully to see if she was inclined to move first.

Rae's eyes closed briefly under his penetrating stare then, marshalled her senses to maintain a semblance of control.

Finally, a smile lifted her lips as the humor of it struck her. "M'lord," she husked, "I feel I must point out that as stubborn as you and I are, we are apt to expire in this position before one of us twitches."

There was an explosion of laughter that nearly drove them apart, but at least got them to move. They were hard-pressed to capture a rhythm after that, and as a satisfaction to their flesh this bout of loving left something to be desired, but as a touching of their hearts, it was everything they craved.

Jericho's seed spilled into Rae, and she trapped him with her long legs, relishing the feel of his weight on her. Slowly she released him, and he rolled from her, propping himself on one elbow.

"Sweet heaven, Red, the next time I make love to you I'm going to put a gag over your mouth. You very nearly had me undone there with your untimely humor."

"Poor man. And what pleasure would there be if I could not touch you with my mouth?" The tip of her tongue teased her upper lip as she gazed at him through drowsily wanton eyes.

"You make it hard to get out of bed," Jericho sighed, eyeing her mouth with a great deal of interest.

Rae's eyebrows wriggled comically as she looked at the sheet lying flatly over Jericho's middle. "I do? It doesn't look—"

Humor vanished from Jericho's face as he grabbed her hand and placed it over him. Through the sheet Rae felt the warm throbbing as blood coursed through him, and she gasped, much struck by this turn of events.

"Oh, surely not, Jericho. Not so soon."

"My body says otherwise, though I've never known the like before. Can you take me again, Red?" he asked, bringing her body flush against him, forcing her to feel her effect on him.

Mutely she nodded and opened herself to him.

"No, dearest, I've no taste for sacrifices. Let me pleasure you."

Rahab did not think it possible that she might feel such intense desire sweep through her so soon after lying with him. Jericho proved her wrong. His mouth and hands were everywhere, on her tingling breasts, the soft curve of her elbow, the damp hair at her thighs, until she reached a pitch of longing equal to his own. When she thought he would come into her, he surprised her again by turning her on her stomach and massaging her back and slipping his fingers beneath her to graze her breasts. He drove strained little murmurs of wanting and need from her, and she found she was no longer embarrassed by the voice given to her body's pleasure.

Her eyes closed as his hands slid beneath her hips, lifting her, and she helped him, bracing herself on her forearms as he thrust deeply inside her. The sounds he could not hold back mixed with her own, and they became one voice as they became one flesh.

Jericho's hand stole around her front, and his fingers stroked her until she shuddered in violent release beneath him, and moments later he did the same. Replete, they lay in absolute silence, senses so full they were deaf to the sound of their own labored breathing.

Rae did not know she had fallen asleep until she felt Jericho's hand on her shoulder, gently nudging her awake. He was dressed now, looking very handsome and rather remote as he leaned over her, as if nothing that had happened still lingered. She sat up, pulling the sheet up to cover her breasts, and cursed the fates that decreed she should look so disheveled and wanton.

"It's time we talked, Red."

"You have me at a disadvantage. May I dress?"

"I want to keep you at a disadvantage, so no, you may not."

At first she thought he was joking, but then he sat on the bed and placed his arms on either side of her legs, effectively trapping her. His face was gravely intent and set on a purpose she did not understand. She could have moved, of course, but he would have hauled her back, and she refused to enact a scene that would shame them both.

"I do not want you to return to Linfield," he said without preamble.

Rae was encouraged that he had not forbidden it, but had merely said he did not want it. "I did not think you would. But I must go."

"Why?"

"Why? I thought your friend explained it to you. I want to find something to stop the duke from bothering Ashley or any of my family."

"That's what Drew told me, but it is not a good reason any longer, if it ever was. I have the means within my grasp of taking back Stanhope and eventually stopping Nigel Lynne. It is not necessary for you to risk yourself under his very nose while looking for something that may not exist."

"But you mean to kill the duke, don't you?"

Jericho was brutally frank. "Do you truly believe there is a lesser means that will work? Have you lived beneath his roof for so long that you have forgotten the sort of man he is? Your father and brothers and I did not plan anything but Nigel's death, and if we're damned for it, then so be it! But even now there could be someone on his way to the landing with no other goal than to bring Ashley here or kill your brother or hurt their children. Is that what you want?"

Rae slapped his face and felt no remorse as his cheek went from white to red. "How dare you ask such a question of me! I am afraid for them, but I also am afraid for you! Tell me what method will you use to kill him?"

Jericho touched his cheek with the back of his hand. She had landed him no ladylike slap. "Naturally, there is a danger to me," he said, striving for calm. "But it is as minimal as I can make it. When the time is right, I will challenge the duke to a duel."

Rae's eyes widened and she shook her head in bewilderment. "That is your idea of minimal danger? My brothers and father accepted that? Of all the cork-brained, misguided, infinitely foolish ideas—"

"Be still, Rahab, and listen." His tone brooked no argument, and Rae fell silent. "Your family knows I am a keen marksman. If the duel is conducted properly, I will not be thrown into Newgate. At worst I would find myself exiled to the Continent, and since I have little desire to live here, that is quite an acceptable risk."

"I cannot like it, Jericho." She blinked back tears.

"I would be hurt if you did," he said honestly, then squashed the hope that sprang to her deep green eyes. "But, no, I will not change my mind."

She looked away from his face and fingered the sheet at her breasts. "Tell me how you plan to regain Stanhope. It was you, wasn't it, that stopped the earl's coach?"

"Heard about that, did you?" he grinned. "Two of Drew's friends and I did that. Twice."

"I had only heard of one time."

"The earl had a married female companion with him the second time, so in deference to the lady's rep there must have been an agreement of silence. Surprising, that. Though how she explained the missing baubles to her husband, I cannot fathom."

"I'm not certain I understand how you are making use of your stolen gains." She touched the soft fabric of his jacket sleeve. "Though I gather you must be spending most of it with a London tailor, I fail to see the purpose."

"It is not the title, but the lands, which I have the opportunity to regain. I believe I told you that Newbrough is a gambler. And a poor one, too. He has lost a great deal over the years, but I had underestimated the size of my father's estate, and it is only very recently that Newbrough has overextended himself. The jewelry I took from him and his companion brought in just enough of the ready that I was able to, at least on the surface, make a presentable appearance at one of Newbrough's gaming halls. Have I mentioned that I show a remarkable talent for gambling?''

Rae smirked. "No, but then I cannot say it shocks me. Do you cheat?''

Jericho pretended to be aghast, then under her hard stare he said sheepishly, "On occasion.''

"I imagine you have a talent for that, also.'

"Regrettably so. The money I have won has been put into a respectable London residence, and Drew and his friends present a rather admirable, though somewhat rough, appearance as my servants. The house is fairly crowded with help, what with wives and all. I'm afraid they find it all a bit of a lark, even while they know the seriousness of the venture.''

"They are trustworthy?''

"Infinitely. Do not concern yourself on that score.'' Jericho rubbed Rae's calf lightly through the sheet. "I have established myself as a regular in some of the gaming halls and find myself much sought after. I think it is the mystery they like, for I am reticent to discuss myself, and it intrigues the others. There are bets in the books that I am recently returned from India where I made my fortune, and I do nothing to dissuade the speculation. I allude to a country estate in the north, and no one has bothered to ask for specifics. As long as my notes are good, and they have been proven to be so, everyone is well enough satisfied.''

"But Stanhope,'' Rae persisted, "what has it all to do with Stanhope?''

"I am gambling for Newbrough's notes, of course.''

Rae realized he thought it explained everything, but she felt all at sea. "So?''

"Dearest rattlebrain,'' Jericho went on patiently, "Newbrough's gambling debts are a veritable mountain of paper spread far afield. Each debt is not so large by itself, but the total is staggering. No one has pressured to collect because it is generally believed he is good for the blunt. If anyone other than myself knew the amount of his outstanding debts, he would be barred from playing. That would not suit my purpose, for I want to play cards with Newbrough, his notes against Stanhope. He must take the wager, because he knows if I choose to collect he will be ruined. If he turns me down he becomes a pariah. Once I have Stanhope, I will have the duke, for it is known he covets some of Newbrough's prime horseflesh. That's where I was headed today when I stopped here for lunch. I want a peek at Stanhope's stables.''

"How long will it be before you possess the bulk of the notes?''

"Two months at most. I will find no shortage of players once word gets out that I am only wagering on Newbrough's debts. He'll hear about it; there is no way he cannot, and no doubt he will try to win some back, but I intend to move quickly. It would help my play if I knew you were safe in my London home.''

She could not help but smile at the appeal in his voice. As your servant or your mistress?''

"As my wife.''

It was the last thing she expected to hear. She buried her face in her hands and began to cry.

"Aaah, Red, don't do that. Please.'' She simply sobbed harder. Jericho hauled her into his arms and lent her his shoulder. "Here. Look at this.'' Fumbling a bit, he unbuttoned his jacket and reached inside, waving a piece of paper in front of her. "This is a special license. We can be married anytime. If you recall, we talked about this on the ship. Why are you crying?''

She knuckled her eyes, wiped tear tracks from her cheeks with a corner of the sheet, and took a deep, steadying breath. "When we spoke of marriage on the ship I did not imagine our lives would still be influenced by the duke. Foolish of me, I suppose, but I pictured us living in comfortable anonymity until someone from the landing arrived for us. I did not think things would become so complicated.''

"Complicated how? What could be simpler than marrying me?''

"Nothing. But would it alter your plans for the duke?''

"No.''

"It would not alter mine, either. I want to stay at Linfield until this thing is at an end.''

"I cannot credit what I'm hearing.''

"I am not going to let you risk your life in a duel if there is another way to stop him. I will not be shut up in some fashionable London dwelling, twiddling my thumbs, while you are at Linfield squaring off at twenty paces.''

Because Jericho knew that he did not want to duel with Nigel in London, as it would bring unwanted attention, he had always thought the event would take place at Linfield. He hated the idea of Rae's being anywhere near when it happened. He wanted her away from the duke, and in this he would not be gainsaid. He grasped her wrists and gave her a small shake, as if to bring her to her senses. "Red, come with me.''

She shook her head, biting her lip to keep from wincing at his hurtful grip. "I would marry you today, Jericho, but I must return to Linfield tonight with Nancy and Jack. Do you not think it would cause a stir if I simply disappeared? Oh, I am not important enough to be searched for, and the duke would not know I was gone, but it would cause comment among the staff. Nancy and Jack will remember you when you arrive at Linfield.''

"What of it?''

"Jericho, I had to explain the circumstances of being abducted by Sam Judge in some way. They think I was a servant at the landing. They know I have a connection with Ashley. If I did not return this evening, you would be astonished at how easily Nancy would determine I left with you, and her speculation, fact or fiction, is not something that would aid our cause.

Should that reach the duke's ears, you would find yourself out in the cold.''

"I think you are making much of nothing.''

"I think I am being prudent.''

Jericho's laugh was joyless. He took Rae by her upper arms and sat her away from him. Then he got off the bed and moved to the window that faced the river, staring out at the white and barren landscape until his eyes fairly burned from the brightness. In his hands he held the special license, and his fingers shredded the paper into tiny pieces that fluttered to his feet like so many flakes of snow. Behind him Rae's harsh sob made no impact. He felt helpless. Surely there was something he could do to make Rae aware of the danger of her position.

Coming to a decision, he jerked off his jacket and tossed it on the chair that had Rae's damp dress draped over it, then he turned the full force of his bitter stare on Rahab. "You've run wild all your life, Red, and you've been given free rein by your father and brothers for so long that you don't know the meaning of prudent. Every scrape you've been in, there has been some man at your elbow to pull you to safety. Never have you been subjected to the full consequences of your foolish behavior. I extracted you from the dangerous, deadly game you played at Wolfe's. Salem's timely arrival saved you from becoming my whore, and make no mistake, that's what you would have been, because I thought you a spy. You acted without caution or discretion when you told Sam Judge you were Ashley, and you paid for it with your abduction and nearly with your life. A simple footman saw to your safety that time.

"I have had enough, Rahab. I will not be taken in by your bravado or your swaggering airs simply because you know how to wield a dagger and shoot a pistol. You are a woman and ill-equipped to pretend you are a match for someone like Nigel Lynne. If you are found doing anything untoward at Linfield, you will have no defense. No servant will lift a finger to help you. Perhaps Nigel will not have you killed immediately upon

discovering you are a McClellan, but he will use you. Think
how much delight he would find in setting you up as his mistress, knowing how it would shame you and hurt your family.

"Does the thought of lying with the duke have some appeal
for you? I understand he is between mistresses right now and
has a vacant house not far from St. James Park."

Rae was sitting up very straight, her legs curled beneath her,
anger born of hurt and fear in every line of her body. Her eyes
glistened, but there were no tears. Two bright spots of color
stood out on her cheeks, but the rest of her face was very nearly
the shade of the sheet that was wrapped around her.

"Does it please you to speak so vilely to me?"

Jericho's eyes narrowed. "Yes," he fairly hissed. "Yes, it
does! Do you know why?" He saw Rae's head give a little
jerk backward at his tone. "Because I want to throttle you. No,
I shall be more specific," he said with deadly calm, advancing
on the bed. "I want—" he paused. His foot struck the pile of
Rae's discarded clothes and he saw the wooden dagger. He
picked it up and handed it to her, slapping the hilt in the palm
of her hand. "Use it, Red. Show me how you will stop the duke
when he surprises you rifling his secret drawer," he taunted.

Rahab dropped the knife. "No. I don't have to prove anything
to you. You've seen me use it before. I killed a man,
remember?"

"I do. But do you?"

Rae put her fingers to her pounding temples and shut her
eyes. It was enough answer for Jericho.

"You don't. You still can't recall what it is like to feel the
end of your knife strike flesh and bone. Your insides don't
crawl at the memory of burying steel into warm muscle or the
blossoming of blood on a chest as you extract your blade. You
think this is a game because you can't remember when it was
real!" Roughly he pulled her left hand from her temple and
thrust the dagger into her palm, holding her hand around the
hilt until she gripped it herself. "Now use it. Show me how

you will keep the duke out of your bed when he decides he wants you!''

She shook her head, the ache behind her eyes nearly blinding her. ''No!''

''Dammit, use it!''

She thrust weakly at him, and Jericho merely stepped back from the bed to elude her.

''You'll have to do better than that. The duke will laugh at that show of protest. Mayhap he will think you like a little sport to make you hot.''

She cursed him for his crudity.

The words slipped by Jericho, making no impact on his implacable expression. He grabbed a loose edge of the sheet that covered Rae and pulled hard. She tried to get it back, even slashed at the material with her dagger, but Jericho was stronger, and she had to choose between being dragged toward him or being uncovered. She chose to scramble to the far side of the bed and watched him warily.

Jericho's boots thumped to the floor and the intent in his eyes were clear. ''It will do no good to scream at Linfield,'' he said conversationally. ''Do you know that Ashley was nearly raped by one of the duke's guests and no one lifted a finger until the old sot passed out? I see you didn't know. Neither did I, until Salem told me the night we planned the duke's murder. He wanted to make certain I knew the sort of man I was going to meet. Are you going to use that dagger, Red?''

''Stay away from me, Jericho.''

''I've taken another name. I am known as Thomas, Lord Adams, now.''

''And your conduct is a shame to both the parents whose name you bear. Leave me be!''

A muscle jumped in his cheek, once, then his face was still. ''I've never taken any woman against her will in my life, Red. I know what it is to be held helpless! Shall I give you a taste of it?''

Rae moved as far as she could away from him, until her shoulder was flush to the wall. Her head pounded relentlessly and her hands shook. "Do not do this thing. You cannot help but regret it."

"You credit me with too many finer feelings." He unfastened his breeches but did not bother to remove them or his shirt. "You'll have to use the knife, Red."

She sprang at him then, fury making her forget caution. The force of her lunge did push Jericho away from the bed just as he was preparing to sit, but it left Rae awkwardly splayed on the mattress. The arm that held the knife hung over the side of the bed, and before she could pull it up Jericho pressed his knee against her elbow until excruciating pain made her drop the blade.

He kicked it across the floor and pulled Rae up by her shoulders and turned her on her back. She kicked and flailed her fists at him, and though he took a good measure of abuse before he wrestled her to exhaustion, in the end he simply straddled her stomach and held her wrists down over her head. She turned her face to one side as Jericho's head lowered.

She expected to feel his mouth on her, so she was surprised when he merely spoke in a strained whisper above her ear. "You've seen the duke, haven't you?" She nodded. "He is a fit man, I believe." She nodded again. "Well capable of disarming you and holding you down thusly."

"Yes. You know he can."

Jericho smiled malevolently. "He won't even have to hold you down for long. Nigel Lynne uses shackles. Had you heard?"

"You're just saying that to frighten me."

"You're damn right I'm saying it to frighten you! But it is not a fabrication. How protected you were in the loving arms of your family! Even Ashley, growing up inside Linfield's cold walls, knowing virtually nothing beyond its boundaries, still was less an innocent than you. She learned as a child of the cruelties one human being can inflict upon another. Why are you looking so bewildered? Has she never told you about the birthmark on her breast?''

''I don't know what you mean.''

''Dear God, Rahab. So sheltered from life's unpleasantries! I wish that Ashley had told you, better yet, shown it to you, just once, while her child suckled at her breast! You needed to see with your own eyes what was done to her, then we would not be having this conversation. There is no birthmark, Red. Your sister-in-law was branded. That is how the Duke of Linfield deals with innocence. She was a babe! A babe!''

''You do love her,'' Rae said, feeling frightened and betrayed by the emotion in his voice.

''No! Can you not understand? I admire her. She has known every sort of brutality at Nigel's hands, and she emerged whole, and clean, and able to love. I wanted that, envied it! Then I stumbled upon you, fresh-faced, saucy, and winsome, and you made me feel those things. Can you blame me for wanting to keep you sheltered from your own recklessness a while longer?''

''No. I don't blame you.''

''Then come to London with me, Red, where there is no chance of your falling into harm.''

''Jericho,'' she said gently, her heart in her throat. ''I need to do this. Perhaps it is time I was unwrapped from cotton wool. I tell you, I am safe at Linfield. Let me be a help to you there.''

Jericho's face was cold, his eyes the icy blue-gray of winter's sky. ''I wish I had never gone to Wolfe's that night,'' he said harshly. ''Go to Linfield, if that is your desire. But know that I will not lift a finger to pull you from any coil you find yourself in. When I leave this room you will cease to exist for me. Does it make a difference to your plans?''

Her voice was choked. ''No.''

''Then there is only one thing more I want from you, Red.''

Rae blinked widely, paling at his words, at the intention she thought she read in his eyes. Afraid of him now in a way she had never been, she sought to protect herself, to fight with the only weapon she had left. "It's bred in the bone, isn't it, Geoffrey?" she said, using his given name deliberately. "You really are naught but a whore's bastard!"

Rae's thoughts had barely been given sound when she realized her grave error. Jericho's face was no longer etched with glacial anger. The moment had passed when he was in full control of his every action. Reason had vanished beneath her stinging words, and in its place was something elemental and primitive, frighteningly ugly. Threats had become promises.

Jericho forgot he had only wanted to frighten her, make her aware of the risk she was taking. Whore's bastard. Whore's bastard. The taunt echoed in his mind, and it was all he heard. Pain was all he felt.

His mouth caught hers brutally, and though she twisted her head she could not completely evade his savage kisses. Not kisses, she thought; they were too punishing to be kisses. There was no hint of tenderness, no real passion, indeed, the emotion that drove him was a tidal wave of anger.

She would never forget how he took her then. And it was a taking, for she gave nothing in return. When his fingers left her wrists, leaving red marks in their wake, she did not lift her arms to shield herself. They remained limply above her, unmoving, as if weighted by the duke's shackles. She had no response for the hard sweep of his hands over her shoulders and breasts or the rough, bruising kisses he placed on her throat.

This was not Jericho, she thought, and she was not Rahab. This violation was happening to two strangers, and she did not think it odd that he was as much victim as she even as she hated him for it.

Jericho's mouth at her breast was not intended to arouse, but merely to show her that he could do as he wanted. His tongue laved her nipples and they hardened slightly, but there was no pleasure in the sensation.

He eased himself down her body, then unstraddled her, placing himself between her thighs. His hands slipped beneath her hips, lifting her, then there was a slight hesitation. Rae's dark eyes sought him out, but Jericho was blind to her pleading, half-pitying glance, and he forced his entry.

Finally one of Rae's hands lifted and she bit the fleshy pad of her palm to keep from crying out. She stared at the ceiling and waited for it to be over. Jericho's hips quickened and the thrusts were deep, painful. She heard him curse violently, then he was withdrawing. She turned on her side away from him and faced the wall.

He left the bed and dressed unhurriedly. In her mind Rae could see him moving with his easy grace. On his way to the door he paused. "My father always had some trinket for his whore. As you say, ma'am, it's bred in the bone." Rae heard him flip a coin on the bed, and what he had not already crushed, caved in at this final humiliation. "Don't tarry in bed. You have to meet your friends soon. Good day."

Rae's monthly courses did not follow in two weeks. At the end of six she could no longer ignore the fact that sometime that afternoon, whether in laughter, love, or violence, Jericho had got her with child.

Chapter 12

The baby changed everything.

Rahab knew that whatever she was willing to risk for herself, she was unwilling to risk any measure that might endanger her child. Jericho could not have foreseen that the one certain way to make her leave Linfield was to give her responsibility for another life, but he had managed to make her yield to his wishes nonetheless. She did not thank him for it.

Even before she knew she was carrying his child, not a day passed that she did not think of him as she had last seen him, ruthless and hurtful, forcing her to acknowledge his command and her own vulnerability. The memories aroused no hatred in her breast, no bitter anger. She felt only a dull ache, and in time that, too, passed.

She supposed in some way Jericho had ceased to exist for her also, in much the same manner he had vowed to put her from his mind. She did not find it difficult to believe he never gave her a thought after leaving the room at the inn; he was more adept at erecting barriers than she.

As she made plans in her mind to leave Linfield, she would idly wonder about the reception Jericho would give her. Rae imagined he would take her in, even marry her once she told him about the child, but it would be an emotionless sort of existence for both of them. She could not imagine them trusting each other any longer with anything so fine and fragile as love, but mayhap they would come to share regard. It would be a marriage for the sake of their child, one of convenience, and lacking passion. She would allow him his mistresses, and some day she might take a lover, but Jericho Smith would never touch her intimately again. The thought of his hands on her body made her feel sick.

Rae gave the china candelabrum in the duke's library a final brush with her duster and glanced around the room to see that it was in order. She supposed Nigel was still eating breakfast with his guest of the last two days, Charles Newbrough. Rae wished the earl had not come to Linfield, because it was a strain to do her work and avoid both men. In truth, the duke was easier to pass by, because he simply took no notice. Newbrough, however, she caught staring after her when she hurried from a room he occupied. Nancy had seen it also and had warned Rae to make herself scarce. Nancy had no idea how seriously Rae intended to take her advice.

Rahab glanced upward and saw that a few books on the topmost shelf had been put away with their bindings facing the wrong way. Newbrough's doing, she thought disgustedly. The duke was not so careless.

Linfield's library held more books than Rae had ever seen. The shelves began at the floor and reached the ceiling on two sides, and because of the enormous height of the room it had been necessary to build a deck about two-thirds up the wall. The highest stacks could be reached by using a small, polished oak stepstool that remained on the loft at all times. There were a comfortable leather chair and a cherry wood table beside it. Two brass candlesticks had been placed there for the ease of a reader who did not want to return to the main floor with his books.

Rahab climbed the first ladder to the deck, pulled the stool where she wanted it, then stood on tiptoes on the top rung to reach the disarranged volumes. Blast and damn, she thought, when her fingers nudged the books and five of them came toppling down around her head. One of them hit her shoulder and nearly knocked her from her perch, but she managed to regain her balance by grasping at the shelves.

Much put out by her own clumsiness, she got off the stepstool and knelt on the deck to gather the books. Two of them were law books and held no interest for her, another was something in Latin which she could not read. The fourth volume she picked up was a slender book, and she supposed it to be a book of poetry until she read the title: *Memoirs of a Woman of Pleasure*. There could be no doubt this was the book Newbrough had been reading. Amused and not a little intrigued, Rae lay on her stomach on the deck and began to thumb through the pages written by an author she had never heard of, John Cleland. Thirty minutes later, blushing to the roots of her hair and feeling a peculiar quickening in her breathing, she knew well enough why no one had ever told her of this book. The heroine, Fanny Hill, was an adventuress, and that was the kindest thing Rahab could think to say of her.

She shut the book and glanced at the last tome lying on the deck near her face. Her blush deepened. It was the Bible. Surely this was no accident, but the Hand of Providence. With the tips of two fingers she nudged Fanny Hill away from her and brought the heavy Bible closer. Strange, she thought, that Nigel kept what was obviously the Linfield family Bible so far out of reach. Not that he was a God-fearing man, by any means. He didn't attend services in the chapel, even though he provided them for his servants, but the book deserved finer care than it had received next to the likes of *Memoirs of a Woman of Pleasure*.

Rae opened the cover and found the Linfield genealogy dutifully recorded in a list of marriages, births, and deaths, all properly noted with dates, and sometimes, in the case of deaths, causes.

Fascinated, Rae forgot about time, her work, or the inappropriateness of her behavior as one of the staff, and traced the history of the Lynnes of Linfield from the beginning of Queen Elizabeth's reign to the present. She saw that Nigel's father had recorded the death of his wife and the birth of his twins on the same day. The ink was smeared slightly by a watermark where she imagined grief had overtaken him. The next entries were in Nigel's own hand, and they puzzled her. He had recorded the death of his father, and a few weeks later, in his same impatient scrawl, he had written the date of his sister's death, recorded the cause as childbirth, and noted the name of the child: Ashley Caroline Lynne. Yet Rae knew the duke let it be believed his twin had drowned and had never told Ashley until her nineteenth year that she was his niece. She wondered why he would give out lies and record the truth.

Thinking about it, Rae idly turned the pages of the Bible, scanning the verses to find something that would be of particular solace to her now. Instead she happened upon the last thing she wanted to find: The Duke of Linfield's last will and testament. Not Nigel's. His father's.

Why, when she wanted to put the intrigue behind her, had she had the misfortune to stumble upon it? Rae hesitated, wondering if she had the strength of purpose to put it from her and pretend this document did not exist. She knew she did not. Fingers trembling, she unfolded the vellum pages with great care.

Robert McClellan had always believed that the old duke had made his daughter Anne the heiress to Linfield, or her issue should she die. Rae's father maintained that Nigel Lynne had never been intended to be the owner of the Linfield holdings, that they rightly belonged to Ashley as Anne's daughter. But without a shred of proof, without the will, it all remained speculation, and Nigel inherited as the duke's only surviving offspring.

When Rae finished reading, her fingers trembled the more and her heart raced as if she had just run the stairs. Her father's words had ceased to be speculation. Here was proof that the old duke had taken measure of his son and found him wanting in every respect, even thinking of him as evil, if the dying man's prose was to be believed. Nigel's father had been willing to let the title die rather than pass it to his son, and the holdings were, without exception, to be placed in his daughter's name.

This document, along with the record of Ashley's birth in Nigel's own hand, offered better hope for destroying Nigel Lynne than a lead ball from Jericho's pistol. She could have wept that she had found it now, when the risk of carrying it away seemed out of proportion to the life she carried within her.

She refolded the pages and tucked them in the book exactly as she had found them. Closing the Bible, she rested her cheek against its leather cover and shut her eyes. So many thoughts raced through her head that she could not hear herself think. When calm finally asserted itself and her mind was blissfully quiet, she realized for the first time that she was no longer alone in the room.

The duke was there with Newbrough, and she supposed it was owing to her position, flush to the deck, that neither man had seen her when they entered. She dared not move now, or even lift her head to see where they were. From the sound of their voices it seemed they were near the hearth, probably seated and enjoying a late-morning cup of tea. Very faintly in the midst of the conversation she could hear the clink of china cups being set upon their saucers. She nearly groaned aloud when she thought of how long they might have been there, and how easily she could have been surprised while reading the will. Worse, how long she had been in the loft. Someone was bound to begin to wonder where she had gone.

Carefully she slipped her cheek from its resting place and laid it against the deck's hardwood floor. There was naught to do but wait . . . and listen.

"I'm telling you, Nigel, I need a diversion. If I must think on what this upstart Adams is doing, I shall go mad. What say you to a hunt? With Lady Georgina as the vixen? It's been a long time since you've had an entertainment here. You used to host the most delicious revels."

"I say the idea bores me. And Lady Georgina? She'd let herself be caught in the thicket just beyond the front door. There is no sport in that."

"But there would be plenty of sport in what follows," the earl laughed wickedly. "I hear she's a near insatiable toss."

"And will open her thighs, I understand, for any man . . . or woman."

"Truly?" Newbrough was much caught by the idea.

"Really, Newbrough, she lacks any sort of spirit. I doubt her protestations as the hunters closed in would be very convincing. She'd be warding us off with one hand and lifting her skirts with the other. No, if I were in the mood for a hunt, I would choose my vixen more carefully than Georgina."

"Lady Catherine Kearns, perhaps? She reminds me a bit of the portrait in your study. Your sister, I believe."

The duke smiled faintly, unwilling to be drawn. "There is some resemblance, I suppose. Cathy intrigues me. Let us leave it at that. Tell me more about this Adams fellow. What do you know about him?"

Newbrough sighed and rubbed the bridge of his hooked nose with his forefinger. "I believe I've told you all I know. He's recently arrived from India, the wags have it, and he's bent on ruining me. What more is there?"

"Quite a lot, I should think. His family, for one thing. Where are his lands and how did he come by his title?"

"Don't know about his family. I spoke to Evans and Lesley on the matter, but they said they were unable to draw him out. The man's a closed one, he is. They say he rarely talks while he is playing and afterwards simply vanishes. It is rumored he came by his title because of his contributions to the royal coffers. Nothing strange in that. And apparently he holds some lands in the north.''

"He's well off, then?''

"Quite. He's won and lost thousands of pounds at the tables. He'll wager on anything, too. Evans said he once laid three hundred on the number of flounces decorating Lord Hardy's mistress's underskirt. He won, of course. Damn lucky fellow. If it had been Hardy's wife, he would have been called out.''

"If he can make so many easy wagers without losing his shirt, why is he collecting your notes? And why yours and no one else's? You're not the only man in London ready to take residence on Dun Street.''

"That's a poser. I can't make it out beyond thinking the man wants to ruin me.''

"Can he?''

Newbrough shifted uncomfortably in his chair and took a quick sip of tea. His hand shook visibly. "I imagine it depends on the cards he's dealt and how his luck holds.''

"It was careless of you to amass debts to so many people, Newbrough,'' Nigel drawled in disinterested accents. "And dishonorable not to make good on them. What are you going to do about him?''

"Do? Why I'm trying to win back my notes, of course.''

"From Adams?''

"No, from the others who still have them. I can't find Adams to play him.''

Nigel smiled at the earl's discomfort. "I have a feeling he'll find you when he wants to collect. Have you many notes still out?''

"That's the hell of it, Nigel. I've more now than when I started. I've had nothing but bad luck with the cards."

"You're no more than an average player," the duke said bluntly. "I should think mediocrity is finally taking its toll."

The earl did not take offense at Nigel's plain speech, for the truth was obvious to him also. "You should know. You have a few of my notes yourself."

"More than a few. Two thousand pounds' worth. Don't panic. I'll make you a gift of them."

Newbrough's tiny eyes brightened. "That's damn generous of you."

"In return for the bay mare I've had my eye on since you brought her home from auction."

"Can't do it," Newbrough said, his shoulders slumping. "She's gone."

"What?"

"She's gone. Stolen, I suspect, though I can't prove it. There was a fire in the stables not above six weeks ago. The grooms got all the horses out, but could not account for some of the best stock when all was over. Said they wandered off, but no one knows where they wandered to. Naturally the men were dismissed, but there's no replacing the prime cattle."

"You *have* had a nasty run of luck. Two robberies, a fire in your stables, your notes being systematically collected. Is it coincidence or Lord Adams?"

"How can I say?"

"I'd make it my business to find out."

"As to that, I was wondering if you might play a few hands with his nibs. You have my notes. He would play you."

"I could lose them," Nigel pointed out.

"What? You don't lose."

"Your confidence warms my heart," Nigel said dryly. "But tell me, why should I wager with this man? What have I to gain? Your notes are virtually worthless. Don't you see, if I won them you would be as indebted to me as you would be to this Adams.''

"Yes, but you wouldn't force a collection. I could honor the notes over time.''

"Years, by the sounds of it. Don't be so certain I wouldn't press my advantage, Newbrough. I only say that to warn you. Do you still wish me to try my hand?''

"Yes. I know you would deal honorably with me.''

"I detect more hopefulness in your tone than conviction. We shall see, won't we? I'll send a man to London and invite Lord Adams here. I've no taste for going there at the moment. I rather think I shall provide you with that diversion you spoke of. Linfield will host an entertainment like none that has been seen in years.''

The earl clapped his hands together. "Capital! When do—''

Nigel cocked his head to one side and held up a hand to stifle Newbrough's question. "What was that?''

"What? I didn't hear anything.''

"I did.'' He rose from his chair and walked toward the door so that he had a better view of the library deck. "Why I think we have had a third party to our conversation. Come down from there, girl.''

Rae thought her heart would surely burst in her chest, but she remained on the floor with her eyes closed and pretended not to hear the stern command then, nor when it was repeated in stronger tones a moment later. She heard the library door open and the duke summon Stephens.

"It appears one of your staff is showing a shocking lack of conscience for her work.'' Nigel pointed in the direction of the loft. "Get her down from there. Immediately.''

Stephens nearly lost his solemn composure when he saw it was Rae sprawled on the deck. The length of her body gave her away. He climbed the ladder stiffly and shook her shoulder. "Get up, girl.'' Rae still did not move. It was then Stephens noticed displaced books and the location of the stepstool. He turned to the duke. "I believe she's been hurt, your grace. She's not merely sleeping. I think some books must have landed on her."

"Don't tell me about it, do something with her."

Rae would have liked to pretend unconsciousness so that she might be carried out without ever having to say anything for herself. But it worried her that the descent from the ladder would be dangerous if she was lifted, and she was mindful that a fall could hurt her babe. When Stephens touched her shoulder again, this time placing her fingers over the place where a book had indeed bruised her, she winced and chose that moment to feign coming around.

She opened her eyes in what she hoped was a dazed and distressed fluttering and immediately put a hand to the back of her head as if to feel for a knot. "Oh, my!" she said, pretending surprise at finding Stephens's face so close to her own. "What? Oh, the books!" She made a convincing show of painful movement as she sat up. At least she had convinced Stephens; she dared not look at the duke or Newbrough, who had left his seat and now stood by the opposite wall that he might also have an unobstructed view of what was happening.

"Can you come down on your own?" Stephens asked.

"Yes, I think I can manage. Let me get the books."

"Leave them. Someone else can put them away."

"But—"

"Leave them."

Rae was loath to do as Stephens requested, for she wanted no one chancing upon what she had found. Still, she had little choice, as Stephens was giving her one of his hard stares that boded ill if she disobeyed. She did stack the books before she followed him down the ladder and tried not to think of Newbrough's beady eyes taking stock of her ankles as she did so.

Without looking at either Nigel or Newbrough, she dipped an apologetic curtsy and hurried across the room. At the door, the duke stepped in front of her, blocking her exit. He moved her to one side, allowing Stephens to leave.

"Not so quickly," he said, when she attempted to follow the butler. "What were you doing up there?"

"I was righting some books, your grace," Rae answered softly, striving for an accent that would not betray her colonial upbringing.

"And what occasioned you to be on the deck with your ear to the floor?"

"Oh, no, your grace, I wasn't eavesdropping! I swear it!"

"Did I say you were?"

"No, but—"

"But?"

"Nothing, your grace," she said meekly. What was it they said about a guilty conscience needing no accuser? Another untimely slip of her errant tongue and surely she would be mousemeat. "One of the books fell on my head and knocked me off the stool. I don't remember beyond that until Stephens touched me."

"Indeed? Then I wonder what noise brought your presence to my attention?"

"I cannot say."

The duke was thoughtful, looking at Rae's bowed head covered in a fresh white mobcap, but whatever he was thinking he kept to himself. "You may go." He stepped aside for her, and once she was beyond hearing he turned to Newbrough. "Watch her for me, would you? You have an eye for that sort of thing."

Newbrough's brow raised in interest. "A pleasure, but why?"

"There is something . . . no matter. Just see that she is not involved in any mischief."

Stephens was waiting for Rahab at the bottom of the servants' stairs. "You very nearly cooked your goose that time, m'girl. If you value your position you'll be more careful in the future."

Rahab bobbed her assent. "May I go? I've the music room to do."

"Yes. Go. But mind that the spinet doesn't fall on your head."

Rae thought she very nearly saw a smile on Stephens's hard mouth. Wonder of wonders.

When Rae reached the music room, Nancy was already there.

"Where have you been?" Nancy demanded suspiciously. Rae's explanation was interrupted frequently by Nancy's expressions of shock and horror. "Are you feeling quite the thing now?"

"Yes. I only have a bruise on my shoulder." She showed Nancy the red mark. "I can finish in here. Leave me your duster. Mine must be in the library. And I'm not going back for it."

"I should say. Forget about it, I may as well help you in here." She handed Rae a polishing cloth. "Give the chairs a good rubbing."

Rae set about her task with vigor, willing herself not to think about all she had heard in the library. But curiosity was eating her, and she finally dared to broach one subject with Nancy. "What is a hunt?"

Nancy's hand stilled, then resumed dusting a shade frantically. "Surely you've heard of a hunt. Foxes and hounds, that sort of thing. They must have them in America."

"Yes, of course, but I don't think they're the same as the ones at Linfield."

"Why do you say that?"

"It was something I overheard and—"

Nancy gasped. "You *were* eavesdropping!"

"No. No, I wasn't, not intentionally anyway. I was lying on the deck and I couldn't move. Can I help it that I heard some things? What would you have done?"

Nancy's appalled expression vanished and she giggled. "Listened to everything," she admitted. "What did you hear?"

Bless her, Rae thought. "The earl suggested that his grace host a hunt. Then he mentioned a Lady Georgina. What do you make of that?"

"Hmmpf. Like as not his lordship wants to hunt for the lady."

"That's what I thought they meant, but I didn't understand."

Nancy's voice became hushed as she knelt beside Rahab and flicked her duster over the spindle-legged chair. "It's been a long time since there was a hunt like that at Linfield. His grace invites all his fast friends and their ladies, mostly demireps, but a few quality whose tastes run to licentious ways. This house fairly swells with guests, I can tell you. The revel usually lasts a week, and I cannot begin to describe the sort of carryings on that go unremarked by the guests." Rae nearly laughed as Nancy then began to catalogue the activities. "Lords and ladies coming and going from bedrooms late into the night, drinking first thing in the morning, and card playing till some of the players fall asleep at the tables. There's dancing, of course, and musicians, and feasting the likes of which you can only imagine. But the hunt is always held on the day before the guests depart. Oh, must you hear it?"

"Yes. I want to know. I suspect I shall find out soon enough, for I think the duke intends to have one."

"Very well, but you'll have to pardon my plain speaking." She took a deep breath and explained in a rush. "On the morning of the hunt the men choose one of the ladies to be the vixen. Most often she is a willing participant, but sometimes not. It makes little difference, for she has no choice but to play. She is given a start on the hunters and freedom to go anywhere on the lands, but to prevent her from wandering too far afield she must wear a collar with bells on it that cannot be removed except by key. There is only one, and the duke has it."

"You are making this up."

"No! I swear it is so! And it becomes worse. When she is

cornered by a hunter, or hunters, if she should be so unfortunate, she must surrender.''

"Surrender? How?"

"She must lie with him . . . or them. It may even be a woman who finds her, for the ladies are free to take part in the hunt if they desire. The vixen is the pet of her captor for the entire day and night and the collar is affixed to a slender chain that leads to her owner's wrist. Once she is found, there is no escape for her.''

"That is depraved!"

"Aye, it is. But the participants do not seem to find it so. I cannot understand it myself. I shudder when I think we might have it here again. It's not decent.''

Rae smiled grimly at Nancy's understatement. "Mayhap it will not occur. The duke told Newbrough he was bored with the idea of a hunt.''

"I hope it is so," she said fervently. "I have known of two of them. It is enough.''

But the duke did not ask his parlormaids' opinions. Footmen were dispatched the following day to deliver his invitations to the revel at Linfield, which was scheduled for some four weeks hence. Rae tried to console Nancy that perhaps this party would not end in a hunt, but neither girl was convinced. Neither were any of the other servants. They shook their heads, whispered among themselves that good Christian folk shouldn't be subjected to such Bacchanalia, but bore the extra duties stoically, too secure in their posts to venture speaking out or attempting to find new employment.

Rahab had no such qualms about leaving. She determined she could depart on a Saturday, some two weeks before Linfield filled with guests, without causing any disturbance. The gold coin Jericho had tossed at her to humiliate her would buy her a seat on the coach to London. She had given the matter a great deal of thought and had concluded there was only one thing she could do. Risk or no, she would arrive at Jericho's residence before he left, with the old duke's will and the record of Ashley's birth from the Bible, and do all that was in her power to convince him not to accept the invitation to Linfield.

It remained only for her to take the documents she needed from the library.

Rae chose her time carefully, waiting for a morning when the duke and Newbrough were out riding. It was under Mrs. Ritchie's directive that she was sent into the library, so Rae thought herself safe enough. She glanced through the letters lying on a silver salver. They were probably responses to the duke's invitations. There was none from Jericho, and she took heart that there was still time to stop him.

Rae made a show of dusting the room, glad she had not gone straight to the Bible because the library was a veritable congregating place this morning. Stephens entered twice unexpectedly, looking for Mrs. Ritchie on both occasions, and Nancy flitted in and out to give her the latest confidences from Mrs. Timms, who was quite behind schedule what with preparing menus, supervising the baking, and still making certain the duke had this evening's meal at the appointed hour. The sweep boy came in to clean the hearth and left a sooty mess that Rahab in turn had to clean. By the time she reached the deck and fumbled for the Bible she had been in the library much longer than she thought proper, but was too afraid that the opportunity to recover the documents might not arise again soon enough for her plans not to take advantage of the situation.

She clutched the Bible to her bosom and descended the stool. Placing the heavy book on the top rung, she opened it and found—nothing. The record of births and deaths had been neatly torn out, and if she hadn't been looking for the frayed edging of the paper she wouldn't have known a page was missing. Quickly she thumbed the chapters to find the will. It was also gone. Desolation swept her as she replaced the book. No doubt Nigel had seen the books that had fallen and had taken the documents as a precaution, realizing if one such as she could stumble upon the incriminating Bible, it could be found by another.

Shoulders slumped, she sat on the stool wondering what she should do next. She thought about the duke's desk with its secret spring, but a healthy sense of cowardice overtook her. It was one thing to go through it when Nigel was in London, quite another while he was in residence. She touched her abdomen gently, hoping her babe would not inherit her timidity.

"Taking another repose from your labors, sweetings?"

The earl's voice so startled her that Rae nearly fell from her perch.

"Careful. You wouldn't want another tragic fall, would you?"

Rae looked down at Newbrough coldly, and she saw his eyebrows raise in surprise at her directness. Remembering her place, she lowered her eyes and slid off the stool. Her hesitancy to come down the ladder with the earl within a few feet of the bottom was clear.

"I can just as well come up, sweetings." He took a step forward to do just that.

His movement decided Rae. She was not about to be trapped on the deck with the likes of the Earl of Stanhope. She descended the ladder with as much caution and modesty as was possible, watching him warily over her shoulder. She faced forward only once, as her feet made to touch the floor, but it was enough opportunity for the earl to steal up behind her and place his hands about her waist. He turned her around and leaned her back against the ladder, then braced his arms on either side of her. The sleeves of his black velvet riding jacket brushed Rae's white blouse and reminded her of thick iron bars. He smelled faintly of horses and horse droppings. The thought that he had stepped in dung made Rae want to giggle hysterically.

"Let me pass, m'lord," she said, looking beyond his shoulder to the door. Please let it open, she thought. Nancy, where are you now?

"In a moment," he said easily. His eyes darted across her face, shoulders, and bosom, then came to rest on her mouth. "Why were you on the deck? Surely there were no more books out of place?"

"No, but I was dusting the bindings."

"Mmmm. With what?"

Rae followed the earl's glance to the mantelpiece where her duster lay. She prevaricated quickly. "That is, I went up there to dust, and was quite put out when I realized I'd left the thing behind."

"And you were deep in the consideration of your own ineptness when I surprised you."

"No, m'lord," she objected. "I was thinking on how tired I was and wondering if Mrs. Ritchie would notice if I were to forgo the upper shelves."

"How unconscionable of you to shirk your duties," the earl said dryly.

"Yes, m'lord, but there it is. May I pass?"

Newbrough's eyes were once again on Rae's mouth. "A penalty is in order first, I think."

"M'lord?"

"A kiss. Mayhap you will not find it disagreeable in the least." He sounded very certain of his prowess as his head lowered. He was rather stunned to find his attentions very much unwanted.

Rae turned her head to elude him and pushed with all her might at Newbrough's chest. While he did not go back far, it was enough to allow her to slip beneath his outstretched arms and run.

"Come back here!"

Rae ignored the command issued in thunderous tones and reached for the door handle. She twisted it, but it did not open.

"It's locked," the earl said calmly enough. He dangled the

key between his thumb and forefinger, then palmed it and slipped it inside his jacket. "Come here, sweetings."

Rae blanched but stayed where she was.

The earl began to advance. "I don't mind a bit of a chase, it adds sweetness to the prize. Is that your thinking, too?"

Rae shook her head and looked about the room for some means of escape. She would be sick if the man touched her again. The windows offered no exit; even if they had been open the drop to the ground was too great.

"Do not think it," he said, taking in her frenzied glance at the window. "Surely a kiss cannot be so repugnant to you. A wench with your looks must have known a man's lips."

Rae's answer was to flee to the armless couch and put it between herself and the earl.

Newbrough laughed. "This has all the possibilities of a French farce if you maintain this posture, girl."

"Please open the door, m'lord, and let me pass. Someone is bound to come and wonder why the room has been locked. Think of your reputation, for it cannot be enhanced by cavorting with one of his grace's poor parlormaids."

"Very prettily said. But you mistake the situation, for there is no one here who will remark upon a dalliance with you. Nigel's a tolerant sort."

And of course the rest of the household's opinion was of no importance. How foolish of her to forget that. "Is it only a kiss you are wanting?" she asked warily.

"My dear," he smiled, "if you're willing to offer more than that on the couch, then by all means let's have at it, but a kiss was all I was asking."

He sounded sincere, and it seemed the only means of leaving the room. "A kiss then, but unlock the door first."

Newbrough rolled his tiny eyes heavenward, much amused by her bargaining. "Come, sweetings, can it be you doubt me?"

"Yes."

''You've a pert tongue and need to be taught your place, but I am a tolerant man myself on occasion.'' He took out the key and made a show of unlocking the door, opening it a notch to show it was indeed unlocked, then closing it again. He even tossed the key on a table. ''I'll have that tart mouth of yours now, m'dear.''

Rae skirted the edge of the couch and waited. Newbrough approached almost without sound. He put his hands on Rae's small waist and drew her to him.

Instinctively she bent backward, trying to avoid his mouth as it lowered. She could not close her eyes, and felt as she imagined a field mouse might, frozen into stillness, watchful and alert, anticipating the talons and deadly grasp of a great, swooping hawk.

Newbrough's lips touched hers, and Rae's stomach churned. She willed herself to be calm and accepting of the kiss that ground her lips against her teeth, but her body would not listen. She pushed at the earl's chest as he deepened the kiss, thrusting his tongue inside her mouth. It was more than she could bear, and she gagged. There was no mistaking the sound for one of passion, and Newbrough reared back his head, unused to having his attentions so reviled.

''Please,'' Rae begged softly. ''Let me pass. You have had your kiss.'' She touched the back of her hand to her mouth, feeling her swollen lips.

Newbrough knocked her hand aside. ''Hardly a kiss, sweetings, for I was the only participant. I want a measure of it returned.''

''No.''

Newbrough dismissed her protest and slipped a hand around the back of her neck, forcing her face close to his. ''You will kiss me this time,'' he whispered harshly, pulling her hair to force her to tilt her head.

Revulsion swept through Rae and her body heaved and twisted. She tried to push away again, but the earl held her

tightly, his conceit making him blind to the exact nature and
consequence of her distress. His head lowered once more, and
that was when Rae lost her breakfast.

Newbrough stepped back quickly enough then, but it was
too late. Rae tossed her partially digested meal on the earl's
black velvet riding coat and pristine white shirt. Bending over,
Rae retched again, this time on the floor at his feet.

There was a terrible silence when she finished being sick.
Rae dared not look at Newbrough as she began to straighten,
touching the corner of her apron to her mouth and perspiring
face. Eyes closed, she never saw the blow that knocked her off
her feet and onto the divan.

"Bitch!" Newbrough's voice was sharp and biting. "You'll
pay for this!" He advanced on her and raised his hand to deliver
another blow.

Rahab's arms went up to protect her face, but Newbrough
knocked them down and landed the flat of his hand with terrible
force against her cheek and temple. Through the tears that stung
her eyes she saw him lift his hand again, and this time she
escaped the punishing blow by rolling to the opposite side of
the armless couch and dropping to the floor. Crouching, her
fingers fumbled beneath her skirt for the dagger she wore against
her thigh. Newbrough rounded the divan as she released her
weapon, though it still remained hidden in her skirt.

"Stay away from me!" she ordered tightly.

Newbrough laughed unpleasantly, looking down at her hunkered figure. "You are hardly in a position to be telling me
what to do." He grabbed her by the collar and pulled Rae to
her feet, determined to give her the back of his hand again.

His hand came up and stayed there, arrested by the sight of
the dagger she brandished. Rae pulled away and stepped back
several feet. "If you touch me again, you will feel the edge of
my blade," she warned him.

"Bravo!" Rae and Newbrough both turned in the direction
of the doorway, where the duke stood, clapping his hands

slowly. "What theatrics! I am certain the London stage has nothing like it!"

Newbrough straightened as a rush of color stained his cheeks. "Your maid's shown an appalling lack of manners, Nigel," he explained haughtily.

One of Nigel's eyebrows lifted in a lazy arc. "So I see ... and smell." He made an impatient motion with his hand and Stephens stepped in from the hallway. "See that someone cleans this up." Stephens left the room without ever looking in Rae's direction, though she felt his displeasure and censure as surely as if he had stared her down. "Newbrough, I think a bath would not be amiss. You, girl, come with me to the study." Giving neither an opportunity to protest, Nigel turned on his heel and left.

Rae began to leave, but Newbrough caught her by the elbow. "See if you don't pay for this piece of work, bitch." He flung her arm aside and strode out of the library. Trembling, Rae slipped her dagger into place and smoothed her skirts, then went to join the duke in his study.

Nigel was seated in a wing chair by the large bay window when Rae walked in. On the table by his side was a serving tray with two delicate china cups and a pot of tea. "Don't hover, girl. Come in and shut the door."

Rae did as she was told, taking a few tentative steps toward the duke before she stopped.

The duke motioned to the tray. "Pour, would you? A cup for each of us, I think. Then sit down, for heaven's sake. I will not conduct this interview straining my neck to see you."

Rae wanted nothing more than to flee the duke's unsettling presence, but somehow she forced herself to obey his wishes. She was amazed she did not spill any tea as she poured, and it appeared Nigel also found her calm remarkable, for there was something akin to respect in his unwavering eyes when she finally sat across from him and dared to meet his studying gaze.

He sipped his tea, unruffled by Rae's stony expression, before he spoke. "You are the same girl I saw in the woods, are you not? The wench that colonial riffraff thought to foist upon me?"

"Yes, your grace."

Nigel's face remained inscrutable. "I thought as much. I can't think why the resemblance did not strike me before, yet I knew it the moment I saw you in the library with Newbrough. Perhaps it was the pasty complexion; you were not looking well the first time I saw you, either."

Rae could think of nothing to say. She was not even sure if she was required to speak. She took a hasty drink of her tea.

"How are you called, girl?" he asked pleasantly.

"Rae, your grace."

"Ray? That is a lad's name, surely."

"R-A-E."

"Unusual, is it not?"

"I cannot say."

"But I think you can . . . Rahab."

Rae's heart squeezed. Nigel knew who she was; he was only playing with her. "Perhaps it is a trifle uncommon."

"Yes. I believe it is. In fact, I only know of one person called by that name: the sister of the man my ward calls her husband. Imagine my surprise when I asked Stephens who Newbrough had cornered in the library and he told me Rahab. It was something of a revelation to open the door and connect that name with your face." Nigel's smile did not light his eyes. They remained as cold as polished stones. "I own to a certain amount of pleasure that you are not stammering prevarications or dissembling for my benefit. I cannot abide mendacity. I know of you from my agent's reports, of course. You are the same girl who lived in New York with Ashley and her children, are you not?"

"Yes." Rae set her cup aside and folded her hands in her lap.

"Are you married?"

"No."

"Then Smith is not your last name, as Stephens would have had me believe."

"It is the name I gave to him and the others when I was brought here."

"Very wise of you. The McClellan name would have been brought to my attention."

"I thought it might."

Nigel looked pleased. "Just so. Tell me how you came to be here."

In calm tones that belied her inner tremblings, Rae told the duke all. Or almost all. Throughout her recital Nigel's face remained grave and thoughtful, giving away nothing of the workings of his mind.

"And what of the man who was taken with you? He was not one of your brothers, was he?"

"No. But he died for pretending he was Salem."

"So the colonials did not lie when they said they had killed him."

"No."

"They have been served justice for the trick they played me," he said easily, taking another sip of the tea. "If it helps, you may believe they paid with their lives for taking the life of your companion. The last of them swung at Tyburn tree not above a month ago."

In her lap, Rae's knuckles whitened. "I find no pleasure in that."

Nigel shrugged and put his cup and saucer on the tray beside Rae's. "I will have your dagger now." Rae's astonishment that he expected her to hand it over without a fight showed clearly on her face. The duke noted it with some amusement of his own. "I can fairly see the wheels turning in your head, m'dear, but let me caution you. I will not go to the floor with you over this matter. Fisticuffs and brawling are not among those things I count as life's pleasures. I cannot say the same for Newbrough, more's the pity. I suspect he would take great enjoyment in disarming you. Now don't pale so. I rather think I will not let him have the pleasure, for he has sadly tried my patience of late. But there are any number of footmen I can call to see to the matter.'' Nigel's eyes swept her coolly. ''Shall I ring for assistance, or will you give me your weapon? You may choose.''

''There is little choice,'' Rahab said, standing. She turned to one side so that he might not see her leg as she lifted her skirt and removed the dagger. Behind her, Nigel came to his feet, and Rae knew some satisfaction that he did not entirely trust her to surrender so easily. She faced him warily, preparing to strike if he should come toward her.

Nigel held out his hand slowly. ''Come, do not be foolish about this. I have no intentions of harming you. Give it over.''

Rae took a step backward. ''What are your intentions?''

Nigel's brows arched in surprise. ''Would you believe me if I told you?''

''I don't know.''

''Then it can only be a waste of my breath to explain anything. Give it over.''

''I cannot.''

''Foolish chit. Do you intend to use the thing on me?

''If I must.''

''Oh, very well,'' the duke said impatiently. He turned his back on her as if she were no threat at all, went to the door and rang for Stephens. ''I gather everything must be a battle with you,'' he told her. Stephens came to the door and blanched when he saw Rae standing at the window, weapon in hand. ''You can see what has come to pass from interference in my affairs,'' the duke said to the butler, pointing to Rahab. ''If the chit had been dealt with according to my wishes in the beginning, you would not be standing here now, gaping like some hooked fish. Bring a footman here and tell him what is toward.

I want the girl's dagger. While that piece of business is being accomplished, have the room next to mine prepared for her and summon a dressmaker from Hemmings—one with enough skill to make the wardrobe my ward left behind fit this chit. See to it, man."

In other circumstances Rae might have laughed to see the shocked look on Stephens's face as he turned on his heel. At the moment she could find no humor in it, nor in the thought that her own countenance was very much a mirror of the butler's.

Rae said the first thing that came to her mind. "I don't want Ashley's clothes."

"There is an expression that seems apt: Beggars cannot be choosers. There is scarcely time for a dressmaker to construct a new wardrobe for you before my guests arrive."

Rae felt as if her head was spinning. "I don't want any clothes."

The corners of Nigel's thin mouth lifted and his hooded eyes grazed her face and tense form. "I will remember that when we are afforded more privacy."

Rae's gasp remained unheard as the footman entered. She paled when she saw it was Jack. He had but to give her one appealing look and her hand loosened around the hilt. She tossed the weapon to him and he caught it deftly, handing it to the duke. Nigel dismissed him and shut the door. "That was hardly worth the fuss," he said coldly.

"I could not harm Jack."

"Jack? Oh, you mean the footman." He shrugged, placing the blade of the dagger beneath his boot. Giving a strong jerk on the hilt, he snapped the weapon in two and kicked both pieces aside. "Now, sit down. I mean to tell you a few home truths about your situation here. Sit!"

Rae's legs fairly buckled beneath her at his stentorian tones, and it was more luck than design that brought her backside against the brocade seat of the chair. She sat very still as the duke crossed the room and took his place opposite her.

"I cannot like that you have found your way into my home by the veriest succession of accidents, nor that you have been underfoot these past months without my knowing it, though to what purpose remains to be seen. But all is at an end. I can see that I may make use of your presence in having Ashley return to me."

"How? My family knows naught of where I am. They think me drowned."

"A situation that can be easily remedied by the letter you will construct in your own hand, asking that Ashley return to Linfield."

"Why would a letter from me make her come back?"

"Because you will outline very clearly that if she does not return your life will be forfeit."

It was not less than Rae had expected, but she had wanted to hear it from the duke's own lips.

"I think I should have killed you," she said sincerely.

"Probably. Why didn't you?"

"I did not think I could get away with it."

"Wise. You could not, of course, and it is the sheerest folly for you to entertain the notion again."

"I will not write the letter."

The duke sighed. "I could compose the missive myself, but it would not be as effective, nor as likely to be believed. I suppose I could send a lock of your hair. Take off your cap and loosen your hair." Rae did as she was ordered, thrusting her chin forward a tad as he leaned forward to examine the mahogany curls. He flicked one strand aside and reclined in his chair again. "It is much as my agent described to me. Unfortunately it is not so unusual that your family will be assured it is yours. Have you any jewelry?"

"No."

"Nothing personal that can be identified as yours alone?"

Rae thought about her pelisse. It had been a Christmas present from her father and specially made for her, but she was not about to share that with the duke. She felt seven times the fool for not taking her chances with Nigel Lynne and knew in her heart it was the babe that held her back. "I have nothing."

"That is regrettable. It leaves you with no choice but to compose the missive."

"I tell you again, I will not write it. I will do nothing to bring Ashley here."

"We shall see," Nigel said, dismissing her words with a negligent wave of his hand. "You will be so good as to explain why you have remained at Linfield this long. I would have thought this the last place a McClellan would wish to be."

"You are right, but I told myself there might never be an opportunity again to stop your single-minded pursuit of Ashley. She wants nothing to do with you. She is happy at the landing and desires only to be left alone."

"Ashley's desires have never been a concern of mine," he said bluntly. "Never say, I've shocked you."

"It is rather surprising to hear you speak with so little regard for her, yet want her here. Your letters—your threats—were most explicit as to what you thought of her and what you wanted to do to her and her family if she continued to thwart you."

"She received them, then."

"No. Ashley never read them. I did. And buried them. They were too vile to be passed on to her. I believe you have a sickness in your mind, your grace." She added the last to taunt him, and it did not go unnoticed.

Nigel's eyes glinted and his mouth thinned dangerously. "I will caution you only once to mind your tongue." His lips relaxed, though there was a strained look in his face. "So, what did you find in the course of your stay here? Have you discovered the means by which I will leave Ashley to the McClellans and the McClellans to themselves?"

Rae wondered at his game. Did he suspect that she had stumbled onto the Bible's contents now that he knew who she was, or was he merely trying to discover what other loose threads he had left? "I found nothing."

"That is because there is nothing to find, Rahab." He used her name silkily, as if she were a lover to be enticed by the sound of it.

Rae's features remained composed even while she marveled that he could lie so easily to her. Now that the documents were safely out of her reach, he had naught to lose by pretending they did not exist. On the other hand, she had everything to lose if she admitted her knowledge of them.

"I believe this interview is at an end," the duke said as he came to his feet. "Come, I will escort you to your new room so that you may think on writing that letter."

"I will not," she stated again, standing and lifting her head proudly.

"Do not be so hasty, m'dear. I will give you some weeks to mull it over. Of course, until it is done I can hardly give you freedom of the house, so your room must be locked."

"A locked room will hardly persuade me to do something against my will."

"Your protestations are tiresome, Rahab," he said, opening the study door. "I hope that by the time of the hunt you will come to your senses."

Rae found it difficult to swallow, and her heart beat wildly in her breast. Almost against her will she found herself looking up at Nigel's austere face. "The hunt?"

He nodded, seeing something in her face that satisfied him. "Good. The servants have explained the nature of the hunt. You will make a most charming and spirited prey."

Chapter 13

Rae kneeled on the wing chair she had pulled over to the window, resting her arms across the high back, and watched the approach of the carriages up Linfield's circular drive. She had no view of the passengers' descent from their coaches because they alighted almost directly below her, but it mattered not, for in her mind she could well imagine their colorful dress, peacock blue and green for the ladies, cool white satin shot with gold threads for the men. The women would dress their wigs with powder and spangles and tease them to the seemingly impossible heights that current fashion dictated. The men would each carry a silver-knobbed cane or a quizzing glass. Rae suspected the former was used surreptitiously to lift a lady's skirt above her ankles and the latter to examine a fair face and bosom.

She thought of the gown the duke had picked out for her to wear this first evening, and distress clouded her green eyes. He had chosen the emerald satin dress with its tightly fitting bodice to punish her. Knowing she was of a modest mind, the duke had purposely set out to find the gown in her redesigned wardrobe that would cause the most comment among his guests.

Rae had tried on eight gowns the day before, parading them in front of Nigel while he sat comfortably in her bedchamber, sipping warm brandy from a crystal goblet and remarking in bored accents about the unsuitableness of each garment until the emerald satin took his fancy. Rae glanced over to the bed where the gown lay and a shudder of revulsion went through her. It looked innocent enough against the white counterpane, but when Rae wore it neither she nor the dress could make any claim of innocence. The panniers that had to be worn under the gown spread the shimmering green material at her hips and made her waist look as if it could be spanned by a man's hand. The bodice fell off her white shoulders and hugged her midriff so tightly that Rae wondered if she could possibly wear it without fainting for lack of air. There had been a lace fichu to wear with the gown, because it had been originally fashioned for Ashley, whose smaller stature did not take up the entire bodice in length. Much to Rae's dismay, she discovered the low neckline cut neatly across her bosom so that one incautious move would reveal more than the swelling curves of her breasts. She had modeled the gown with the fichu, but Nigel asked her to remove it. Her stammering first refusal, then the high color in her cheeks when he tore it from her shoulders, convinced him it was the gown she should wear when he introduced her to his guests. He would never have to say the word mistress, he told her. His friends would know.

She almost had reminded him that whatever his friends suspected, it would be a lie. At the last moment she held her tongue, afraid her sharp words would bring about a reenactment of the harrowing scenes that had occurred the first three nights of her imprisonment.

Nigel had come to her on each of those evenings for the sole purpose of bending her to his will. Rae thought he looked like Satan himself in his blood-red dressing gown, standing in the shadows between his room and hers. He had talked to her for a long time that first night, telling her in explicit detail what he intended to do to her, explaining in quietly seductive tones that while he found her attractive, he found the thought of using her because she was a McClellan infinitely appealing. She would not merely be the means by which Ashley would return to him, she would also be the means of his revenge on her brother and father. It would give him great pleasure, he said, to have her beg for his attentions, and there was nothing in his voice that hinted it might be otherwise.

He had approached her bed then, pausing only to draw the curtains and snuff the candles. He slipped beneath the sheets and reached for Rae's trembling arms. His hand fell upon her breast and his thumb brushed her nipple.

Unlike with Newbrough, Rae warned the duke that she was going to be sick. Nigel's folly was that he did not believe her. The first evening he returned to his own room while Rae retched over the side of her bed.

On the second night he plied her with spirits, hoping to relax her sensibilities. He forced her to curl beside him on the small couch in her chamber while his fingers teased her hair and fondled her shoulder or thigh. When he began to remove her diaphanous shift she paled to nearly the color of the thing she wore and heaved the contents of her stomach over the arm of the couch. Disgusted beyond words, the duke left her alone.

No food was sent to Rae on the third day, and she understood the significance of the duke's order. When she heard him in his own chamber preparing to come to her, Rae prepared herself for his assault. He would be done with having her beg for him. Now he would be only concerned with having her. Rae had intended to fight him, to draw blood if she had to, but the aftermath of Jericho's rape was more powerful than even she had credited, and once again she stopped the duke with a fit of painful dry heaves when he tried to force himself upon her.

It was enough for Nigel. In the following days her morning

and afternoon meals were brought to her regularly, and he never approached her again for the purpose of lying with her. There were other changes also. In the evening Nigel escorted her to the dining room, where she ate at his side while Newbrough watched with narrowed eyes from across the table. Rae understood immediately by the duke's actions, his absent petting of her arm, the way his gaze sometimes fell upon her mouth, that he was presenting her to Newbrough as if she was indeed his mistress, and that she could only suffer by doing anything that would make the earl aware of the truth.

Rae did not know how Nigel explained her leap from lowly servant to the exalted position as his mistress, nor did she care. She admitted to a certain satisfaction that the earl believed Nigel had been successful where he had not, but she found no cause for gratification that others accepted it of her.

Rae could well imagine that the household staff was buzzing with the news. She only saw Nancy twice, and both times her friend had given her pitying glances that made Rae grit her teeth to keep from shouting the truth. She supposed they knew she was a McClellan, for she remembered how quickly the servants learned the duke's business, and she suspected Mrs. Timms was reminding everyone how she had known from the beginning that Rae was nothing if not trouble.

Rahab moved listlessly in her chair, thinking she had not the energy to cause trouble for anyone. Outside, the carriages continued their procession through Linfield's gate, and Rae watched as if spellbound, wondering which one, if any, carried Jericho Smith.

"I thought you would be ready by now," the duke said from the doorway to his room.

Rae spun in her chair nervously, as if she had been caught in some clandestine act. Her fingers played with the hem of her short shift, trying to pull it over her knees. In contrast to her skittishness, Nigel looked infinitely at ease, handsomely turned out in teal-blue satin breeches and waistcoat. His neckcloth was a veritable waterfall of ivory lace, and the ruffle on each sleeve covered his hands to his knuckles. His hair was covered with a flattering white wig that made his eyes seem almost black and gave his hollow cheeks a hint of color. He tapped the floor lightly with his cane to get Rae's attention.

She pulled her eyes away from him, embarrassed for even thinking that in spite of what she knew him to be, there was something attractive about him. "Oh, I would be ready, but no one has come to help me dress. I cannot manage that gown on my own."

"Nor should you have to." He disappeared into his room and returned after he had rung for a maid. "My apologies, Rahab. I thought I had told someone to see to you."

Rae believed she hated him most when he was being pleasant. His considerate manner could set her flesh crawling because she knew it was naught but a polished veneer, covering all manner of evil designs.

"It is hard to believe the guests are upon us," he said smoothly. "Have you given consideration to my request?"

Rae knew he meant the letter. Not a day passed when he did not remind her of it. "My answer is the same."

The duke smiled thinly and walked farther into her chamber. Standing in front of her chair, he lifted his cane and drew its tip across her collarbone, pressing it lightly in the hollow of her throat. Rae did not move nor cast her expressionless eyes from his watchful ones. "Do you know that I am not sorry to hear your reply? I have come to look forward to the last day of this revel, when you will become some other man's property."

"Then you do not intend to snare me for yourself," she said coolly. "I had wondered."

The duke gave her a little poke with the cane for her insolent attitude, then turned on his heel and made himself comfortable on the sofa. "Snare you? My dear, I shall be happy to give you over to any number of men who are not as fastidious as myself. Or mayhap a woman. It occurred to me that your regrettable penchant for losing your meals may be only because you shun the male sex.''

"I might have known you would put such meaning to my natural disgust of you and the earl.''

"I would beat you for that remark if I were not concerned the welts would show. The others have faded, I see.'' There had been four thin, bruised lines on her upper arm and back where Nigel had viciously snapped her with his riding crop for answering him sharply once too often. That had occurred nearly a week ago, and today was the first evidence the duke had that the effects of the beating were wearing off. "I caution you not to ply your tongue with careless sharpness, for I can use a crop on your flanks just as simply, and no one will be the wiser.''

Rae's retort hovered on her lips, but the maid's entrance kept her from saying it. "Will you go, your grace, so that I may dress?''

"No. I think I'd rather stay and watch the preparations. I find a lady's toilette rather fascinating.''

Rae fought to pretend his presence was of no account, knowing well the pleasure he could derive from ruffling her. The maid was little help, for the young girl was all thumbs under the duke's keen eye and became more so as he leveled criticisms upon her hapless head. He was not satisfied with the way the panniers were fastened or the quality of the undergarments the girl had chosen. Rae retreated twice behind the silk screen, murmuring encouragement to the poor maid while she changed into a gossamer chemise and adjusted the panniers herself. Three lacy slips were fastened to her waist before she stepped out from behind the screen.

The duke's brows rose slightly in appreciation, and the look he leveled on her was one of desire. "You quite take my breath away, Rahab. I may consider taking part in the hunt, after all.''

At her side she felt the maid stiffen, but for herself she pretended not to hear. Rae eased into her gown and bade the girl not close the back until her makeup was applied and her hair dressed. She seated herself at the vanity and touched rouge with a light hand to her cheeks and lips. She had never worn any sort of cosmetics before and thought the artifice made her look the veriest sort of doxy. She did not mention this to Nigel for fear he would make her apply the color more deeply to emphasize her tawdry view of herself.

Rae's glorious hair was pinned closely to her scalp and the maid slipped an artfully sculpted white wig over her head. Rae did not know the woman who stared back at her through the glass. Thick finger curls dusted with silvery powder hung to one side of her neck and lay softly against the creamy skin of her bare shoulder. Her eyes were brighter than she thought they should be, her lashes and brows darker. Her own flush heightened the color in her cheeks, and her lips parted in surprise when she saw she no longer looked a tart, but a woman of high fashion and some beauty.

Nigel dismissed the maid and came to stand behind Rae, looking at her in the mirror. "Lovely." He fastened the tiny buttons at the back of her gown and watched with interest as Rae's breasts swelled about the tight line of the bodice.

Rae's eyes lifted and met Nigel's in the mirror. She did the one thing she promised herself she would not do: she pleaded. "Do not make me go below like this," she begged softly.

In answer the duke extracted a choker of emeralds from his waistcoat and laid them across Rae's throat. "I think these will do nicely. I have never had a tight purse where my mistresses were concerned." He lifted a few of the silver curls and fastened the necklace's catch.

"Please. I cannot do this thing." She touched the slender stem of her neck and felt the cool stones. It reminded her of the collar she would wear on the last day of the revel.

Nigel's hands rested on her shoulders. "At one time I would have said you only have to write the letter to be relieved of your duties as my hostess, but events have changed while you procrastinated."

Rae half expected him to say that he wanted her to sleep with him, so she was a little startled, though immeasurably relieved, to hear him announce that he required her assistance at the gaming tables.

"My assistance? In what manner? And more to the point, why should I render it?"

Nigel's fingers tightened on Rae's shoulders. A little more pressure and he would leave bruises. At her soft gasp he released his grip. "I believe that answers your last question first. Unless you have a penchant for pain, you will do as I ask. Am I understood?"

"Yes."

"As to the manner of your assistance, I wish you to watch a certain player's cards for me and apprise me of their worth."

"How will I do that?"

"The necklace has four large stones. From your left to right they will signify the spades, hearts, diamonds, and clubs. You have only to tap them the appropriate number of times to give me a fair idea of his cards."

"Perhaps he will not let me see them. Most good players would not allow someone to stand over their shoulder."

"It will be up to you to see that he does."

"Why is this so important to you? I have heard Newbrough say that you are nearly unbeatable at cards. You trounce him regularly in the evening after dinner."

The duke's smile was genuine as his fingers brushed Rae's fragile jawline. "Newbrough would not know how to play his hand if I diagrammed it for him. That is why I am playing for his gambling notes this week."

Rae remained very still, afraid the slightest move would give her away. Until this moment she was not certain that Jericho was the player the duke intended to cheat. She feigned innocence. "But Newbrough is no match for you. Why must you cheat?"

"It is not Newbrough I shall be playing against, but another gentleman, one Thomas Adams. His lordship has collected nearly all of the earl's notes and is threatening to ruin him. I mean to win them back. He sent his acceptance of the match only this morning and promises to arrive this evening.''

"It is very decent of you to help your friend."

Nigel laughed. "You, of all people, I did not expect to mistake my motives as decent ones. Or to suppose that Newbrough is really my friend. He is a convenience, nothing more, a human joke who amuses me from time to time."

Rae pretended to think that over. "I see. Then you intend to win the notes and ruin the earl yourself."

"Clever minx. Actually, I have not yet decided which way I will go. I may choose to lose the bundle to Adams and have him do the thing himself."

"And deprive yourself of so much pleasure? Surely I have heard wrong."

"Naughty puss," Nigel said, not unkindly, giving her cheek a pinch. "I only know now that I want the choice. That is what you will provide for me by keeping a careful eye on my opponent's hand."

Rae nodded. "As you wish, your grace."

"So docile and compliant of a sudden," Nigel remarked. "Can it be you hate Newbrough more than me?"

"Please don't ask me to choose, your grace, for I'm sure the pressure of it would send me into a faint."

Nigel helped Rae to her feet and escorted her to the door. Her skirts rustled against his thigh. "Mind your tongue, Miss Saucebox, else I will turn you over my knee in front of my guests."

For all that it was said in a teasing manner, there was nothing light about the harsh fingers on her elbow. Rahab knew he would do it if she crossed him in public. Gathering the remnants of her much abused pride, she lifted her chin haughtily and waited for him to ease his grip. He surprised her by laughing at her show of disdain and led her down the hallway to the grand staircase where they made a regal descent to greet the guests who were milling about the ballroom.

Jericho had arrived at Linfield some ninety minutes earlier and like other early arrivals had been shown to his room in the great house's west wing so that he might freshen before the dancing began. Unlike the other guests, he had used most of his time to prowl the corridors, hoping to catch sight of Rahab among the flurry of black-skirted females who moved with frantic purpose through the hallways, fetching fresh linens and water and tisanes for an aching head.

When he returned to his room, Drew Goodfellow, who was serving as his valet, saw that the tour had been without reward. He shook his head at the pain clouding Jericho's eyes and set about laying out his evening attire.

"I'll have a look meself as soon as you've gone to the ballroom," he said. "It will be safer for me to find her and not so remarkable if I should stop to talk to her."

"Tell Rae that I must see her." Jericho sat on the edge of the bed, his head in his hands. "Convince her, even if she swears she will have none of me."

"Now why would she say that?"

Restlessly Jericho moved from the bed to the window. "I treated her most vilely when I saw her in Hemmings. She has good reason to want nothing to do with me."

"And that's the reason you've been goin' about whipping yourself these past weeks. Why didn't you speak of it?"

"And give you disgust of me too?"

"I do not think you could do that."

"If you did not think less of me for what I did to Rae, then I would surely think less of you."

Drew was silent as he considered Jericho's softly spoken recriminations. "So that's the way of it," he said at last. "You thought to use force when persuasion would not suffice."

"Aye. And was most bitterly cruel before. . . and after."

"I see. Then Rae is the reason you wrestled so long with

the duke's invitation to play for Newbrough's notes. I wondered
why you did not leap at the chance.''

Jericho nodded. ''I thought to lure the duke to London when
it became clear Rahab would not leave Linfield. I still do not
know if I have done the right thing in coming here. Of late
everything seems to be going awry. I originally thought to play
Newbrough for the titles to his lands, but it appears the wily
fox has chosen Lynne to champion him. I strongly suspect the
duke hopes to wrest the bulk of Stanhope's debts from me.
The letter accompanying his invitation said as much.''

''The play will not be dull.''

''Without question,'' Jericho said dryly.

''Well, let me turn you out, laddie, and then I shall see to
the errant miss. I've got a smooth tongue when I've a mind
for it, and I'll take care not to give her more offense of you
than she already has.''

Jericho allowed himself to be turned out, as Drew suggested.
He cut a fine figure in ivory breeches, white stockings, and
black shoes with a large silver buckle. His waistcoat was also
ivory satin, with a delicate pattern of flowers raised in silver
thread. He wore a neckcloth arranged in a simple fall, and his
jacket was ice blue, which could not fail to draw comparison
with his eyes. Jericho noted his appearance in the cheval glass
critically and decided he looked every bit a blue blood. He
picked up his ebony cane and made a ridiculous courtly bow
to his valet.

Drew laughed, taking a moment to arrange the ruffle at
Jericho's wrist. ''You'll do, laddie. Take yourself off and let
me find Red. Good luck with your play.''

The lilting strains of violins from the stringed orchestra
threaded in and out of the gay conversation of the duke's guests
as Jericho entered the ballroom. It gave every appearance of
being quite a squeeze, and economy played no role in the
elegantly decorated ballroom. Bright silks hung from the walls
and the chairs looked to have been recently covered with com-

plementing colors. Lush hothouse greenery was arranged on a number of tables and in the corners of the room, giving one the sense of being out-of-doors.

Jericho was announced at the door by Stephens and quickly swept into the reception line by a trio of London acquaintances. "Wait until you meet the duke's latest amour," one of them whispered in Jericho's ear. "She's a stunner." Jericho found himself smiling at their enthusiasm, and the smile served him well, for it aided his composure as he was introduced to the duke.

Jericho and Nigel took their full measure of each other in but the blink of an eye, and for his part the duke welcomed matching wits at the gaming table with an adversary of some strength. Jericho's thoughts were not so dissimilar, but he had no real liking for the match that lay ahead of him.

Jericho's head tilted slightly as the duke turned to the woman at his side. "My dear, may I present Lord Thomas Adams. He is, for all intents and purposes, our most honored guest. His lordship and I will be playing for Newbrough's notes. Adams, permit me, this lovely lady is my hostess, Miss Rahab McClellan."

There was an infinitesimal pause before Jericho acknowledged Rae's curtsy by making a leg of his own. "Your servant," he said coolly, even as he marveled that he could speak the words. He sounded as if he had ice water in his veins, when in truth his blood was boiling. Thoughts tumbled through his head over which he had little control. Folding her in his arms and kissing her senseless vied with reaching for the slender stem of her white throat and strangling the life out of her. The duke's hostess, indeed! She had become his whore, and if he was any judge she appeared to be enjoying the notoriety.

"Honored, my lord," Rae said calmly, her composure never slipping. She had an advantage over Jericho, because not only had she been expecting him in the ballroom, she had watched him from the corner of her eye long before he realized it was she standing by the duke. "It was kind of you to accept the duke's invitation. Many of our guests would have been sadly put out if you had chosen not to come. They have remarked upon looking forward to the play between you and his grace."

"Surely no more than I, Miss McClellan," Jericho responded pleasantly. He turned to the duke. "But how is it that your guests know my business?"

"As to that," Nigel explained, "you only have to look at Lord Newbrough for the answer."

"I might have known. I suppose there is nothing for it, though I can't say I like our game being made a sideshow."

"I assure you, there will be privacy. I have invited only a select number of friends to view the playing, and you may choose any of your own friends to watch. Of course, the earl will be there. They are, after all, his notes. Miss McClellan will escort you to the library where the play will take place, and you may inspect it at your leisure. If there is anything not to your liking, I will alter it, if you but bring it to my attention."

"You are generous," Jericho said. "I am certain the accommodations will be most satisfactory. Do not fear that I will keep your hostess long, no doubt you wish the first dance with her."

"Indeed, I have claimed that honor."

"Then mayhap she will give me the second." Jericho's composure was pushed to new limits when Rae did not respond of her own accord, but looked first to the duke for his permission.

Upon seeing Nigel's nearly imperceptible encouragement, Rae smiled serenely at Jericho. "I will look forward to it." She placed her hand on Nigel's arm briefly. "If you will excuse me, your grace, I'll show Lord Adams the library."

Jericho and Rae said nothing until the library doors were closed behind them, and even then their tones were hushed.

"You would do well to keep your voice down," she told him, breaking his tight grip on her elbow and moving several

steps away. ''There is no telling who is on the other side of
the door.''

''I own to some surprise that you would mention it to me.''

Rae turned on him sharply. ''What do you mean by that?
Do you think I would betray you?''

Jericho shrugged, his eyes wandering about the room. ''You
are his mistress now and seemingly comfortable in the role. I
know not what to think.''

''You ass,'' she hissed. ''If I am his mistress, then you are
King George!''

''What are you saying?'' He looked directly at Rae, his
cerulean eyes boring into hers, searching for the truth.

''I am saying you quite ruined me for becoming any man's
lover. I cannot stomach even the thought of being fondled by
any of your sex, and the duke has discovered this on three
separate occasions. It is quite a situation, is it not? Nigel cannot
touch me because of what you did to me, and it is difficult to
know whether to be grateful or sad. I see you do not know
what to make of it, either. No, do not come near me, else I
swear I will toss my dinner at your feet. An odd form of
protection, isn't it, but I assure you its efficacy cannot be
denied.''

Jericho's arms lowered slowly and he took a step backward.
Inwardly he recoiled from the scorn and rejection in Rae's face
and voice. He had not expected her to leap into his arms, but
neither had he anticipated such virulence. She was right about
his not knowing what to make of the tangle he had trapped her
in. His heart leapt with gladness that she was not the duke's
paramour, but he could not rejoice that he had given her such
a disgust of intimacy. ''Mayhap it is only the duke who causes
you to react in this way.''

''You would like to believe that is so, for it would do much
to ease your conscience, but it happened with Newbrough also.
And it matters not who the man is, because it is your face I
see when I am touched! Your nerve is only surpassed by your

conceit! You are the only man who has ever made me his whore! Make what you like of that!''

"Red." It was the merest whisper of sound, achingly soft and imploring, filled with regret.

Rae felt as if her heart was lodged in her throat and she could scarcely breathe. "I never intended to tell you these things in this manner; they would have been better left unsaid, but when you believed I could actually like the role of Nigel's mistress I became undone. Forget what I have told you, for there is nothing that can be done. Come, we must go back to the ballroom, for we have tarried overlong. And know this last thing: The duke has asked me to watch your cards. He is undecided if he shall allow you to win the notes or whether he will choose to ruin Newbrough himself.''

Rae turned on her heel and began to leave, but Jericho caught her arm. "I care naught for any of it, Red."

Rae shook off his hand. "You must care. Stanhope could be yours by the end of the week."

"And you?"

Her smile held no warmth. "Me? At week's end I can be anyone's."

With that enigmatic response hovering between them, Rae led Jericho back to the ballroom. Nigel met her at the door and escorted her onto the floor as the musicians struck up the first dance.

"I never thought to ask if you could dance," the duke said to her as he led her through the intricate patterns of the country dance. "But I can see you are quite good." After the first few bars of music other couples took their place on the floor, and soon the ballroom was filled with an arresting array of color moving in splendid orchestration.

"A shade out of practice, your grace, for there has not been much cause for dancing in my country of late."

The duke nodded. "Did Adams find the library satisfactory?''

Rahab had no idea if Jericho had even given the matter any thought, but she said that all was to his liking.

"What do you think of the man?"

"My opinion matters?"

"More than you know," Nigel said with a certain gentleness.

Rae nearly lost her step, so startled was she by the duke's tone. She looked at him warily.

"Come, do not be so shocked. Surely you must know that I find much to admire about you. It grieves me only that you are a McClellan and completely unworthy of my attentions."

"And completely unwanting of your attentions." Nigel laughed, and heads turned at the sound. "Be careful, your grace, for your guests are bound to think you are enjoying yourself."

"I find that I am, my dear, for you are playing your role to perfection. Might I hope that by Friday you will reconsider the letter?"

Rae blanched at his cruel reminder of the hunt, and this time her steps did falter noticeably. She recovered, but thereafter her movements were stiff rather than graceful. "Damn you," she swore under her breath while smiling pleasantly beneath Nigel's sharp gaze.

"Tell me about Adams," the duke said, as if he had not heard her.

"La! What do I know of the man's character? He seems a serious sort, and rather remote. I should think you are well matched. And might I say I hope he trounces you?"

"But he won't, will he?" Nigel asked smoothly. "I have you to see to that. I want you to put the man at his ease. Anything short of shaming me in order to make him feel comfortable in your presence."

Rae did not answer as Jericho came toward them to claim the next dance. Under the duke's watchful eye she smiled in welcome and allowed herself to be led into the new steps as the music started.

"It is quite a crush, is it not?" she said, her smile firmly in place.

"Yes. I had not known the duke would invite so many people."

"By the accounts of the duke's previous entertainments, this is a small gathering. I understand they all will not stay for the entire week."

"That is a relief."

"Yes. I hear that by Friday only the most jaded will still be in attendance. Does that include you?"

"My invitation is for the entire week."

"I feel in need of some refreshment, my lord."

Still puzzling over Rae's distancing conversation, Jericho led her off the floor. After they each had a glass of champagne, he dutifully followed her to a less crowded corner of the ballroom where they could sit in plain view of the guests, but with less danger of their conversation being overheard.

"Nigel has asked me to be pleasant to you," she explained. "So pretend that you are quite enamored of my conversation."

"I assure you, I am."

Rae laughed gaily. "You ought to be, for your life may well depend upon it." It was odd to see Jericho smiling genially, chuckling occasionally, as she explained about the documents in Nigel's family Bible, but he managed to give nothing away as she told him the whole of it. "I dare not spend another moment with you now, or there will be talk."

"By all means, Miss McClellan, see to your other guests," Jericho said, coming to his feet.

Rae circulated among the duke's friends, frustrated that she could not explain everything at once to Jericho, and equally determined not to let it show. Several times she caught sight of him deep in discussion with the duke and wondered what they could possibly be talking about. She also saw he managed adroitly to avoid any introduction to the Earl of Stanhope, which she was sure must be sending Newbrough into fits. Rae was never lacking for partners, and she became adept at turning the conversation away from herself, finding all manner of innocuous subjects to discuss with the men who plagued her for her personal history. But the playacting took its toll, and by the time the guests were called for the late supper she felt as if her nerves were a veritable Gordian knot. She ate little of the repast, though she made a show of moving the delicacies about on her plate. Her conversation was divided equally between Lord Lesley on her left and Lord Evans on her right, who both declared they were much put out with Nigel for keeping her existence a secret from them. Though the tone and manner of each was deferential, Rae wondered frankly if they expected the duke to share.

At supper's end most of the guests returned to the ballroom, but others were shown to the music room or the study where tables had been set up for cards. A select few accompanied the duke to his library, and Rae found herself once more at Jericho's side, having no idea how she would survive this evening.

The playing table was set up in the near center of the room, and eight wing chairs had been arranged for the spectators equidistant from the table. Jericho had declined to have any one of his acquaintance attend the match, and Rahab was the only woman in attendance. Rae chose a chair at Jericho's back and to one side, so that if she stood up on occasion, and if he permitted carelessness, she would see his cards. Charles Newbrough took up a similar position on the duke's side, and the others fell in between. A fresh full deck of cards sat untouched between the players, and a footman in new livery served drinks with the rectitude the situation required.

"Before I outline the rules of play as we have discussed them," the duke said, leaning casually in his chair, "I wonder if you would share with us the reasons you have gone to such lengths to secure Newbrough's notes."

"Can it make any difference to the play?" Jericho asked easily, as if he had anticipated the question.

"No."

"Then it will remain my affair. But you mistake that it has been a troublesome thing," he added, looking directly at Newbrough. "It has given me naught but pleasure."

Rahab held her breath, half-expecting that the earl would call Jericho out on the spot. He did nothing, however, except to give Jericho the fullest measure of his beady stare. Jericho seemed not the least perturbed, while Nigel nodded as if he understood.

"Then let us begin," the duke said. "First, for the benefit of our audience, let me outline the play. The game will be two-handed whist, each player receiving thirteen cards. After each trick we will both draw one card from the stock until it is exhausted; then we will play out our hands. Lesley will be keeping score as well as providing fresh cards. Rather than make unlimited wagers and perhaps end our ... pleasure in one night, Adams and I agree that each point will be worth ten pounds until Friday, when each point will be worth one hundred pounds. The winner of the entire match is the one possessing all of Newbrough's notes, and only the notes are good for this wager. Since I begin with but two thousand pounds, and Adams has considerably more, it is conceivable, though unlikely"— here the duke shot Jericho an amused glance—"that I could lose it all in the first two nights of play. Either of us may call a halt to the play for the evening at the end of any single game, and there will be a break every fourth game that may last not above thirty minutes." The duke looked around, glancing back at Newbrough, then at Jericho. "Have I explained it to your satisfaction?"

"Yes."

"Very well. Let us begin. We will draw for the deal, Ace high." He waved a hand at Jericho to draw first. Jericho lifted about one-third of the deck and showed everyone the bottom card, a jack. The duke drew a seven and Jericho swept up the cards and began shuffling. He dealt their hands smoothly, one card at a time, and placed the remaining cards in the middle of the table, but not where they would interfere with the taking of the tricks.

Both men were highly skilled players, and neither dallied overlong determining which card would be laid out. The winner of each trick collected it in a single sweeping motion, and Rae understood at last how the game derived its name as the cards were whisked from the table. Rae concentrated on the game and waited for some sign from Nigel that she was supposed to signal Jericho's cards, but it never came. She surmised that at present he did not require any assistance, because when the first break was called he had added Ł400 to his coffer.

Rae excused herself from the library at the beginning of the break and wandered back into the ballroom to watch the dancers. There was an enormous amount of gaiety in this room compared to the other, and she wished she might find a reason not to return to the library. Even as she thought it she saw Nigel approaching her and knew she must go back.

"My dear, you must remember not to fidget with your necklace," he said to her when they were alone in the hallway. "It is most disconcerting."

Rae's hand dropped abruptly from her throat as she realized she was guilty of the absent movement as they talked. "I'm sorry . . . I had not realized. Was I doing it before?"

"Incessantly."

"Oh. But you won anyway."

Nigel looked pleased. "Yes, I did. However, I would rather you did not toy with that thing. I may have need of you yet."

But he did not look to her once during the second set of games, even though Rae sat with her hands folded in her lap and Jericho proceeded to win back Ł300. Rae felt as if she were a single exposed nerve, though she knew she looked the picture of calm reserve. Indeed, upon glancing about the room she saw that there was only one person who appeared at all affected by the tension of the game and that was Newbrough.

The earl never allowed the obsequious footman to pass without relieving the man's silver tray of one glass of spirits.

The clock on the mantelpiece had already struck one when Jericho announced an end to the evening's play. Rahab sighed thankfully, for which she received a glaring look from the duke and an amused chuckle from his opponent.

"It would seem our hostess is ready to retire," Jericho said pleasantly, gathering the well-thumbed cards and shuffling them idly. He glanced over his shoulder. "My apologies, Miss McClellan, for keeping you this long."

Embarrassed by her show of tiredness, Rae flushed. "If you gentlemen will excuse me," she said, coming to her feet and motioning them to remain seated. "I bid you good night." It was not until she reached her room that she realized she had not heard Lesley announce the evening's final tally, though she suspected Jericho had got the better of the duke.

As she readied for bed she could still hear the melodic strains of the violins from below and she wondered if the dancing would go on until dawn and if the duke seriously expected her to stay up until the last of the guests had retired. She had just slipped into bed when she heard the key turn in her door and knew the duke was locking her in for the evening. A few minutes later he entered her room from the connecting door to his own chamber.

Rae pulled the covers up to her neck as she sat up in bed. Nigel carried a single candle and the light flickered across the gaunt planes of his face. He stood in the doorway for some moments, studying Rae's protective posture as if it puzzled him. "I merely came to thank you for being so charming to my guests this evening. I have no designs on your body. Mayhap you wish it were otherwise?"

A small shudder made Rae tremble. "No."

Nigel frowned. "You've made it quite clear. Again. Then you will not be jealous if I seek pleasure elsewhere this evening."

"Hardly."

"I've locked your door so that others might not suspect you are fair game."

"How considerate of you."

"I only wish to heighten the anticipation of Friday's hunt, m'dear. For my guests . . . and for you."

"Leave me."

"On this occasion I'll bow to your wishes. Tomorrow evening wear the silver gown. It will go well with the necklace. And be prepared to make use of it. I am not going to let Adams take me on the second day of play." With that he withdrew from the room, leaving Rae more awake than she had been in some hours. After tossing and turning, thumping her pillow and twisting her covers into complete disorder, sheer exhaustion overcame her.

Jericho stood over Rae's sleeping form for long minutes before he came to a final decision and deposited the key to her door in his waistcoat pocket. Carefully, so as not to have her awake screaming, he lowered his hand over her mouth and whispered her name in her ear.

Rae's eyes flew open, and unable to make out the shadowed figure hovering over her, prepared to put her vocal cords to a true test. Her eyes widened as she tried to draw in a healthy breath of air and found herself nearly suffocated in the process.

"Rae! It's Jericho!"

But she already had her teeth sinking into the soft flesh of his hand before the words registered, and now Jericho had to stifle his own cry of surprise and pain.

"Jericho?" Her question was muffled, owing to the fact that she held a ridge of skin between her teeth.

"Yes. Let go, will you?"

Rae released him, and as her eyes adjusted to the room's poor firelight she saw him massage his sore hand. "Are you mad? What are you doing here?"

"Probably," he answered her first question, sitting on the

edge of the bed as Rae raised herself on her elbows. "And I've come to talk to you. Please don't send me away."

"I cannot even credit you are here. Is this a nightmare?"

"No, Red. I'm real enough." Tentatively he touched the palm of her hand where it lay open at her side, heartened that she did not pull away from him. "May I stay?"

"To talk?" she asked uneasily, feeling as if his touch was burning her hand. She willed her insides to cease their roiling.

"Yes. Only that. My word on it."

"How did you come to be here?"

Jericho let out his indrawn breath slowly, taking her response to mean he could remain. "My valet stole Stephens's key from the rack belowstairs and replaced it with a similar one."

"Your valet?"

"Drew Goodfellow, the tinker."

"You brought him here as your valet? Isn't someone likely to recognize him?"

"He's a different man in his livery. I doubt you would know him. But I did not come here to discuss Drew, though he sends his regards."

Rae smiled weakly. "Return my own."

"Depend upon it." He hesitated, searching for the right words, wondering what had happened to the speech he had rehearsed once he had discovered the duke was spending the night in another's bed. The fingers that lay in Rahab's palm trembled. "Red, I'm sorry. If I could undo my cruel treatment of you, believe that I would."

"I believe you," she said quietly. "If you recall, you mocked me when I said you would come to regret it."

"I said so many things that afternoon that I did not mean!" he whispered harshly. "I only meant to convince you that you should not come here."

"It was more than that, Jericho. You wanted to control me."

"I wanted to protect you!"

"It is an odd sort of method you chose, to hurt and degrade

me, to use me against my will so that I might experience helplessness at your hands. If you came here to be forgiven, Jericho, then know that you are. But if you are asking for more, if by chance you are asking me to forget, then I can only say I have not yet forgotten, nor can I say if I ever will."

For all that her words were gently spoken and lacking in malice, they tore into Jericho as lashes across his naked flesh. "Just say that you will not leave me, Red. Don't put me from your life when we are safe from this place. I want to make amends."

"For me or for yourself?"

"For both of us."

Rae's thoughts drifted to the child they had made and her answer was less for herself and Jericho than it was for the life within her. "I will not leave you. You should know that I had already decided to leave Linfield before Nigel discovered my identity."

"You were coming to me?"

There was an incredulous sort of happiness in Jericho's voice that Rae knew would vanish when she explained the reason. She found herself curiously loath to tell him of their babe. "Yes. I was coming to you."

He gave her hand a gentle squeeze. "I thank you for telling me that. It is something to hold on to."

She almost told him then but held her tongue, wishing, she supposed, that the babe had not made her decision and that she might have gone to him not out of necessity but because it was the wisest choice. "I don't know if I can stand it," she managed to choke out, "but if I can, would you hold on to me? Oh, Jericho, I have been such a fool!"

"Hush, darling."

Rae pushed herself up from her elbows and waited for Jericho to take her in his arms. When he did not she realized with some shock that he was afraid. Well, he was not the only one afraid, and if the truth be told, not the only one who had said things in order to hurt. "I lied about seeing your face when the duke touches me. I did it to—to—"

"I understand," he said quietly. "I deserve far worse punishment than being put in my place." He lifted his arms tentatively, reaching for her but not quite touching. "You need to decide if this is where you want to be."

Rae scooted closer so that if he were to close the circle of his arms she would be wrapped in his embrace. It was like testing the waters before taking the plunge, she thought as her hand slowly lifted to touch his chest. Her palm rested flat against his linen shirt and she could feel the racing of his heart and the warm heat of his body. Did she really want to be comforted in *his* arms? she wondered. Was it weakness that made her turn to him, or the strength of the love she had borne him? She wasn't certain; not even when her head rested against the curve of his shoulder did she completely understand what made her want Jericho to ease her hurt. She only knew that when his arms finally eased around her she felt a stillness within her breast, a sense of peace that had been lacking for more weeks than she cared to remember.

Though Jericho wanted to envelope Rae, he forced himself to hold her loosely, alert to even the smallest indication on her part that she wanted to be free of him. "Is it all right for you here?" he asked at last. He wondered if she understood how much comfort he derived from the feel of her smooth cheek sliding against his shoulder as she nodded her head in assent. "You know it will never happen again, don't you?"

"I never believed it would happen in the first place," she told him with bitter honesty. "I have lost count of the times I've asked myself if I was to blame. I think: What if I provoke him again with my willfulness? Needs must he repeat the lesson?"

"No!" he swore softly.

Rae's head lifted as she sought his sharp profile in the darkness. "I know you mean that now, but when the situation is upon us, how can you know you will not want to assert your strength again?''

"I know because I would sooner take a pistol to my head."

"I'll prime the thing for you," she said, meaning it.

"It would be a kindness," he said. "I have never known so great a misery than these weeks since Hemmings."

"I thought you meant to put me from your mind."

"A thing easier said than accomplished."

"And what of your promise not to lift a finger to help me from a tangle of my own making?"

"No promise, that. Another lie."

She sighed, lowering her head once more to his shoulder as her pride battled with her common sense. For the moment her pride won, because Jericho's words of that fateful afternoon still stung. He had pointed out too clearly that someone had always come to her rescue, and just once she wanted to prove that she could stand without him or any man. She would find a way to escape the hunt without his help; then he would never doubt her ability to care for herself again. She bit her lip, mulling it over, and when she spoke it was of something else.

"Have you given any thought to the documents?"

"Yes." Jericho did not share Rae's dilemma of pride's warring with common sense. He was able to admit that the old duke's will offered a much better way of discrediting and disposing of Nigel than calling him out. "I am prepared to look for the papers. I've discussed it briefly with Drew, and he agrees with me that it is the sane thing to do. You say the documents are in the duke's study?"

"I think they must be. His desk there is where he keeps important papers. It will be difficult to get into, what with so many guests about, but I think it can be accomplished at night."

"I expect I can count on Nigel to be seeing to the pleasures of any one of his female guests."

Quite against her will Rae's mind formed a picture of the duke sliding into her own bed, touching her with his cold,

impersonal hands, kissing her mouth with passionless lips and
bent on making use of her because of the hatred he bore the
McClellans. She shivered.

"Red?"

"It will pass in a moment." But it did not, and she lifted
her head in the same moment Jericho brought his closer to
question her. His lips touched her cheek and a wave of nausea
swept her. "Dear God," she whispered, covering her mouth
with her hand. With her free hand she pushed Jericho away
and leaped from the bed, running to the chamber pot behind
the silk dressing screen. Minutes later, recovered from her bout
of sickness, she returned to her bed, unable to decide if she
were relieved or desolate that Jericho was no longer in the
room.

Chapter 14

The duke's study was without even a fire in the hearth to
light Jericho's progress from the door to the desk. He paused
after taking a few steps inside and bumping against the sharp
edge of a walnut end table. He cursed softly while he waited
for his eyes to take advantage of the pool of moonlight filtering
through the large study window. Drew Goodfellow waited on
the other side of the door, ready to alert Jericho if there was
any danger of the secretive breaking and entering being chanced
upon. Even with Drew's presence to warn him, Jericho felt the
need to move quickly. He sat in the duke's chair and ran his
fingers along the face of the drawer, feeling for the lock. Finding
it, he took a small pick from his waistcoat pocket and fiddled
with the tiny opening in the brass plate. At the same time his
free hand slipped along the underside of the desk, searching
for the hidden spring that would release the drawer in concert
with his makeshift key. The scratching of the pick sounded
unbearably loud in the quiet room, and the spring's final clicking

seemed deafening. Jericho found himself holding his breath as he slowly slid the drawer open.

The room was simply too dark to permit Jericho to examine the content of the papers he found. He gathered them, prayed he could return them to their proper place, and carried them across to the window, holding them up to the pale silvery light. It only took a few minutes to determine the documents Rae had told him about were not among those he held in his hand. Still, he took the time to go through them twice before he returned them to the drawer. He searched the desk again, hoping to find a more cleverly concealed place where the duke might keep important papers. He was very pleased with himself when he found it and smiled with grim satisfaction as he lifted the contents. The smile vanished as he leafed through the papers and found nothing but a continuation of the kind of threatening correspondence Nigel had determined would bring Ashley and the McClellans to their knees. The most recent missive was dated but a week earlier, and Jericho scanned it, stopping to read it carefully only when he came across Rae's name.

Jericho's face was a terrible thing to see, devoid of expression save for the muscle jumping in his cheek as he read the duke's description of the humiliation he had planned for Rahab. Hands trembling, Jericho returned the letters to their hiding place, then slipped out of the study, abandoning the search for the will and birth record, recognizing the futility of trying to find them if they were not in the desk.

"Nothing," he said tightly in answer to Drew's questioning look. "Let's go." Jericho followed Drew down the empty hallway and up the servants' staircase. Outside the door to his room Jericho stopped. "I have to see Rahab."

"Are you mad, laddie? The duke's sleeping in his own bed this night."

"I'll be quiet."

"You'll be dead."

Jericho waved his hand impatiently. "I must talk to Red. It cannot be helped."

Drew shook his head, certain his young friend was showing a foolish lack of regard for his own skin. "Do what you will, but mind that you tread softly. And whatever you do, don't upset the poor girl like you did the other night. Keep your hands in your pockets."

Jericho took a steadying breath, thinking that no one had ever dared to speak to him in such a fashion in recent years. If anyone but Drew had thrown salt on his open wounds Jericho would have laid him out. Instead he jammed his thumbs in the waistband of his breeches. "I'm unlikely to touch her ever again, old man. I don't need you to remind me what I do to her." He turned on his heel and strode off to the wing of the house that held Rahab's room.

It was four in the morning when Rae woke, sensing that she was not alone any longer. Almost immediately she was alert, sitting up against the headboard and knuckling sleep from her eyes. Blinking to clear her blurred vision, she saw Jericho sitting in the damask-covered chair beside her bed, looking for all the world as if there was nothing alarming about his presence in her room. Somehow she had not expected him to seek her out again. He must have been revolted by her inability to control herself, she thought. In the past two days he had gone out of his way to avoid her, so much so that Nigel had asked her what she had done to give him disgust of her.

Rae offered an explanation that suggested the duke's honored guest had overstepped the boundaries of good taste by asking her to share his bed. Rather than being offended by the news, Nigel studied Rae's tense features thoughtfully, as if contemplating the merits of giving her to Lord Thomas Adams himself. Why not, Rae considered; it was apparent from the recent play in the library that Nigel was going to give his guest the game.

For two nights running Rae had dutifully followed Nigel's orders to indicate Jericho's cards, and Nigel had chosen to lose to his opponent. Rae did not like to think about the reasons the duke had decided to allow Jericho to win, for she suspected that Nigel found something to admire in the younger man. It bothered her not a little that Nigel supposed he and Jericho were two facets of the same diamond, glittering cold and hard with an icy self-possession that could serve up a cutting glance as easily as if it were cutting glass. It bothered her because in the last two days she had entertained similar thoughts, having now been on the receiving end of Jericho's aloof and disinterested gaze more times than she cared to remember. She admitted it frightened her that he might indeed be ruthlessly dismissing her from his life. Still, she was not entirely unsympathetic. There was a part of her that envied Jericho's ability to do what she could not: completely sever the bonds of love.

"How long have you been here?" she whispered, certain he could see the yearning in her eyes and wishing it were not her lot to want what she could not have.

"A few minutes."

"The duke is—"

"Yes, I know. It was necessary I talk to you." Jericho's fingers itched to touch the white column of Rae's throat, to stroke her gently and ease the note of fear he heard in her voice. Instead his hands clenched the arms of the chair until his knuckles were bloodless. "I went to the duke's study. There was no evidence of the documents."

Rae closed her eyes a moment as if feeling a blow. She did not insult him by asking if he was certain. Jericho was nothing if not thorough. "What is to be done?"

"I have not yet decided. I only came from there. I could call Nigel out for cheating at cards, though it would be hard to make a case when the man is bent on losing to me. I doubt that killing him would be viewed in a very favorable light under those circumstances. If he continues as he did tonight, I will have his notes tomorrow. Have I made my cards visible enough for you?"

"Yes. But what would you do if Nigel decided he wanted to win?"

"The same. Stanhope is not the important thing here, Red. It is, and always has been, a means to an end. If I withheld my cards from your view it is you who would suffer. I will not have more of your suffering on my conscience."

"Jericho . . ." There was a hint of pleading in her tone.

"There is another matter I wish to discuss," he said coldly. "A matter of some import. Though I did not find the documents, I did stumble upon—"

"Ssshh!" Rae said urgently, scrambling to her knees and cocking her head toward the connecting door. "I heard something."

Jericho had heard it also, the sound of a harsh curse in the adjoining room, and he was already moving toward the door, anticipating the duke's entry. A second raised voice stopped him, and he and Rae realized at the same time that the curse was not directed at anything that was occurring in their room.

Rae slipped into her dressing gown as she padded across the room and came to stand at Jericho's side. He warned her to be quiet by raising a finger to his lips, then both of them moved to the door. It was not necessary to press an ear to the wood or an eye to the keyhole to recognize the owners of the angry voices as Nigel Lynne and Charles Newbrough.

It startled Rae to hear the duke's chilling tones unleashed in a red haze of fury. She thought that if Nigel's letters to Ashley had a voice, this would be the sound of them. She could not imagine what Newbrough could have done to prompt Nigel to show so much naked emotion.

"How dare you threaten me!" Nigel fairly screamed.

"A threat? Is that how you see it, old man?" The earl was much more in control. "I prefer to think I am merely apprising you of some facts."

Nigel ranted on as if Newbrough had not spoken. "In my own home! How dare you abuse my hospitality and my privacy!"

"Really, Nigel, you are carrying your act as the insulted host a bit beyond bearing when the reality is that I am the injured party."

"You? You deserve to lose more than your lands, you sniveling blighter!"

"Are you thinking of calling me out?" Newbrough asked uninterestedly. "I can't think what it would serve. Not when my seconds would be instructed to release the documents in my possession. I cannot conceive what made you keep your father's will, Nigel, though I would venture that it was no mere oversight, but further proof that you believe yourself above the touch of the law. It's just as well for me, for you have provided me with the means of control. Do you seriously believe I would have asked you to play for me if I had no way of managing you?" Newbrough laughed then, a pitying sort of laugh that was meant to grate on Nigel's nerves. "You don't have to answer. I can see that you did. Poor Nigel, so shocked that someone other than yourself has some leverage."

"Shut up. I will not let you take Linfield from me."

"You mistake my meaning in coming here if you think that is what I want. I don't want Linfield. I want two things from you, and neither of them is your title or your lands. I want to retain Stanhope. Did you think I would not notice you are purposely losing to Adams? Your actions have forced my hand now. If you had won my notes and returned them to me I would never have mentioned what I discovered in your family Bible. In fact, I had every intention of leaving those documents in their place, relying on your honor and hoping I would not have need of them. But you may recall your mistress was overzealous in her duties as a maid. When I realized someone might chance upon them in much the way I had, I knew I had to remove them."

"What have you done with them?"

"They're safe enough. And yours again as soon as you deliver my notes to me."

"You don't deserve Stanhope," Nigel said, recovering a measure of his composure. "You are naught but a peasant who happened upon a great title simply because the estate was entailed."

"People who reside in glass houses," Newbrough said warningly. "Our situations are similar, don't you think? But there is one important difference. I own Stanhope, and I made certain there is no one else to lay claim to my lands. You were foolish not to dispose of your ward, excuse me, your niece, long ago. Why didn't you?"

"It is not your affair. You said earlier that you wanted two things, yet you have spoken only of the notes. What is this second demand of yours?"

"Anxious for this interview to end?" the earl asked smoothly. "And I was enjoying it so."

"On with it, man, or I swear I'll kill you now."

"That would not be wise. Your secret would become very public upon my untimely death. What with the way you've been shouting, I shouldn't be surprised if a dozen of your guests don't know of it now. Oh, very well, Nigel, there is no need to pitch daggers at me. In addition to the return of my notes, I want you to guarantee that I shall capture Rahab during the hunt."

"Is that all? You may have her now, if it's your desire."

Rae reached blindly for Jericho's arm, leaning on him weakly. Her terror was so great that she did not hear Newbrough's response, but she was certain Jericho did. His body was coiled with tension as he scooped her up and carried her back to the bed. After he helped her out of her dressing gown, Rae huddled beneath the covers at the head of the bed. Jericho's hands fell uselessly at his side, and he despised his inability to comfort her. From the other room he heard the door being slammed in the earl's wake and the sound of glass shattering as Nigel gave full vent to his rage.

"You have to leave here, Red," he said, leaning over and

placing a hand on either side of her. "Drew's friends are at Blackamore's in Hemmings. You have only to present yourself and they'll see to your safety. Will you go?"

"Yes," she said wearily. A heavy tiredness settled over her and she was incapable of protest even if she had wanted to voice one. "Shall I leave now?"

"No. It will be light soon. You must wait until tomorrow night. Drew or I will let you out of your room."

Rae shook her head. "It would be better if I left during a break in the card playing. Then no one would suspect I had assistance. You can stay here without fear of being implicated in my departure."

Jericho saw the wisdom in that. "All right. But the breaks are only thirty minutes long. It is not much of a head start for you."

She laughed without humor. "More than I would get in the hunt."

"You've known about it all along, haven't you? And I only found out this evening when I was reading the duke's letters. Why didn't you tell me that Nigel had such a thing planned?"

"A matter of pride, I suppose. I wanted to prove that I did not require your assistance. You made a point of telling me I was incapable of caring for myself."

That set Jericho back on his heels. "Surely you must know I said that in order to keep you at my side."

"Nonetheless, it is true."

"Then it is true for me as well. Think you that I could have survived Yorktown without your help? No, I see it never occurred to you. I wish to God there was time to settle this, but I must go. Take nothing with you when you leave tomorrow night, and for your safety stay off the main road, to the left if you can, for I believe the cover is better. Do you climb trees, Red?"

"Not well," she said, thinking of the scar on her knee. "Why?"

"If you hear a search party coming for you, climb a tree and stay put until they pass. I doubt anyone will think to look for you overhead."

"I can do that."

"Of course you can," said Jericho encouragingly. "And when you get to Hemmings, seek out Tom Jenkins at the inn. He will see that you get to my London home without mishap. I will join you when all is finished here." He searched her face to make certain she understood, then straightened and left Rae's chamber as silently as he had entered it.

Rae stared at the door long after Jericho locked it behind him, wondering at the sense of loss she felt upon his departure. What a burden she had come to be she thought sadly. It occurred to her that he did not smile anymore, and that it had been forever since she had heard him laugh with genuine amusement. If she had made him happy once, it was true no longer. Her willfulness had not aided their cause, rather it had added to their problems. She was a yoke about his neck, a weight that he could do without. Yes, she would leave for Hemmings tomorrow night, but perhaps there was one last thing she could give him before she went. The least he deserved for all his effort on her behalf was Stanhope. Her hand went to her throat as if touching the green stones that usually lay there. She could give nothing of herself, but she could give him Stanhope.

Rahab took her usual seat at Jericho's back before the beginning of the play, smoothing the folds of her gold satin gown over her lap and studiously avoiding the sharp and faintly hungry eyes of Charles Newbrough. Throughout the day he had been more forthright in his attentions than he had been recently, and Rae took pleasure in snubbing him, knowing if she had done else she would have aroused suspicion. She could practically hear the thoughts of revenge forming in his mind as he considered he would best her in the end. It would not have been easy to pretend ignorance if she hadn't been prepared to leave. Under the circumstances, it was difficult not to gloat.

Nigel looked comfortable and relaxed as he sat down to play, but Rae knew his unconcerned air for the act it was. While she was dressing he had once again come into her room and reminded her of what he required. Even if she had not overheard him talking with Newbrough the night before, she would have known then that he had changed his mind about permitting Jericho to win. She pretended ignorance, assured him she would go on as she had from the beginning, and attended to her toilette as if she had come to enjoy her role as Nigel's mistress. It was not until Nigel was out of the room that she filed the clasp on the emerald necklace.

Rahab took a glass of champagne from the passing footman's tray and sipped it with what she hoped was nonchalance. She smiled faintly as the drink slipped smoothly down her throat. She would have given almost anything to get her hands on Esther's jug liquor. That heady brew was guaranteed to calm her brittle nerves and quell the uneasy excitement that made her heart thump alarmingly in her breast. It was only as the duke began to deal the first hand of cards that a blessed numbness stole over her and she gave herself up to the task she had set for herself.

As he had done with nearly every hand, Jericho made it easy for Rae to view his cards, and Rae dutifully fingered her necklace for the duke. Nigel won the first four games with ease, and Jericho congratulated him on his skill at the break. Rae schooled her features not to show her disgust as Nigel accepted the praise as if it were his due, but decided at that moment she would not put off ridding herself of the hateful necklace.

It was during the first game of the second match that she managed to give a surreptitious tug, breaking the flimsy clasp. The necklace slid to the floor before she could catch it, and she apologized prettily for the noisy interruption of the play.

Lord Lesley gallantly offered to replace it around Rae's neck but found the clasp would not hold. After some fumbling on his part Rae took the necklace from him and held it in her lap. The angle made it impossible for Nigel to see the stones, and Rae felt immense pleasure as white lines of tension appeared at the corners of the duke's mouth. She hid her satisfaction by smiling at him nervously as if to assure him this turn of events was not her fault. She studiously avoided Jericho's speculative gaze.

The next four games were split evenly between Nigel and Jericho, and at the break Rae excused herself from the room. Nigel caught up with her at the bottom of the stairs.

"I hope you are on your way to repair that necklace," he said.

"That is exactly what I am going to do," she assured him, praying all the while that he would not ask to examine it. "Though I believe you can win without my help."

The duke was not immune to having his own opinion bolstered. "I believe I can also. But I would rather there not be the slightest doubt as to the outcome. Secure that jewelry any way you can." She turned to go, but Nigel placed a hand on her bare shoulder. "Have I mentioned that you are looking exceptionally beautiful this evening? There is a certain glow about you that I had not noticed before."

Coolly she said, "Please remove your hand from my shoulder."

"As you wish, m'dear." His hand slid from her shoulder to her breast and he did not retract it until he felt her shudder. He tapped her nose with a slender forefinger. "Repair that necklace."

Rae gave the duke's order all the attention she considered it deserved once she was in her room. She tossed the necklace toward the bed, and when it narrowly missed landing on the coverlet and skidded instead under the four poster she did not give a thought to retrieving it.

Pitching the necklace aside was the last motion Rae wasted as she prepared to leave Linfield. In a matter of minutes she had completely undone the hours she had spent readying herself to meet the duke's guests. She removed her gown and filmy undergarments and replaced them with the uniform she had worn in the duke's service. Her wig was added to the pile of discarded clothes and she scrubbed her face free of lip and cheek rouge. She caught sight of herself in the mirror as she slipped the pelisse about her shoulders and decided it was unlikely that any of the duke's friends would recognize her. To her own eyes she looked unremarkable, and she paused long enough to give thanks for an appearance that to her own way of thinking was nondescript and every bit common. In her anxiousness to flee she could be forgiven for this delusion, but the man who saw her slip from her chamber and hurry toward the servants' stairs thought she had a look of rare loveliness about her.

When she disappeared from his sight, Stephens decided Linfield was darker than it had been in months, but that he would pray for her safe flight. No one, least of all Rae, deserved what Nigel Lynne had planned for her. Turning on his heel he went to the library to inform his employer that Rahab was still experiencing some difficulty with her attire but promised to join him at the next break.

As the play was ready to resume, Nigel had to be satisfied with his butler's report and was forced to rely on his own considerable skill. He chafed at the slowness of Jericho's play, for it seemed to him that his opponent had been quicker in his deliberations in the past, yet Nigel recognized that his own playing was more thoughtful without Rae's presence to guide him.

Jericho felt Rae's absence more keenly than the duke, though he was just as careful not to show it. He knew she had set a different course for herself as soon as she had managed to be rid of the necklace. He understood immediately that she was giving him back his chance to win Stanhope. There was nothing for it but to prolong the play and hope Rae had the good sense to leave. If she dared return to the library with a bare throat Nigel would make her answer for it.

Jericho concentrated on the cards as they fell, making a mental note of the contents of each trick. It would have been the utmost foolishness not to take advantage of the opening Rae had left him. Although Nigel played his hand well, there was a certain recklessness in his manner that Jericho took pleasure reining in. It was obvious to Jericho that Nigel was still relying on Rae's return to give him an edge. By the end of the next round Jericho had recouped his earlier loss to the duke, and only £300 remained in Nigel's coffers.

Jericho anticipated the duke would go in search of Rae himself when the break came, and there was nothing he could do to prevent it from happening. Far from looking anxious when Nigel left the room, he gave every appearance of enjoying himself immensely as he chatted genially with Lord Evans. His expression did not flicker when Nigel returned to the library and took Newbrough away, though he could well imagine the gist of the conversation taking place in the hallway. He was certain now that Rae was no longer in the house, and he felt as if a weight had been lifted from his shoulders.

It was but a momentary respite, because the duke's announcement upon reentering the library would have knocked Jericho to his knees had he been standing.

"Gentlemen," Nigel addressed them calmly. "I wish to call an end to this evening's play and begin a game of a different nature. It has been customary to hold the hunt on the last day of our festivities, but our lovely hostess has convinced me of the pleasures and challenge of a night pursuit."

Even as he pretended bewilderment, Jericho felt a chill race down his spine. "I must protest," he drawled. "Can't say that I like the idea of prolonging the inevitable racing to the hounds."

The murmurs of interest that had accompanied Nigel's announcement gave way to amusement at Jericho's innocence.

"You misunderstand," Evans told him. "There are no hounds in this hunt, and the fox is of the two-legged variety. Who is it to be this time, Nigel? Did I miss casting my vote?"

Nigel smiled thinly. "I've taken the liberty of choosing this hunt's vixen."

"Who?" asked Lesley. "I hope it ain't Georgina. Don't think I'll take part if it is. Heard she has the pox."

"Not Georgina. Rahab."

Jericho wondered if his face mirrored the eagerness of the men around him. Newbrough, who had finally rejoined them, was the only man who looked unhappy at the prospect of hunting for Rahab, and Jericho realized it was because there were no longer any guarantees that he would be the one to find her. "I can see everyone is anxious to be underway," he said, "but I wish someone would explain what the deuce is going on."

Lord Lesley explained in very explicit terms the game that was about to begin, and Jericho was torn between landing him a facer or thanking him for delaying the start with his ribald recitation of the rules.

Then Nigel spoke. "There are only two things I would like to add to Lesley's account. I have decided that in order to make the hunt more sporting, Rae will not wear the collar, and I have given her no boundaries. She will be a difficult quarry to corner." He smiled again, but it did not touch his cold eyes. "However, I have complete faith in your ability to bring her in, and because you are my closest friends and Lord Adams is a new acquaintance, you may have a start on the others. If you'll excuse me, I'll attend to my other guests now."

"Damn!" Evans said in the tone of a man who could not believe his good fortune. "What a piece of luck this is!"

Standing, Lesley laughed and spoke to the others. "He's been racking his brain trying to think of a way to assure Miss

McClellan's victory in the voting. I take it you're ready to put your mind to the task of catching her, eh, Evans?''

"Like this.'' He snapped his fingers. ''Are you coming, Adams? Don't force yourself, man. The fewer of us, the better chance I'll have.''

Jericho laughed as he was expected to. ''No, I'm coming. I've never fancied a hunt before. But this? This is something else again.''

Rae, mindful of Jericho's directives, kept to the left side of the road where the protection was better. Even having no idea that Stephens had seen her leave or that he had lied to give her more time, she was beginning to feel confident that she was well beyond the reach of the duke and any search party he might send. Occasionally she glanced toward the moonlit road and wondered if she dared walk along its edge, thinking she could make even better time if she were not hampered by the darkness of the wood. In the end caution asserted itself and she kept to her path, looking beyond the overhanging branches for the candlelit windows in Hemmings that would mean her safety.

Jericho parted ways with Lesley and the other hunters soon after mounting. It appeared they were of the opinion that Rahab had entered into this game willingly, and they were going to look for her on the grounds first. Newbrough was the only rider who set off for the main gate, and Jericho held back, circling round so that it would not seem obvious he was following. Still within earshot of the house, he heard the high-spirited, slightly drunken laughter of the guests who were now making their way to the stables in search of horses for the hunt. Jericho did not know if Nigel was among them, but he felt sure he must be. Too often in the past the duke had found that others failed to bring him what he wanted. Nigel was not likely to leave the trapping of Rahab to the drunken pursuits of his friends.

Jericho and Newbrough made the same mistake in following Rae: both underestimated the time she had been gone from Linfield. They both left the road too early in search of her trail, and Newbrough compounded his error by choosing to cut into the woods on the right where the going was easier for his horse. Unfortunately it was a case of two wrongs making a right, for when he realized Rae had not come that way he shot back onto the road and down to the left, well ahead of Jericho now.

Newbrough went forward about two hundred yards and began to reconsider Nigel's advice to search along the road to Hemmings. Yet the duke had been adamant that Rae was clearly trying to escape, so he took the advice, deciding Nigel would not lie to him when the girl was part of the bargain for his silence. He pressed on in spite of his doubts and was rewarded for his trust by the sight of a ribbon of lace fluttering at the thorny end of a briar bush. He reined in his horse and leaned over to examine the bit of material. He could not be certain it belonged to Rahab, but it gave him hope. Grinning, he took the piece of lace and tucked it in a buttonhole, then pushed ahead.

Rahab did not know how Newbrough missed the shaking branches above his head, for she had expected her trembling to alert him to her presence. Having no idea how much farther Newbrough would go before he realized he had lost her, she was afraid to move from her perch and afraid not to. It was the most accursed piece of luck that in her haste to climb the tree she had torn her slip on the bush. She caught her breath on a sob and nearly wondered aloud how long it had been since she had done something right. Her damning thoughts were interrupted by the approach of another rider, and Rae was frozen into stillness this time. She hugged the slender tree trunk, too weary to tremble any longer.

For a moment she ceased to hear anything except the drumming of her own heart, but gradually she became aware of the rustle of leaves as the horse trampled them underfoot. Then there was another sound, totally unexpected, yet infinitely welcome. Anyone else could be forgiven for thinking Jericho's whistle was merely a tuneless ditty, but Rae knew "Yankee Doodle" when she heard it.

She feared calling out to him, thinking it might attract Newbrough, so she waited for him to come within her sight. It was the most terrible sort of waiting she had ever endured, and her eagerness as she spied his silhouette was almost her undoing. It was only as she opened her mouth to speak his name that she heard another rider coming up behind Jericho. Her gasp could not be entirely stifled, but if Jericho heard it he gave no sign. His attention was all for the newcomer, and she saw him turn his horse to greet the rider.

"I'm rather surprised to find you here, Adams," Nigel said.

"I hope so," Jericho answered, his voice amused. "Else I might be threatened by that pistol in your hand."

Nigel looked down at the weapon as if he had forgotten he carried it, then smiled good-naturedly as he tucked it in the waistband of his breeches. "It doesn't pay to go into these woods without protection. I'm sorry I frightened you."

"I didn't say I was frightened," said Jericho. "I am not without my own resources." Jericho saw the duke's head tilt to one side and knew he was trying to make out where the weapon was secured. Jericho was not about to tell Nigel his steel blade was resting comfortably in a sheath fitted inside his riding boots. "But tell me, dare I hope your presence here means I may be close to Miss McClellan?"

"I was going to ask you the same. I would have thought you'd stay with Lesley and Evans."

"I might have if I hadn't seen Newbrough going in this direction. I recalled you talked to him before announcing the hunt. I supposed he was privy to information not given to the rest of us."

"That was observant of you. I take it you wish to best him in this as you have in everything else."

Jericho laughed. "Are you conceding that I've won the last of his notes? I warn you I am anxious to play for Stanhope once I have them in hand."

"As anxious as you are to have my mistress in your bed?"

"Now there's a question to encourage a man to think. I'll grant you she's a fair one, but I admit to wanting her because Newbrough wants her more."

"I thought as much."

"I know you did; that's why I don't mind telling you. And you, have you come to secure her for yourself, or are you doing Newbrough's work?" Jericho intended for Nigel to take exception to his words, and he was not disappointed.

"I work for no man," he said coldly.

"Then it is friendship that prompts you to claim for the earl what he cannot claim himself."

Nigel did not comment directly. "What is your interest?"

"It is self-interest, I assure you. If I find your mistress, I want her for myself. I cannot say that I like the idea of your taking her from me only to pass her along to Newbrough. In this instance, I would not find it sporting."

Nigel heard the underlying threat in his guest's soft voice. "You would call me out?"

"I cannot say I would proceed that formally if you were to cross me."

Surprisingly, Nigel laughed. "Damn, but there is something I like about you, Adams. There's an uncivilized element that I never thought I could admire, but I find it suits you well."

Jericho was hardly flattered. Indeed, it did not take a leap of the imagination to know that Nigel was wondering how they could join forces and defeat Newbrough. "I have your word then, that your mistress is mine if I find her?"

"My word," said Nigel solemnly. "She is yours until the gala is over, of course."

"Of course. I have no desire to steal her from you."

"I feel I must point out that you have to find her first."

Jericho's even teeth glowed whitely in the moonlight. "I already have. Miss McClellan, you may come down. And if you have a mind to hesitate, you will have to choose between me and Newbrough, for I hear him coming now."

Rahab also heard the earl's noisy approach as he returned to the site where he had found the lace. There was no choice to be made, but she was afraid Nigel would suspect something if she went too easily to Jericho.

"She's not a willing wench," the duke said. "She has a mind of her own."

"I thought as much when I followed Newbrough out the front gate. It struck me odd that she would even suggest a hunt at night, though I suspect she envisioned some other woman as the prey. No matter, I look forward to having the taming of her." Jericho urged his horse around and forward, stopping when he came to the base of Rae's tree. Grasping a sturdy lower limb, he gracefully pulled himself up into the boughs. In a matter of seconds he was at Rae's side. "There is no choice. None. You must come with me. I fear the others would have found you."

From Nigel's point of view it appeared Jericho was whispering encouragement in Rae's ear. "Have done with it, man. Get her down from there."

"I cannot come without a fight," Rae whispered back, ignoring Nigel.

"Flail away. I won't let you fall." He wrapped her waist firmly in one arm and made to lift her from her branch.

Rae took Jericho at his word and fought him in earnest, frustration at being captured so close to her goal making her arms work like small windmills. Her fists pummeled his shoulders and back and she landed several painful blows on his legs with her feet. It was only when she realized part of her enjoyed the one-sided battle that she was careful to miss more often than she connected.

"What is toward?" Newbrough demanded sharply as he

reined in his horse beside Nigel's. His anger mounted as he was forced to watch helplessly while Jericho dragged Rahab from the tree. "You said I could have her!" he hissed.

"I cannot help it that you could not find her. You must have passed right beneath her if you came this way."

The earl did not care for having his failure pointed out to him. "I want her, Nigel."

"Call him out. Say you found her first and he took her from you. I'll support you."

Newbrough snorted in derision. "Think I am such a fool as that? It would suit you very well if I were to get myself killed in a duel." He dismissed the duke and turned his attention on Jericho as Rae was finally subdued. "Do you really suppose she is worth the trouble?"

Jericho shrugged. "It is apparent you think she is, my lord. That was the only recommendation I required." He urged his horse forward until he was beside the earl. The hand that lay casually at Rae's waist slid possessively to the underside of her breast. "I shall try not to spoil her for you, Newbrough."

"You conceited lout!" Rae spit, twisting in Jericho's arms in an effort to free herself. "I want none of you! You are not a whit better than the company you keep! Put me down from here!"

"I'd advise you to consider your alternatives." Rahab quieted instantly. "The lady has made her decision, Newbrough. I bid you good evening." Jericho gave his horse a kick and started off in the direction of the road. The hand that had rested beneath her breast slid back to her waist. "I am sorry for the crude display," he said stiffly. A litany of curses rang in his head as he held her loosely in one arm and wished he could offer the comfort of two. He willed himself not to be moved by the fragrance of her hair as soft strands of it swept across his mouth. "It seemed necessary to convince Newbrough that I mean to keep you."

Rae shifted in the saddle so that she could see Jericho's

profile. It appeared harsh and unyielding in the moonlight, as if sculpted from white marble, and retained all the warmth one might expect from that stone. She could find no cause for his coldness other than in response to something she had done. "Are you angry with me?" she asked.

"No."

"I see," she said in a tone that clearly showed she did not. "Did I hurt you when you pulled me from the tree? I thought to make it a realistic struggle, but I confess in part I wanted to strike at you."

If anything his profile became bleaker. "Don't refine upon it. I deserved it and more." Behind him he could hear the duke and Newbrough following, and he urged his mount to a quicker pace. "Red, do you understand what awaits us when we return to Linfield? It was no mere search party the duke sent for you. He covered your disappearance by beginning the hunt."

She looked away from his face, unable to meet his grim glance. "I thought as much," she whispered. It was difficult to swallow and her throat felt raw when touched by the cold night air. "Do you think I shall have to wear the collar?"

"I shouldn't be surprised," said Jericho tightly. "But there is another matter that should concern you more. By capturing you I have claimed the right to have you in my bed."

"Any other man would have said he had claimed the right to bed me. I thank you for making that distinction."

"You don't have to worry that I'll touch you, Red. I wanted you to know that before we arrived. In front of the others I may have no choice but to treat you in a certain manner; in private you will choose how you wish to be treated. I won't let any harm befall you at my hands or the hands of others."

"I believe you, Jericho." Her slender fingers slipped from beneath her pelisse and covered his hand holding the reins. "I truly do believe you."

Jericho would have liked to have pulled her closer then, feeling the narrow contours of her back against his chest, and offer more than the protection of his promises. He leashed the impulse, afraid that in spite of her confidence Rae would misinterpret his gesture.

After leaving his horse at the stables, Jericho escorted Rae across Linfield's wide lawn, their steps dogged by Nigel and Charles. At the entrance they caught up to him, handed their cloaks to Stephens, whose daring disapproval was wasted because no one gave him a glance, and followed Jericho into the library.

Newbrough poured a stiff drink immediately upon entering and nursed it while watching Jericho offer Rahab a chair with a solicitousness that set his teeth on edge. "There's no need to grovel for her, man. She's yours. You could take her now, and no one would stop you."

Jericho straightened, his eyes pinning the earl to the wall. "Is that why you followed me? Had you hoped I might flip up her skirts and have at her here?" Jericho laughed. "I admit to wanting her, but not so much that I will entertain an audience." He turned his back on the earl, dismissing him, and addressed Rae. "Would you care for a drink?"

Rae shook her head. The look that she saw pass between Nigel and Newbrough made her mute. It struck her that Newbrough intended to be privy to what happened in her bedchamber. She nearly disgraced herself by being ill at that moment.

Jericho eyed her keenly, wondering what had brought on her sudden pallor, but a small negative movement of her hand told him to dismiss his inquiry. He moved away from her and poured his own drink, offering one to the duke.

Nigel refused. "You must excuse me for a moment. I wish to make my other guests aware the hunt is over."

As soon as he left the room Newbrough spoke up. "I want her, Adams. She was promised to me."

"That is unfortunate. But for the time allowed by the rules of this game, she is mine. I have no intentions of giving her up." As Jericho talked he stepped closer to Rae, until he stood at the back of her chair.

"You do well to guard your captive," Newbrough said sneeringly. "Any man can challenge for her until she wears the collar. That is also part of the rules."

The loud report of a pistol firing somewhere on the grounds startled Rae. It seemed that even before she jumped Jericho's hand was on her shoulder, calming her. "I think that is our host's signal the game is at an end," he told her. When he gave his attention back to the earl he did not remove his hand, but allowed his fingers to insinuate themselves intimately in the neckline of Rae's blouse. It was a gesture of ownership and had but one purpose: to remind Newbrough that he had been bested again. "Do you wish to challenge me, my lord? I doubt that I would kill you, for it would deny me the pleasure of wresting the title of Stanhope from your hands. But wounding you? Now that would be something to savor. Mayhap I would allow Miss McClellan to choose where the lead ball should lodge. Though the lady has no liking for me, I think she has even less for you. What say you, Newbrough? Shall I find my seconds?"

Rather than answer, Charles Newbrough flung his empty glass at the hearth and stalked from the room.

Rae drew an uneven breath. "I fear you are goading him beyond reason. He may not say nay to your next challenge."

"Do you think I care?" demanded Jericho in a strangled whisper. "I would like to strike him down every time his hot glance rests on you." Unwittingly his fingers pressed harshly on her throat, and her small wince made him pull back as if burned. "Forgive me," he groaned feelingly.

There was no time for Rahab to console him, because Nigel returned carrying the collar in one hand. The musical tinkling of its tiny silver bells would have been pleasant had they been meant for any other purpose than to remind everyone that Rahab was naught but a possession.

''Newbrough insisted,'' said Nigel as he handed the collar, key, and chain to Jericho.

Rahab's laugh was filled with contempt. ''Tell your honored guest the truth, your grace. You fully intended that I should wear this bit of jewelry from the beginning. It has always been your determination to shame me.''

''Would that it were a muzzle, my dear,'' the duke said pleasantly, seemingly unperturbed by her vehemence. ''It would become you more. Still, it would be better if you entered into the spirit of the thing. Lord Adams has won you fairly.''

Rae flinched slightly as Jericho fastened the collar about her neck and the bells sounded gently, giving her movement away. ''I doubt there was anything fair about it,'' she said, as Jericho attached the chain to the back of the collar and then slipped the bracelet end of it on his wrist. He returned the key to Nigel's open palm. ''No doubt you took great delight in giving him my direction.''

''Have a care,'' said Jericho. ''Accuse me of cheating again and I'll not answer to the consequences. I can see why the duke chose you for the hunt. It will give me great pleasure to return him to you a bit subdued.''

''Vain coxcomb! Both of you are bastards!'' Though she was expecting Jericho's retaliation, knew that he had to respond so that Nigel would not suspect there was anything but enmity between them, she was still surprised when he jerked his wrist sharply downward, causing her head to bow in an attitude of subservience. When she tried to lift it she discovered she could not because he had wrapped the chain around his hand, shortening it until only a few links were free between her neck and his fingers.

''Her tongue is too sharp by half,'' said Jericho, giving the chain a little jerk so that Rae's head bobbed against her will. ''See, she agrees.''

Rae twisted her head within the collar and glanced upward at Nigel, loathing in her narrow gaze. Her movement clearly accused him rather than the man who held her. She saw in his thin-lipped smile, in the icy glitter of his dark stare, that he was well pleased that she had been brought to this pass. She doubted that he would honor his bargain to release her now even if she penned the letter in front of him. Her abortive escape this evening had finished all that, his complacent stance seemed to say. If he was concerned about Newbrough's not having her, he did not indicate it. It was as if he sensed a certain ruthlessness in Jericho that he thought she would do well to experience.

"It is not yet late," said Nigel, as Rae looked away from him and studied her folded hands. He felt immense satisfaction that she had known it would do no good to plead with him, though he admitted he would have liked to hear her entreaties. Had he found her in the woods she would have felt the sting of his riding crop for trying to thwart him and make him a fool in front of his guests by taking her leave. "The others will be returning shortly. Do you wish to resume play, or would you rather retire?"

Jericho brought Rae's head up, forcing her to look at him while he pretended to examine the familiar features of her face. "I am in no hurry to retire, but I confess I am anxious to have the last of Newbrough's notes in my possession. I would like to see if my luck will continue to hold. What say you, Miss McClellan? Can you possibly put a hold on your enthusiasm to share my bed?"

"Go to hell."

"I doubt that I would be admitted," he said with complete sincerity. "Yes, your grace, I rather think I'll play a few hands."

The card game began thirty minutes later. Lord Evans told Jericho, only half in jest, that he was queer in the attic for not taking Rahab immediately to his chamber and commencing a little slap and tickle. Though Rae blushed deeply at the slight, she held her tongue while Jericho shrugged off the comment good-naturedly. It was then that Rae realized that the respect she was accorded as Nigel's mistress did not extend to the captive of the hunt. It seemed that every man save Nigel wanted to slip the bracelet from Jericho's wrist and attach it to his own. She survived the humiliation of the deliberately rude and speculative stares by entertaining thoughts of making every would-be stallion a gelding.

Unaware of the designs upon their manhood, all the observers were seated in their usual places, with the exception of Rae, who had no choice but to sit at Jericho's side. The length of the chain made it difficult for Jericho to gather his tricks without pulling on Rae's throat, and rather than remove the bracelet from his wrist, he ordered her to take in his cards. That she did so without demur won a salute of delighted murmurs from everyone but Newbrough. The earl had lost interest in Rae for the time being and only had eyes for the fall of the cards as Nigel continued to lose hand after hand to his opponent.

Rae did not understand Nigel's purpose, for it appeared to her that he was deliberately allowing Jericho to win, though it was done with such skill that she suspected the observers put it down to successive unlucky deals. She was certainly giving him no assistance, and when she dared to glance about the room she could find no one who had taken her place. It did not make sense to her that he would give up Newbrough's notes when the earl had threatened to disclose to London at large that Nigel was not the rightful owner of Linfield. Jericho was of no help, for his face was at its most inscrutable, giving nothing away of his innermost thoughts. His deep blue eyes remained hooded, while his mouth neither lifted nor turned down at the corners, no matter what the outcome of the cards.

The room was so quiet as the last hand for the notes was dealt that Rahab was loath to breathe for fear of setting the bells at her throat to tinkling. Jericho broke the spell by pulling her close and kissing her full on the lips. The bells jangled wildly, masking the thumping of her heart. "For luck," he said, but Rae thought she surprised something in his eyes that said it was not for luck, but love. It was only as Jericho fanned his cards in front of him that Rae realized his intimate touch had caused an alarm of a different nature than she had been feeling of late. His mouth on hers had sent a shiver of pleasure through her. Unconsciously one of her hands fluttered to her abdomen, as if assuring her babe that everything was as it should be.

Jericho momentarily lost his concentration as he caught the shudder of what he could only perceive as revulsion sweep Rahab. Out of the corner of his eye he saw her hand fall to her stomach, and he wondered if she was going to be sick. Cursing himself for the weakness that made him want to touch her, he gathered the shreds of his wounded pride and appointed himself to the task of taking this last hand.

He very nearly did not win because of his early careless play, but Nigel made an equally careless blunder by reneging on his hand, and the win went to Jericho. Lord Lesley announced the final score, and Jericho accepted the notes Nigel handed to him with none of the satisfaction he might have felt had the circumstances been different.

Jericho stood, bringing a bewildered Rae to her feet. The jingling of the bells as she twisted her head to look from him to Nigel to the earl attested to her confusion. "Have you won all, my lord?" she asked as Nigel extended his hand to Jericho.

Nigel answered in Jericho's place. "He has won the notes, m'dear, but not Stanhope. For that he must play on the morrow. Unless you have changed your mind, Adams, and propose to collect."

Jericho looked past Nigel to where Newbrough was sitting, still with shock and an ugly menace in his wide-set eyes, and said, "I wish to play for the title to the lands." His statement was given in the manner of a man throwing down a gauntlet, for it was issued clearly to remind everyone in the room that the earl did not possess the funds to honor the total of his debts. By extending this last opportunity to Newbrough to save his estate, Jericho had shown his complete contempt for the earl of Stanhope.

"Till morning, gentlemen," he said coolly, giving Rae a nudge to move toward the door. "I hope the remainder of your evening is as pleasant as mine."

Rae closed her mind to the rude speculation that followed her exit from the library. She silently thanked Jericho for keeping his chained wrist at her waist as they mounted the stairs. If he had dropped his hand to his side she would have had to bow her head to keep from straining at the collar. She despised the weakly submissive posture that she had been forced to endure for the sake of the charade.

At the top of the stairs she turned out of habit toward her room in the east wing. Jericho's hold brought her up short, and the hateful bells jangled in response.

"I'm sorry, but my rooms are this way," he said, pointing to the left.

"Of course. I wasn't thinking." She put one hand to her throat to still the bells. "Please, let's go. I want to be rid of this accursed thing."

"I had to return the key to Nigel," he reminded her.

Rae had forgotten, and her disappointment was clearly etched on her face. Her attempt to shrug it off was unsuccessful, and though Jericho's heart went out to her, he offered little in the way of comfort. Other than release the bracelet from his wrist, there was nothing he could do.

Once they were in Jericho's bedchamber, however, Rae would not let him take off the bracelet until she had satisfied herself that they were indeed alone. Leading him about this time by the wrist, she checked under the bed, in the mahogany wardrobe, and in the dressing room. When her search yielded nothing, she drew Jericho along all the darkly paneled walls, running her hands over the polished woodwork until she was satisfied there were no secret doors or sliding panels that could subject their privacy to an intrusion. Her fingers slid along the intricately carved marble mantelpiece and found no movable objects or hidden springs. There were three paintings in the room, and she looked behind each one and tapped the elaborately scrolled frames.

"What has this been in aid of?" asked Jericho as he helped her replace the last painting.

"I feared that Newbrough had planned to spy on us. It is in his style. Yet I cannot see how it could be accomplished in this room. I believe it is safe to talk."

Jericho slipped off the bracelet and gave it to Rae. She put it on her own wrist and felt in control of herself for the first time since Jericho had taken her from the wood. Rae stood in front of the fireplace and picked up the poker, stirring the fire. Every movement was accompanied by the gentle peal of the tiny bells.

"I doubt I shall ever like the sound of bells again," she said lightly. Directly behind her she could feel Jericho's solid presence. It seemed there was more heat at her back than in front of her. She ached to feel his loving warmth closer to her and willed him to put his hands on her shoulders and draw her near.

Jericho's hands remained at his side as the courage to take Rae in his arms failed him. He tried to match her light tone and failed. "I have no liking for them, either."

"I almost made it to Hemmings." She turned to one side, her smile wistful.

"I hope you are not discouraged. It was a good attempt. If Nigel and Newbrough had not suspected your direction you would be there now, safe with Drew's friends. I regret I was not able to give you more time."

"You kept me from Newbrough's hands. I cannot thank you enough for that." It occurred to her that they were treating each other with the mannered politeness of strangers. Rae put aside the poker and brushed past Jericho, seating herself on the blood-red ottoman that was placed beside one of the large wing chairs. She idly smoothed the folds of her black skirt until the contrast of the bright silver links of the chain caught her attention, and then her hands were still. "What was Nigel's purpose in allowing you to win this evening?"

"I suspect he wanted to have done with the notes and play for larger stakes. He does not understand that I know he made errors calculated to permit me to win. The duke believes I will underestimate his ability when I play for Stanhope. In his place I would have used a similar strategy, especially when you made it clear you would no longer help. Remember, I am good with the cards myself. He would have been hard-pressed to have won all my notes, even if the stakes were raised beyond the ten-pound and hundred-pound limit. But tomorrow it will be all or nothing. When the game begins again he will be in earnest. He may have some trouble convincing Newbrough he still means to secure Stanhope for him, but Nigel has a way of getting others to fall in with his plans. My cousin is probably half-convinced by now that it was his idea to proceed in this fashion."

"I understand why Nigel has a modicum of respect for you. I had not realized how you were possessed of such similarly clever minds."

"That is not a compliment. I have no wish to be thought of in the same way you think of Nigel Lynne, though I know I have brought it upon my own head."

Rae's head jerked upward, startled by the bitter anger in his voice. "I don't think of you as I think of the duke," she denied. "You are not cast from the same mold as Nigel! He is domineering, driven by an obsession to make others subject to his will. He would stop at nothing to achieve his ends!"

"And I would? Can it be my fondest hope has been realized and you have forgotten your treatment at my hands? No, don't answer. I know you have not forgotten. Tonight, using that collar and chain for an excuse, I found the courage to kiss you and saw with my own eyes how you shuddered and clutched yourself to prevent being ill!'' He turned away from her and slammed his fist on the mantelpiece.

Rae watched a delicate porcelain figurine sway under the force of the blow, then topple from the mantel's edge. A serene smile shaped the curves of her lips as Jericho bent, one hand sweeping out like a stroke of brilliant lightning, to catch the exquisite piece and cradle it in his palm before he replaced it on the mantel.

Softly she said, *"There* is the difference between you and Nigel, if you would but open your eyes to it. You saved that piece from the consequence of your violence; you will always take to your heart those in need of protection, though you may deny it even as you draw your last breath. I could not love you so well if you had not at least tried to save the figurine.'' She rose from the ottoman and stood beside Jericho, touching his forearm with her hand to bring him round to face her. ''You mistook what you saw earlier this evening. It was not revulsion that made me shudder, but pleasure.'' She drew his hand to her abdomen and held it there. ''And I was not clutching my stomach, but communicating with my babe, as mothers are wont to do.''

Jericho blinked. ''A child?'' His hand flattened as he sought proof of her words and found it in the unfamiliarly rounded contours beneath her skirt.

Rae held her breath, biting her lip as she anxiously examined Jericho's face. ''I hate it when I cannot tell what you are thinking! Will you please say something? Do something? Should I have not told you? Are you—''

He smiled then, that youthful grin that held joy in its wide curve, and pulled Rae into his arms, holding her in an embrace that was as fierce as it was loving. ''Is it all right to hold you?''

''I will only object when you put me away from you.'' Her arms wrapped around his waist and her cheek pressed against the silken threads of his brocade jacket. ''I want a finish to the painful things we have said—''

"And done."

"And done," she repeated reluctantly, "to each other. I want you to know I love you, even when I swore it was otherwise there must have been part of me that would not let go. I do not know if I feel this way because I lack all sense or because I am stubborn and refuse to give up what was so fine between us. I do know that I want to be with you."

"Is it the child that makes you speak so?"

"I should do you grievous injury for that remark." Rae bent back at the waist so she could look up at him. 'The answer is no," she said severely. "When I first realized I was carrying your child I was going to return to you and settle for a loveless marriage of convenience. I imagined you with your mistresses, myself with my lovers, sharing our lives with our child and merely tolerating each other. Then your first night here you risked everything to come to my room, and I began to understand I was foolish for being willing to settle for so little. Just as I began to hope you turned cold again, watchful, as if you could not bear to see me."

"You were sick when I touched you. Remember? If I was aloof it was because I was afraid you could not tolerate my presence."

"There is something you should know about that night. Although you were holding me it was not your presence I was feeling, but Nigel's."

Jericho frowned. "That is not precisely a comfort."

"It was not meant to be. If I were trying to comfort I would fabricate some reason that would excuse us both. What I am trying to do is begin an understanding. I told you truthfully that I could forgive more easily than I could forget. That has not changed, except that I place less importance on the one time you were hurtful and recall with fondness all those moments you caught me as deftly as you did that figurine."

It occurred to Jericho that he had been correct in thinking he did not deserve anyone like Rahab, but he knew better than to voice his doubts. If she did not realize it already, he promised himself he would do nothing to give her cause to think it. He pressed her head to his chest and his fingers tangled in the warm silk of her hair. He held her just so for the longest time, cradling her as gently as if she were porcelain, while savoring the fact that she was not. His hand touched her throat and the bells jangled softly. He groaned, "I had forgotten."

"Make me forget. Please, Jericho, make me forget."

"Are you certain, Red? I don't—"

She shut him up by placing two fingers over his lips. After a moment's hesitation his tongue slipped out to touch the soft pads. Her fingers slipped to his chin, stroking the hard line of his jaw. There was just a hint of a stubble along his cheek and she liked the contrast against the back of her hand. She reached higher, tracing the arch of his dark brow with her thumb. His lashes brushed her, tickling her skin. He made no overt move, but his eyes were watchful, scanning her face carefully to assess her mood. She smiled inwardly at his reticence. His willingness to offer her control was endearing.

Standing on tiptoe, Rahab gave Jericho a kiss that delivered little and promised much. Just when he would have deepened it she drew back, not out of fear, but to tease his patience.

"Never think I shall fall willy-nilly into your arms, m'lord. You must woo me with clever phrases and loving nonsense."

Without missing a beat, Jericho quoted wisely, " 'Such a war of white and red within her cheeks! What stars do spangle heaven with such beauty, as those two eyes become that heavenly face?' "

Rahab's hands dropped to the front of Jericho's jacket. Laughing, eyes sparkling like the stars he compared them to, she fiddled with his buttons, then drew the jacket off his shoulders. "Enough. I had not given a thought as to how it would sound. Consider me wooed."

Jericho did not even feign hurt; he was too relieved. He finished shrugging out of his jacket and tossed it on the ottoman.

Rahab had no warning of his intentions as he scooped her up, raising her close to his chest and carrying her to the bed. Her arms circled his neck, and when he would have dropped her to the mattress she held him fast, kissing his mouth fully before she released her grip.

For a moment Jericho forgot what he was about; her kiss had rocked him back on his heels. He set her on her feet and eased her slowly onto the bed, then followed her, renewing the kiss until they were lying side by side, one of his arms circling her back and keeping her close.

Rahab tugged at Jericho's shirt until she could slip her hands under it and stroke his smoothly muscled chest. In a short time it was not enough for him and he sat up, hastily removed his neckcloth and shirt, and slid back beside her, slightly out of breath. The tiny bells gave sound to Rae's otherwise silent laughter.

"Do I seem a trifle eager?" he asked, carrying her palm to his heart.

"Mayhap a trifle. Do not refine upon it. I don't." Her head bent and her mouth found the faint pulse in his throat while her fingers teased his nipples, arousing them as he would hers. She felt his murmur of encouragement against her lips before she heard it. When she raised her head his mouth unerringly found her lips, tasting her with a sweet gentleness that left her completely in his thrall. That was why she was surprised when he rolled away from her after breaking the kiss.

"We don't have to make love," he said huskily. "Holding you now would be enough."

Rae knew he was giving her an opportunity to set the pace, retreat if it was her desire. But it was not her desire, though she answered in another manner. She slid out of bed and took the bracelet from her wrist. Turning her back on Jericho she pulled her blouse over her head, slipped out of her shoes and stockings, then unfastened her skirt. Jericho had a shadowed view of the long, seductive curve of her slender back as she rolled her shoulders to push the straps of her chemise over them. Before she turned she pinched out the candle flames on the night table, then wriggled out of her chemise.

The firelight accented Rae's wickedly sensuous smile as she faced him. Jericho glimpsed it once, then his eyes dropped, following the fragile line of her white throat that supported the hateful collar to her shoulders. Her small breasts were fuller than he recalled, and he ached to touch them with his hands, his mouth, to see if this change was real or part of his fevered imagination. His cerulean eyes dipped to the inward curve of her high waist and lower, to where his child lay protected in her womb. It seemed a startling thing to him that her body was nurturing another life, that her narrow hips already cradled their child.

Desire stirred him as Rae knelt on the edge of the bed, her long, slender legs curled beneath her. She bent forward slowly, so that her hair fell over her shoulders and cheeks and curtained both their faces as she brought her mouth to his. She kissed him with infinite gentleness at first, then deepened it to show that desire moved her, too.

"Hold me if you want, m'lord, but know that I intend to have my way with you," she whispered against his mouth.

There was a heady mixture of pleasure and pain in Jericho's groaning surrender. He sat up and helped Rae remove the remainder of his clothes, though the task took longer than usual, since she was intent upon making explorations of her own as his body was uncovered. In the end he had to take her by the shoulders and bear her down to the mattress before he lost all control.

Quite by accident the silver chain was trapped beneath Rae, and the links and bracelet pressed uncomfortably into her skin. "Wait," she said as she turned to free it. Pulling it forward, she took Jericho's hand and slid the ring on his wrist. "Now I've bound you to me."

Jericho marveled at the way she had turned the tables, for

he hated the chain when it was meant to signify that she was only his chattel. He looked at the bracelet and then at her, his eyes alight with a memory. "In truth, I believe it was that fine spring day we spent on the Hudson that bound me to you. No woman had ever offered to dig worms for me."

"You did not act as if I had done you any favor," she reminded him tartly. "You were insufferable."

"I know."

Rae grew restless as he trailed kisses on her brow and cheeks with the same lazy intent she remembered so well from that hot day. His tongue touched the sensitive spot behind her ear, then slid along the exposed cord of her neck as her throat arched. His head moved lower, and when he licked her nipples she gasped at the powerful, fiery sensation. It was different from anything she had known before, but not unpleasant, though it verged very nearly on pain.

Jericho drew back when he felt a tremor pass through her. "Have I hurt you?" he asked anxiously.

Rae shook her head in denial. "No, not that. They're so tender. I hadn't thought how it would feel when you touch them. Please. Touch me again."

Gently Jericho's tongue flicked across the swollen tips of her breasts, eliciting a tiny sound of pleasure from her throat. A hand cupped the underside of one breast and it seemed to harden, filling his palm. The chain scraped lightly across the other nipple and she shivered in reaction to the sensation. Her thighs parted as his legs tangled in hers, and her hips lifted in anticipation of the moment he would come to her.

He filled her slowly, watching her watching him. When he was in her deeply her lashes fluttered downward shyly, hiding the pleasure darkening her green eyes. "Let me see," he said. "I love to look at your eyes when I am inside you." Rae's lids lifted in response to the husky command in his voice and saw her desire mirrored in Jericho's own dark gaze and echoed in the beating of his heart. She was drawn to the face above her that for once hid nothing of his thoughts and feelings. There was no place for a mask between them now.

Nothing of the outside world intruded upon them as he made love to her. His movements were unhurried, but never denied his need. She twisted beneath him as his mouth touched her shoulders, her infinitely sensitive breasts, then settled on her mouth, muffling the soft cries of her pleasure.

Her hands slid along his back and his taut buttocks as her legs curved around his. She held him as lovingly inside, welcoming his thrusts and contracting about him even as she wondered how long this seduction of their senses could last. Almost as soon as she thought it, sensation, hot and liquid, rippled through her. Jericho's mouth did not cover this satisfied cry, and it sounded louder in the room than the bells at her neck. Rahab clutched his shoulders, burying her face against the curve of his throat as Jericho's hips flashed in the involuntary movements preceding his own release. She arched hard to meet his final thrust, and then they both lay still, much struck by the completeness of their loving.

Afraid he would crush her, but reluctant to leave, Jericho pulled away by slow degrees and drew a long sigh from Rae. To keep from going too far, she turned on her hip and trapped him with one leg.

Chuckling softly, Jericho held up his chained wrist. "You doubt this is sufficient to keep me by your side?"

She smiled sleepily. "I am not taking any chances."

Jericho propped himself on one elbow and stroked the damp dark strands of hair from Rae's cheeks. "I will be relieved when this business is at an end tomorrow, or rather today. It's quite late."

Rae's brows drew together over her closed eyes. "How can you be certain it will end?"

"Because I have every intention of regaining my inheritance tomorrow. Have you given a thought to what my cousin will do when that happens?"

"He'll expose Nigel."

"And isn't that precisely what we have wanted to do?"

"Well, it's what I wanted to do. I believe you wanted to take more severe measures."

"It is not only a woman who may change her mind," he told her smartly. "If you would but recall, I saw the merits of your plan once the existence of the documents was more than a fancy of yours. What does it matter if the earl has them? He will achieve our ends for us."

"If you win Stanhope."

"*When* I win Stanhope."

Chapter 15

A small circle of sunlight touched Rae's cheek and she welcomed the warm kiss with a faint smile and a lazy stretch. The smile vanished when she felt the collar and chain restrain her movement. Turning on her side to face Jericho, she slipped the bracelet from his wrist so she could get out of the bed. That she was able to do so without waking him spoke to his complete exhaustion, and she realized for the first time the full extent of the strain these last weeks had been on him.

In sleep nothing of it showed on his face. There were no tiny white lines cutting the corners of his thickly lashed lids nor any hint of tension about the relaxed curve of his mouth. The easy cadence of his breathing was a comfort to her, and it took every bit of Rae's will-power not to climb back in bed and thread her fingers in his bright yellow hair and touch her lips to the gentle pulse in his throat.

She remembered how she had awakened in the middle of the night, an unfamiliar heat resting on her abdomen, and how she had feigned sleep while Jericho slowly explored the contours of her body, first with his hands, then later with his mouth. Somehow he knew the moment she was aware of what he was doing, and it became a game between them to see how long she could pretend to be unaffected by his lazy caresses. Surrendering was not the same as losing, she thought as she gave herself over to his loving.

Reluctantly she left the side of the bed and dressed as quietly as she was able to, given the accompaniment of the bells. Rae's only purpose in leaving Jericho's chamber was to return to her own room to bathe and change her servant's garb for something clean. Once she was refreshed and out of her torn and slightly soiled garments she would return to Jericho's room with no one the wiser. It was early yet when she left his side, and she knew none but the duke's staff would be up at this hour. That she only heard the soft padding of her own feet as she walked through Linfield's quiet corridors seemed to bear this out.

It was not until she opened the door to her chamber and a cold hand was clamped over her mouth that she realized her confidence had been without substance.

Struggling to free herself as well as to breathe, Rahab was lifted off her feet by the strong arm about her waist and carried into her room. The hand on her mouth slipped a little, and as she gasped for air she was assailed by the strong odor of spirits. She nearly gagged at the smell of the hot breath befouled by liquor, and her momentary weakness effectively cut off her chance to scream. Behind her the door was kicked shut.

In an effort to escape, Rae twisted wildly in the arms of her captor, kicking backward with her feet. Though her arms were restrained on either side of her waist, she used her fingers to pinch the hard thighs that trapped her from behind. Several pained grunts attested to the distress she was causing, but the arms around her were like iron bands and refused to give quarter.

Rae had no need to see her assailant to know it was Newbrough, but there was no satisfaction in the knowing. She could feel herself becoming light-headed from lack of air, and as her strength waned her terror grew. When it became clear that the earl's direction was the giant four-poster bed in her chamber, she went slack in his arms.

Rae's dead weight caused Newbrough to pause in his stride. As he shifted his hold to gain better purchase on her unwieldly body Rae shoved backward with the last of her strength and managed to stumble free of his arms. Newbrough leaped forward to grasp the chain and bracelet that dangled at Rae's back, but she spun on her toes suddenly and he was left flailing drunkenly at the air. While he was recovering his balance, Rae slipped the bracelet on her own wrist and put a spindle-legged chair between herself and the earl.

Newbrough merely laughed unpleasantly at her delaying tactic. "Do you think that bit of furniture is going to keep me from what I want? I've been waiting all this long night and morning to have you. A few sticks of wood aren't going to stop me."

Rae drew in long draughts of air, trying to calm herself and think where she could go from here. The path to the door that opened on the hallway was partially blocked by Newbrough. Even foxed as he was, she did not think she could best him in a scramble for that exit. He would not be taken in by her fainting ploy a second time, and she feared that if he held her again unconsciousness would be a thing too real. Her glance traveled to the connecting door to Nigel's room, but even as she considered it the earl put a period to her hopes.

"It's locked and Nigel is sharing another's bed. If he were there he would not help you. He promised that I could have you, and so I shall." He took a step toward the chair, and like a frightened faun Rae became wide-eyed and still. "I did not believe you would stay with Adams," said Newbrough conversationally. "I knew it was only a matter of time before you found a way to escape him. And I waited. I could pity the man for being made insensible in your embrace if I did not loathe

him so. He's tried to make a fool of me as you did that day in
the library. My presence in your chamber now is proof that I
will be no one's fool. Mayhap he will heed the lesson I intend
to serve you.''

The earl's bloodshot eyes held but one purpose as he
advanced on Rae. Blinking once, as if to rouse herself from
her arrested posture, she pushed the chair forward so that its
seat hit Newbrough squarely in the knees. He grunted once,
shoved the piece aside and continued to advance as Rae cautiously retreated to the fireplace. Unwittingly she backed into
the poker and andirons and they fell over, the sudden noise
surprising her. Newbrough took advantage of her disorientation
and lunged for her as she watched the heavy poker roll out of
her reach. She screamed once, spinning away as the earl's hands
clawed at her skirt. The fasteners on the waistband tore under
the harshness of his grip, but as the material was rent Rae had
enough freedom to fumble for the brass candlestick on the
mantelpiece. Newbrough caught her frantic movement in time
to avert his head and escaped having the blunt end of the
instrument brought down on the back of his neck. The candlestick connected with his shoulder with such force that numbing
pain shot down one arm and his fingers loosed their grip.

Rae yanked her skirt away from Newbrough's other hand
while his explicit oath echoed in the room. She threw the
candlestick at him, and not waiting to see if it made its mark,
ran for the door. Her palms were so clammy that it took two
tries to turn the handle. On the second twist the door opened a
few inches, only to be slammed shut by Newbrough's powerful
hands on either side of her head.

Shouting for help, Rae ducked beneath his outstretched arms
and was halfway to the other side of the room when the earl
tackled her. The weight of his body bore her down and she
skidded along the hardwood floor, coming to an abrupt halt
when her head met the fireplace's marble apron. Dazed, the
breath driven from her lungs, it was several minutes before she

could move. She watched helplessly as Newbrough recovered first and took the bracelet from her wrist and slipped it on his own.

Rae's eyes were nearly blinded by the ache behind them as she thought of thrusting a steel blade between Newbrough's ribs. The terrible pain in her temples was the first sign that the threads of her repressed memory were returning. As Newbrough jerked her to a sitting position, then half-dragged, half-carried her to the bed, she remembered being led up the narrow stairs of Wolfe's Tavern, away from the crowd of drunken soldiers ready to hang her for killing one of their own. She remembered Jericho's indolent inspection of her body as he lifted her skirts and commented on her legs. Though she had been angered at the time, his look was nothing compared to the earl's piercing gaze, which stripped her of her dignity as well as her clothes.

Newbrough straddled Rae, and when she attempted to beat off his hands as they tore at her blouse he yanked hard on the collar so the bells rang wildly and the leather chafed her tender skin. She clawed at the collar with her fingers to prevent herself from choking, but the earl slapped her viciously across the cheek and her hands fell uselessly to her sides. The pressure on her throat was relieved the instant Newbrough had her compliance.

Impatient fingers ripped through Rae's blouse, then her chemise, uncovering her breasts. Rae closed her eyes, unable to bear the sight of Newbrough's slack mouth and hot gaze as he stared at her. Something of the sickness she was feeling showed on her face as he cupped her breasts and kneaded them with rough intent. He stopped what he was doing, grasped her chin in one hand, and slapped her lightly with the other.

"It would be folly to toss your stomach now, sweet bitch," he said tightly. "I mean to have you regardless. Open your eyes. I want you to see what manner of man you're getting now."

Seething with revulsion and loathing, Rae opened her eyes.

Far from being angered by the hatred in her glance, the earl
smiled and drew his palms along her naked shoulders and arms
until his fingers circled each of her wrists. Slowly he lifted
her hands and forced her to caress his velvet-covered thighs.
Controlling her as easily as if she were a marionette, he made
her hands stroke the hard length of his legs as he stayed straddled
over her. His neck arched as he brought her hands closer and
closer to his arousal and finally settled them on the hard bulge
in his breeches.

Taking a deep breath, Rae squeezed as hard as she could.

Newbrough screamed in pain, doubling over to hold himself
as Rae struggled to be free of his weight. Newbrough rolled
away from her, but the bracelet on his wrist kept her a prisoner.
She attacked him then, clawing at his face and drawing blood,
beating him with her fists. At first he was vulnerable to the
attacks and only hunched his shoulders to ward off the blows,
but as he recovered he retaliated with bruising fists, and it was
the one he delivered to Rae's midsection that left her breathless
and fearing for the life of her child. She pulled at his chained
arm and tore at his wrist, trying to roll the bracelet over the
fist he had made. Out of the corner of her eye she could see
his free hand raise to strike her down again. A voice from the
doorway gave him pause.

"Lower your hand one inch, m'lord, and I will cut you down
so that it never lifts again." Jericho stood in the open doorway,
light from the hallway shadowing his features but not the menace in his voice. His left arm was extended straight in front of
him, and in his steady hand he held a pistol aimed directly
at Newbrough's head. "Now relax your fist and allow Miss
McClellan to take back the bracelet." The earl's hand unfolded
and Rae carefully freed herself from him. "Stand by the fireplace, Rahab." Rae scrambled from the bed, crossing her arms
in front of her as she went to the other side of the room. From
the hallway other voices could be heard, and she turned her

back on the doorway, hiding her naked shoulders from the curious with the long fall of her hair.

"What is toward?" demanded Nigel as he stalked down the hall belting his burgundy dressing robe. "I thought I heard an animal scream." He stopped at the open door to Rae's room where several guests had gathered, drawn not by Rae's early cries for help, but by Newbrough's shout of pain.

"You did," said Jericho, never taking his eyes from the earl. "Miss McClellan surprised a wild beast in her room. Isn't that the way of it, Newbrough?"

The earl made no reply, but continued to hold one hand in the air while the nostrils of his hawkish nose flared angrily. The scratches Rae had scored on his thin face dripped blood on the snowy coverlet.

Jericho lowered his weapon and he jerked his chin toward the door. "Get out of here, Newbrough. Consider the gauntlet thrown. Is the morrow too soon to see this thing done?"

Newbrough's hand fell to his side, and with great dignity he climbed from the bed and advanced on Jericho. "Not soon enough, m'lord, but I would have Stanhope firmly in my possession before I end your life, so the morrow it shall be." After a significant look at the duke he brushed past Jericho, and in the corridor the crowd that had gathered parted for him, then closed in once more.

Nigel Lynne stepped into the room and shut the door on the other guests. He gave one glance to Rae as she looked over her shoulder to see if she was alone with Jericho, then dismissed her as if she was of no import. He did not ask for an explanation; Rae's state of deshabille explained everything to his satisfaction. "Why the challenge, Adams? Surely the chit is not worth it."

Rae and Jericho were both curious as to why Nigel would be cautious about the duel. He had every reason to want the earl of Stanhope dead.

"Newbrough's a poor shot," Nigel continued. "He won't

choose pistols, you know. He's an astonishingly good swords-
man. Can you say the same?''

Jericho almost laughed aloud as he realized Nigel's concern
stemmed from the fact that he feared Jericho could not best
Newbrough. ''I can handle my own with a sword,'' he said
easily. ''Don't concern yourself for my safety.''

Nigel almost said he never had been, then caught himself.
''As you wish. Mayhap Lesley will act as your second.''

''I'll speak to him.''

The duke nodded and glanced in Rae's direction again.
''Keep her by your side, Adams. I cannot want to see you
challenging every one of my guests who covets your possession.
I take it she proved more amenable to you than she did Newbrough.''

Knowing it would goad Nigel as well, Jericho answered not
with words, but with a secretive smile that said much of his
enjoyment of the evening past. After a moment's hesitation
Nigel quit the room, unable completely to conceal the flash of
jealousy that darkened his eyes.

As soon as Nigel was gone Jericho crossed the chamber to
Rae. His hands rested lightly on her shoulders. ''Are you all
right?''

She nodded as he turned her round and raised her face.

''My God!'' he swore, and then a shutter came down over
his blue eyes so that he might not reveal the damage that had
been done to Rae's face. Her right cheek was discolored and
beginning to swell so that already one eye looked slightly
smaller than the other. Around the edge of the collar he could
see her skin was chafed, and there was a long angry scratch
on her shoulder. The places where Newbrough had landed his
fists had not begun to bruise, but Jericho could guess that her
arms and chest would be marked with livid spots before long.

Self-consciously she touched the back of one hand to her
swollen lip where she could taste blood at its corner. ''I think
the earl looked worse,'' she said shakily.

"But I do not care about the earl," was all Jericho would say.

The next half-hour passed in a blur of silent activity as Jericho rang for a maid and ordered a bath for Rahab. Nancy came and looked at Rae with pitying eyes, but never spoke a word. While the bath was being prepared Jericho helped Rae out of her torn clothes and into a silk dressing gown, then gently washed her cuts from a porcelain bowl that Nancy brought him. Dismissing her with a wave of his hand, Jericho assisted Rae into the hip bath and proceeded to wash her with strokes as soft as velvet.

"That maid was your friend, wasn't she?" he asked. It was not what he intended to say, but it bothered him that the girl would not speak to Rae. He folded the wet cloth in his hand and squeezed drops of water on Rae's shoulders, watching those that slid like tears to the high curve of her breast. "Why didn't she say anything to you?"

"She was afraid," Rae said simply.

"Of you?"

"Of you. Didn't it occur to you that Nancy would think you had done this to me? Why wouldn't she think you might treat her the same?" Rae bit back a smile as Jericho cursed softly. "Do not think your rep has been maligned forever, m'lord. She'll hear soon enough how the thing came about."

"I don't care a fig for my rep," he ground out. A moment later he said sheepishly, "You were teasing."

"Of course."

He nodded thoughtfully, trailing water along the slender arm she had placed along the edge of the copper tub. "What possessed you to come here, Red?"

"I wanted a bath and a change of clothes. I thought to be back in your room before you awoke. It never occurred to me that Newbrough would be prowling the hallways waiting for me to leave your chamber. Thank God you came!"

Jericho's eyes closed briefly on his pained thoughts, then

realized there was no reason to dwell on what had happened. "I know," he agreed softly. "I saved Newbrough's life."

"You saved Newbrough's life? Oh, you are teasing." She splashed water at him with the tips of her fingers and winked at him with the eye that was closing rapidly. "I did give as good as I got, didn't I?"

"Better." He kissed her temple, then finished bathing the last vestige of Newbrough's touch away, first in the copper tub with the soft linen cloth, then in her bed with his velvet-soft mouth.

Much later Rae asked, "Jericho, can you really hold your own with a sword?"

His brows shot nearly to the line of his bright yellow hair. "After what we just did, my love, can you doubt it?"

Rae pinched him on the thigh as a rosy blush stole across her face. "That was not what I meant, and you know it! If Newbrough chooses swords, can you defeat him?"

"It most likely depends on whether I learn how to fence between now and then."

Rae only had to close one eye as she groaned. The other was shut completely now. "I suspected as much. What are you going to do?"

"Do not refine upon it. First things first. There is still Stanhope to be won."

Rahab sat stiffly at Jericho's side while waiting for the card play to begin. She refused to allow her collar to make a sound and attract the attention away from Nigel as he explained the rules for the final match. She had already had her fill of the other men's trying to see beneath the lacy fichu that covered her shoulders. It did not seem enough that they could clearly see the shiner she sported on her right eye. It was as if they intended to compare her bruises with the earl's and determine the winner of the uneven bout. Only Lord Lesley looked at her with something akin to sympathy in his clear eyes; the others saw her with new interest, intrigued that she would fight so hard against the earl's advances.

"This match will be the best of seven games," the duke was saying. "All will be finished before the night is over. Adams is laying the whole of his notes, some fifty thousand pounds, against the Stanhope estate."

Jericho slid a packet containing all his notes on the table and at the same time Nigel took an envelope from his waistcoat containing the title to Stanhope and laid it on top of the packet. Lord Lesley left his chair and took both items for safekeeping until the winner should be determined.

Rahab watched Newbrough while Lesley gathered the prizes. She had avoided looking at him since coming into the room, but now that his attention had been diverted, she felt safe in staring.

For a man who was in danger of losing all the trappings of the life he had embraced for the last twenty years, Rae thought the earl of Stanhope looked remarkably calm. The glass of wine at his side remained largely untouched, and he appeared more sober than Rae had seen him in days. Nothing had changed about his vanity. He had used makeup to hide the worst of the scratches on his face as well as the bruise on his chin. Rae flexed her stiff fingers and swollen knuckles and wondered wryly who was hurting the more.

Rae's eyes drifted from Newbrough's discolored chin to the tiny scratches that disappeared beneath his snowy linen neckcloth. Ready to turn away from him, her attention was suddenly caught by the corner of yellowed parchment sticking out above the edge of Newbrough's blue velvet vest. His waistcoat was open, and she could follow the rectangular line of what lay beneath his vest. She understood now why Newbrough was at his ease. He was carrying the documents that would expose Nigel Lynne, and she was certain the duke was aware of it.

The irony of what lay ahead struck her again. Neither Nigel Lynne nor Charles Newbrough had any right to the estates they were trying to protect, while Jericho was being forced to chance losing the lands that were rightfully his. So caught up was she by the sight of the will and birth record on the earl's person that she never looked lower to where two silver mounted pistols were tucked in the waistband of his breeches. Later, when she looked in his direction he was studying her with his reptilian eyes and she turned away, only noting that he had buttoned his velvet jacket.

Nigel won the first deal, shuffled, and offered Jericho a cut. Rae kept her eyes averted from Jericho's cards as he picked them up, afraid she would give something away. She was not even hurt when she realized the same thought had occurred to Jericho, for he kept his hand close to his chest throughout the game. He gave her a small, nearly imperceptible nod when he wished her to collect the trick he had won. Unfortunately during the first game it was not often enough, and Nigel scored his first win.

When it was Jericho's turn to deal, he shuffled the cards slowly. Rae wondered at his thoughtful interest in the deck, but she forgot it when he dealt them out, fairly snapping them on the polished table. He played the next game with more consideration than was his usual style, but it did him no good. Nigel easily took the majority of the tricks.

Rae saw that the duke looked confident, but was in no way gloating over his two easy wins. Jericho appeared unruffled by his losses. There was something about his indolent grace under pressure that reminded her of the day they had gone fishing on the Hudson. He had been so unconcerned with catching his dinner that it had puzzled her until he revealed he had laid a better trap. That memory gave her pause.

There was a break in the play following Jericho's third loss. Nigel asked to speak to Rae alone while Jericho talked with

Lesley about the arrangements for the duel. Jericho handed over the bracelet and the duke led Rahab into the hallway.

"I've but one game to win," Nigel reminded her. "Have you considered what it would be like going to Stanhope as Newbrough's mistress?"

Rae strove not to make her repugnance visible. "You are supposing that not only will you win the match, but also that Lord Adams will lose the duel. Do you really think both things are likely?"

Nigel gave Rae's chain a less than gentle tug. "Listen to me, Rahab! After this evening's match I will consider the festivities at an end. Adams only holds you until then. It makes no difference to me that he's called Newbrough out over you. You will be my mistress again, and I shall decide if I want to keep you or allow Newbrough to have you. If you do not want to mar the other side of your face you will do something about the letter I asked you to write, and you will do it tonight!"

Rae lifted her chin and eyed him scornfully. "You are naught but a bully, Nigel, and if you think I shall bow to your dictates at this late date, then you are a stupid bully as well."

Nigel's face paled alarmingly, then flushed with angry color. "How dare you!"

Rae was not certain how she dared. If she had called him wicked or evil, perhaps likened him to Satan, he might well have been flattered. But to name him a bully—and a stupid one, at that—was to announce that she thought him nothing more than a willful child. She stood her ground because the chain bound her to him. There was nothing for it but to go on as she had begun, so she maintained her look of reproach and disdain. "Another time perhaps, your grace, but your guests are waiting for you to resume the play. Tell me," she asked ingenuously, "are you cheating?"

Nigel looked as if he wanted to strike her dead on the spot, but he chose to yank on the chain and pull her roughly into the room. Jericho accepted the bracelet without comment, but his eyes questioned both parties as to the cause of their anger. Neither Nigel nor Rahab deigned to answer.

Jericho sat down and began shuffling the cards. "While you were talking with Miss McClellan I took the liberty of selecting a new deck of cards. I trust there is no problem in that."

Rae thought she saw Nigel's tightly etched features sag a bit even as he brushed aside Jericho's announcement. So he *had* been cheating! Before she could wonder why Jericho hadn't told the room at large about the duke's dishonorable tactics, he was offering Nigel the cut and dealing the cards.

The tension in the room increased as Jericho successfully kept Nigel from winning his fourth hand. When the score became three games to two, Rae noticed the duke's smile was strained, and at three all, it was nonexistent.

Everything rested on the outcome of the seventh game. Rae's heart sank as Nigel elected to choose a fresh pack, for she knew he would choose a marked deck. Lord Lesley might as well hand over the packet and the title to Newbrough, she thought desolately. Jericho had lost his last chance to regain his lands.

She gathered in Jericho's tricks with none of the briskness she had used previously, thinking to prolong the inevitable as long as possible. It took a gentle tug on her chain to make her realize that the pile in front of her was growing. Jericho was playing his hand with more assurance than he had shown thus far, and, incredibly, he was winning more of the tricks! Newbrough looked as if he could hardly stay seated as she collected another pair of cards, and the duke's fingers visibly shook around the three remaining cards in his hand.

One by one they floated to the table to lie against the card Jericho had led. Each time, Jericho's card took the trick. Rae swept the last pair away slowly, her slender hand gliding across the table. With her somewhat dazed attention on the cards, she never saw Jericho's clear blue eyes narrow dangerously in Nigel's direction. The duke looked as if he wished he could slam his fist on her fingers and snatch away the proof of his opponent's victory.

Lord Lesley stood and offered his hand to Jericho, then the packet and the title. Rae had to stand as Jericho got to his feet and accepted Lesley's silent congratulations along with his winnings. No one spoke in the room. No one. It was so quiet that Rae thought she could hear the pages of the books decaying. She wondered what the others were thinking, whether or not they felt anything for Newbrough's loss or any lessening of respect for the duke of Linfield because of his failure. She was careful not to let any of the relief and elation she was experiencing show on her face.

Nigel pushed back his chair, scraping it on the hardwood floor, breaking the terrible quiet that permeated the library. There were white lines about his mouth and eyes, and Rae was not the only one who thought he suddenly looked much older than his years. It was as if the decades of his libertine existence had chosen this moment to mark his finely chiseled face.

Standing, he leaned across the table and offered Jericho his hand. "You are a superior player, Lord Adams," he said, his voice strained. "My congratulations." Before Jericho could comment, he removed his hand and went to the sideboard at Jericho's back where the footman was pouring wine for the assembly.

Several of the men gave their condolences to Newbrough, then quit the room, but Lesley and Evans remained with the earl, who was now rooted to his chair in palpable shock.

"Do you know," Nigel said, looking past Jericho's shoulder at the earl, "I would still like to hear his lordship's reason for wanting your estate, Newbrough. Aren't you the least bit curious as to why he would desire to ruin you?"

Rae frowned, questioning the duke's reasons for bringing up Jericho's purpose again. A delaying tactic against Newbrough's revealing the documents in his vest—or something more?

Newbrough was standing now, and though his features were

bleak, even pleading, his polished eyes were riveted on Jericho's expressionless face. "It's the least you owe me, don't you think?" He unfastened a few buttons on his jacket and fanned himself with his hand as if he were hot all of a sudden.

"I fail to see that I owe you anything, but there is no reason I can't tell you now, in front of witnesses. My father was Lord Thomas Hunter-Smythe, my mother, Elise Adams. I am Geoffrey, cousin. Have I really changed so much since the day you took me from school and put me onboard the *Igraine?* Can you tell me you never once suspected my identity?"

Newbrough's surprise was real. His mouth fell open before he collected himself.

Jericho's laugh was not pleasant. "You never did think of me again, did you? No doubt you forgot me as soon as you pulled away from the dock in my father's carriage. You were too anxious to claim what belonged to me to give me another thought."

"Stanhope was never yours. You were a bastard."

'My parents were married," Jericho corrected him. "And my father claimed me."

"Is this true, Newbrough?" Lesley asked.

"Don't be ridiculous!"

Jericho turned on Nigel. "Tell them, your grace. You've suspected for some time who I am. By the time I arrived at Linfield you had more than suspicions, else why would you practically hand me Newbrough's notes if not to help me regain what was rightfully mine?" Jericho's smile was a sly curve, daring Nigel to say his motives were prompted by something other than decency. "I imagine it was difficult at first to discover anything about me, but you are nothing if not persistent."

Nigel raised his glass to Jericho. "You are right. It was difficult. In fact, impossible. I learned who you were by delving into Newbrough's past. You were the right age to be the bastard issue that had disappeared, and your actions would indicate revenge. Until this moment, however, what I lacked was confirmation. There is a gap of twenty years that only you can account for. However, you're correct about your parents. My man found the proof of their marriage in a parish church not far from Stanhope. You are indeed the owner of the estate.''

"No!" Newbrough shouted. "That's a lie! You're both lying!" He reached for the documents in his vest and flung them on the table. "Have you forgotten these, Nigel?''

"Not at all," Nigel said smoothly. He put his drink aside and walked past Jericho and Rae. Right under Newbrough's stunned countenance Nigel picked up the yellowed envelope and page from his family Bible and tossed both of them into the flames burning brightly in the fireplace. They writhed and crackled as Nigel walked away. He took up his drink again and raised it in mocking salute to Newbrough. "Now I have forgotten them. Can you say the same?''

Jericho was watching the duke again, but Rae had never taken her eyes from Newbrough. She grew wide-eyed in horror as the earl drew a pistol from his breeches and was too startled by the sight of the second weapon still lodged there to scream a warning. She had no idea whether Newbrough intended to shoot Jericho or the duke, but it was Jericho who made the clearest target. Even Newbrough, no matter what his skill as a marksman, could not fail to miss at this distance. Terror lent her strength, and Rahab grasped the chain that held her to Jericho, yanking on it hard as she threw herself on the ground. Someone else shouted as Jericho toppled on Rae and a flash of light and smoke issued from Newbrough's weapon.

Rae and Jericho both glanced up in time to see the disbelieving expression on Nigel's face fade and be replaced by pain. Simultaneously, a blossom of blood appeared on his ivory vest. The glass of port in his hand fell to the floor and shattered, spraying the floor with crystal and droplets of wine.

"Not at all the thing to do, Newbrough," Nigel said slowly, carefully enunciating each word. "Should have called me out. You . . . never were . . . fit to hold a . . . title." He collapsed then and his life's blood mixed with the blood-red wine on the floor.

Jericho slipped his wrist out of the bracelet, left Rae, and knelt at Nigel's side. Lord Evans fled the room in search of someone to help, while Lesley stood at the door blocking New-brough's escape. In the corner the footman cowered, and Rae had to help Jericho turn over Nigel's body.

The duke looked at Rae with eyes that were not yet sightless, but held the knowledge that they soon would be. "You'll tell Ashley that it's . . . hers now. I was . . . only saving it for . . . her. Loved her . . . in my way. She should be here now. Where . . . she has always belon—"

It was the end Rae had wished of late for Nigel, but she could find no gladness that it had finally been done. She turned away from him as Jericho closed his lids. When Jericho stood to face Newbrough, Rae stayed on her knees, staring at her folded hands and wondering why she should want to weep for a man like the duke of Linfield.

From the doorway she heard Lesley say, "I'm going to tell Evans it's too late for help." He slipped out the door.

As the door clicked shut something clicked in Rae's brain. Her fingers were insinuating themselves in Jericho's left top boot even as Newbrough was pulling out his second primed weapon. She felt Jericho tense, though whether it was caused by the sight of Newbrough's pistol or his awareness of what she was doing, she could not say.

The intent in the earl's eyes was clear as he judged Jericho's posture as if anticipating which way the younger man would jump. His gaze was so steady on Jericho that he did not see Rae's movement. A second later, when the gentle tinkling of the belled collar caught his attention, it was too late.

The pistol fired harmlessly at the ceiling as Charles New-brough was sent reeling backward by the force of the dagger thrown squarely at his heart.

Jericho bent down and grasped Rae by the shoulders, holding her close as he escorted her from the library. Shielding her from the eyes of those who had gathered in the hallway, he guided her up Linfield's grand staircase.

Epilogue

Rahab wiped a film of mist from one of the small panes of glass that made up the cabin's window. She sank down on the hardwood bench and peered through the glass, watching without comment as England slipped away from her view. When the blue-gray serenity of twilight descended and she could no longer distinguish between the water and the sky, she turned away from the window. Expecting to see Jericho still asleep, Rae was surprised to find him on his side watching her.

"You look a little melancholy," he said, patting the empty space beside him. "I had thought you would be happy to see the last of England. I thought at times the business of Stanhope would never be settled."

She crossed the cabin, not so sad that she couldn't enjoy the way Jericho's eyes followed the clinging lines of her white shift, and slipped into bed. After dinner, when she had yawned hugely and admitted to being tired but too restless to sleep, Jericho had lain down with her, stroking her hair until she relaxed against him, He had often done so during the six weeks they lived at Stanhope, napping with her when it seemed their child drained her of all energy. Now Rae warmed the soles of her feet against the length of his calves as he pulled the blankets up around her chin. His hand warmed the rounded shape of her abdomen as she turned on her side to face him, snuggling close for his warmth. Rae had a sudden longing for the hot Virginia sun, which she believed must be different from the one hanging over the North Atlantic in summertime.

"I shall miss Drew," she said. "He was very good to us. I'm glad he agreed to become the caretaker of Stanhope. I should always worry about him otherwise."

"I know. In part, that's why I offered him the position."

"And Nancy and Jack?"

He nodded. "Jack will make a fine head of staff, and Nancy a most excellent housekeeper. Didn't you tell me so at least twenty times a day?"

"I never knew if you were listening," she said sheepishly. "Do you have regrets about leaving?"

"No. It will be there for our children if one of them desires it. I imagine Ashley will do much the same with Linfield. Why are you asking now? I thought this was settled weeks ago."

"It was," she sighed. "But you cannot blame me for wanting to be certain."

"The truth," he teased. "Give over. You secretly liked being Lady Hunter-Smythe. Once we're in America you'll be Mrs. Smith. Not quite the same, is it?"

"It will suit me just fine," she said tartly. "And my parents better. I hope you have time to make explanations before they see my belly. You'll have a lot to answer for. As you pointed out once before: My family is not likely to think ill of me."

He groaned softly. "Don't remind me. It is my fondest hope that they receive our letter before we arrive, else I suspect you will be picking buckshot from my posterior for a month of Sundays."

The thought of Jericho running from her brothers and father

was too outrageous to be believed. She chuckled deeply and cuddled closer. "That's unlikely, not when you faced Nigel and Newbrough so bravely. Do you know you've never told me how you won that final game against Nigel?"

"You never asked."

"I've been trying to figure it out for myself. I hate to admit that I cannot."

"Remind me not to play cards with you, for I would dislike taking advantage."

"Beast! Tell me how it was done. Nigel was using marked cards, wasn't he?"

"Yes. I suspected during the first game and confirmed it when I shuffled for my deal. There was no sense making a fuss over it, because as long as Nigel did not know I knew, I had the upper hand. Do you follow?"

Rae shook her head no and answered yes.

"Poor Red." He continued patiently. "It took me the second and third games to learn the markings on the cards. It was not so difficult, as we were drawing from the stock and I had the opportunity to see nearly half the deck. I selected an unmarked deck at the beginning of the fourth round and beat Nigel fairly for the next three games. I knew if I could tie the score he would panic and change decks."

"And, of course, he would choose another marked one. But since you already knew how it was marked it was like being able to see into his hand. You trounced him with fair unfairness."

"Actually, I was going to say he was hoist with his own petard."

"Isn't that what I just said?" she demanded.

He laughed, kissing the furrowed line of her brow. "More or less."

"Did you truly suspect Nigel knew who you were?"

"How inquisitive you are of a sudden! One would think you knew the lecherous bent of my mind and were trying to put me off." He could see by the firmness of her expression that she would not be gainsaid. "Oh, very well. Yes, I suspected. It fit what I knew of the man. Nigel prided himself on knowing the secrets of others, so why shouldn't he know mine. He understood an emotion as basic as revenge."

"It's odd, isn't it, how he never knew you were interested in Stanhope only as a means to reach him. None of it came about the way we had planned, yet it all came about. I think Newbrough went a little mad at the end."

"A little? He was very nearly rabid when I told him who I was! If I had known he was carrying two primed pistols I would have saved my explanations. I'm glad you were on my side, Red."

"One of us had to be."

"You have a sharp tongue," he observed, studying the pink tip as it moistened her lower lip.

"So I've been told." She leaned over and flicked her tongue along the curve of his ear.

Jericho shivered. "Perhaps sharp is not what I meant."

Rae's mouth slid lower, tracing Jericho's strong jawline. When she reached his chin he dipped his head and caught her lips with his own. His hands framed her face, fingers curving around her cheeks and the soft pulsebeat in her temples. He deepened the kiss, and desire seemed to curl Rae's toes. She told him that, and they laughed while making rather a clumsy mess of discarding their nightclothes. That was the last thing they did with any haste, until they drove each other to pleasure's edge with their patient explorations.

Jericho's bright hair lay against Rae's breast, his arm around her waist. Idly she stroked his shoulder, savoring the contentment that clothed her like a silky garment.

Jericho lifted his head suddenly, a hint of mischief about his mouth and eyes. "One thousand, four hundred, sixty-three," he announced. Immediately his head returned to his comfortable pillow and waited for his meaning to strike Rae.

It did not take long. She wailed unhappily to hide her laughter. "Never say you really counted them!"

He nodded. "Not all at once, of course. I had to concentrate on one area at a time. I had not fully comprehended what a distracting sort of business it was."

"I knew I shouldn't have let you drag me on that picnic at Stanhope. A light lunch, you said. A cool dip in the lake, you said. Never did you mention the sun was coercing these horrid little spots to appear all over my body."

"I warned you of my intentions once."

"Hmmmph. You probably counted wrong. I can't have as many as that."

Jericho raised his head, an eyebrow arched wickedly. "Are you challenging me, madam?"

"No!"

"Little liar." He kissed the gentle slope of her shoulder. "One," he announced grandly. His mouth traced the edge of her collarbone. "Twenty-six."

"Horrid creature! That was an estimate!"

Jericho merely shrugged, and Rae gave in graciously, holding the irrepressible boy as dear to her heart as she held the man. Her spirit knew a gladness that could not be suppressed as the wind-filled sails above them strained to carry them home.

ABOUT THE AUTHOR

Jo Goodman lives with her family in Colliers, West Virginia. She is the author of nineteen historical romances (all published by Zebra Books) including her beloved Dennehy sisters series: *Wild Sweet Ecstasy* (Mary Michael's story), *Rogue's Mistress* (Rennie's story), *Forever in My Heart* (Maggie's story), *Always in My Dreams* (Skye's story), and *Only in My Arms* (Mary's story), as well as her Thorne Brothers trilogy: *My Steadfast Heart* (Colin's story), *My Reckless Heart* (Decker's story), and *With All My Heart* (Grey's story). She is currently working on her newest Zebra historical romance, MORE THAN YOU WISHED (to be published in April 2001). Jo loves hearing from readers, and you may write to her c/o Zebra Books. Please include a self-addressed stamped envelope if you would like a response. You can e-mail her at jdobrzan@weir.net and visit her website at www.romancejournal.com/Goodman.

BOOK YOUR PLACE ON OUR WEBSITE
AND MAKE THE
READING CONNECTION!

We've created a customized website just for our very special readers, where you can get the inside scoop on everything that's going on with Zebra, Pinnacle and Kensington books.

When you come online, you'll have the exciting opportunity to:

- View covers of upcoming books

- Read sample chapters

- Learn about our future publishing schedule (listed by publication month *and author*)

- Find out when your favorite authors will be visiting a city near you

- Search for and order backlist books from our online catalog

- Check out author bios and background information

- Send e-mail to your favorite authors

- Meet the Kensington staff online

- Join us in weekly chats with authors, readers and other guests

- Get writing guidelines

- AND MUCH MORE!

**Visit our website at
http://www.zebrabooks.com**